"You aren't what I expected, Lady Catherine. You're different."

His voice was low and hesitant, his expression more intense.

Cathy's breath caught at the back of her throat. "You can't even imagine how different I am, Rory. Take my word for it, you have never met a woman like me in your life."

He silently walked on, taking in her words. Suddenly he said, "Before you were saying that you would give anything in the world to go home to America. You didn't want to come to Ireland? I had heard you did."

She almost grinned. "What else did you hear? That I couldn't find a husband? That Lady Montrose was going to play matchmaker for me and get me married?"

He looked embarrassed. "I beg your pardon, Lady Catherine. I apologize if anything I said offended you."

Surprised, she looked at him and saw that he was sincere. When he smiled, his eyes actually sparkled, showing tiny yellow flecks. How long had it been since she'd felt this attracted to a man? Ever since she woke up at the cairn and saw his face above her, she had trusted this man, and he hadn't disappointed her.

The question was, could she trust him again?

—From "Irish Eyes"
by Constance O'Day-Flannery

Secret Loves

Constance O'Day-Flannery

Wendy Haley

Cheryl Lanham

Catherine Palmer

BERKLEY BOOKS, NEW YORK

SECRET LOVES

A Berkley Book/published by arrangement with
the authors

PRINTING HISTORY
Berkley edition/March 1994

ISBN: 0-425-14124-1

BERKLEY®
Berkley Books are published by The Berkley Publishing Group,
200 Madison Avenue, New York, New York 10016.
BERKLEY and the "B" design
are trademarks belonging to Berkley Publishing Corporation.

PRINTED IN THE UNITED STATES OF AMERICA

10 9 8 7 6 5 4 3 2 1

Contents

Irish Eyes • 1
Constance O'Day-Flannery

Midnight Daydreams • 67
Cheryl Lanham

Masquerade • 135
Wendy Haley

Behind Closed Doors • 215
Catherine Palmer

Secret Loves

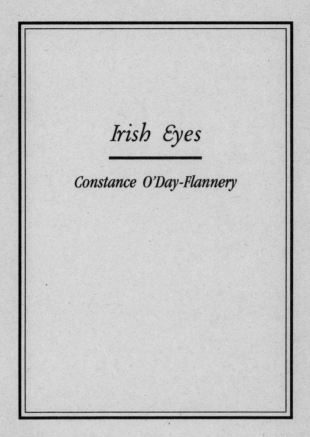

Irish Eyes

Constance O'Day-Flannery

chapter

one

She had no one to blame but herself. The entire trip was turning into a fiasco. One did not plan the vacation of a lifetime on the spur of the moment. And that was just what she'd done. Ireland . . . It had called out to her since she was a young girl, in pictures and movies and music. Always quietly, almost sadly, the land whispered to her subconscious of a homecoming. But she wasn't coming to anything, not really. She was running away.

Cathy Connelly swore under her breath as she jammed on the brakes. Two horses stood in the middle of the road, their reins or harness or something, hanging from them. Impatient, she looked down the narrow road for their owner and, not seeing anyone, swore out loud.

"Damn it. This isn't cute anymore." When she'd arrived three days ago and rented a car, the sheep and cattle in the road had seemed a novelty. The guidebooks had been accurate. Animals did have the right-of-way. She'd actually smiled with patience while waiting for the livestock to pass by and had waved to the owner who'd seemed in no hurry to catch up with his herd. But now she was lost. Not just lost as in the States, where within five miles she could find a gas station or a 7-Eleven and ask for directions. This was major, big-time lost—on a mountain where the directions were in Gaelic, and the last human being she'd seen had been fifteen miles back when she'd asked if she were going toward Killarney.

The old man had chuckled and told her, "Some blackard must 'ave turned the sign around again. Just you turn

3

around, missy, and cut through the mountain. You'll pick up the main road soon as a whistle."

Soon as a whistle? She had no idea what that meant, but she did know from the past three days that there were very few main roads. Most of them were barely wide enough for two compact cars. And the towns . . . Cars were parked half on the sidewalk, half on the road. She'd already side-swiped two of them by bumping their rearview mirrors. Driving on the left side of the road was unnatural and—

She stopped that line of thinking and took a deep breath while waiting for the meandering horses to pass her. She didn't want to become the Ugly American by being critical. Ireland was also beautiful. She saw it in the land and in the faces of the people. It was like America thirty years ago, before drugs and violence had gotten out of control. She hadn't seen one homeless person. There were poor people, but they lived off the land, or families took them in. Everyone was friendly. In three days she hadn't passed by one person, either in a town or walking in the country, who hadn't tipped a hat or waved in greeting. At every hotel and restaurant, she was treated as if she were royalty. The Irish were definitely a polite people. It was her own fault that everything wasn't turning out right. She'd had this ridiculous fantasy about finally arriving in Ireland and finding solace, but nothing was going to take away the pain and humiliation that she carried around like extra baggage.

One of the horses stopped and seemed to inspect her car. When he looked into the window at her, a chill ran down her back, and she shivered as a light mist began. Giggling with nervous laughter, she turned on the windshield wipers and waved to the horse. She was a city girl, through and through, and the only animals she'd seen with any regularity were dogs and cats. But there had been something weird in the expressions of the sheep that casually grazed next to some of the ancient ruins she'd inspected. And now these horses. Something about their eyes . . .

Dismissing the sensation, Cathy eased her foot off the

brake and slowly drove on. Out of habit, she looked in the rearview mirror and was surprised that the horses were out of sight. Shrugging, she drove down the mountain and breathed in the crisp air. Swallowing unclogged her ears, and she heard the unmistakable sound of rushing water. That wasn't unusual. She'd seen a number of small waterfalls during her tour of Ireland. But this sounded stronger than any of the others. She saw a sign ahead and hoped it was in English. It was.

Crestkell Cairn.

Torrec Waterfall.

Smiling, Cathy pulled her car to the side of the road and glanced at the clock on the dashboard. This was her reward for getting lost and making it through the mountain. She could stop and explore, and still make her reservation at Ardrare Manor before dinnertime. She turned the car off and grabbed her raincoat, for she'd learned that a light mist could explode into a rainfall at any moment, even when the sun was shining.

The roar of the waterfall filled her ears and sent a ripple of excitement through her. After all the hours sitting in a car, she needed the exercise and quickly started climbing the stone steps, eager to reach the top ... to actually see what she could already hear.

It was a magical place, a faerie forest of green. Moss dressed the trees and overhead branches in Erin's shade. Ferns grew large and feathery amid stones that were worn smooth from centuries of water rushing over them. Cathy felt her heart expand with exhilaration as she climbed higher and higher, the crisp spring air filling her lungs.

White frothy water ran with an incredible force over the stones, creating a roar in her ears. Awed, Cathy stood for a moment, and leaned against a high stone wall. It was worth the climb. It was worth the entire trip to feel this good, this in tune with something so primitive, so primordial, that it made her feel as if she were part of the universe. You couldn't get this feeling sitting behind a desk arranging appraisals for estate auctions.

Standing with her back against the stone wall, Cathy

tried to memorize the scene so she could pull it out from the recesses of her mind the next time she felt sad or insignificant. Considering what was waiting for her at home, the memory would be recalled frequently.

Adam . . . Just thinking his name caused her stomach to twist with dread. How could she go back and face him? What do you say to an ex-lover who tells you he doesn't love you? Why did she even call him a lover when there was no love involved? But she'd thought there was, at least the beginning of it. Her mood altered; Cathy turned away from the waterfall and read the sign for Crestkell Cairn above the stone wall. It was one of Ireland's best megalithic court cairns, a burial area and open-air court where rituals had been performed around 2500 B.C.

Glad to have something so exciting to take her mind off her problems, Cathy hurried up the wide stone steps and was rewarded with a sight that few human beings ever see.

It wasn't as big as Stonehenge, but it was more intricate. As she walked up to the ruin, visions danced around in her brain of Druids, the ancient people of Ireland. She had heard about them from her grandmother who'd left Ireland at eighteen and had missed her birthplace every day of her life. There was a powerful bond between Ireland and those who were born on her land, and neither an ocean nor seventy-one years ever diminished the connection. Just that morning in Kenmare she'd seen the tiny house where Nana Maeve had been born. There were no relatives left, at least none that she could find, but she enjoyed walking around the pretty village, knowing her grandmother had walked the same streets as a girl.

Entering the round court area, she sat down on a lower wall and regretted that she'd left her camera in the car. This would make a fantastic picture, she thought while running her hand over the stones. Druids . . . the priestly, learned class among the Celts. They were judges and lawmakers and advisors to their people. Even the Romans who defeated most of Europe couldn't conquer them. Nana Maeve had been very proud of that. As a young child, Cathy had heard about these ancient people—the old ones, her grandmother had called them—and she wondered what rituals had been performed in this holy place two thousand years before Christianity came into being.

Cathy felt a loose rock in the low stone wall and pulled it out. Holding it in hand, she experienced an odd surge of power race through her body, and when it left, she felt weak. Glad that she was seated, Cathy slipped the rock into her pocket, thinking it would make a great souvenir to bring home.

Home. She didn't want to go back. Returning to the States meant she would have to deal with her life, and wasn't that what she had run away from? Dear God, why had she fallen in love with someone she worked with? How could she go back and face him? After almost a year of dating, Adam had coldly informed her that he was in the market for a wife, and she didn't fit his requirements. At thirty-six, she was five years his senior and too old. She didn't have the right background, which meant she couldn't bring him the social prestige he craved like a drug. And he never really said he loved her . . . that was his way of justifying his position, and the statement that hurt the worst.

She had thought he did love her. She had told herself that he was just unsure of committing himself out loud. She had *believed* that he loved her. How naive. And how foolish. Even after three months she still felt wounded. It was as if when Adam walked out of her apartment that last time, he had carried her self-esteem in his back pocket. He took her confidence, her belief in herself, along with him. She felt old and unattractive, and every feminist instinct hated the fact that she could only see herself reflected in his eyes.

Wiping away tears, she stared at a patch of clover by her feet. It was cowardly to run away to Ireland when Adam was scheduled to conduct an audit at her firm, but she couldn't face him. She didn't feel strong enough yet. And that was how they had met a year ago. Her company had switched accounting firms, and Adam Kline had walked into her life. Within two months he'd been spending weekends at her place. After a year, why wouldn't she think he was falling in love with her? When did she suddenly become too old? And too old for what? Marriage? Children? Her worth as a potential partner was based on being a breeder? Shaking her head, Cathy reached down and picked a shamrock by her boot. She'd been through the whole process. The shock and grieving stage, when getting up and getting dressed was an effort. The anger stage, when she believed all men were rotten. Now there was acceptance. Adam didn't love her. He never had. And now she didn't love him. Perhaps she never had. Women looked at relationships differently from men. Like most women, she needed to feel something for the person next to her in bed. Otherwise it was just sex, which was unacceptable. Why couldn't women handle sex like men? Why couldn't she? In the last three months, she'd examined the relationship and realized that she had tried to ignore certain aspects of his personality that bothered her. When they went to the theater, for example, Adam hadn't really paid attention to the play. He looked around, seeing who was there and making sure he was seen. If they were at dinner with others, he tipped lavishly. Alone with her, he reverted to his bean-counter accountant personality. They socialized with his friends, never hers. He made statements that were borderline prejudiced, and when she argued with him, he called her a misguided liberal.

Sitting in that ancient ruin, Cathy made a startling discovery—she didn't even like Adam Kline. If she were to meet him for the first time at a party, after five minutes of honest conversation, she'd walk away. So why was she carrying around all this emotional baggage for a man she didn't want as a friend, let alone a lover? It didn't make any sense.

She threw her head back and laughed with joy. Suddenly she felt lighter and happier than she had in months. The knot in her stomach disappeared, and the muscles in her shoulders finally relaxed.

She was free.

Closing her eyes as the mist turned into a light rain, she

put her hands into her pockets and touched the flat rock. She silently thanked her grandmother and the "old ones," for she felt healed. She felt whole. Lighthearted, she stood up and walked out of the cairn, anxious to continue her journey. No longer was she running away from anything. She was running toward the rest of her life.

Dizzy with happiness, she nearly ran down the moss-covered steps toward the waterfall. Her world was right again. She had left the past behind and was free to do anything she wanted. Everything made sense and—

Suddenly her foot slipped on the wet step, and she felt herself falling. Panic-stricken, Cathy held out her hands to break her fall, but she was tumbling forward toward the stone wall and the water. She heard a sickening crack, as her head banged into the wall. There was a moment of surprise; then pain ripped through her skull, taking away her breath and her control.

The last thing she remembered was the roar of the waterfall and the blinding pain, as oblivion wrapped its comforting dark robe around her.

"Can you hear me? Where are you hurt?"

Something cold was placed at her forehead, and she tried to pull away from the freezing pain.

"Don't move," she was ordered in a deep male voice, heavy with an Irish lilt. "Open your eyes if you can."

Her lids fluttered open, and she stared in confusion at the face above her. A man was kneeling next to her, his black hair plastered against his skull from the rain. Water dripped from his face onto hers as he stared at her with worried blue eyes.

"I . . . I fell," she muttered, blinking away the rain.

His mouth softened with a smile. "Aye, you took yourself a good fall, judging from that bump on your head." He lifted his red handkerchief away from her scalp and wrung it out, adding, "But there's no blood, praise be. Where else do you hurt?"

"All over," she mumbled with embarrassment. How humiliating to be in this position in front of a stranger. A good-looking stranger, she mentally added, and immediately became angry for noticing. Hadn't she just promised herself that a man's opinion of her would never again supersede her own? "My head is killing me."

"It won't kill you," the man answered matter-of-factly. "Can you move?"

"I think so," Cathy said, and tried to sit up. She sucked in her breath with pain. "My back . . . and hip. I . . . I must have injured them." With surprising gentleness, he eased her down to the wide stone.

Looking at the waterfall and the path leading toward the road, he said, "I could try carrying you, but for the rain. If I should slip, we'd both be in a fix. And to try and find help at this point would waste too much time. You have to get out of this rain . . ."

Through her pain she could see how hard he was thinking, and she wanted to apologize. "I'm very sorry. Look, maybe you should just go and call for help. I'll be all right. It's isn't as if I'm going anywhere." She tried to laugh, but it came out sounding like a moan of anguish.

The sound spurred him on. "Where exactly does it hurt?"

He sounded so much like a doctor that she quickly responded, "My lower back and my right hip." She tried to show him, but moving only produced more pain.

"Do you mind if I touch you?" he asked, wiping rain from his eyes. Light blue eyes, the color of the Caribbean. Kindness and concern were reflected in them.

Stop it, Cathy Connelly, she warned herself. How could she be writhing in pain and still notice the color of a man's eyes? He was only being polite. Very polite. And he didn't have to help her. "I suppose it would be all right," she murmured. "I . . . mean, I'm already indebted to you for finding me up here."

"Then let's try to roll you to your side, facing me. We'll do it slow, and tell me if the pain increases."

He had to be a doctor, she told herself, though why he was turning her to face him rather than the other way around was a puzzle.

He pulled her raincoat up to expose her back and hip, and she felt his hands slowly move over her blouse and jeans.

"Pardon me, Lady Catherine. It is necessary to determine your injury."

Lady Catherine? The Irish were certainly formal, but that had sounded more than polite. And no one had called her Catherine since the nuns in grade school. "How did you know my name?" she asked, trying not to concentrate on his hands and how they slid over her body, applying pressure every few inches. Suddenly she yelped in pain, for it felt as if he had touched a raw, exposed nerve.

"I'm sorry, but now we know what's wrong."

She tried to regain her breath. "And what's wrong?" she finally was able to ask. "If that pain was any indication, I'll never walk again."

"You'll walk again, Lady Catherine," he said with kindness in his voice. "Now I'll ask you to lean toward me, as if you are falling off a cliff. I won't let you fall."

She glanced up at him. "What are you going to do? Are you a doctor?"

He looked back at her and shook his head. "No, and I should have introduced myself. My name is Rory Egan, and I'm the stable master at Ardrare Manor."

"That's where I was going," she said, and then thought for a moment. Was she that late for her reservation that they had sent someone out looking for her? Impossible. No hotel would do that, even in Ireland, where guests were treated like nobility. Then his last words hit her. "You take care of horses?" she asked with disbelief.

"That's correct."

"But I'm a person, not an animal. Do you know what you're doing?"

He appeared insulted. "Muscles are muscles, Lady Catherine, whether they're yours or a Connemara pony's. Now, you'll either have to trust me to help you, or wait here until I find others to carry you down to the road. Of course, if I have to do that, there's a good chance that you could contract pneumonia from lying in the rain for well over an hour. Naturally the choice is yours."

He was right, and she really didn't want to stay on this cold stone. She had to trust him, but . . . "Are you at least a vet?"

"I beg your pardon?"

She shook her head and closed her eyes, resting her cheek against the slick rock. No need to further antagonize him, but what if he did something wrong? What if she became paralyzed or something—

He interrupted her thoughts. "Have you made a decision?"

She didn't even open her eyes. "Tell me what to do," she said in a weary voice.

"Lean against me and then take a deep breath. I promise I won't let you fall."

She did as she was told, smelling the wet wool of his jacket, hearing the roar of the waterfall in her ears. This was an odd position to be in, pressed up against a stranger. A handsome stranger at that. Mentally shaking the thought from her head, she felt him positioning his hands on her lower back, and suddenly, without any warning, he twisted her body. "Oh, my God!" She heard a weird crack in her back and her breath rush out of her with her plea to the Almighty.

"I'm sorry, Lady Catherine, but there's just no way to prepare someone for that."

She tried to find her breath and her voice. "What did you do to me?" she demanded.

"I aligned your muscles. I've done it before when someone's thrown from a horse. My father taught me. And his father taught him. It's a very ancient method called meridian therapy. Now, let's try and sit you up. Ready?"

She wasn't ready, but she did cooperate. Actually she had little choice in the matter as he supported her into a sitting position.

"How does that feel?"

She blinked away the rain from her face and realized there wasn't any pain . . . so far. "All right, I guess."

"Good. Now we'll stand. Slowly . . . lean on me for assistance."

He pulled her upright, and she was shocked to find that it wasn't torture.

He stared at her. "How are you?" he asked with concern.

Holding on to the high stone wall, she took a step forward. Immediately she smiled with gratitude. "There's no pain!" she said in astonishment. "I feel a little achy, but there's no pain."

He nodded. "Good. You can take care of any aches at the manor, but now we can get down to the road."

She was shaking her head in amazement. "This is incredible. It's a miracle! Thank you . . . I mean, how can I ever thank you? I thought I'd be in traction for weeks."

"You can thank me, Lady Catherine, by coming with me now. I have no great desire to nurse a cold myself."

"Yes. Of course. I'm sorry. And, please . . . you can drop the Lady Catherine thing. My name's Cathy." She held out her hand to him. "I'm really very grateful to you for finding me. I could have been up here for days."

He appeared puzzled and a little awkward as he accepted her hand and placed it on his arm for support. Leading her down the steps past the waterfall, he spoke more loudly. "How did you get up here?"

"I walked up. I could hear the waterfall and I wanted to see it." Her head was starting to throb again as she moved, but she tried to ignore it as she concentrated on her steps.

"I don't understand. You came to see a waterfall after your accident?"

"What accident? My car is down by the road." He couldn't be talking about bumping rearview mirrors, could he? They were flexible; they bounced right back into position. She didn't think there was any damage. Great, now she was involved in a traffic accident in a foreign country. What next?

"Your cart and your driver, Lady Catherine, were found this morning. We've been searching for you ever since."

She stopped walking and turned to him. "I think you've

made a mistake, Mr. Egan. I didn't have a driver. I drove myself. And there wasn't any damage. C'mon, I'll show you when we get down to the road. You can check my car."

Now she took the lead, anxious to prove her point. When her foot started to slip over the heavy moss, he grabbed her shoulders and righted her before she could fall.

"Be careful! Lean on me, and we'll get down together."

He held her shoulders and slowly walked her down toward the road. She could have sworn there was a paved path coming up. And the foliage had looked more dense. What was going on? They weren't taking another path, were they? Confused, she decided not to figure out this puzzle just yet, but then other weird thoughts entered her brain. She could feel the strength in his body, which surprised her since he wasn't a heavy man. He looked as if he were built like a runner. Tall, lean, and muscular . . . But what could she tell under the heavy clothes that he wore? Tall, that's all she knew for sure. Of course, those big heavy boots must have added three inches to his height. But still, her head only came up to his chest. Judging by the wrinkles in the corners of his eyes, she guessed he was in his early forties. His skin was ruddy, weathered by the climate, and his smile—when he smiled—had been quite nice.

She actually shook her head, as if to dislodge the thoughts. Stop it, she scolded herself again. He's a Good Samaritan. Maybe she could buy him dinner or offer to repay him. Yet she didn't think he would take kindly to that suggestion, for there was an unmistakable air of Irish stubbornness and pride about him.

"Why are you shaking you head?" he asked. "Does it hurt again?"

She nodded. "Like hell," she answered, and saw a horse tied to a tree limb. "Hey, is that yours?"

He appeared startled by her language, but then she knew that Irish women hadn't wholly embraced the feminist movement yet. There wasn't even divorce in this country.

When people married, they did so for life. Cathy thought there must be a heck of a lot of unhappy people here with no way out of bad situations.

"The horse is mine, madam. He'll take us both to the manor house."

"I can use the car," she hurried to tell him. She had never ridden a horse in her life. "So can you. I mean, you don't want to ride in this rain."

"I would never leave a horse like that. And may I remind you that you don't have a cart. Your trap was found on Cromaglen Mountain, and . . . I'm sorry to tell you this, but your driver was killed."

They had reached the road, and Cathy turned to him as quickly as her bruised body could maneuver. "Mr. Egan, I'm sorry this man died, but I have no idea what you're talking about. I *did not* have a driver. I'm perfectly capable of driving myself."

She looked around for her car. It was gone.

She looked at the road. It, too, was altered. No longer was it paved, but a sea of mud.

"Something's wrong here," she muttered, turning around in a circle. "We must have come down a different way. My car isn't here."

He stood quietly in the rain and said, "There is no other way down from the cairn."

"But my car isn't here! I left it parked over there," she cried, as a feeling of panic enveloped her. "No, maybe it was over here," she said, looking at a huge tree that she didn't remember. "This doesn't look right. I mean, it does . . . the waterfall is in the same place. But where's my car?" Everything was in it. Her clothes, her purse, her money, her passport. How could she have been so stupid as to leave her purse, even in a locked car? She reached into the pocket of her raincoat and pulled out the car keys. They were attached to a small green plastic shamrock. "See, I have the keys," she said in a high voice as she held them out to him.

He looked at them but didn't take them from her hand. "Madam, I have no idea how you managed to walk this far from Cromaglen. Or why you were even there when you were supposed to come into Cork, instead of Mizen Head, but I would suggest you discuss this matter at the manor. Your trap is gone, and standing here in the rain isn't going to—"

"I didn't have a trap," she interrupted with near-hysteria and felt the burning of tears at her eyes. "How many times do I have to tell you? And I didn't come into Cork or Mizen Head. I flew into Dublin from London!"

He continued to stare at her, as if trying to control his patience. "I beg your pardon? You *flew*?"

What was wrong with him? "Yes. Flew. As in an airplane?"

He merely stared at her, blinking a few times, before looking heavenward for help and walking away to his horse. Holding the animal by its reins, he led it up to her. "Your head injury seems to have confused you. I suggest we get to the manor as quickly as possible."

He continued to stare at her as if she'd lost her mind. Defensive, Cathy stood her ground. "Look, I know Ireland is . . . How shall I put this? A little backward. It seems like the 1950s here, instead of the 1990s, but even here you must be familiar with flying." She issued a nervous laugh. Maybe he was mildly retarded and the hotel let him work with horses because he had trouble grounding himself in reality.

"Lady Catherine," he said gently, softly, as if she were the one with the mental problem, "people can't fly. And it is the year of Our Lord, Eighteen Hundred and Seventy-One."

chapter

two

She was going to sit very still and not say a single word until they reached the hotel. She didn't care how good-looking he was, or that he had "rescued" her and miraculously cured her back—this man was weird! He actually thought he was living in the last century!

He seemed to have the same opinion of her, for he hadn't said anything to her since putting her on the horse behind him and telling her to hold onto him. That she did, with a death grip, for she was afraid of falling off the animal. Holding on wasn't easy because of the rain and because she wanted to keep her distance from Mr. Egan's back.

As the thick drops pelted her, she closed her eyes and prayed that he was really taking her to the hotel. She was at his mercy, and if he were crazy, then he could be taking her anywhere. She had no identification, no money—nothing but the clothes on her back.

They rode through iron gates with the monogram of an A and M intertwined, and Cathy sighed with relief. Finally. Ardrare Manor. She wasn't going to be abducted. Mr. Egan was weird, but he wasn't threatening any longer. They passed a stone house, and a man appeared at the doorway.

Holding his jacket over his head to protect it from the rain, he shouted, "Praise be, Rory, you found her!"

Cathy felt Rory's lungs expand as he shouted back, "Call off the search, Liam. Bring the boys back to their fires."

The man nodded and rushed into the house. "Liam

Fermoy, the gatekeeper," he informed her as they continued up the road.

Bring the boys back to their fires? Who talked like that anymore? And why was there a search party looking for her? How could they know she was hurt? It was too confusing, she thought as she looked around her. The hotel grounds were immense. She observed several neatly trimmed gardens of evergreens with purple and white flowers that bowed their heads in the rain. They would be lovely in the sunshine. Too bad she was only spending the night, Cathy thought. If they let her spend the night. She didn't have money or a credit card on her. She just needed a telephone to start everything in motion. She'd call the police to report the stolen car, American Express to replace the plastic, and the American Embassy for a new passport.

Peeking around his shoulder, Cathy saw the house and sucked in her breath. It wasn't a house. It was more like a castle! "Dear God," she muttered. "It's beautiful!"

Rory didn't say anything, but she could feel his body tense as they rode up to the huge front doors. Immediately the doors opened, and two people emerged—an older man holding an umbrella over an equally elderly woman.

"Catherine! Thank God they found you. We've been frantic, positively frantic with worry." The woman broke into tears and reached out her hands to Cathy. Rory dismounted and gently took her off the horse.

Shivering in the rain, Cathy wasn't sure what to do. The woman was dressed in an old-fashioned costume . . . a . . . a gown of some kind, and she was wearing a fringed shawl over her shoulders. Her graying hair was pulled up in a braided coronet, and she had the strangest expression on her face.

Before Cathy could decide how to proceed, the woman startled her by enveloping her in a strong hug.

"Oh, Randolph, do keep the umbrella over the child until we get her inside. Can't you see she's soaked through?" Not waiting for an answer from the old man, the woman began pulling Cathy toward the huge double wooden doors. "My dear, I would know you anywhere, with that red hair and those freckles. You look just like your mother. Thank God I didn't have to write her with any more bad news. You're found, and after a few days of rest, you'll be just fine."

Totally confused, Cathy allowed them to lead her, but as she got to the doors, she turned around and looked at the man who had brought her here. "Thank you for helping me," she said sincerely.

His eyes locked with hers, yet he merely nodded his head as the man named Randolph spoke. "Yes, of course, Mr. Egan. Thank you. Please come by the house later this evening to fill me in."

She thought it was an odd exchange between the two men, but turned her attention to the entrance hall. It was the ultimate vacation experience. She had heard about places like this, magnificent old homes where the furnishings were authentic, and even the maids, who stared at her with curiosity, wore black floor-length gowns with crisp white aprons. Mounted heads of animals lined the high walls with names under them: Irish Red Deer, Japanese Sika, Wild Goats from Torrec Mountain. Even the huge antlers over a mantelpiece bore the name Great Irish Deer. Strange . . . she didn't remember booking a hotel that was ever a hunting lodge. She hated hunting. Looking up into the eyes of the Red Deer, she could only think of Bambi's mother.

"My dear, do let Maureen have your cloak. You're soaked to the bone." The older woman summoned a young maid, who quickly came when her name was called.

Cathy took her raincoat off and handed it to the girl. When she turned around, everyone was staring at her jeans.

The woman who seemed in charge put her hand to her chest, as though embarrassed, and then cleared her throat. "My, what unusual riding attire," she said to fill the silence. "American tastes are so forward, so advanced," she corrected, as if fearing she had insulted their guest. "Aren't they, Randolph?"

"I really wouldn't know, my dear," the man said, clearly uncomfortable with the question. "Perhaps Catherine would like to see her room?"

As if recovering, the woman came back to life. "Why, yes. Of course. Here I am going on about foolish things when you've been through such a terrible experience." She turned to the maid. "Maureen, please take Lady Catherine to her room. And draw a warm bath. Have Tess prepare a tea service and—"

"Excuse me," Cathy interrupted in a polite voice. "I really do have to use your telephone. I've lost everything, and I need to report it."

"Telephone?" Randolph asked, his brows knitted together in puzzlement. "Do you mean a telegraph? There's one in Killarney, if you'd like to send a message to your mother. I'll have someone ride in with it when the weather breaks."

"And Catherine, dear, you haven't lost everything. Your trunks were recovered. They're in your room."

"I think there's been a mistake. I'm not Lady Catherine. Everyone keeps calling me that. My name is Cathy—"

"Of course," Randolph interrupted. "Americans don't go in for titles, do they? That's just something your Aunt Margaret will have to get used to." He put his hand to her back and steered her toward the stairs. "Welcome to Ardrare Manor, Cathy. Why don't you get settled, and we'll all speak again at dinner."

It wasn't a question, but more a polite order.

Aware of a pounding headache and the wet clothes clinging to her skin, Cathy decided she might as well go to her room and figure out what to do next. These people were as confusing as Rory Egan—even more so, for they actually acted as if they were related to her!

Rory curried the horse and gave him extra oats as a reward, but his mind wasn't on his job. He was thinking about the woman he had brought off the mountain. He had only met one other American and had liked him. He wasn't sure he liked Lady Catherine. She was a Montrose by her mother's sister marrying one, and therefore she was the enemy. All English were the enemy. They had raped the land, taking away its innocence forever. Hadn't his father told him that? And his grandfather, and his father before him. The Egans owned this land, had since the time of Brian Boru. His ancestors had fought with the high king against the Vikings at Clontarf. They had fought against Dermot MacMurrough and the Norman soldiers he'd recruited with Henry II's help. He knew the history well, for it had been repeated throughout the generations, the father always wanting his children to know that they were descended from princes. No matter how many English monarchs pronounced otherwise, this was Irish land and would one day be held by the Irish again. England might have taken away their land and given it to British noblemen; they might have passed laws that prohibited ownership of land, education, voting, and the practice of their religion; they could sit in their huge homes and watch nearly a million people starve to death during the famine without offering assistance; but they could never take away the burning resentment that blazed in every Irishman's soul.

Randolph Montrose might think his family owned the land, but they were only tenants. Just like all the other English for the last six hundred years of oppression. This land belonged to the Egans, and one day he or his sons, or their sons, would regain it. He was the last Egan; his entire family had been wiped out in the potato famine thirty years ago. And he couldn't remember the faces of his parents, or his brothers and sisters. At forty-two years of age, it was time for him to take a wife and rebuild the Egan name. He owed it to those who had gone before him. He owed it to himself.

Leaving the horse to its oats, Rory walked out of the stable and stood for a moment looking at the house. Maureen worked as Lady Margaret's personal maid. She was young and she'd shown her interest in him on several occasions, but she was vain and calculating, sneaky as a fox. In fact, it was Maureen who had told him about Lady Margaret's niece. She had overheard the Montroses' discussion of a letter from Lady Margaret's sister in Boston, begging Margaret to take her daughter for the spring and summer. Catherine apparently could not find a husband, and her mother feared she never would. At thirty-one years, she was officially a spinster, and her mother hoped her prospects would improve in Ireland.

Rory wondered why Lady Catherine had never married. She wasn't a homely woman. Quite the opposite. She was tall and full of figure. His hands had felt her woman's curves. Her hair was red, her nose and cheeks sprinkled with fading freckles. If he hadn't known her ancestry, he would have thought her Irish, but that could only be the Viking strain coming out. Still . . . there was something odd about her. She actually thought she could fly! Perhaps what he had blamed on the fall was really simplemindedness, and no man wanted to take her for fear of it being passed on to children. Or she could be one of those women he'd heard about, women who dressed like men yet didn't want to marry one. Whatever the answer, it wasn't his business.

Shrugging, he walked toward his cottage, eager for a hot bath and a warmed shot of whiskey. He had earned it.

She sat in the velvet-cushioned chair by the marble fireplace and stared at the periodical in her hands.

The London Review, 14 March 1871.

The clothes the maid had shown her in the inlaid wardrobe were all of the last century. The wardrobe itself was a genuine Sheraton, one of his earlier works, and a priceless piece of furniture. From all of the estate auctions she'd arranged, she had acquired more than a working knowledge of antique furniture. But this didn't look antique, and it wasn't a copy. She knew the table holding the tea service was mahogany in the French style of the Louis Philippe period. If it wasn't an antique, and it wasn't a copy . . . then what was happening? How could any of this be real?

Glancing down, she reread the editorial about the death of Dickens in the previous year and the sale of the painting he had commissioned from W. P. Frith, depicting the heroine of *Barnaby Rudge*, and how it was influencing current fashions, making a woman resemble a rococo shepherdess by concentrating on the curve of the bustle.

Rory Egan had said it was the year of Our Lord, 1871.

The people downstairs, Margaret and Randolph, dressed and acted as if they were living in the last century. Since coming to the beautiful room, she had discovered that there was no electricity, no central heating, no telephones or televisions. Not even a radio.

This wasn't a hotel. It was someone's home.

The maid checked the fire, and Cathy looked up at her. She was young and pretty and moved gracefully in her long gown. "Maureen, may I ask you a question?"

"Certainly, ma'am." Maureen turned around and faced her.

"What year is it?"

The girl looked startled and stood very still. "I beg your pardon, madam."

"Can you tell me the year?"

"You don't know?" the girl whispered in fright.

Cathy pointed to the paper in her hand. "This says 1871 and—"

"I can't read," Maureen interrupted as she backed away toward the door. "I'll just call your aunt for you."

"I would rather talk to Mr. Egan," Cathy said. He was the one who had found her. Maybe he could explain.

"Mr. Egan?" Maureen's tone was defensive. "He has nothing to do with the house. Mr. Egan is a fine man who risked life and limb today."

"I realize that," Cathy hurried to say. "And I don't think I thanked him properly for finding me. Could you please tell him that I'd like to see him? Or tell me where to find him?"

Maureen lifted her chin, and her lips tightened. "Yes, madam," she said stiffly and left the room.

Cathy stood up and walked around the bedroom. Never in her life had she been surrounded by such beauty in one place. The Turkish rug beneath her feet was in shades of blue and gold. Gilt wainscoting graced the ceiling, and beveled crystal windows looked out onto an intricate maze of evergreens below.

She touched the heavy brocaded curtains and wondered what kind of beautiful dream she had entered. The nightgown and robe she wore belonged to someone else, someone two sizes larger, someone with money, for Victoria's Secret never carried anything as fine.

"They were woven in Brussels for Queen Victoria and Prince Albert's visit here ten years ago."

Cathy dropped the curtain and spun around from the window. Margaret was smiling at her.

"There were two beds in here then, but I had one removed to prepare for your visit. Come sit with me by the fire, Catherine, and tell me of your mother. How I long to see her once more. Is she happy living in America all these years?"

"My mother?" Cathy asked in a frightened voice.

Margaret took her hand and led her back to the chair by the fire. "Here, sit down, my dear, and rest. Maureen tells me you are confused. Where did Mr. Egan find you?"

Cathy sat down, and Margaret put a robe over her lap. "He found me by the waterfall."

"Not on Torrec Mountain?" Margaret asked, horrified.

"Yes. I had left the cairn, and it was raining, and . . . and I fell. I hit my head on a stone wall and . . . and I must have been unconscious, because the next thing I remember is someone calling out to me. He was kneeling next to me and telling me not to move because of the injury to my head." Cathy touched the lump under her hair and hissed with pain at the contact. "But I couldn't because I had also injured my back. He did something to it, fixed it somehow, and then he helped me down to the road."

Margaret reached over and felt the size of the bump. "Oh, dear . . . Randolph sent for the doctor as soon as we saw Mr. Egan bringing you to the house. He should be here shortly. You poor thing. What an ordeal you've been through."

"I'm afraid you don't understand," Cathy said as tears

came into her eyes. "Everything was gone. Everything had changed ... Please," she begged, letting the tears roll down her cheeks. "Please tell me what year it is!"

Margaret's smile seemed to freeze on her face, yet she quickly recovered. "It's understandable why you're confused. It's April twelfth, dear, 1871."

Cathy stared at the woman's kind face. She wasn't lying or trying to play a role. Ever since she'd woken up at the waterfall, everyone she met, everything she saw, had told her she'd awakened in a strange place. It wasn't her world, her time. Everyone couldn't be crazy.

It had to be her.

She looked at the fire and felt mesmerized by the flames licking at the charred wood. She was having a nervous breakdown. None of this was real. It wasn't happening. It was a nightmare, a horrible, horrible nightmare ...

"Catherine? Catherine, say something!"

She wouldn't speak; she wouldn't participate in the nightmare. If she were very quiet and went along with it, then it would go away. *They* would go away.

There was a knock on the door, and Margaret rose to answer it. "Thank God, you've arrived, Doctor! She's very confused, and when she asked what year it was, she seemed to go into some sort of trance. She just sits there and stares into the fire."

Margaret told the doctor about her injuries, and Cathy sat very still as the man touched her and looked into her eyes. He asked her questions, but, convinced that participating would only prolong the insanity, she refused to answer.

"She should be in bed, Lady Margaret. The mind is a fragile muscle, and your niece has been through an extraordinary trauma. From what I've been able to piece together, she and her driver were involved in an accident on Cromaglen Mountain." Although they had moved away from her to the window, Cathy could still hear their whispers. "The driver's body was found at the bottom of Cromaglen, along with the trap and your niece's belongings. Somehow Lady Catherine survived and had been wandering in the mountains for two days until Mr. Egan found her injured. For anyone, especially a gentlewoman, any of those circumstances could produce such a reaction. Just as the body needs rest when injured, so does the mind. It has simply shut down to rejuvenate. Do not be alarmed by her confusion."

"But what can I do, Doctor? This is my only sister's daughter. What should I write to her mother?"

"I would suggest patience. Put off informing her mother, for it would only cause unnecessary concern at this point. She could wake up tomorrow, or the next day, and be recovered. Come, let's put your niece to bed and then we'll go over instructions for her care."

In silence Cathy did everything she was told. When she was in bed, Margaret bent down and kissed her forehead.

"Rest now, Catherine, and I'll be back soon."

Margaret walked the doctor out of the room, and when the door was quietly shut, Cathy closed her eyes and cried.

This wasn't happening to her.

She couldn't be living, breathing, talking to people in the last century!

Sleep . . . that's all she needed. When she woke up, she would be in her own time, her own world.

Please, God. *Please?*

chapter

three

Cathy awoke to sunlight. If she was correct, this was the second morning she had spent in the nightmare. Yesterday she had allowed them to take her into a bathroom and bathe her. She had listened to the pride in Margaret's voice when she explained that it was the first indoor commode in the whole of County Kerry. They had put a clean nightgown on her and sent her back to bed. There she had listened to Margaret's voice as she told her the family history, dating back to Norman noblemen named the Earls of Kildare, and the Montroses' distant connection to Henry VIII and Edward and his daughters, Mary and Elizabeth, up to the present Queen, Victoria.

None of it was real. Cathy listened, merely blinking, hoping she would wake up in her own bedroom in Pennsylvania. She didn't eat anything or drink the liquids that were presented to her. She felt weak and fragile, and temporarily insane.

"Here's your breakfast, Lady Catherine," a young Irish maid said in a soft voice as she placed the tray over her lap. "There's porridge and a fry of bacon and eggs, and soda bread with marmalade. And tea, of course. Won't you try to eat?"

Cathy closed her eyes, though the smell of the food enticed her. Her stomach twisted painfully, and she fought off the urge to grab the bacon and shove it in her mouth.

"The poor thing," the girl whispered. "She's starving herself."

"No need to whisper. She's off in a trance. I heard the doctor telling Lady Montrose. I don't think she can hear

27

you." Cathy recognized Maureen's voice answering the young girl.

"I heard about this, during the famine. Mothers who watched their children starve would go off to a place in their minds and die, too. I thank God I wasn't alive then."

"Well, she didn't go through starvation, like in the Great Famine. This is her choice. I don't think she was ever happy."

"How can you say that? You don't know her."

"I know about her. She's thirty and one years and can't find a husband. That's why her mother sent her here. As if the pickin's would be better across the ocean. There aren't enough men as it is. What with the famine, and an equal amount leaving Ireland for America and Canada."

"I wouldn't be thinkin' they'd be lookin' for an Irish husband for her, Maureen. He'd have to be English. The Montroses are well connected, and that's the reason, I'm sure. No need to tell you that from May until September we have our share of holiday guests here at the manor."

"Aye, that's so, but it was Rory she was askin' about the evening she came. And you should have seen the look in her eyes. I think something happened out there on the mountain. He found her, you know, coming down from the cairn."

"The *cairn*?" the young girl asked in a horrified voice.

"And you know what can happen in that place."

"It's just old tales . . ."

"Old tales, you say? Tales of the old ones is more like it. Didn't Mistress O'Sulliebhain go up there lookin' for her goat? And didn't she drop her babe three months early? And wasn't he born with a clubfoot?"

"Yes," came the terrified whisper.

"And didn't Brian Donahey go up there on a dare to paint his name? And didn't he die of fever five weeks later? And what of Eamon Boyle bringing Nora Quinn up there? Didn't she discover she was with child and her da beat her so bad for shamin' the family that she got sick and lost it? Don't you be tellin' me of old tales, Eileen.

Somethin' strange happens up there, all right. And I don't want Rory involved."

"You act like Rory Egan is your sweetheart, and the man doesn't say more to you than good morning. You're always runnin' after him. I say he'd get in more trouble from you, Maureen Larkin, than any goings-on in the cairn."

"A lot you know, Eileen. Why, I could tell you—"

Maureen stopped speaking and stared across the room. "Look, she's eating!"

Cathy smiled at the girls and picked up another slice of bacon. "Could you please call Lady Montrose?" she asked in a husky voice. She really was thirsty and quickly dropped a spoonful of rock sugar into her tea.

Maureen and Eileen ran out of the room.

Cathy dug into her eggs and murmured appreciatively when she tasted them. Of course, Maureen was right. It was the cairn. Why hadn't she thought of that? She'd taken a rock and then fell. It was her own fault. She never should have done it; everything had gone wrong after that. The rock belonged to the cairn, to Ireland, not to her. All she had to do was explain everything and get back to the waterfall and the ruin. It had brought her here and it would take her back.

That was the only answer. And her only salvation.

Margaret rushed into the room, an ecstatic expression on her face. "Catherine. Thank God. You're eating!"

Cathy put down her cup and smiled at the woman. "Mrs. Montrose, please sit down. I have to speak with you."

"Of course, dear. But, please, call me Aunt Margaret. Thank God you've come back to us. I've been so worried." She pulled a chair close to the bed. "Now we can get to know one another, and you can tell me all about your mother. How is my sister? Has that auburn hair I so envied turned as gray as mine?"

Cathy experienced a moment of guilt, for she knew she had to tell this woman the truth. "I can't call you Aunt Margaret because I'm not your niece."

Margaret looked shocked. "Catherine, what are you saying?"

"I'm trying to tell you that I don't belong here. I belong in the . . . the future. 1994, to be exact. I shouldn't be here. This isn't my time. It's lovely. I've never been anywhere so beautiful, but please understand," she hurried to explain, seeing an expression of horror on the woman's face. "Something happened to me when I fell at the cairn. I mean there was all this energy and—"

"Oh, dear God!" Margaret stood up so abruptly that her chair fell to the rug. She grabbed Cathy's hand and squeezed it tight. "I will go into Killarney myself to see Dr. Bowers. Right away. I promise I'll find you the best doctors in Europe. This is all my fault. If we had met you at the ship, none of this would have happened. The accident. That poor man's death. And now this . . ."

"No, please," Cathy begged. "Don't do that. A doctor isn't going to help. You aren't listening. I know this sounds crazy to you. If someone told me this story, I would laugh in their face, but I promise you I'm telling the truth. I don't know how it happened. I mean, I think it's because of the rock, but I have to return it. It's my only chance."

"Finish your breakfast Catherine, and then rest. Perhaps you would like to read, or tour the house. I'll have Maureen accompany you." Margaret's voice was low and controlled, as if she were speaking to a child. "I'll be back this afternoon, and then we can discuss this further if you wish."

"Margaret, please listen to me," Cathy whispered, but she could see the woman was fighting to control herself as she left the room.

I tried, Cathy told herself, feeling terrible for causing Margaret such pain. But she had to tell the truth. She couldn't impersonate the woman's niece. What would happen when the niece turned up? Wouldn't deception have hurt more?

She had to get out of here, before Margaret returned with a doctor. Did they have shrinks in 1871? It didn't matter. Even Freud wouldn't have been able to make sense out of this.

No longer hungry, Cathy got out of bed and walked into the bathroom. Completely tiled in white marble, it was as large as her kitchen back home. It even boasted a fireplace. Talk about luxury. If she had to land in the past, thank God it wasn't the Middle Ages. She never would have survived. Knights in shining armor might sound romantic, but rushes on the floor infested with bugs, and relieving oneself out of a window blew the romance to shreds. She didn't even like camping in her own time. If she had anything to be thankful for during this insanity, it was this bathroom.

Ten minutes later, she stood at the bedroom window and watched Margaret and Randolph ride away in a large black carriage. She simply had to get back to the waterfall and the cairn, and there was no better time. She had no idea which direction to go. Surrounded by mountains, she could be lost for days trying to figure it out.

And then the picture of Rory Egan's face flashed through her mind. He knew. He could take her there. But would the handsome Irishman do it? She remembered the stubborn tilt to his chin. She also remembered his beautiful blue eyes, eyes that seemed to look inside of her and connect with her soul. She shook herself, as if to dislodge the ridiculous thought. Connect with her soul? She hardly knew the man. And being attracted to someone who lived a hundred and twenty years ago was just plain stupid. She didn't need a handsome man right now. She needed help. But how could she get him to agree?

He would if he thought she were Lady Catherine.

She silently prayed that she could pull it off and, when Maureen came into her room, Cathy turned from the window and said in a calm voice, "It's so lovely this morning. I think I'd like to go for a ride. Would you please tell Mr. Egan to ready a horse for me?"

Maureen stiffened. "Lady Montrose said I was to take care of you. If you want to see the house, I'll do that. I don't think you should go horseback riding. No, not that."

Cathy forced a smile, wondering if the girl were really worried about Lady Montrose's orders, or the fact that she had asked for Rory Egan. "Why, I'm just fine, Maureen. Please do as I have asked. I believe I asked you once before, and this time you will kindly do as I've requested." Would a lady speak like that? She hoped so. Yet she was also an American, and believed in equality, so she added, "I'll take full responsibility. I'll even write a note absolving you of any blame. Now, where are my clothes, the ones I was wearing when I came?" She was getting pretty good with this authority thing.

Maureen was bewildered, obviously unsure what she should do. "Vincent is cleaning them. The . . . the trousers are not yet dry."

Damn, her jeans would have been a heck of a lot more comfortable while she tried to stay on a horse. Improvise. It was now or never to make her escape from this gilded cage. "All right," she said patiently. "Is there something else I could wear?"

The girl looked to the wardrobe, yet didn't move. Cathy walked over to it and opened the heavy doors. Inside were the most beautiful clothes she had ever seen. Good Lord, she felt like Cinderella and sighed loudly, regretting that she would never have the opportunity to wear the silks and fine muslins.

"There must be something in here," she mused, pushing aside the lovely gowns until she found a plain brown one. "Here, this should do. What's this one for?"

Maureen appeared startled by the question. "It's your riding habit, madam."

Cathy grinned. "Of course. I forgot." You're allowed to do that when everyone thinks you're crazy, she figured. Seeing all the buttons and laces, she added, "Please inform Mr. Egan about the horse, and then would you come back? I believe I'm going to need your help."

If this works, she thought as she descended the steps into the entry hall, then she was going to look like one hell of a fool when she returned to her own time dressed in this getup. The outfit consisted of a long-sleeved jacket with twenty-six buttons down the front, over a draped skirt with a train in the back. At least she had her car keys and the rock in the pockets of the skirt. How did women ride with all this material? she wondered. It was hard enough not to trip down the stairs. To all of this was added pale yellow kid gloves, a bowler-type hat with a long yellow feather, and a riding crop. Maureen insisted that no lady would dare ride without the gloves, the hat, and the crop. Cathy intended to ditch them as soon as she could.

The servants stood in the hall, staring at her, and she had the impression that if she said, "Boo," the lot of them would run screaming. They probably thought she should be locked away in the room, and here she was preparing to gallivant around the countryside.

Seeing Rory holding the reins of two horses, Cathy smiled as she walked through the doors and down the steps. Just as she was about to greet him, her skirt caught on the heel of her boot, and she tripped.

Again he came to her assistance, righting her, and she tried to regain her balance along with her composure. "I'm not used to this," she muttered while looking up into his eyes. She expected to see ridicule for being so clumsy. She hadn't exactly given this man the best impression so far.

"Yes, I know," he answered with a hint of a smile. "You really do want to ride?"

Cathy straightened the silly hat on her head and nodded as she pulled back her shoulders. She must remember that she was Lady Catherine now. "Yes, I do. It's such a lovely day, and I'd like to see the countryside. Is this one mine?"

He dropped the reins of the large brown horse he had ridden the other day and brought a slightly smaller version up to her. Cathy had to force herself not to back away from the animal. She had never ridden in her life, but she would do anything it took to get back to her own time. Even bluffing her way through this.

Aware of the servants still watching her, she took the few steps to the side of the horse and looked up. Where was the saddle horn? There was only a little stump. She had nothing to grab onto! It was a damn English saddle.

Rory laced his fingers together and offered assistance, using his hands as a makeshift step. When she didn't move, he looked up at her. "Are you ready?"

Cathy took a few deep breaths and then muttered, "As ready as I'll ever be." She hiked her long skirt up to her knee and placed her boot in his hands. Without further thought, she grabbed hold of either side of the saddle and jumped.

It worked! She was sitting on the horse. Her skirt was tangled, and she pulled it from under her as Rory kept the animal still. Pleased with herself, she looked down at him and grinned.

He wasn't smiling. He, along with everyone else, was staring at her legs.

"What's wrong?"

Aware of the others, he came closer and said in a low voice, "You're supposed to sit sidesaddle. Swing your right leg over that short horn."

He had to be kidding. She was going to have enough trouble staying upright without taking away half her balance. "That's all right," she said, hoping to put some authority into her voice. Ignoring the short stirrup by her left leg, she let her right leg dangle free. "This is the way women ride in America." How would they know if she was lying? She pulled the skirt down to cover any exposed skin and straightened her hat. Holding the crop in her hand like a wand, she pointed to his horse. "Whenever you're ready, Mr. Egan."

He handed the reins to her, and she could have sworn he was biting the inside of his cheek to keep from laughing. She envied the ease with which he swung himself into the saddle, but reminded herself that this was his only means of transportation. He would be awkward and afraid if she sat him behind the wheel of an automobile.

Rory pulled on the left rein, and his horse turned toward the drive. Following his example, Cathy did the same and said, "Giddyap." That was the only horse language she knew, and she was amazed when her horse followed his. This isn't hard, she thought, as they walked the horses slowly away from the house. But at this rate she'd never get to the cairn. And now that she was out of the house, she was eager to return the stone. It was going to work. She knew it. That was the only thing she had done to bring on this craziness. She had insulted the "old ones." It didn't matter that she never believed any of that New Age stuff. She had laughed at Shirley MacLaine and crystals and past lives as kooky. No normal, intelligent adult would accept such nonsense . . . And she still didn't accept it, but how could she explain *this*? Something had happened to her that was beyond the realm of her perception, something totally unexplainable.

"Have you ever ridden before?"

Pulling herself out of her daydream, Cathy realized Rory had pulled up next to her and was staring. She cleared her throat. "Of course I have." Did merry-go-rounds count?

"Then we can increase our gait?"

Did that mean go faster? "Why, yes. I was just thinking that myself. But first, in which direction is the waterfall where you found me?"

He looked at her strangely before pointing across the field toward a huge mountain.

Good Lord, it seemed so far away. Rolling hills and pastures separated her from it, but there was a road winding up, and she had to find it. "Will you take me there?"

His expression revealed his surprise. "Absolutely not. I was told by a housemaid that you were not to leave the estate property. Lady Montrose's orders."

Cathy didn't know if it was the order or who had told him that made her spine straighten with indignation. Before she could figure it out, she blurted, "Oh, really? Did your little sweetheart tell you that?"

His head jerked up. "I beg your pardon."

"Maureen. Quite pretty, but she seems to carry a great deal of authority for a young woman working in someone else's home. And she's too chatty about something that isn't any of her business."

He actually smiled. "That does sound like Maureen, and

she isn't my sweetheart. It wouldn't be the first time she's overstepped her boundaries. But are you saying what she told me wasn't true?"

"Well, I don't know what she's told you," Cathy countered, glad that they were still walking the horses. And he was smiling . . . Maybe she could change his mind about taking her to the cairn.

He seemed to think about her statement for a few seconds before saying, "I was told that you had been sick for the past two days, and your head injury has left you confused. The Montroses were very concerned when they left this morning for Killarney."

"Yes, well . . ." She didn't know how to answer. "Fresh air is good for me, and it's such a beautiful day . . ." She was rambling, yet she couldn't figure out how to convince him to take her. Obviously it was time for Lady Catherine to reappear. "I'd like to see the waterfall again, Mr. Egan. You may take that as a polite order, but an order nonetheless."

Perhaps she had gone too far, for his lips tightened and there was anger in his eyes. "Why don't we see how well you ride first? Torrec Waterfall is a goodly distance. Shall we take the horses into a cantor?"

Without waiting for an answer, he bolted away from her, and her horse immediately followed. Startled, Cathy dropped the crop and grabbed hold of the horse's mane as the animal took off after the brown in almost a gallop. Frightened, she fought to hold her balance and instinctively gripped the horse with her legs and leaned forward. She was terrified of the power beneath her. She could feel the massive muscles working and felt helpless to control them as the horse broke into a full gallop. The animal had a mind of its own, running without any direction, and she passed Rory while holding on for dear life.

Terror raced through her veins as quickly as the horse raced through the field. She was out of control but could hear Rory behind her yelling, "Steady! Pull back on the reins. Half halt! Stop gripping him with your legs. You're making him go faster!"

Frozen in fear, she couldn't make her hands let go of the mane, nor could she relax the muscles in her legs! Every instinct she possessed told her to hold on or fall.

She saw the low stone fence ahead and knew the horse was going to jump it. She could feel it in the way the animal tensed. She would never make it! She couldn't! The reins slipped from her grip, and she closed her eyes to shut out the sight as the horse leapt into the air.

Suddenly she, too, was in the air, suspended alone for a silent, timeless moment in space, and then she fell away from the horse to the ground. Stunned, Cathy stared at the clover by her face, as sound and senses returned.

She heard Rory stop his horse, and when he jumped over the fence, she expected him to yell at her stupidity. "Are you all right?" he asked, bending down.

She pushed herself into a sitting position and glanced up at him. "I couldn't stop him," she muttered, still dazed by the fall.

"I thought you said you could ride," he accused as he pulled her upright.

"I . . . I lied," she admitted as she pushed her hair off her forehead and looked up at him. "It seems you're always coming to my rescue."

It passed between them again, that male-female thing, that quick, hot spark of recognition and attraction. It started at her knees and worked its way up the inside of her thighs to settle in her stomach.

He seemed to catch himself and was the first to break the gaze. Looking to his left, he whispered, "Oh, no . . . ," and, dropping her hands, he walked away.

Cathy turned and saw the cause for his dismay. Her horse was limping about thirty feet away. One of his back legs was injured. There was a long gash, and blood stained the shining brown coat.

Picking up her skirt, she ran after Rory and stood next to him as he examined the animal.

"It's okay, boy," he murmured, running his hands gently down the horse's leg to check for further injury. When he lifted the long limb, he said, "Thank God, it's not broken. He didn't clear the fence."

"Rory, I'm so sorry. I can't believe I've done this. Here . . ." She hiked her skirt up and ripped the fine cotton slip. Handing the length of material to him, she said, "Maybe you can wrap his wound with this. I . . . I wish I could do more. I wish I had never come here!"

Sitting down on the low stone wall, Cathy let the tears come as she stared at her boots. Nothing as working out. She couldn't even get to the mountain, let alone the cairn. How was she ever to get back to her own time?

He looked over at her. "Are you all right?"

She lifted her gaze. "I'm fine. But my God, what about the horse? What have I done?"

Rory tied a knot to secure the makeshift bandage and stood up. Walking over to her, he said, "I'll ride back to get you a trap and then I can take you home."

Home? She sniffed and wiped at her cheek. "I'd give anything in the world, Rory, to get home again. The manor isn't my home. Ireland isn't my home. America is. And I might never see it again."

"Will you be all right here until I get back?" he asked, uneasy with her sudden declaration. "Cully isn't going to go anywhere the way he is."

Cathy got up and walked over to the animal. No longer afraid, she reached out and ran her hand down its nose. "Is that your name?" she asked in a whisper. "I didn't even know your name. I'm so sorry I did this to you. But I was desperate to get away . . ." She looked over at Rory. "Forget about going back for me. Let's take care of the horse. This is my fault. I'll walk back to the manor."

"It's a lot further on foot, and we'll have to go around this fence."

She looked once toward the mountain and then back at the man. "I'll do it." She picked up Cully's reins and waited for him.

Together they led their horses in silence through the pasture, neither one of them knowing what to say to the other. Something was different now. Acknowledging an attraction had changed both of them. And they had shared something . . . twice. Once in the mountains and now here. Experiences bind the most unlikely people together.

He stopped walking and bent to pick something up from the ground. "Here," he said, extending his hand toward her. "You dropped your riding crop."

Cathy took it and said, "I don't know how anyone could use this thing on an animal. I know I couldn't."

"If you're good enough, and understand the horse, then you don't have to."

She threw back her head and laughed. "Well, we know I don't qualify on both counts. What a terrible actress I am. I can't even stay on the back of a horse."

He did that thing with his eyes again, making them seem as if they were looking inside of her, seeing the real person and not the facade she presented to others. "You aren't what I expected, Lady Catherine. You're very different."

His voice was low and hesitant, his expression more intense.

Cathy's breath caught at the back of her throat. "You can't even imagine how different I am, Rory. Take my word for it, you have never met a woman like me in your life."

The corner of his mouth lifted in a smile, one that he was trying to control. "I believe you are correct, Lady Catherine. You are unique. I have never met an Englishwoman quite like you before—"

"I'm not English," she interrupted. "I'm American."

"Oh, yes. American. Women must be very different there."

"We are. We're very different from the women you're used to. I think you'd be shocked by how much."

He silently walked on, taking in her words. After half a minute he suddenly said, "Before you were saying that you would give anything in the world to go home to America. You didn't want to come to Ireland? I had heard you did."

She almost grinned. "What else did you hear? That I

couldn't find a husband? That Lady Montrose was going to play matchmaker for me and get me married?"

He looked embarrassed. "That is none of my business. I'm sorry I asked, madam."

"Well, it's not true. If I had wanted a husband, I could have found one. I'm not ready to get married." She thought about that last statement. "I mean, I'd like to meet somebody, but so far it's not in the cards. I am *not* a spinster, however. What a word!"

"I beg your pardon, Lady Catherine. I apologize if anything I said offended you."

Surprised, she looked at him and saw that he was sincere. The longer he stared at her, the more she felt that strange pulling in her legs. No wonder Maureen was jealous. He was handsome, and when he smiled, his eyes actually sparkled, showing tiny yellow flecks. And he was so . . . so male. How long had it been since she'd felt this attracted to a man? Not even Adam had produced this powerful, instant attraction. Ever since she woke up at the cairn and saw his face above her, she had trusted this man, and he hadn't disappointed her.

The question was, could she trust him again?

Taking a deep breath, she decided she didn't have any other choice. "Remember when I told you I was American? Well, I'm an Irish-American. My grandmother was born in Ireland. Kenmare, to be exact. So you can drop the Lady Catherine thing once and for all. I'm not the Montroses' niece. My name is Cathy Connelly. I'm thirty-four years old and I live in Philadelphia, Pennsylvania. In the good old U.S. of A., I work at an office on Locust Street, and I live at 462 Walnut Street, Apartment 2B. My phone number is 215-555-5383. I was born in the year 1959. And on May twenty-third, I will be thirty-five years old."

He had stopped walking to stare at her. Shock and disbelief were written on his face.

"Yes, Rory Egan, I am a unique woman. When you found me, I had left the year of Our Lord, nineteen hundred and ninety-four."

chapter

four

"Let's get back to the house." Rory started walking away from her.

Cathy slowly led her injured horse and called out after him, "Now do you understand why I must get back to the cairn? I took a rock as a souvenir, and I have to put it back. Once I do, I just know everything will turn around. I'll go back where I belong. Or should I say forward . . ."

He spun around to face her, and he was clearly angry. "The only thing about you that I understand is that you have a fantastic imagination. And that, Lady Catherine, is being polite."

"I've told you," she insisted. "I'm not Lady Catherine. I'm a very ordinary woman who finds herself in an extraordinary situation. But I am not crazy. If I were, I wouldn't remember all those details of my life. And I want to get back to it. That's why I need your help."

"My help? Madam, I would say—" Rory stopped speaking and turned his head toward the main road and the carriage quickly approaching. Closing his eyes, he muttered, "I must be cursed. Ever since I saw you at the cairn, nothing has gone right. It's the Montrose carriage."

"From Killarney? Already?" Cathy looked toward the sky, as if for help. "If you think your life is cursed, Rory Egan, you should try living mine."

The carriage rolled to a stop in front of them, and Randolph Montrose opened the door and stepped down to the road. Margaret leaned out, a horrified expression on her face.

"Catherine, what are you doing away from the house?" Randolph demanded as he walked up to them.

"I was riding," Cathy answered. "And . . . I fell."

Margaret made a strangled noise and held her chest. Randolph turned to Rory. "Where are your senses, man? The woman is sick and shouldn't be out of bed."

"Please," Cathy interrupted. "Mr. Egan was only following my orders. This is entirely my fault."

Randolph's white mustache twitched as he tried to control his temper. "Catherine, are you hurt?"

"No, I'm not. But my horse is. I tried to jump a fence and didn't make it. I'm very sorry."

"Please get in the carriage with your aunt," the elderly man instructed, then turned to Rory. "Mr. Egan, you and I will discuss this further."

"Don't blame him," Cathy said. "I told you I gave him an order. If you're angry with anyone, then it should be me." She turned to the man next to her and whispered, "I'm sorry, Rory. I didn't mean to get you in trouble."

"Catherine?" Randolph waited at the carriage door.

"Go ahead," Rory said and took the reins from her hand. "It's all right." He turned away to the injured horse.

Cathy shook her head and sighed before walking toward the carriage. Once inside, she sat back against the leather seat and looked at Margaret. The old woman was dressed in an elaborate gown with a heavy gray cloak over it. A ruffled bonnet in the same color sat on her head, and she clasped her gloved hands together in her lap, as if to control them.

"I'm sorry," Cathy said to her. "I've been so much trouble since I came—"

"We'll speak of this later," Margaret interrupted. "We have conferred with Dr. Bowers, and he is going to contact a colleague of his in Dublin and perhaps one in London. But you must stay at the house, Catherine. It's for your own good. You simply can't go off on your own until this . . . this situation is remedied."

"I'm afraid I will have to demand that you respect your Aunt Margaret's instructions, Catherine."

Cathy looked down at her lap and the silly riding hat. She wouldn't answer Randolph, for she didn't want to lie. She had every intention of leaving at the first opportunity.

She was in bed. Again. It seemed that every problem brought the same solution. Bed rest. She was sure the entire staff had heard about her adventure, for Maureen had come into her room with the jeans and blouse. Putting them away in the armoire, the girl had muttered under her breath about how Rory could lose his job because of Lord Montrose's anger.

As the sun began to set, it created a prism of colors through the beveled windows in the bedroom. She had spent the rest of the afternoon trying to think of some way to get back to the cairn, and absolve Rory Egan of any transgression. When Margaret joined her for dinner, Cathy tried once more to tell the woman that Rory wasn't to blame for anything that had happened.

Margaret delicately wiped the corner of her mouth with the crisp linen napkin and sat back in her chair. "Catherine, perhaps this is a good time to speak with you about certain things. Please, finish your wine. Dr. Bowers said it was permissible."

Cathy brought the crystal goblet to her lips. The wine tasted slightly bitter, but she wasn't exactly a connoisseur. She, too, sat back in her chair, forgetting the delicately seasoned salmon. "But I want you to understand that Mr. Egan isn't to blame for anything that happened. It was all my fault."

Margaret cleared her throat. "My dear, you need to understand that a certain amount of decorum is necessary when dealing with those under you. I realize formalities have broken down in America, but you are in Ireland now. Becoming overly friendly with the stable master is unthinkable."

"I wasn't overly friendly," Cathy said in her own defense. She hadn't even touched Rory, let alone come on to him. Maybe that snoop, Maureen, had told Margaret something.

"Your mother wrote to me of your . . . difficulty in finding a proper suitor. I can understand," Margaret hurried to add when Cathy opened her mouth to reply, "how a woman of your age must feel without a home and children of her own. And it will happen, I'm sure. But to associate with the hired help, and an Irishman at that, is simply not done. The servants are beginning to speak of your strange fondness for this man."

"I'm sure you're talking about Maureen," Cathy said and gulped the rest of her wine. "I think the girl is jealous."

"Now, this is just what I was speaking of. Catherine, I suppose the man is handsome in a rugged sort of way, but you must not be discouraged by your past inabilities so that you consort with those beneath your station in life. Your fascination with this man must end. I forbid you to see him again."

Her lips felt warm and tingly, as if she'd had three or four quick drinks, and she ran her fingertip over them. How strange that Margaret should think Rory beneath her. Most of the men she had dated in her lifetime wore three-piece suits and held down respectable jobs. They were suitable, but they had never made her feel the way Rory did by just looking at her.

"Are you listening to me, Catherine?"

Cathy raised her chin and tried to concentrate. "Yes . . . It's just that I feel . . . I don't know . . . strange." She ran her tongue over her lips, wondering how to tell Margaret, without further shocking her, that she felt drunk.

"That's to be expected, my dear. Dr. Bowers gave me a packet to mix with your wine. It will make you sleepy so that you can rest properly. He said that sleep restores energy to the body, particularly to the brain."

"A packet? What was in it?"

"Morphine. We picked it up at the chemist when we were in Killarney."

Cathy merely blinked, not believing this was happening to her. "You gave me *morphine*! You drugged me!"

"Calm down, Catherine. I assure you it's quite safe when used properly."

Cathy stood up and held onto the small table that separated them. "I'm very tired, Margaret. I think I'd like to rest now."

"Certainly," the woman said as she rose. "Would you like me to help you into bed?"

"No, thank you. I can manage."

"Rest well, my dear," Margaret whispered as she kissed Cathy's forehead. "The maids will remove the table shortly, and tomorrow we shall continue our conversation."

As soon as the door was shut, Cathy grabbed the teapot and poured herself a cup. She didn't bother with cream or sugar, but gulped down the strong, hot liquid. Gasping for breath, she poured another. They probably didn't know that tea had even more caffeine than coffee, or they wouldn't have let her have it. And she needed all the stimulants she could get into her now.

Morphine! God, they could kill her and not realize what they were doing! How long did she have before it took full effect? Could she fight it off? What was next? A straitjacket and a padded room? Just the thought of a nineteenth-century mental institution sent a shot of adrenaline pumping through her veins.

She drank the second cup of tea and walked to the wardrobe. Inside she found her jeans and her blouse. Feeling for the stone and her car keys in her raincoat, she thanked God that she had remembered to remove them before Maureen took away the soiled riding habit earlier. She checked for her boots and her underwear. Everything was there. Now all she had to do was wait until they came for the table. Since it was dinnertime, everyone would be busy in the kitchen. Margaret would be telling Randolph of their conversation, and together they would be planning their next move. It was now or never.

Cathy went into the bathroom and poured water into a basin. She splashed it over her face and rubbed it into her skin in the hopes that it would wake her up. She was get-

ting out of here. And she was going to do it before night
fell.

It was almost too simple. The house was quiet and everyone was busy. Only once did she have to flatten herself
against the wall and hide behind the large cabinet in the
entry hall, when Randolph's manservant walked by carrying a silver tray with brandy on it.

She waited until the man entered another room before
gathering her raincoat about her and heading for the door.
With her escape from the house complete, Cathy ran
toward the small thatched cottage next to the stable.

She was nearly out of breath when she pounded on the
door. Dear God, please let him be here, she prayed. He
was her only hope.

The door opened, and he stared at her with shock.

"Please. You have to help me!"

"Go away," he said in an exasperated voice. "I'm in
danger of losing my position because of you."

"Please," she begged while fighting back tears.
"They've drugged me with morphine."

He looked around the yard, and then, sighing, opened
the door wider to allow her entrance.

She rushed into his cottage and spun around as he
bolted the door behind her. "You must help me, Rory. I
have to go back to the cairn tonight. I know where the
mountain is now. You showed me today, but I can't saddle
a horse. I need you for that. I won't ask you to go with
me. I know how much this job means to you."

Shaking his head, he said, "You can't possibly know."

"I do," she said urgently. "I've seen the poverty in this
country. I wouldn't ask you to jeopardize your job. I know
it's important."

"It isn't the job," he said angrily. "It's the land!"

"The land?" She was confused and looked around the
small room. "Do you have any tea? I need something to
stay awake and fight off the drug."

He stormed over to the fireplace and took a cup off the

mantle. "Here. Sit down," he said in a gruff voice as he poured the tea.

She did as he asked and looked up at him. "This land?" she asked. "Ardrare Manor?"

Jamming his fists into the pocket of his trousers, he stared into the fire. The muscle in his jaw moved as he clenched his back teeth together. "Before there ever was a manor house, this land belonged to the Egans," he finally said. "Before Ireland was invaded by Vikings or the Normans, this land belonged to the family of Egan. And it will again. A time will come when rightful ownership is restored. If not by me, then by my children. And if not by them, then by my great-grandchildren. We have waited seven hundred years. We will wait as long as it takes." He turned his head to look at her. "If I help you, I will be forced to leave. And I can't leave the land."

She didn't say anything for a moment as she acknowledged the passion in this man's soul. She wanted someone to feel that way about her ... Surely it was the drug and the fire that made her wish it could be him. Breaking the powerful gaze, she said, "I know you don't believe what I told you this afternoon about being from the future, but you must listen to me now. I can't remember much history. It wasn't one of my best subjects. But my grandmother would tell me of Ireland. Something called Home Rule came into effect right before World War I, but the Irish don't get their country back until 1940 or 50. I can't remember ..."

His jaw dropped, and his eyes widened with shock. "World War?"

She rubbed her forehead, trying to think clearly. "It happens in 1914 or 15, but don't you see, Rory, that's fifty years from now. You may not even be alive to see Irish people unite and stand up for their rights. And win. Even in my time, a hundred years from now, England still has a hold in Northern Ireland. If you want to own land, then go to America and make your fortune in ..." She racked her brain for a solution. "Gold! It's discovered in the West. Wyoming, I think. And oil. This should be around the right time. Oil in Pennsylvania. That's my home state. But maybe that's before the Civil War. I can't remember. And telephones. Alexander Graham Bell. Remember that name. Invest in telephones. And gas and electricity. If you ever hear of them, sink everything you've got into it." She held his startled gaze. "I don't know what else to tell you, except it will never happen here ... the English handing over the land. If you don't believe anything else I've told you, believe that."

"Who are you, Cathy Connelly?" he asked in awe.

She smiled. "Finally you've got the name right."

"And you're not related to the Montroses?"

"I'm not."

"And you're not English."

"Not a trace. My grandmother would turn over in her grave."

"Then why are you here?"

"I don't know ..." She stood up and walked around the small room. "I've tried to figure it out. The only thing I can come up with is the rock. I never should have taken it." She stopped pacing and stood before him, placing a hand on the mantle to steady herself. "Will you saddle the horse for me? I'm getting very tired and dizzy."

He put his large, warm hand over hers and whispered, "Aye, Cathy Connelly. I'll do better than that. I'll take you there myself."

He pulled her into his arms, and the space between them vanished. Their mouths met instantly, hungrily, in a kiss that finally united them. It was possessive and voracious, as if they had been starved. He tasted her, inhaling the scent of her. The kiss left her breathless and clinging to him for more.

"I've wanted to do that since I found you on that damned mountain," he whispered into her mouth, while running his hands down her back slowly, gently.

There was a heat curling around her flesh that had nothing to do with the fire. It was hypnotic, and she wanted to melt into him, to pull him to the narrow cot and let him wrap his arms around her. To make love to him and discover every inch of him. To sleep in his arms forever. Her eyes again filled with tears, and her voice was thick with emotion. "I think I've been searching for you all my life, Rory Egan." She kissed his mouth, knowing she was losing herself in this man, and not caring.

His arms wrapped around her, pressing her breasts into him, and her body molded itself to his, as they clung together against everything, everyone, that would pull them apart.

There was something so bittersweet and right about it that Cathy pulled her mouth away and rested her cheek on his chest. Breathing heavily, she tried to control the tears that were beginning to sting her eyes. How could this have happened *now*? And was it the drug that was making this seem so extraordinary?

He kissed her hair, again breathing in the scent of her. "Stay with me, Cathy. We'll find a way."

She pulled back to see his face. "I ... I can't," she cried. "This isn't my time. Come with me, Rory! You wouldn't believe the 1990s. There's so much for us there. For you!"

A sharp knock sounded at the door, and both of them froze.

"Over here," Rory whispered, pulling her to the wall behind the door. Holding his finger to his mouth in warning, he nodded once and released the latch.

"Ahh, Rory, the gates of hell just opened," a man pronounced.

"What is it, Liam?"

"Jack Sweeney just rode up to the house, tellin' Lord Montrose that the widow Sullivan over on Cromaglan has been carin' for a woman that claims to be the Lord's niece. I'm tellin' ye, Rory, there's somethin' mighty strange goin' on. I'm to tell you to be ready at first light for Lord Montrose. Can you believe he's goin' hisself?"

Rory didn't say anything for a moment, then lowered his voice. "Liam, I need your help."

"What is it?"

"Will you saddle my horse and bring it here, without asking any questions? I'll explain later if I can."

There was a pause, and then the old man said, "Aye, lad. I'll do it. God watch over ye, in whatever you're doin'."

Rory closed the door and looked at her. "They've found the real niece."

"I heard," she whispered. "Now I really have to get out of here. Margaret and Randolph will think I was impersonating Lady Catherine. They could have me arrested, or . . . or put away!" She hurried to the chair and sat down, holding her head in her hands. "What if it doesn't work at the cairn? How could I ever live in this time? How would I survive?"

He stroked her hair and pulled her to him. There was gentleness, yet security, in his touch. She wrapped her arms around his waist and leaned her head against him.

"There, now, Cathy, girl, we have no time for tears yet."

She wiped at her cheek. "It's the morphine. I'm so tired . . . and I feel dizzy, as if I've had too much to drink. Oh, God, am I crazy, Rory? Is all this a bad dream?"

"What you're asking me to accept is so . . . so amazing. Anyone would think I was daft for believing you. But I do, Cathy Connelly. I believe you."

She raised her head, and relief washed through her. Someone believed her. He believed her!

They heard Liam bringing the horse around, and Rory pulled her up to him. "We must hurry. Soon they'll discover you're gone, if they haven't already. Can you ride? Can you hold onto me?"

"I can do it," she said, determined to fight the effects of the drug.

He nodded once, grabbed his tweed jacket, and led her to the door.

The wind whipped through her hair, and she wrapped her arms around him as they rode toward the sunset, leaving Ardrare Manor behind.

It was almost dusk when they reached the waterfall. Cathy could hear its roar as they climbed the mountain toward the cairn. He held her hand, encouraging her, supporting her, until they reached the ancient ruin.

It stood before them, as it had stood for four thousand years ... a mystical place of meeting.

Cathy breathed heavily as she stared at it. It was more defined than she remembered, less of a strange pile of huge rocks. She looked around and sighed. "It's so beautiful here. The mountain and the waterfall. When I first saw it, I felt as if I had finally discovered the magic of Ireland. It gave me such peace ..." Still holding Rory's hand, she reached into her pocket with the other hand and felt the rock.

"Do you know that you look almost exactly the way you did when I first saw you?"

She smiled and turned her head to him. "I looked like a drowned rat."

"You looked frightened, and even though I thought you were English, a part of me was touched by what I saw in your eyes. I didn't want to care for you, you know? You were the enemy. I didn't want to lie in my bed at night and think about you. But you captured my mind. What an odd woman, I thought. So strange. So beautiful. So gentle. So determined."

"Unique," Cathy whispered in a thick voice. "That's what you called me. No one has ever said that to me." She took a deep breath and continued, "When I was first here, I was running away from myself. I thought I'd never find happiness. Poor Lady Catherine ... I know just how she feels. Too old for any chance at love. I wish I could talk to her and tell her that it's all right. That she's all right. That love comes at the most unexpected times."

He stared into her eyes, and she wanted to lose herself in him. "Don't say anything, Rory," she murmured as she came into his arms. "This has happened so fast that I don't want to examine it. Not yet. Just kiss me. Please ..."

A gentle wind out of the west ruffled Cathy's hair, creating a soft halo of reddish gold around her. Rory gently held her face between his hands as his mouth took possession of hers in a wild, hungry meeting. Cathy kissed him back, leaning closer to him, feeling the cadence of his heartbeat against her own. It took her breath away, made her legs weak, and she held onto him for support.

He gently pulled his lips away from hers and smiled. "If we stand here much longer," he whispered, "I'll take you down to the sweet clover and make love to you."

"Make love to me," she whispered back, wanting him more than she had ever wanted a man.

"This is neither the time nor the place, Cathy. Soon a search party will be looking for you." The gentle smile still reflected in his eyes as he took a step back from her, creating a barrier of air between their bodies.

"But there may never be another time or another place! Come with me, Rory."

He held her shoulder as he led her into the cairn. "Where is the rock?"

She reached into the pocket of her raincoat and brought it out. Suddenly dizzy, her steps faltered, and Rory sat her down on the low wall. He held her hand tightly and said, "Now put it back."

She hesitated. Looking up at him, her heart actually ached with fear. "What if it doesn't work? And what if it does? What if I lose you? I couldn't wait to get here to do this and now . . . I'm afraid."

That tender smile returned to his face. "Don't be afraid. I'm with you."

Holding his hand in a tight grip, Cathy placed the rock back into the wall. Immediately she felt infused with a tingly energy. She felt it enter her fingers and work its way up her arm, circling inside of her body, passing through her and down her other arm to his hand. She stared at him, saw the shock on his face as he felt the intense force, and cried out when he broke away from her.

Standing by the entrance to the cairn, his expression turned from shock to anguish. "I didn't really believe it, Cathy. I didn't! I can't do it . . . I'm . . . I'm sorry. I can't leave the land!"

Terrified, Cathy pushed herself off the wall and tried to reach him, to touch him, but her legs felt rooted to the ground. Dark clouds blocked out the last of the sun's rays, and a wild wind blew up around her, bringing fat droplets of rain.

"*Rory!*" she screamed, sinking to her knees.

When she looked up, he was gone.

chapter

five

Cathy pushed the wet hair away from her eyes and fell back against the wall. Tears streamed down her cheeks, yet she ignored them, letting them mingle with the driving rain. She felt confused, disoriented . . .

What the hell was she doing on the ground of the ruin? Pushing herself up, she sat on the low wall for a moment until she felt steadier. Her hand touched something flat and rough, and she looked down to see a gray-and-white rock. Instinctively her fingers pulled away from it, and she immediately stood up.

"This is crazy," she muttered as she wrapped the edges of her raincoat around her and carefully made her way out of the cairn. Had she fainted? She had never done that in her entire life. But what could explain her being on the ground? It didn't make sense.

Wanting to get out of the rain, she walked in the direction of the waterfall, hearing its roar as she hurried toward it. About to step down the moss-covered steps, she stopped and, for some reason, held onto the high stone wall for balance. She felt a sudden ache in her scalp and wondered if she had fallen on her way up. And if she had, why couldn't she remember?

Just get to the car, she told herself, as she headed down the paved trail to the road. It would soon be dark, and she prayed she wouldn't fall on the slick walkway. Despite her careful steps, she slipped twice and had to grab hold of a tree branch to right herself. By the time she saw her car parked on the side of the road, she was exhausted, far too tired for such a short descent. Reaching into her pocket, she pulled out the keys to the rental car and sighed with relief. She couldn't wait to get to the hotel and a hot bath. And sleep. She felt she could sleep for days.

Fumbling with the door lock, she finally managed to open it. Once behind the wheel, she started the car, turned on the heat and defrost, and leaned back against the headrest. What a strange afternoon . . . Maybe she should see a doctor, she thought as she waited for the car to warm up. Something had happened up there. The last thing she remembered was coming to a peace about Adam. She had been happy. She'd even said a little prayer of thanks to her grandmother and the old priests who had built the cairn, for she had felt as though she'd gotten her life back on track. How could she have wound up on the ground in the rain? And why did she have this headache?

She'd figure it out at the hotel when she was warm and dry and rested. Nothing was going to come from sitting on the side of the road, except a possible cold. Letting out her breath in a frustrated rush, Cathy turned on the headlights, shifted the car into drive, and pulled out onto the road.

She drove in silence, not bothering with the radio. She kept her gaze on the winding narrow road, yet her mind kept wandering back to the waterfall. It was frightening to think she could lose time and memory like that. Maybe she was having a nervous breakdown—all the pressure she'd left in America had only followed her, and it was starting to show.

She slowly applied the brakes as her headlights illuminated a large set of iron gates with an A and an M intertwined.

Ardrare Manor.

She hadn't looked at any signs, or even the map, to get here. How had she known the way? she wondered as she passed the gatekeeper's house. She had the strangest impression of a short, wiry man standing with his jacket over his head at the doorway. Now, that was frightening. Shaking off the silly notion, she continued up the drive.

For some reason she knew that once she made this last turn, the house would appear beyond. Her breath caught in the back of her throat when she saw it. It was a mixture of shadows and lights, yet she knew that the house would be magnificent in daytime. Maybe she had seen a picture of it in one of the brochures when she'd planned the trip. She wouldn't think about it anymore. Not until she was inside a room, in a hot tub. She parked the car in front of the house, picked up her purse, and walked up to the huge double doors.

A uniformed attendant immediately appeared at her side. "May I be of assistance, madam?"

Cathy stared up at the array of antlers and animal heads that lined the walls of the entry hall. She experienced a weird feeling of déjà vu, that she had known they would be there.

"Madam?"

Cathy blinked a few times and turned to the man next to her. She smiled nervously. "I'm sorry. I have a reservation for the night. Cathy Connelly."

"Very good, madam. If you'll follow me to the desk?"

She nodded, and he escorted her to a long desk and introduced her to the girl sitting behind it.

"Now, if I may have your car keys, madam," the man asked, "I'll bring your luggage in and park your car. It's the red Toyota?"

"Yes," Cathy said, handing the keys over to him.

The girl stood up and came around to her. "Here, let me take your coat before you're chilled. Would you like a cup of tea?"

"Yes, thank you." Cathy gave her the wet raincoat and looked around the room. She thought the wallpaper was different, and the rug was Oriental instead of Turkish. The huge cabinet had been removed to make room for the desk . . . She caught herself and shuddered. How ridiculous to think that.

"Would you like cream and sugar, or lemon?"

Turning, Cathy forced a smile. "Sugar and lemon, please." She sat down in the chair, and the girl handed her the tea and asked her to fill out a registration form.

Cathy did so and took out her American Express card.

Sliding both back across the desk, she gazed around her into the beautifully decorated rooms beyond, where people were meeting and having cocktails under vast stone arches.

"It's a lovely hotel," she murmured.

"Why, thank you," the girl answered while making an impression of the credit card. "It was in the Montrose family for years before being bought and turned into a hotel. Actually it was the first home of this size in Ireland to become a hotel. Ahh, here's Andrew with your luggage." She handed Cathy a large key and added, "Your room number is 223. Will you be joining us for dinner tonight?"

At the thought of food, Cathy's stomach muscles tightened. She was starved. "Maybe I'll just have room service," she said, envisioning a hot bath and climbing into bed.

"Unfortunately there might be a long wait for room service. We're fully booked tonight. Sixty-four travel agents from the United States are staying with us as our guests."

Cathy looked out to a group of laughing women that had grown in number. They were dressed to the nines, and she felt like a wet dog in comparison.

"Of course, our other guests, such as yourself, are invited to dine in the manor's private dining room. It's quite lovely and very quiet," she added, glancing at the loud women.

"Thank you," Cathy answered, standing up. She'd just take a hot shower instead of a bath. "I'll be down in less than an hour."

"Of course, madam. Don't rush. Our chef will be on call late this evening."

"Thank you," Cathy said. She turned to the man with her luggage and led him across the room and up the stairs.

When they were in the hallway, Andrew asked, "Have you stayed with us before, madam?"

She glanced at him as he stopped in front of her room. "Why, no. This is my first trip to Ireland."

"It's just odd," he said as he took the key from her hand and unlocked the door. "Most guests go straight for the lift, but it was as if you knew the lift doesn't stop on the second floor. It stops on the third because that leads to the newer section of the house, where most of the rooms are."

Standing in the middle of her room, Cathy opened her purse and took out a punt, the equivalent of an Irish pound. Placing the coin in the man's hand, she said, "I don't know why I assumed we were taking the stairs. Maybe because I needed the exercise after riding in the car all day. What a pleasure to finally be here, though." She looked around the luxurious bedroom and sighed with satisfaction. Maybe she could afford two nights here, and to hell with her itinerary.

He hung up her wet raincoat in the large wardrobe and walked to the door. Smiling, he said, "Enjoy your stay with us, madam."

Cathy smiled back. "Thank you. I'm sure I will."

Alone in the room, she started exploring. The wardrobe was a good copy of an early Sheraton piece. The two chairs in the alcove by the fifteen-foot, stone-mullioned window appeared to be copies of Louis Philippe. She spun around and looked at the king-sized bed with longing. She couldn't wait to slide under the covers. Above the bed, at the high molded ceiling, was a Latin saying in gilt letters. *Omina Aliena Sunt, Tempest Tantum Nostrom Est.*

She must remember to ask someone to translate it, she thought, as she left the bedroom and walked into the bath. She stood at the doorway, touching the thick, heavy white robe that hung from a hook, and stared at the beautiful room. It was huge, completely done in white marble. She walked up to the tub, turned on the hot water, and picked up a tiny plastic bottle of bath gel. Pouring it in, she heard a woman's voice in her head telling her that this was the first indoor plumbing in the country.

Her hand froze over the tub, and she glanced toward the fireplace. Pine cones and dried lavender and heather rested in the grate, but she could remember it burning with wood, filling the room with warmth.

Frightened, she shook the thoughts out of her head. "This is nuts," she muttered, replacing the bottle on the marble enclosure and walking back into the bedroom.

"You have never been here before. You've been driving too long and you're stressed out, that's all. You merely have an overactive imagination, spurred on by years of listening to tales from an Irish grandmother."

She threw her huge leather bag onto the bed and almost laughed. Anyone who heard her talking to herself would surely think the cause was more than an overactive imagination. All she needed was to soak in the tub ... get warm, get dressed, and get some food in her stomach. She glanced once more at the Latin saying before gathering up her makeup, hair dryer, and underwear.

It was time to get her act together.

She sat alone at a small table in the corner of the room by the fireplace. She could feel the heat on her legs and was glad that she had decided to get dressed and come down for dinner. After so many days in jeans, she enjoyed wearing pretty clothes again. The olive silk skirt and jacket were perfect for dinner at a mansion, and for the night she was going to pretend that it wasn't a first-time experience. Several couples were eating at the long, formal dining table, and she wondered if they realized they were seated at an original Chippendale. Surely the hotel didn't use this room often. Maybe she had lucked out by arriving with all the travel agents that she could hear talking and laughing in another room.

Smiling, Cathy brought the wineglass to her lips. It was funny how she had changed on this trip. Eating alone in the States was so uncomfortable. Everyone seemed to be in couples. She had always felt inadequate, as if something were wrong with her that she should find herself alone at dinnertime. Here, in Ireland, she appreciated the peace. She found out that she actually liked her own company.

"Did you enjoy your dinner, madam? Would you care for dessert?"

She grinned as the young Irish waiter took her empty plate away. "The poached scallops were delicious, but no, thank you. I'll just have coffee. Decaffeinated, please."

"Of course. Perhaps you'd like to take your coffee in

the library or the drawing room. They're reserved for our private guests."

"That would be very nice. Thank you." She wiped the corner of her mouth with the crisp white napkin and rose from the table.

A few couples were in the library, immersed in conversation. When she entered, they looked up and smiled a greeting, but she didn't want the company. Not tonight. Tonight was for herself. Stopping to check out a few of the titles that lined all four walls, she realized almost all were devoted to agriculture, religion, or philosophy. Too heavy for bedtime reading, she thought as she left the library and walked into the most beautiful room she had ever seen in her life.

Rose-colored velvet sofas faced each other across the long expanse of Oriental carpet. A rosewood piano stood in front of two Venetian mirrors in the corner. And by the lit fireplace was a games table, inlaid with mother-of-pearl. Running her fingers over the surface, Cathy smiled with appreciation. Why did the hotel allow guests, even paying guests, to use this room? It was filled with priceless antiques. Like the Georgian cabinet containing a service of crystal and Royal Worcester tea and coffee cups. But what drew her attention were the many portraits of men and women, all with dark hair and piercing blue eyes.

She was staring at one when the waiter found her.

"I'm so sorry," he said as he placed a silver tray down on a mahogany end table. "We have a large group of travel agents with us this evening."

Cathy smiled. "I've heard."

"Normally this room is reserved for our regular guests, but now that they've finished dinner the hotel manager is taking them for a tour of the house."

"Would you like me to leave?" she asked as she heard the voices coming closer.

The young man appeared surprised. "Oh, no, madam. I merely wanted to prepare you for—" He turned as the travel agents gathered at the entrance to the room. "For this," he added with a smile. "They'll be off to the Tack

Room in a few minutes for a night of wine and song. It happens once a year."

She could tell by the man's voice that he couldn't wait for tranquility to return to the manor. "It's fine," she assured him. "I'll just sit here and have my coffee."

"Very well, madam. Enjoy your evening. I added a small plate of biscuits to tempt you."

Biscuits in Ireland, she discovered, meant cookies. She grinned as she picked one up. "I believe you've succeeded. Thank you."

Taking a bite, she marveled at the service at this hotel, for they made her feel like royalty. It was wonderful to be pampered, especially after days of driving alone in a car. Suddenly the trip to Ireland wasn't such a disaster, and she decided to splurge and definitely book for another night. She fixed her coffee and sat back in the chair, ignoring the men and women and the flashes from their cameras. Nothing could spoil the moment for her. She had come to Ireland to run away, and instead she had found herself. Not bad, she thought. It was okay to be thirty-four and unmarried. She wasn't exactly a spinster.

Spinster? Where had that word come from? It must be this place. She felt transported back in time . . .

"I'm sorry if we disturbed you."

Startled, Cathy almost spilled her coffee at the sound of the male voice. She looked over her shoulder at a man making his way around the sofa. He was dressed in a navy blue gabardine suit that fit his tall frame perfectly.

"No . . . not at all," she said nervously, placing the cup and saucer back on the tray. "Are you one of the travel agents?" What a stupid question, she thought, wiping her hands on a napkin. He spoke with an Irish accent.

He smiled, and his eyes lit with amusement. "No, I'm not. My name is Terrence Egan. This is my hotel." He extended his hand to her.

She had to force herself to move her hand to his. His palm was strong and warm, and she felt as if she had done this all before. Stop it! she mentally scolded herself. This déjà vu thing was going make her look like an idiot. Remembering her manners, she said, "How do you do? I'm Cathy Connelly. Would you care to join me?" Was that bold or polite?

It must have been polite because he didn't look shocked. In fact, he seemed pleased as he thanked her and sat down at the end of the sofa.

"It's a beautiful hotel," she said, anxious to find something to say instead of staring. Dear God, the man was good-looking. His thick black hair was combed neatly back, making his eyes that much more riveting. And his smile seemed sincere. He was the perfect host for this place . . . the perfect gentleman.

"Thank you again, though I can't take any credit for it. It has been in my family for many years."

"Centuries, I would imagine. Before the Norman Conquest . . ." She almost bit her tongue. Damn it! What would make her say such a thing?

He appeared surprised. "Why, yes. As a matter of fact, it was. Not counting, of course, the six hundred years the English laid claim to it."

Egan . . . Egan . . . Why was that name so familiar to her? So important? Why did her heart ache at the thought of it, as if she had lost a lover? She blinked a few times, trying to get her brain working properly again. "But your family regained it?"

He sat back and looked around the room with appreciation. "Yes, it's quite an interesting story. My great-grandfather once worked here for the Montroses as their stable master . . ."

She didn't hear anything else he said as the muscles in her body tightened with dread. "Do you have a picture of him?" she interrupted in a whisper.

"Why, yes. His portrait is right there." He pointed to a large oil painting by the piano.

Forcing her legs to move, Cathy got up and walked over to it.

She gasped with shock and recognition. Immediately everything came back to her. Margaret and Randolph. Maureen. Liam. And him. *Him* . . . Tears welled up in her eyes, and she had to hold the edge of the piano for support. She would have known him anywhere . . . in any time. Although the painting portrayed him in his sixties, the stubborn tilt to his chin was there. And his eyes . . . they were the same. Those laughing Irish eyes.

"Rory Patrick Egan," the voice behind her announced. "He was quite a man, from everything I've heard."

Rory. His name filled her brain, and instantly she remembered everything about him. The touch of his hands on her body. The feel of his lips on hers. The shock and anguish in his face when he let go of her at the cairn and yelled to her about the land. His eyes pleading for understanding. She brought her hand up to her mouth and pressed hard, to stop from crying. My God . . . what had happened to him?

Taking a deep breath, she stared at the painting and made herself ask the question. "How did he get the land back?"

"That's what's so interesting." The voice was closer to her, and Cathy realized the man had moved to the piano. "There was a scandal. Something about the Montroses' niece, and my great-grandfather had to flee the country. He went to America and worked his way to Wyoming, where he discovered gold. Then he came east to Philadelphia and, at your country's Centennial Exposition, came into contact with Alexander Bell. He invested with Bell and in 1887 became the silent partner of Edison and Swann in producing Ediswan Electrical Lamps. That's how he made his real fortune. At the age of fifty-nine, he came back to Ireland and bought Ardrare Manor from the family that had employed him in their stable."

She wiped the tears from her cheeks and asked, "He married, of course?"

"Not until late in life. I think he was fifty. He married an American woman named Nora Groghan. They had one son, my grandfather."

"He was happy, then," she whispered. "He finally had his land back."

"But he wouldn't live in this house. To Nora's horror,

he turned it into a hotel and built his own home by Torrec Waterfall."

She spun around. "He built another home?"

He seemed surprised by the emotion in her expression and her voice. "Yes. I live there. He called it Catherine's View. Much to the chagrin of my great-grandmother. You see, Catherine was the name of the Montroses' niece."

She caught her breath and turned back to the picture to hide the fresh tears that suddenly sprang into her eyes.

"My father told me his grandfather hated this place, but he left orders in his will that it was to be maintained throughout the next century exactly as it had been bought. The only thing he changed at the time was adding the Latin saying to each bedroom."

"I saw it above my bed," she murmured while gazing with love at the painting. "What does it mean?"

"It's taken from the work of Seneca, a Roman poet. Translated, it means: Nothing is ours, except time."

She couldn't hold back the tears and let them come as she reached up and touched the heavy frame. *I got your message, Rory,* she silently called out to him. *And I love you for it. Thank you for that, for making me believe again in love and commitment. I'll keep the secret, our secret. I promise . . .*

She turned back to face Rory's great-grandson and laughed, suddenly lighthearted. "Goodness, I must seem quite odd to you. I'm sorry for falling apart like this. It's just such a . . . a romantic story."

"Yes, it is," he said and reached into his breast pocket for his handkerchief. Handing it to her, he added, "I think it's quite remarkable in this day and age to be so open with your emotions."

She took the handkerchief and wiped her face. "Thank you. That's a very kind way of dealing with a weepy woman."

He chuckled and then asked, "Tell me, Cathy Connelly, how long are you staying?"

"Well, originally just for the night. But I decided at dinner to stay longer, if you have room."

He walked around the piano and extended his arm to her. "As the proprietor of this establishment, I can assure you that you can stay as long as you like. Now, shall we see to that?"

He has Rory's eyes, she thought, those wonderful Irish eyes that seemed to sparkle and laugh with pleasure. And she knew those eyes so well. She had fallen in love with them once. But she could never tell Terrence about his great-grandfather. He would never understand. No one would. Rory would remain in her heart and her mind forever. He had remembered her, even left her signs of his love . . . that was all that really mattered. But Rory Egan was part of a mystical past that had brought her to the present. Her future was ahead.

Smiling, she threaded her hand through Terrence's arm, and he walked her out of the room.

"Perhaps you would care to join me tomorrow for a tour of the grounds? They're really lovely this time of year."

She looked at his left hand. No wedding ring. "I would like that very much, Terrence," she said, realizing she wanted to know this man beyond the instant attraction.

"Wonderful!" he proclaimed. "Do you ride?"

Cathy threw back her head and laughed.

Some things even time couldn't change.

Midnight Daydreams

Cheryl Lanham

chapter

one

"Yo, baby. Where'd you get that body?"

Ignore them, Anna Trask told herself. She refused to look at the gang of youths clustered in front of the liquor store across the street.

"Hey baby, over here," one of them catcalled again in a singsong voice.

She kept her gaze straight ahead and gripped the rental application tighter. They're just kids, she chided herself firmly. There's no reason to be afraid. They're only a bunch of boys showing off for each other.

One of them gave a long, low wolf whistle, and she felt herself blushing. Despite the hot August sun, Anna wished she'd worn a high-necked long-sleeved blouse instead of this skimpy tank top. She felt half-naked. But if she were going to live in this neighborhood, and considering her circumstances she couldn't afford to live anywhere else and still go to school, she'd better get used to dealing with the locals.

Steeling herself to ignore them, she stepped off the apartment house steps and onto the pavement. The boys started laughing, and she heard the sound of footsteps. If she could just make it to her car. Turning, she started briskly up the pavement, telling herself not to panic. For goodness' sake, it was broad daylight and they were just kids. It might be a lousy neighborhood, but it would soon be her home. She didn't have any choice anymore.

From the corner of her eye, she saw a black pickup truck turn the corner and cruise slowly past her. Startled, Anna came to a dead stop and gaped at the vehicle. What on earth was *he* doing down here? Even without the distinctively lettered sign on the side that read "Martell Construction," she'd have known that truck anywhere. She'd seen it often enough in the past three years.

As the truck pulled up next to her own car, a shaft of pure heat shot through her. Heat that had nothing to do with the hot sun and the ninety-degree temperature. She closed her eyes briefly, willing herself to stay calm. But the instant her lids fluttered shut, the sweet, forbidden images flicked to life from the back of her mind and began tormenting her anew.

Images of *him*. Images that had been haunting her for months. She could suddenly see his mouth on hers, his hands moving slowly, sensuously over her skin, their bodies entwined on a huge bed with white silk sheets.

Anna's eyes flew open. Stop it, she told herself firmly. This is getting ridiculous. You've got to learn to control yourself. You're acting like a moonstruck teenager with rampaging hormones. Do you want to embarrass yourself completely? No matter how much you fantasize about him, John Martell isn't interested. He's merely a nice man who had business dealings with your late husband. Whatever John's doing in this neighborhood, it has nothing to do with you.

Anna watched him get out of his truck. She continued lecturing herself fiercely as he walked toward her, refusing to allow his six-feet-two-inches of masculine grace to fluster her into making a fool of herself.

But as she stared at him, her throat went dry. John wasn't a conventionally handsome man. His face was too harsh, his cheekbones too sharp, and his jaw too determined.

"Hello, Anna," John said softly, taking off his sunglasses and brushing a lock of black hair off his forehead. His clear gray eyes studied her intently.

"Hello, John," she replied. "Are you doing a project down here?"

He shook his head. "No, I came to find you."

"To find me?" she repeated, astounded. "What on earth for?"

"I needed to talk to you."

"How did you know where I was?" Anna asked curiously. She was even more curious about why John wanted to see her. She hoped it had nothing to do with Roger's drywalling business. She thought she'd paid off all of her late husband's business debts.

"Jodie told me," John said. "I called over there to talk to Nick, and she happened to mention you were apartment hunting." He broke off and frowned at the boys in front of the liquor store. "You're not seriously thinking of moving into a place down here, are you?"

"Down here is all I can afford," she admitted candidly.

John scowled. "That's not a good idea. This area has one of the highest violent crime rates in Long Beach."

"Yeah, but it's cheap," she replied cheerfully. "Besides, I'm a big girl. I know the drill. I keep my doors locked and look in the backseat of my car at night."

He glanced at the rental application she had clutched in her fingers. "Have you actually signed anything yet?"

Confused, she stared at him. "No, but . . ."

"Good, then let's get going." He took her arm and started for his truck.

"Hey," she yelped. "My car's over there. And where are we going? What's going on here?"

John stopped and sighed but didn't let go of her arm. "Please, Anna, I'd like you to come with me to a nice restaurant down at the Marina. I'll wait here while you get in that accident-waiting-to-happen you call an automobile, and then you can follow me. Okay?"

"No, it's not okay," she said. His nearness was doing dangerous things to her nervous system and her pulse rate. But she stoically ignored the effect he had on her and kept her mind focused on the task at hand. John Martell was one nice guy. She had a funny feeling he was playing the knight errant again, and this time she wasn't going to allow it. She'd done enough of that when Roger died. Anna refused to take advantage of John's kind heart again.

"John," she began firmly. "I have to find an apartment and I have to do it fast. Jodie and I have to be out of our place on Saturday. She and Nick are getting married, remember? Charming as your offer is, and much as I'd love to go have a drink with you, I don't have time. I have to keep looking."

"Come down to the marina with me and you may not have to look at all."

"Huh?"

John gave her a long, slow grin. "Let's just say I've got a proposition for you. One I don't think you'll be able to refuse."

Anna continued lecturing herself as she followed John's truck down Pacific Coast Highway. She wouldn't read anything at all into John's rather peculiar behavior. He was probably just being a gentleman again. No doubt Jodie had launched into a hysterical tirade about Anna's decision to find a studio apartment in the cheapest part of town. No doubt the man was only doing what he thought was his duty in coming to her rescue. He certainly hadn't shown up because he had any interest in her as a woman. She sighed deeply and flipped on the turn signal indicator as they swung onto the road leading to the marina. No matter how many midnight daydreams she had about John Martell, she would be letting herself in for a bitter disappointment if she let herself believe he had any real feelings for her. According to Jodie, John liked his women chic, sophisticated and flashy. He certainly wasn't interested in a widowed waitress trying to work her way through college.

John congratulated himself on having had the foresight to pick this particular restaurant. Anna was so busy gawking out the window at the view that she didn't notice him staring at her.

God, she was so lovely. He studied her profile. Small, delicate, slightly upturned nose, high cheekbones, ivory skin and dark brown hair piled atop her head in a casual knot. Several tendrils had escaped and curled around her neck. His gaze dropped to her shoulders. He swallowed heavily as his body responded. That pale peach tank top she wore covered her decently enough, but he could see the beginning of the top swell of her breasts. His hands suddenly tingled as one of those midnight fantasies he had had about Anna flashed through his head.

She turned and smiled hesitantly, and he silently cursed himself. He had no right to think these kinds of erotic thoughts about this woman. For God's sake, her husband had practically dropped dead at his feet. John knew he wasn't responsible for Roger's death, but he still felt like a heel, even after all these months. He was haunted by guilt. Because the first time he'd met Anna Trask, he'd fallen for her like a ton of bricks.

The waitress brought their drinks. John waited until Anna picked up her glass of sherry and then cleared his throat. "I suppose you're wondering what this is all about."

"Yes, as a matter of fact." She smiled and deliberately tried to sound lighthearted. "I hope you didn't discover an unpaid bill of Roger's. The only thing I have left to sell is that old Cadillac of his, and we both know what you think of that car."

"I've never hounded you about Roger's bills, have I?" he replied with a scowl.

Embarrassed, she hastily dropped her gaze. "No, I'm sorry. You've been very understanding." He'd been more than understanding; he'd been her savior after Roger died. He'd helped her liquidate the company and pay off all the creditors. He'd even arranged for her to move in with Jodie when she needed a place to live.

John reached for his scotch and took a sip to give himself time to think. Anna was turning beet red and staring at her lap. He shouldn't have snapped at her. This situation was starting to deteriorate before he had even made his offer. Damn, that was the last thing he wanted.

"Like I told you," he said. "I've got a proposition for

you. But I want you to promise to hear me out before you say anything. Okay?"

Anna lifted her gaze to meet his, her expression puzzled. "All right," she agreed.

"First of all, Jodie told me you're determined not to have another roommate, is that true?"

Anna nodded. "It's about time I lived on my own, don't you think? Roger's been dead for fourteen months, and Jodie's getting married. I decided it was time for me to stand on my own two feet."

"I understand." Actually, John was delighted about her decision. It made his plan so much easier. "But without a roommate, you'll have to live in a pretty cheap place, right?"

"I was thinking of a small studio. I don't have much stuff anymore, just my teapot collection and my personal things. That apartment downtown is very reasonable and it's furnished too."

"I don't like the idea of you living there," he said bluntly. "It's too damned dangerous."

"John," Anna began, "I appreciate your concern. But they've cut my hours at work, and there just aren't that many jobs around these days. I refuse to give up college. So there's no alternative but to cut my monthly expenses."

"Yes, there is," he countered, then paused and forced himself to slow down. He didn't want to scare her off—he was afraid that if she guessed his true feelings she wouldn't come within a mile of him. And he was determined not to let her live in a slum!

John didn't harbor any illusions that his offer would make her eventually fall in love with him. But it would keep her safe. And who knew what might happen if they saw each other every day? There was always a chance she might come to care for him. It was a slim chance, but one he was prepared to take. "You can rent my place."

"What?" She gazed at him in confusion.

"I just finished converting that little cottage behind my house into a small apartment," he explained. "You'd be an ideal tenant."

Anna's emotions seesawed wildly. For one reckless moment she almost said yes, then she realized why he was making this ridiculous offer. Roger. Darn. Why couldn't he have asked her for herself? But he hadn't. It was all because her dear departed late husband had keeled over with a heart attack in poor John's office and Mr. Super Citizen still felt like he owed her something.

"John, that's very kind of you," she began hesitantly, "but I can't continue to take advantage of your generosity. I couldn't afford to—"

With an impatient wave of his hand, he cut her off. "Look, don't worry about what you can or can't afford. I need a good tenant, someone I know and can trust. I'm willing to knock some off the rent to get that kind of peace of mind."

She wanted to laugh. She wondered how much peace of mind he'd have if he knew the kind of daydreams she'd been having about him for so long. Ruthlessly, she pushed those tantalizing fantasies to the back of her mind and concentrated on getting out of this awkward situation.

"But you'd be losing money," she said earnestly. "I can't let you do that."

John's eyes narrowed thoughtfully. "You haven't even asked me how much I was going to charge, nor have you seen the place. How do you know you couldn't afford it? What's that fleabag downtown asking?"

She told him.

He grinned.

"But the studio downtown is furnished," she protested, feeling trapped, "and I have to have a furnished place."

"My place has a stove and refrigerator. What happened to all your furniture? You and Roger used to have a houseful."

Anna flushed with embarrassment again. She didn't want to admit that when Roger died, she'd not only had to sell his company assets but their personal belongings as well. "Er . . ."

"Never mind," he interjected quickly. "I've got plenty of my grandmother's old furniture stored in the garage.

There's no reason you can't use it." He nodded at her sherry glass. "Finish your drink, and we'll run over there now."

"But, John." She started to argue. But he was already downing his scotch and signaling the waitress for the check. Anna couldn't think of a graceful way to back out.

And she was tempted. More tempted than she'd ever been in her life. The idea of being near John Martell, even as just his tenant, was too potent to resist.

chapter

two

The house was too good to resist too. Anna stood just inside the living room and thought she'd died and gone to heaven. John had done an excellent job of converting the old cottage into a bright, airy and cheerful home. The walls were painted a boring white, but she didn't let that stop her. The place had tremendous possibilities. She glanced down at the thick beige carpet and wondered why he'd put such expensive flooring into a rental. But that was like him, one of the reasons he was such a successful contractor. He always used the best materials.

"How do you like the kitchen?" John asked. He walked across the living room and gestured at the gleaming white countertop. "Everything's brand new. I know the fridge is small, but that's all this unit needed. The dishwasher is built in and the stove is gas."

Anna smiled. "It's lovely. Who picked out the flooring?" The linoleum was white squares interspersed with pale blue sailing ships. "It's gorgeous."

"I did," he replied. "I picked out everything. Didn't see much sense in bringing in a decorator. I mean, this is just a rental . . ." His voice trailed off and he felt like biting his tongue. This was a helluva lot more than just a rental unit. Every single moment he'd been working on it he'd dreamed of her living here. He'd even hurried to finish when Nick and Jodie had moved up their wedding date and he'd known Anna would be looking for a new place to live.

Anna nodded. She walked briskly across the carpet to

the tiny hallway leading to the bedroom and bath. He followed.

"Oh, this is nice," she said, standing awkwardly in the bedroom door and peering inside.

"Go on in," he encouraged, coming up to stand behind her. He could smell the faint scent of a flowery perfume, and without meaning to, he inhaled deeply, dragging the fragrance inside his lungs. "Take a good look around. There's a built-in closet over there and plenty of electrical outlets."

Anna felt him standing behind her, and for a moment she couldn't move. His body heat radiated off him like warmth from a flame. Her flesh broke out in goosebumps. Her nerve endings did a hat dance. She could feel his breath on the back of her neck.

She forced herself to move away.

Dutifully, she checked out the closets and counted the number of electrical outlets, aware of his eyes on her the whole time. She'd be a fool to move in here, but her will to resist was melting by the minute.

It wasn't just John that tempted her either. She coveted this cottage. It was perfect. Clean, cozy, a great neighborhood and John living a mere fifty feet away. She glanced up from the outlets she'd been pretending an interest in and saw his gray eyes regarding her steadily from across the room.

"You interested?" He leaned his large body against the door frame and crossed his arms over his chest.

"John," she began hesitantly, "this house is wonderful. But I really can't afford to pay you what it's worth. I told you what my rent budget is. You could get a lot more than that for this house."

"Let me worry about that," he said bluntly. He straightened from the wall and came toward her. "I told you, losing a few bucks off the rent is well worth the peace of mind I'll get from having a tenant back here who won't give me any hassles. Jodie claims you're neat and clean and you don't throw wild parties."

"You've been discussing me with Jodie?"

"Only insofar as finding out what kind of tenant you'd make," he lied. He'd been pumping Jodie on the sly for months for information about Anna. And what he'd learned had confused him. Knowing the kind of party animal Roger used to be, he'd been genuinely surprised when Jodie reported that Anna was a real homebody. She hadn't even dated since Roger's death. He wondered if it was because she hadn't gotten over losing him.

Anna laughed. "And what did she say?"

"That you're a wonderful roomie." He grinned. "You do the dishes, don't leave your clothes lying all over the place, never bring home strange men and always come up with your share of the rent. What more could a landlord want?"

Anna gave in. The temptation was too strong to resist. "Well, in that case, I'd love to rent this place."

"Good." He turned and started for the door. "Let's go out to the garage. You'll need to pick out some furniture to use. I hope you don't mind. It's pretty old stuff, but it's in great condition."

"I don't mind at all," she replied as she followed him. "I love old things."

The "old stuff" turned out to be gorgeous late Victorian. Anna almost swooned with pleasure as John uncovered a hand-carved mahogany sofa upholstered in faded blue velvet. There were matching wing chairs and two small tables with delicately curved legs.

"There are two beds back there," he said, pointing to some sheet-draped headboards leaning against the wall of the garage. "A single and a double."

"Oh, the single will be fine," she replied, thinking of the small bedroom.

He gave her an enigmatic smile. "Okay. Whatever you say." John put the covering back on the sofa. "I'll take care of getting this stuff moved in and set up for you. Let's go to my place. We might as well take care of the business end of this over a cup of coffee."

* * *

John gazed steadily out of his living room window, watching for Anna's car. He glanced at his watch, realized it was only one o'clock and told himself she probably wouldn't be here for another couple of hours. He'd wanted to offer to help her move in, but he hadn't quite worked up the courage. He'd never been this hesitant with a woman. But then, no other woman had ever affected him the way Anna did.

From the moment he'd first seen her, he'd fallen hard. She'd been married and off-limits. But she was widowed now. Maybe he had a chance. Then again, maybe he didn't.

Women, he'd always thought, tended to go for a certain kind of man. If Roger was the kind of man that Anna went nuts for, then he was plain out of luck. John had no illusions about his attractions to women. He'd had more than his fair share of relationships, some of them good, some of them not so good. But he knew he was basically a hardworking, not very exciting, stay at home and read a book kind of guy. Roger, on the other hand, had been a sophisticated smooth talker who knew how to show a woman a good time.

He reached for his mug of coffee and took a sip as a familiar bronze van turned the corner. It was Jodie's van, and Anna was behind the wheel. Still clutching his mug, John headed for the back door.

Anna was home.

Anna flushed as she climbed out of the van and saw John standing by the back gate. He was holding a coffee mug and watching her with that strange, enigmatic expression that sent pleasurable shivers up her spine. Funny, she couldn't remember him staring at her like that before. Then she realized that wasn't true. He'd worn the same expression just a few days ago, when he'd shown her the rental. "Hi. Looks like we're in for another hot one."

John's gaze flicked down her body, and she felt her cheeks turn pink. She was wearing a pair of short cutoffs and another tank top. He was dressed in a pair of jeans and a short-sleeved shirt.

"At least you're dressed for it," he replied mildly.

Anna hurriedly unlocked the door of the van and pushed it open. "Yeah, well. Uh, I'd better get started. Jodie needs the van back in a couple of hours."

"Let me help you," he called, walking over to the back porch and putting his mug down.

"Oh, that's all right," she muttered, dragging out a box of books. "You've done enough for me already."

John ignored her. He came up behind her, reached past her, and their bare arms brushed lightly. Anna swallowed as she tried to manuever away from him in the small area. She stumbled slightly, righted herself and heaved the box up in her arms.

He was right behind her. No matter how much she tried to protest, John continued to "help."

As they came out to get the last two boxes, she started to reach for the one marked "Pots," but he beat her to it.

"I'll get that one," he said, gently shoving her to one side. "You look beat. Go on inside and sit down. I'll bring these last two in."

Anna bit her lip. His big hands were already reaching for her most precious possessions. She couldn't help it. "Be careful with that one. It's got my pots in it."

"Pots?" he asked archly.

"Teapots," she explained. "And some cups and saucers too. I collect them." She broke off as an amused smile crossed his face. "Go ahead and laugh," she said. "I know it's sort of a funny hobby. But I enjoy it."

"I wasn't laughing at you," he said.

But Anna knew he probably was. No doubt he was used to women that were far too worldly and sophisticated to collect something as corny as teapots. Then she realized she was being ridiculously sensitive, smiled weakly and headed for the house.

John muttered a curse as he watched her stiff back. Not here an hour and already he'd made a mistake. He hadn't been laughing at her hobby. Heck, he thought collecting teapots was kind of cute. Homey. Not at all the sort of hobby a party girl would have. Why in the hell had she been married to someone like Roger Trask? John pushed these speculations to the back of his mind. He had what he wanted now. Anna Trask living right beside him. He had plenty of time to find the answers to all the questions he had about her.

By six that evening Anna was exhausted. She unloaded the last of her teapots from the box and placed it carefully on top of the bookcase. A bookcase she hadn't asked John for, but which had mysteriously appeared in her living room while she was returning Jodie's van.

She sank down on the carpet, too tired to move. John had disappeared inside his house right after bringing the last of the boxes inside. She hadn't seen him since. It was just as well. He wasn't interested, and it was best she accept that now, she told herself.

Her eyes closed and she relaxed, allowing her mind to drift off into its own little world. No sooner had she let her defenses down than the daydreams started. And they were so wonderful she couldn't find the will to stop them. Anna sighed.

In her mind's eye, she could see John standing close to her, his mouth moving slowly toward hers, his gray eyes smoldering with passion, his hands stroking sensuously up and down her arms. He pulled her close and brushed his mouth against hers. Softly, slowly, his hands stilled on her arms and drifted around her back until he was cradling her close to his hard, warm body. Anna shivered.

There was a loud knock on the door. Her eyes flew open and she leapt to her feet. "Come in," she called.

It was John holding two glasses of white wine. "I thought you could use a drink."

"You thought right," she said, wincing at the unnaturally high-pitched note in her voice. "Have a seat."

John handed her a glass and took a long, thorough look at the room. He smiled slightly, satisfied that she'd settled in so quickly. Then he settled himself into one of the wing chairs while she perched daintily on the edge of the couch. He couldn't take his eyes off her. She was still wearing that damned tank top, and the material was so thin he could see the outline of her nipples. He shouldn't look, but God, he couldn't help it.

Anna was going to drive him nuts.

"Uh, it was really nice of you to set up all the furniture for me," she said.

"No problem." He took a long swig from his glass. Now that he was here, he wasn't sure what to do next. Darn. This was ridiculous. He was thirty-four years old; he'd been dating women for years. Why was he suddenly tongue-tied around this one?

"But there's something I don't understand." Anna smiled hesitantly.

"What?"

"Why did you put the double bed in? The single would have been fine with me."

He tried not to smile. He'd put the double bed in because he had high hopes, but he could hardly admit that to her. "The headboard on the single was cracked," he explained. It wasn't exactly a lie. The thing *was* splintered in places. "And the double had a much better mattress."

"Oh." Anna was suddenly, deeply embarrassed. Why on earth had she mentioned that damned bed? It only reminded her of what she'd been thinking just moments before he showed up. She'd been having an outrageously graphic fantasy about him. And he was just being kind. Decent. A gentleman.

She glanced around the room at the borrowed furniture, her gaze skimming her collection of teapots. For a twenty-eight-year-old woman, she sure didn't have much to show for her life. Anna didn't feel sorry for herself. She'd made her choices and taken her chances in life, just like everyone else. But she was damned if she was going to let John feel any responsibility or guilt toward her. She'd spent four years of her life tied up in a relationship where she'd been manipulated by guilt, and she wasn't going to do that to someone else. John Martell was her landlord, nothing more.

And she was going to stop these ridiculous secret fantasies too.

"Have you had a chance to get to the grocery store?" John asked. He knew she hadn't, and he also knew the boxes they'd carried in had contained only the barest of cupboard staples. Anna would no doubt be very hungry, and he knew of a nice little restaurant down in Seal Beach.

"Not yet. But tonight I'm too tired to worry about it. I'll go tomorrow before work."

"You're working tomorrow night? But I thought you told me they'd cut your weekend hours."

"They have," Anna said. "But I'm covering for a girl who wants to go to her cousin's baby shower." She sensed a pity invitation coming and quickly headed it off. Anna yawned widely and then forced herself to smile. "I'm so tired tonight, I think I'll just take a hot bath and crawl into bed."

Lucky bed, John thought as he got up to leave. He wasn't totally stupid. The woman was telling him to take a hike.

chapter

three

The heat of the summer night didn't help her sleep.
Anna rolled over on her stomach and bashed her pillow a couple of times. She felt ridiculous. John Martell
was sleeping less than a hundred feet away, and she
couldn't get him out of her mind. She had to get some
sleep; she had things she needed to do tomorrow.

Anna closed her eyes for the tenth time, took a deep
breath and commanded her muscles to relax. School would
be starting in a couple of weeks, and she had to keep her
mind on her goals. Not on her landlord. Damn it, she'd
spent most of her life living through fantasies, and she
wasn't going to do it again. After finally learning to control this habit, she wasn't going to get sucked back into it
because of John Martell. From now on, she was *living* life
for real, not through her imagination.

The barest hint of a cool breeze came in through the
open window and wafted across her heated flesh. She
stretched and rolled over to the far side of the double bed,
searching for the coolest spot on the sheet. She sighed into
the sultry night air, wishing she were more disciplined,
wishing she hadn't wasted so many years drifting aimlessly. Anna smiled wryly. If wishes were horses, then
beggars would ride. She couldn't change the past; she was
smart enough to know that. But she could determine her
own future, and that future didn't include fantasizing a
one-sided relationship with anybody.

For once in her life she was committed to her own
goals. For once in her life she knew exactly what she

wanted. For once in her life, she wasn't daydreaming the minutes and hours of each and every day completely away.

Getting her B.A. degree was the first thing on her list of priorities. A wave of bitterness washed over her, but she quickly squashed it. It wasn't Roger's fault she'd quit school. Maybe if she'd put her foot down when they were married and insisted on her right to an education, he'd have done a better job of running his business. But she hadn't. She'd let him do as he pleased, and Roger, being Roger, had taken the path of least resistance. He'd continued running the drywall business his father had left him. Even when she'd realized he just wasn't much of a businessman, she hadn't had the heart to say anything. She'd continued working as a secretary to pay the rent and put groceries on the table while Roger tried to salvage the failing business. But Roger had done too little, too late. And she hadn't said a word. How could she nag someone with a heart condition?

Bull. Roger used his heart problem to his own advantage and only when it suited him. The rest of the time, he totally ignored his doctor's warnings. Roger had smoked like an exhaust pipe, drunk like a fish and partied like a frat rat. The reason she hadn't made any demands on Roger was simple. She was drifting through life, just as she always had. When she got bored, she daydreamed. Her job hadn't been too bad, Roger hadn't minded microwaved dinners, and the minute he'd go out to meet a potential customer, which he did practically every night, she'd stick her nose in a book. It hadn't been much of a life, but she hadn't realized that until she was so stuck in a rut she couldn't even see the walls.

Pushing thoughts of the past aside, she sucked in a gulp of hot night air. She had to make plans; she had to keep focused on her goals. She'd spent most of her life daydreaming, true. But now she'd finally found the drive and discipline to go after something for herself. And she wasn't going to let it be spoiled by fantasizing about a man she couldn't have.

Yeah, she thought, as an image of John wearing the

swimming trunks at the company barbecue two years ago flashed into her head. Easier said than done. She couldn't even close her eyes before he was laminated to the back of her eyelids.

Sighing, she flopped over onto her back and mentally went over the list of resolutions she'd made when she'd agreed to become John's tenant. One, no taking advantage of the man's good nature. Two, no buzzing over to his house for every little thing. If there was something that needed doing or fixing around her house, she'd write him a note. Three, and most importantly, no more sexy fantasies.

Anna intended to keep these resolutions, even if it killed her!

John Martell wasn't interested in her. She wasn't his type and she knew it. She'd be darned if she would forge a relationship with the man just because she happened to pay him rent on the first of every month. If she'd learned one thing from her marriage to Roger, it was that forcing someone into a relationship they didn't want was wrong. She ought to know.

Hadn't Roger manipulated her? Hadn't he clutched her hand that night in the emergency room. The very night she'd planned on telling him they weren't suited to each other. He'd begged her to marry him. And Roger had known darned well he wasn't dying.

Anna sighed again. It was impossible to hate her late husband, even for pulling a stunt like that. Roger had been too charming. Too nice. Too damned sweet to hate. Heck, she'd even come to love him after a fashion, and she'd been a good wife too. But that didn't change the facts. Roger Trask had used his heart condition to force her into a marriage she hadn't wanted. He'd manipulated her with guilt and then trapped her with pity. She'd never do that to anyone. No matter how much she loved him.

John angrily kicked the sheet off and stared straight up at the dark ceiling. The air was hot, heavy, bearing down on his naked body and making him conscious of every single nerve ending. A trough of tropical air was streaming up from Baja and bringing with it the highest humidity levels anyone could remember. But it wasn't the damned heat that had him so restless. John snorted. It was the woman sleeping less than eighty feet from him.

Anna.

She was finally here, close at hand. He squeezed his eyes shut as he remembered how she looked when they were moving her things inside. Those beautiful eyes of hers were cautious, wary; several strands of hair had slipped free of her ponytail and come down to curl around her delicate neck. Even the old clothes she wore couldn't hide her shapely legs and slender ankles. And that tank top! Every time she'd leaned over to pick up another box, it had dipped enough to give him a quick peek at her lushly rounded breasts. My God, her breasts.

His flesh responded instantly. John groaned and rolled onto his stomach. Hell, he thought in disgust, he was as bad as a horny teenager in the backseat of a car with a willing cheerleader. He had no business lusting after Anna like this. She wasn't just a body. She was a person. A woman. She was kind and gentle and intelligent, and he'd been crazy about her for a long time. But Lord, he thought, as the ache between his legs intensifed, with half a chance he could really love that body of hers.

Half a chance? John pushed himself up on his arms. His mother's words when he was a little boy came drifting back to him. "If you want something bad enough, John," she'd said, "you just have to keep working until you get it."

In the darkness, a slow, sexy grin spread across John's face. Mama was always right.

Anna speared another lump of hard-packed dirt to one side and tried to ignore the heat searing into her back. She knew she should wait until the cool of the evening before digging up the small flower bed outside her front door, but she was too restless to wait. Too angry. Damn it, why did it have to happen now?

She heard the slam of John's back door and stiffened, then told herself not to be such a fool. It was his backyard; he could come out here on a hot Sunday afternoon without asking her permission. She'd been living behind John for a week now, and except for a brief exchange on Tuesday night when he'd granted her request to plant flowers outside her door, she'd only glimpsed him a few times, coming home in the evenings. Usually when she was on her way out.

"Hi, how's it going?" John asked.

She jammed the trowel into the dirt. "Fine. How are things with you?"

"Busy. We've got a big job up on Spring Street." He knelt next to her.

"Good," she replied with forced cheerfulness. "Sounds like business is booming." His shoulder brushed hers, and she could smell the faint scent of coffee and after-shave. His nearness coupled with the rotten news she'd gotten before leaving work last night rattled her so badly her hands almost shook. Anna attacked the flower bed with renewed vigor.

John watched her slash at the dirt, her fingers clenched so tightly around the trowel her knuckles were white. Without thinking, he reached over and laid his hand across hers, imprisoning her fingers between his flesh and the wooden handle.

Startled, Anna turned and stared at him. He smiled, but made no move to release her hand. "Hey," he said softly. "Did you get up on the wrong side of the bed this morning or is something wrong? You keep hacking at that dirt like that and you're going to have a stroke."

"Nothing's wrong," she replied tartly. She tried to tug her fingers from beneath his, but instead of letting her go, he gently increased the pressure. "Hey, what're you doing? Let go . . ."

"Anna," he interrupted firmly. "Now I know something's upset you. You've been bashing at this flower bed for half an hour. I know. I've been watching you from the kitchen window. Now, we can either spend the rest of the day kneeling here like a couple of penitent sinners, or you can tell me what's wrong. The choice is yours." She glared at him. He grinned. "I like holding your hand. It's all warm and soft and . . ."

"Oh, all right," she snapped, too confused by his outrageous behavior to try and keep a lid on her temper. "Let go and I'll tell you."

He obediently released her hand, and she jerked it back and sat back on the lawn. "I never realized you were so nosy, John."

John shrugged. Let her think he was just a snoop. As long as she told him what the problem was, she could think anything she liked. He'd tried to stay away from her, tried to give her time to adjust to living here, but he was out of patience now.

It was time to start the courtship.

And a woman wouldn't notice she was being courted if she had other worries on her mind.

"Maybe you don't know me as well as you think you do," he replied. John rose gracefully to his feet, reached down and pulled her up. He loved touching her. "You can tell me all about what's bugging you over a cup of chocolate raspberry flavored coffee."

"Chocolate raspberry," she repeated. Her lips quirked in a sudden smile. "That's my favorite. I love flavored coffee." But at over six bucks a pound she wasn't able to afford it.

Keeping her fingers firmly entwined with his, he pulled her up the stairs and into the kitchen.

When he released her hand to make the coffee, she felt oddly bereft. She took refuge in examining his kitchen. "Wow, this place is gorgeous. Did you do it yourself?"

He looked up from the coffeemaker. "Of course. This was originally three little rooms. What do you take in your coffee?"

"Just black, please," she murmured. The room was bright and airy, with spotless white appliances, flooring exactly like the linoleum in her place, and a huge bay window looking out over the backyard.

John nodded toward a polished oak dining set next to the window. "Have a seat."

Suddenly nervous, Anna pulled out a chair and sat down. She watched him pick up the coffee mugs and move with that unconscious masculine grace of his toward the table.

Setting a mug in front of her, he sat down. John regarded her steadily. "Now, why don't you tell me what's wrong?"

"It's no big deal," she said, forcing a casual smile to her lips. "I'm just a bit annoyed because they cut my hours at work. Again."

"A bit annoyed," he repeated in disbelief. "Come on, the way you were mutilating that dirt out there it looked like you were ready to take on an army of muggers and the IRS singlehandedly."

Anna shrugged nonchalantly. "You misinterpreted my body language." She refused to let him see how badly losing those hours had really hit her. She didn't want his sympathy. "Maybe you don't know me as well as you thought you did," she said, repeating his earlier words back to him and hoping it would make him smile.

It didn't. John continued to stare at her.

"I see," he finally said. "How many hours are you going to work now?"

Anna's embarrassment began to turn to anger. "Enough to pay the rent."

"I wasn't worried about that," John said flatly. "Answer my question."

Instead of telling him to mind his own business, she found herself answering. "Ten to twelve a week. With this economy, the restaurant doesn't need me except on weekends." She forced life into her voice. "But I'm not worried about it. With my experience, I can find something to keep the wolf from the door. And if that doesn't work, there's always Aunt Hilda in Alameda."

"Aunt Hilda?"

"My mother's sister, she lives up in the Bay area. Ever

since Roger died, she's been trying to talk me into moving in with her and finishing college up there."

The thought of Anna moving four hundred miles away from him filled John with panic, but he was too good a negotiator to let his emotions show on his face. "You're not seriously thinking of doing that, are you?"

Anna shook her head. Much as she loved her aunt, she didn't want to live with her. "No, I like it here. Cal State Long Beach is a good school, and I'm already enrolled there. Besides, they have a Physical Therapy Department. The only school up north that has one is Stanford, and short of winning the lottery, there's no way I could ever afford to go there."

"That's what you want to do?" He took a sip of coffee. "Be a physical therapist?"

"Eventually," she replied. Her eyes suddenly gleamed with enthusiasm. "It's going to take me a while. I mean, working your way through college isn't easy, and I've still got two years' undergraduate work to complete, but I'm going to do it. I've never wanted anything more in my life."

He wanted her to have it too. John realized that if it had been in his power to give it to her, he would have. And suddenly it was.

"Wanting something badly is half the battle," he murmured. "Believe me, I know. And you don't have to worry about hustling out and trying to find another waitress job."

"I don't?" Anna stared at him in surprise. Then her stomach tightened in dread. Surely he wouldn't try and reduce her rent.

"You can come and work for me."

Oh no, she thought, I'm doing just what Roger used to do. Fishing for pity. A wave of hot, humiliating shame swept over her. "John, that's very kind of you . . ."

"It's not kind at all." He cocked his head to one side. "Can you type?"

"Huh? Oh, yes," she answered. "Of course I can type, but really, you don't have to offer me—"

He brushed her protests aside with his hand. "Good.

Maggie's been nagging me for more help for months. How many hours a week were you working at the restaurant?"

"Twenty-four, but, but . . ."

"Good. I can give you twenty-five. If that's too much, we can cut back to fifteen or twenty. You'll need time for classes and studying. And you've got to have time for a social life."

"I don't need a social life," she protested and then realized she should have told him she didn't need the job. Oh, good grief, what was she going to do? Living this close to him was bad enough; despite all her intentions and her constant lectures, she still couldn't keep him out of her mind.

Anna's head spun in a tangle of conflicting emotions. She didn't want his pity. She needed a job. She wanted to go to school.

"Nonsense," he replied firmly. "All work and no play makes Jill a dull girl. When can you start?"

"Er . . ." She really didn't want to live with Aunt Hilda. "I'll have to give a few days' notice at the restaurant."

"Fine." He sat back in his chair and gave her a slow, satisfied grin. "You can start a week from Monday."

c h a p t e r

_____

f o u r

_____

Anna's maroon Caddie backfired as she was turning
onto Redondo Avenue. She ignored the surprised
glances of the other motorists and kept her eyes straight
ahead as she pumped the gas pedal and prayed the engine
wouldn't stall.

"Please," she murmured under her breath, "don't quit
on me now. Not now. I've got to get to work; I'm already
late." The car must have heard her, because despite the occasional groan and belch from the engine, she made it into
the parking lot of the industrial park where John had his
offices.

She plastered a phony smile on her face as she dashed
up the walkway and through the door. Maggie Jones,
John's office manager, was sitting at her desk, her dyed
black hair sprayed into a football helmet and a cigarette
dangling from her lips.

"Don't sweat it, kid," she yelled as she saw Anna
glance nervously at the clock on the wall. "The boss ain't
here, and you're only five minutes late."

"Oh, Maggie, I'm so sorry." Anna dumped her purse on
her desk and flopped into her chair. Lifting the cover off
her typewriter, she sighed. "It's been a miserable day. My
car's acting up . . ."

"Acting up," Maggie hooted with laughter. "Jesus, kid,
you oughta be grateful the old thing even starts."

"Yes, I know. It started all right, but it doesn't seem to
want to make left turns without backfiring. On top of that,
I went over to school, and I've found out the darned fees
have gone up."

"Tough break," Maggie said sympathetically. "Why don't you take a minute to pull yourself together? You look like hell."

Anna brushed a lock of hair out of her face. She'd only been working here four days, but she already loved Maggie Jones. "Thanks."

"Get a cup of coffee, kid." Maggie picked up a computer printout and tossed it onto the top of the filing cabinet beside her desk. "It's fresh and I could use a cup myself."

Anna knew a hint when she heard one. She hurried over to the small cubicle at the back of the office and poured two cups. Carrying one over to Maggie's desk, she said, "Er, Maggie."

"Yeah?" She stubbed out her smoke and reached for the cup. "Spit it out. Something else go wrong today?"

"Well, not exactly." Anna pushed a stack of papers aside and perched on the edge of Maggie's desk. "It's just that when John hired me, he said if twenty-five hours a week was too much, we could cut it back to twenty."

Maggie arched one dark eyebrow over the rim of her glasses. "If your school fees just went up and your car is on its last legs, I'd figure cutting your hours would be the last thing you'd want to do."

"It is, but the restaurant called, and well, they don't want me to quit. I still want to keep this job. I mean twenty hours a week would be great, but with the extra money I'm going to need for tuition, twelve hours a week at Manuelo's plus tips might just let me swing things."

"It's fine with me," Maggie replied. She studied the young woman shrewdly through her glasses. "But John won't like it."

"Why should he care?" Anna was truly puzzled. John had turned out to be a considerate landlord, wonderful boss and ideal friend. Since becoming his tenant, she'd discovered they had a lot in common. They saw each other practically every evening. Usually it was just for coffee out in the backyard, or maybe they'd watch a movie on TV. They weren't dating or anything, but they'd become friends. "I won't let my work here suffer. I'm sure he'll understand. Besides, it's just Friday and Saturday nights. That's no big deal."

"Maybe not to you, but John won't like it."

"John won't like what?"

Anna jumped, almost spilled her coffee and whirled around to face the man she was still having torrid daydreams about. "Oh, hi. We didn't see you come in."

He grinned. "Obviously. Now, what was it that I'm not going to like?"

Anna quickly explained about the restaurant and the additional tuition fees. "So you see," she finished, "I can't really quit there yet."

"I thought you quit last week."

"Well, I kinda did."

"Kinda?"

"I gave them my notice, but I told them if they ever needed someone to work an extra evening shift, to give me a call," she explained hurriedly, wondering why she felt so guilty. Like a kid caught lying about the dog eating her homework assignment.

John gave her a long, steady look. "I see."

"I'm going to cut her hours down to four per day if it's all right with you," Maggie put in. She glanced from Anna's face to John's.

Finally, he nodded. "All right. I'll be out at the Spring Street job if you need me," he said. "I just came in to pick up my beeper." He stopped when he reached the door and turned. "I'll see you tonight, Anna."

Though the words were polite enough, Anna suddenly felt a little nervous.

"Enjoy it while you can," Anna muttered to herself as she sat the square of pink yarn on her lap. "After tomorrow night you won't have enough free time to pick up a crochet hook."

She glanced at the clock on the table and sighed. It was past eight, and John still hadn't come by. She hoped he wouldn't give her another lecture about overdoing things. She'd already heard that one.

There was a light knock on the door. "Come in," she called.

John stepped inside, his face creased in a frown. "How many times have I told you to keep that door locked?" he demanded.

"Lots, but I knew you were coming over, and I didn't want to have to get up." Anna held up the square of afghan she was crocheting. "See. What do you think?"

John tried not to smile. He couldn't have cared less about her project, but he thought she was adorable. That didn't mean she wasn't still in for a lecture, and this time, by heaven, she was going to listen. "It's nice. But I'm not here to look at your knitting."

"It's crocheting," she corrected. "Would you like some coffee?"

"No, I want to talk . . ."

"How about a cup of tea?" Anna's tension level shot up.

"Nothing." He quickly took a seat on the couch. "Anna, I want you to listen to me. How come you're even considering working nights at that damned restaurant?"

She looked up from her lap. "I told you. I need the money. Tuition has gone sky-high, my car is on its last legs, and I've got books, lab fees and who knows what other expenses coming up next week when school starts." She hastily dropped her gaze back to the hook held limply in her hand. This was embarrassing. Having grown up in an average middle-class family, she wasn't used to being so broke and even less used to having to admit that fact publicly.

John resisted the urge to shout. "Times are tough for everyone," he began, forcing himself to stay calm. "But that's no reason to kill yourself. No one can carry a full load at school and handle two jobs."

"Lots of people have done it," she insisted, picking up a strand of yarn and loping it onto the hook. "Besides, it's not like I've got anything else to do on Friday and Saturday nights."

Yeah, he thought angrily, and as long as you insist on working the weekends, you'll never be free to do anything else. Least of all, go out with your landlord. John felt his temper start to slip. She was twenty-eight years old, and she deserved something better than constant work, studying and pressure. But Anna was too damned stubborn to listen. Or maybe it wasn't just plain cussedness; maybe she really was desperate for money. But surely she had something to fall back on? Roger Trask hadn't been much of a businessman, but John had thought he'd at least left a small life insurance policy. Something.

But what if she were really broke? The question haunted him. He hated thinking of her doing without, working herself to death and worrying constantly about money. And she shouldn't have to. He had plenty; he didn't need the damned rent money. Maybe if he offered to cut her rent ... But as he gazed at her sitting there in that old wing chair, her lips compressed into a flat line and her eyes glued to her lap, he suddenly realized he'd better keep his mouth shut. Anna wouldn't appreciate charity. He'd already figured that out. Anyone who worked as hard as she did wouldn't want a handout. But he had to do something!

He took a deep breath and tried again. "Listen, you don't have reliable transportation," he pointed out reasonably. "That heap you drive could break down anytime, and you could find yourself stuck on Pacific Coast Highway at two in the morning without a gas station in sight."

"I'll call a taxi."

John's hands balled into fists. "You know there are alternatives to working yourself to death. You could cut down to one class a semester and come to work for me full-time."

She smiled but shook her head. "Thats a nice offer. But one, you don't need me full-time, you've got Maggie, and two, I've drifted along long enough, it's time to get serious about my future. With one class a semester it would take ten years to get my degree."

"Future," he argued. "What future? With the kind of

pressure you're putting yourself under you'll be lucky you don't end up a walking zombie. Two jobs and a full school schedule? Stop kidding yourself. You'll be burned out by Christmas."

Anna suspected John might be right. But darn it, it wasn't as if she had any choice in the matter. Didn't he understand? She had to do this, she had to prove to herself that she could make something of her life. Besides, there were lots of people who worked their way through college. She wouldn't be the first. If she had to, she'd slow down. But she wasn't prepared to pull back before she'd even started.

"Don't be such a pessimist," she said, forcing a lightness into her voice she didn't feel. "It won't be all that bad. If push comes to shove, I can always drop one class."

He snorted derisively. "Oh, that's really going to help. One class out of what, five? And what about your social life? You know most people like to have a little fun on the weekends."

"Like I said," she was beginning to get angry, "it's not like I've got anything better to do."

John could think of a lot of better things to do on a Saturday night than hustling margaritas and enchiladas. "You could spend that time resting," he said, knowing he was lying through his teeth. He fully intended for Anna to spend those nights with him.

"I agree," she said grimly, clutching the hook so tight her fingers hurt. "But right at the moment rest is a luxury I can't afford."

Because he knew that was true and because he couldn't think of any possible way out of this dilemma, he exploded and attacked the one man he thought responsible for Anna's predicament. "Jesus Christ, didn't Roger leave you anything?"

Her cheeks flushed as pink as the yarn as she tried to keep her temper in check. "The only thing Roger left me," she snapped, "was a lot of bills and that stupid old car."

"What the hell was the matter with the man?" John

yelled. "What about life insurance? What about social security?"

Anna leapt to her feet. "Life insurance? Are you serious? What insurance company in their right mind would have insured someone with a heart condition? And as for social security, forget it. Roger was self-employed. Only unlike a lot of people, he didn't pay that particular tax." She laughed harshly. "Believe me, the IRS sure rectified that little boo-boo after he died."

"He didn't pay his taxes," John said in disbelief. Then he realized it was probably absolutely true. Charming as Trask had been, he'd also been the kind to take shortcuts. John knew that from bitter experience.

"No, he didn't pay his damned taxes." Anna glared at John. "Not that it's any of your business. I know you're trying to help, but I wish you'd back off. This conversation is very embarrassing and far too personal. My money problems are my own. I'm your tenant, not your sister."

For a long moment, they faced each other down. Anna stared at him in confusion and anger. John saw the hurt and the pain and knew he'd been the cause of it. He took a hesitant step forward and gently placed his hand on her shoulder.

The minute he touched her he knew he was lost. He'd avoided letting his hands get anywhere near her for that very reason. His feelings toward Anna were so intense, so powerful, that he was sure he'd lose his head and scare the daylights out of her. But he was willing to risk that now. Whatever else she felt, he knew Anna wasn't afraid of him.

With his eyes locked onto her face, he lowered his head and brushed his lips against hers. Beneath his fingers, the bare skin of her arms was soft and silky. The light, flowery scent she wore filled his nostrils, and he could feel her breasts against his chest as he pulled her closer and grazed his mouth against hers.

She started in surprise as their lips skimmed lightly together. John drew back and stared at her for a moment. In her eyes he saw surprise and something else . . . something it took him only a flash of a second to identify.

Desire.

He took her mouth again, only this time it was no light brush, no hesitant testing of the waters. John pulled her close against him, groaning with pleasure as her delicate form molded itself so perfectly against his body, and kissed her. Her lips were closed, but it took the barest of coaxing with his tongue to get him inside. He tasted her fully, his tongue plunging inside and stroking, teasing, tangling with hers. His arms tightened.

Anna's shock gave way to passion, and she clasped him tightly around the waist as he deepened the kiss and began to run one hand up and down her back.

They were so absorbed in each other that neither of them heard the car pull up in the driveway. "Hey, John," a voice yelled from the backyard. "Where the hell are you?"

Slowly, he lifted his head as the loud voice intruded. "Damn," he muttered. "What's Ted doing here?"

Dazed, Anna stepped back, folded her arms over her chest and took a deep breath. "Uh, hadn't you better go see what he wants?"

"Yo, John!" Ted shouted again.

John ignored the voice of his buddy and kept his attention on Anna. God, kissing her, holding her, had shaken him to his very core. But he needed to know how she felt. "Anna?"

A car horn honked.

"You'd better go see what your friend wants," she said hastily, heading for the door and throwing it open before he could move.

John could take a hint. But his instincts told him she'd been just as shaken by the kiss as he was. He headed for the door but stopped right beside her. She wouldn't look at him. John gently lifted her chin so she'd have to meet his eyes.

"Don't hide from me, Anna," he said softly.

"I'm not," she protested. Actually, she was surprised she

was able to answer coherently at all. "It's just, I'm not used to kissing my landlord."

He grinned, leaned over and gave her a quick kiss. "Don't worry. There's plenty of time for you to get used to it."

chapter

five

John quickened his step as he saw Anna waiting in front of the restaurant. His lecture hadn't completely fallen on deaf ears. Anna had agreed to give up her restaurant job and to cut back by one class. But she'd insisted on working tonight. He'd just as stubbornly insisted on picking her up.

"I thought I told you to stay inside until I got here," he said, frowning at her.

Anna shrugged, and the movement caused her hot pink off-the-shoulder blouse to dip dangerously low over her bosom. "Easier said than done. They had to lock the front door. Besides, there's half a dozen people in there. One good scream and they'd come running."

He took her arm as they crossed the darkened parking lot to his truck. It was all he could do to keep from tripping over his own feet. He was having a hard time keeping his eyes on where he was going and not on her.

That uniform! My God, if he'd known she wore a skin-tight green skirt and frilly pink peasant blouse when she worked, he'd have been eating at Manuelo's on a regular basis.

"Yeah, but you still should have waited inside," he grumbled. "A woman standing alone in a parking lot at this time of night is asking for trouble. It looks like she's waiting to be picked up."

"I was waiting to be picked up," Anna replied. She laughed. "But I guess that's not what you meant."

"Dressed like that," he raked her with a glance, "do you get a lot of hassles?"

"Not really. Nothing I can't handle anyway." Anna was suddenly terribly self-conscious about her uniform. "The place is known for its food, not the bar. The clientele is mostly families or couples on dates. It doesn't attract singles."

Good, he thought, as they approached his truck. He released her arm and unlocked the door. Anna grabbed the side of the door and tried to swing gracefully into the front seat. Her skirt rode up, and she knew, she just knew, that John was probably getting ready to laugh himself silly.

"God, it's a wonder you can sling hash in that outfit," he muttered as his hands clamped around her waist and she felt herself being lifted onto the seat.

"Thanks," she murmured.

John hurried around and slid into the driver's seat, glancing at Anna as he shoved the key into the ignition and turned on the engine. He was momentarily distracted by the fetching sight of her stocking-clad knee and thigh, revealed by the slit in her skirt. "Did you tell your boss you were quitting for good?"

"Yes. He wasn't particularly happy about it, but he understood." She took a deep breath. "You know, I really appreciate all you've done for me. I mean, giving me the job and letting me rent your house, but I don't want you to think you've got any responsibility for me. You were right about me not being able to handle working at Manuelo's every weekend, that would have led to burnout. But I did agree to be available if they ever get shorthanded and need a shift covered, sort of on an emergency basis . . ." She saw his mouth tighten, but she pressed on. "Look, I guess what I'm trying to say is that I don't want you tying up your time thinking you have to come and get me." She paused and drew in a deep breath of air. None of this had come out as she'd planned. She'd wanted to sound appreciative, but casual. Grateful, but sophisticated. But she'd ended up sounding exactly like a prim little schoolmarm thanking the local sheriff for helping out the poor little widow.

"Tonight wasn't a problem," he mumbled, concentrating

on pulling out onto the busy highway. "I was out anyway. And we'll worry about other nights when and *if* they happen."

"Well, uh, thanks for picking me up tonight. I'm glad it wasn't a hassle for you."

"Like I said, I was out anyway." He flicked her a quick, unreadable glance.

Anna wished she could read minds. She'd have loved to know what he was thinking. "I figured that," she replied lightly. "You don't normally spend your Friday nights in a three-piece suit. But I'm sure Mike will call every now and then for me to fill in, and, well, I'm sure you'll have other plans on those nights. So I decided that if my car wasn't up to par, I'd take a cab home."

Over my dead body, John thought, but he was smart enough to keep his mouth shut. Building a relationship with Anna was more difficult than he'd first imagined, but he was satisfied with the progress he'd made so far. Her reaction to his kiss the other night had convinced him she was interested. Wary, a bit nervous, but definitely interested.

"Er, uh, did you hear me, John?" Anna prodded. "I said that from now on if I work a night shift, I'll take a cab home." She slanted him a quick glance from the corner of her eye. He'd obviously been out on a heavy date tonight. No one dressed in a spiffy gray pinstripe to sit home and watch television! Who was he seeing? she wondered. And why did she care so much?

"I heard you," he muttered.

Anna couldn't think of anything to say. She'd been surprised and pleased when he'd told her at work this afternoon that he'd pick her up. She'd almost convinced herself it was because he was coming to care for her. Then she'd seen him in that damned suit and known he'd probably had a hot date with someone else. Someone tall and sophisticated, someone as successful as he was.

"So, was it a good night?" John asked. He wished she'd move a bit closer.

"Good tip night," she said, pushing the flash of jealousy

aside. "I probably cleared enough to buy half of my text-books."

"Your evening sounds more productive than mine was."

Anna couldn't stand it; she had to know. "Bad date?"

"Worse than that." He sounded amused. "It was a boring business dinner. Lots of lumpy mashed potatoes, stale rolls and long-winded speeches."

Exultation shot through her, and she laughed. Not a date! "Do you go to those things often?"

"Not if I can avoid it," he said lightly, flipping on the turn indicator and pulling into the right lane. "But I agreed to go to this thing months ago."

John knew his admission made him sound as exciting as a tree stump, but he wanted her to know he hadn't been out with anyone. He hadn't seriously dated a woman since Roger died, and if he were completely honest, he hadn't seriously been interested in any woman since he'd met Anna.

He'd deliberately kept his romances casual during that period. One part of him knew it was wrong to get involved with one woman while his heart so firmly belonged to another. At times he'd wondered what he would have done, how long he would have continued like that, if Roger hadn't died. But it didn't matter anymore. Anna was free now.

John pulled into the driveway and parked behind Anna's car. He quickly got out and hurried around to help her down, but he wasn't fast enough.

The light from John's back porch wasn't strong enough to illuminate the driveway. Anna's foot suddenly slipped into the depression between the concrete and the grass, and she tripped. Strong arms caught her before she fell.

John drew her against him. "Are you all right?" he asked.

"I'm fine. My foot slipped." Her heart was beating like a jackhammer. His hands on her arms were firm and warm. She could smell the tangy scent of his after-shave; she could feel the outline of his thighs against her own.

She lifted her gaze and saw him staring at her, his eyes gleaming in the dim light.

Slowly, he lowered his head and kissed her. As before, Anna was lost. The moment his mouth touched hers, she was opening to him like a flower spreading its petals toward the sun. His tongue darted inside, his hands tightened around her back, and the kiss exploded into raw need.

Anna was spun into a web of passion so fast and so furious she couldn't think. Despite all the hours of daydreaming of him, about being in his arms and touching him, holding him, kissing him, nothing had prepared her for the reality of it.

Their tongues clashed, retreated and danced a savage mating ritual in the warm, moist cavern of her mouth. Her head was spinning, her pulse racing and her body molding itself to his so closely that at every contact point her nerve endings were writhing with sensation.

Suddenly it was over. John drew back and held her at arm's length. Anna's eyes were wide with shock, her face pale and her lips half-parted. She lifted her fingers to her mouth. "My goodness, that was quite a kiss." She cringed. What a stupid thing to say.

John smiled slowly. "Yeah, it was. You know, I think something's happening here."

Anna desperately wanted to agree with him, but something stopped her. She and John didn't really know each other. This kiss, like the one the other evening, could mean nothing. Or everything. She didn't much trust her judgment when it came to figuring out how a man felt. After all, look what a mess she'd made with Roger. She'd read him wrong from their first date!

When she said nothing, John felt a flash of fear. Then he quickly quashed the notion. She hadn't exactly been fighting him off—she'd responded to him. Yeah, his conscience whispered, she's a lonely widow and maybe she just needed a little human affection.

Anna cleared her throat and made up her mind. If she were reading his intentions wrong, she wanted to find out quickly. The best way to do that was to talk to him. But tonight wasn't a good time. They were both too tired. "John, would you like to come over tomorrow afternoon? For tea."

Relief shot through him. A woman didn't issue invitations unless she was interested. "Thank you, Anna," he replied formally. "I'd like that very much."

Anna sucked in her stomach and tugged the stubborn zipper up the last two inches. She buttoned her skirt and stepped back to examine herself in the mirror. The skirt was tight, maybe even too tight. But the sleek-fitting olive-colored garment was the only thing she owned that went with her favorite high-necked, pale green Victorian blouse. She'd just have to suffer and remember not to make any sharp turns or moves.

The oven timer dinged, and Anna forgot about her appearance. She ran toward the kitchen, wincing as she came out into the living room. Darn! It was still hot as blue blazes in there.

Opening the oven, Anna carefully lifted out the tray of scones, and smiled her relief. They looked fine. Unlike the pineapple upside-down cake she'd made this morning, which was now in the garbage disposal because it looked more like a pancake than anything else.

Sweat trickled down between her breasts, and she could feel the band of her skirt pressing hard against her waist. She put the scones down and looked at the kitchen window, wondering if she could open it any wider. She couldn't. Damn. It was so hot in here, she was sweating like a horse. Why did she have to invite him for tea? Why couldn't she have used her head and invited him for a barbecue and a beer? Because she'd wanted to impress him, that's why. Because she'd always wanted to have an afternoon tea, and she'd never had the chance before. But this wretched heat was ruining everything.

Another trickle of sweat rolled down between her breasts just as she heard John's back door slam. She cast one quick glance at the elegant china tea service on the table and prayed that scones, ham sandwiches and brownies would be enough. He was such a *big* man.

"Hi." John paused in the open doorway. "Can I come in?"

"Sure, it's all ready." Wearing a welcoming smile, she started forward when she heard a ripping sound. Anna froze. She quickly dropped her hand to her hip and then skimmed the back seam of her skirt. Nothing ripped there, she thought in relief. Must have been the lining.

"Uh, I'm sorry I didn't dress up," John said sheepishly, taking in the sight of her in an elegant blouse, form-fitting skirt and high heels. "But with this heat, I guess I just figured you'd be real casual."

Anna felt a flush creep up her cheeks. John had on a loose white tank top, a pair of denim shorts that showed off his long, sleekly muscled legs to perfection and a pair of flip-flops. "Let's not worry about how we're dressed." She tried for a light, sophisticated tone. "Please, have a seat. I'll just pour the tea."

John squeezed his legs into the tiny space between the couch and the table. Anna had crowded both end tables into the area in order to have her tea party. As he sat down, his knees brushed dangerously close to the edge of the table loaded down with things that looked breakable. He was afraid to move.

Glancing quickly around the cottage, he saw that Anna had gone to a lot of trouble. Both tables were covered with fragile lace cloths, dainty teacups, gleaming silver, a platter of elegantly stacked brownies, sliced ham sandwiches and a bowl of . . . He squinted at the white lumps in the green bowl and finally decided it must be cream.

"Uh, this all looks great," he called. "I've never been to a tea party before." He could hear the kettle starting to hum.

"Thank you," Anna replied. Things weren't going well at all. John looked as nervous as a toddler waiting to get a shot. She smiled formally as she carried the platter of scones to the table. Her smile froze as she tried to think of a way to bend down without the accompanying sounds of ripping fabric.

"Here, let me help you with that," John offered eagerly, sensing the awkwardness in the air and wondering what the hell had gone wrong. He lunged forward, intending to take the scones from her, but he forgot about his cramped position, and his knee banged hard against the wood.

"Oh no," Anna yelped, as two brownies toppled off her carefully arranged stack, bounced against the rim of the plate and then flopped onto the floor. Her precious teacups clattered noisily against the saucers, and the spoons rattled together.

Fearing more damage, John jerked back. "Uh, maybe I'd better let you handle this."

"Perhaps that would be best," she murmured, wanting, but not knowing how, to put him at ease. She put the scones down, grabbed a fancy napkin and hurriedly scooped up the brownies. Luckily, the Gods decided to be kind and she didn't hear her skirt lining rip any further. Getting to her feet, she tried for a cheerful smile. "I'll just get the tea."

John racked his brain for something to say. He blurted out the first thing that came to his mind. "Isn't this weather weird?"

"You mean all this humidity?" Anna picked up a pot holder and reached for the teakettle.

"Yeah. Feels more like the South than the Southwest out there. According to the weatherman, there's a lot of tropical moisture pouring in from Baja. That's how come it's so humid." He ran out of things to say. Good God, talking about the weather? Anna was staring at him blankly. She looked supremely bored. He didn't much blame her.

"You know," he continued desperately, determined to get some kind of conversation going. "You're doing a great job on those flower beds."

"Thank you," she said, pouring the boiling water into the teapot. "I enjoy gardening."

"Yeah, well, you seem real good at it too. But I don't want you thinking you've got to do everything out there," he said. "There is a gardener that comes in a couple of times a month."

Carrying the teapot, Anna headed for the table. "But I'm only doing the flower beds," she said, not realizing how defensive she sounded. "Not the lawn."

"Oh sure, that's fine. But I didn't want you thinking that just because you're paying cheap rent, you've got to do it all."

Anna stared at him stupidly. Then she carefully put the pot in the center of the table. "I didn't think that."

"Well, good." Hell, he thought miserably, this was going from bad to worse. Maybe he should get up, go out and come in again. And keep his mouth shut. Instead, he blundered on. "But I saw those two big bags of potting soil you bought, and I, uh, didn't want you overdoing it."

"I see." Anna sat down in one of the wing chairs. She bent over and had started to reach for the teapot when John's beeper went off.

Without thinking, he leapt to his feet. This time the table didn't just shake, it went over with a loud crash. "Damn, I'm sorry."

His beeper buzzed again, and John knew it was urgent.

"Oh no, my teapot." Anna dropped to her knees. A loud rip accompanied the movement as she scrambled in the ruins, looking at her most cherished possession.

"God, I'm really sorry." John stepped gingerly over the mess and headed for the door. No one beeped him on Sundays unless it was an emergency. "Jeez, Anna, I'm really sorry about all this. But I've got to go." He reached into the pocket of his shorts and drew out a wad of bills. Tossing the money onto the couch, he said. "This should take care of anything that's broken."

Then he turned and raced for the door.

Anna shoved the ice tray back in the freezer and slammed the door. She picked up her ice water, tilted her head back and rubbed the cool glass against her neck. What a fiasco today had been. Anna closed her eyes and cringed in remembered humiliation. She started to get mad all over again.

From outside she could hear a soft rain begin to fall. Jerking the icy glass off her skin, she smiled wryly into the darkness. What a day. Rain in August in California, and she making a fool of herself in front of John. She didn't much blame him for running out.

Anna sat the glass on the counter and began to pace the room. There was only the dim light of a candle burning. She had thought the candlelight would make her feel better. Much as she'd have liked to blame him for everything that had gone wrong, she couldn't. It wouldn't have been fair. Between the heat, humidity, nerves, her ridiculous clothes and her inability to say more than six words consecutively, what had she expected? God, she'd probably scared the man off for good. No doubt he was convinced she was desperate for companionship or on the prowl for another husband.

But he didn't have to fling money at me, she thought defensively as she reached the end of the room, turned on her heel and started back the way she'd come. He wasn't flinging money at you, her better nature argued, he was in a hurry and trying to make amends for wrecking your china collection. Anna stopped and turned toward the kitchen, where her precious teapots and saucers were neatly stacked on the counter. She'd have to remember to give him the bills back. Despite the chaos in the middle of her living room floor, nothing had been broken.

The rain began to pound harder. Anna sighed and knew she should get to bed. She'd be dead on her feet tomorrow. She cringed at the thought of facing him. Oh God, this was all a mistake. She was crazy about a man who could care less. Even worse, she was living in his backyard and spending every afternoon right under his nose. What a mess. John was such a gentleman that if she tried to extract herself gracefully from what was proving to be an impossible situation, he'd probably try to stop her.

Despite those two heavy kisses they'd shared, he really wasn't interested. He'd been ill at ease from the moment he'd come in today. Obviously, her invitation had made him uncomfortable. Obviously, she'd read him wrong last night. She sighed again. John was only being nice because Roger had once been his drywall contractor. He was just being kind to the widow. Trying to do the right thing, act decent. Roger always said that John was like that. Too bad she hadn't listened closer. If she had, she wouldn't have had this stupid, disastrous tea party, and she wouldn't be dreading the moment when she had to look him in the eye again.

Anna wandered over to the open window. The way this rain was pouring, she figured she'd better close the damned thing. As she reached for the sill, she glanced out into the well-lighted backyard and squealed. The rain was a torrential downpour now, and a stream of water was gushing out of the drainpipe on the side roof of the house, directly onto the bags of potting soil she'd bought yesterday. The pressure was so hard that the water, instead of running off, had dented a channel in the bag and was draining directly onto her newly planted seedbeds.

Mindless of the fact that she was only wearing a flimsy nightgown, Anna rushed out the front door. She was determined to salvage something from this miserable day. Water beat hard against her as she ran across the yard. Kneeling down, she pushed her hair out of her eyes and tried to tug the bags away from the flow of the drainpipe. They wouldn't budge. Anna gritted her teeth, dug in her heels and tried again. Her foot slipped from beneath her, and she yelped as she came down hard on her ankle.

John's back door crashed open. "Who the hell's out there?" he yelled, coming out onto the back porch. "Jesus, Anna. What the dickens are you doing out here? It's pouring!" He leapt off the porch, and Anna wished the ground would open up and swallow her.

"I can see that," she snapped, overcome with humiliation and anger.

John knelt beside her. "Are you hurt?"

"No." She tried to get up, but her ankle hurt. "Yes. I hurt my ankle. I was trying to move those bags. They're ruining my plants. The water's going to drown them. Then I fell, and now my damned foot hurts . . ."

Without another word, he scooped her into his arms and started for his back porch. "Let's get you inside and see if anything's broken."

"Oh, that's not necessary," she protested, but he ignored her and took her on inside. A moment later, she was sitting in the kitchen and John was cradling her foot in his big, warm hands.

They were both soaked. Anna's hair hung limply against her shoulders, her scanty nightgown was plastered to her like a second skin, and one of the tiny spaghetti straps was falling off her shoulder.

John could barely keep his eyes off her. She looked so beautiful, half-naked and soaking wet. He cleared his throat and forced his attention back to the foot. Gently, he ran his hands over her ankle. "Does that hurt?"

Anna sucked in her breath. "Just a little." God, she couldn't keep her eyes off him. He'd come outside wearing nothing but a pair of jeans. Water glistened on his muscular shoulders and arms. "I think it's just twisted." She avoided meeting his gaze, sure that her thoughts were written all over her face.

"You'd better stay off of it for a day or so." He twisted her ankle slowly to one side and then another. "It doesn't appear to be broken. But if it still hurts in the morning, we'll take you to the emergency room." His fingers stroked the ankle. He didn't want to let it go; he didn't want to break the contact with her flesh.

Anna was staring at the floor. He let his gaze wander over her body. The silence stretched and tightened, his breathing quickening as his body began to react to hers. John lifted his eyes to meet hers. She was staring at him.

They sat like that for a few moments, each of them locked in private thoughts, private wants and desires. Suddenly, John couldn't stand it anymore. He stood up and pulled her to her feet, using his arms to support her so that she wouldn't have to put her weight on the sore ankle. Lowering his head, he kissed her. Hard. There was no tentative probing with his tongue, no hesitant brush of his mouth to hers; there was nothing but raw need and frustrated desire as his lips touched hers and he gave in to the overwhelming compulsion that had been driving him for months.

Anna kissed him back. Her mouth parted and her arms came around his neck as she clutched at him. His big, warm hand slipped down her spinal column, molding her close and sending shivers up her back as he stroked her through the thin nightgown.

John could feel her softness, her warmth through the silky fabric. Her breasts pressed hard against his chest, and her sweet mouth and stroking tongue were driving him wild. He slipped his hand to her bottom and pulled her tightly against him, wanting her to feel how desperately he needed her.

Days of having her living so close at hand, nights of knowing that she was lying only a few feet away, years and months and days of wanting her had finally taken their toll. He didn't want to stop. He wanted to make love to her.

Anna gasped as her soft flesh made contact with the hardness between his thighs. Her eyes closed and her head fell back, exposing her neck. John didn't need an engraved invitation. His lips traveled down, dropping tiny kisses on her cheek and chin. While his hands continued their tender assault on her bottom and back, he nipped her gently on the vulnerable spot where her neck joined her shoulders.

She cried out softly. His head dipped lower, his mouth showering kisses on the top of her chest. Unable to stand the hot sensations flooding her, Anna whimpered.

John smiled in satisfaction and quickly skimmed his hands up to the straps of her nightgown. He slid them down her shoulders, and the gown dropped to the floor. Without giving her a moment to think, he lowered his head and kissed her breast. She shivered and clutched his arms as her whole body tingled with pleasure.

Abruptly, John straightened and looked down into her flushed face. Dazed with passion, she could only stare at him. Then he picked her up and carried her through the darkened house into his bedroom.

John lay her in the center of the king-sized bed and stripped out of his jeans. He was too aroused to take it slow, too excited to shower her with whispered words of love and praise for her exquisite body. He needed her now.

Climbing in beside her, he drew her into his arms, finding her mouth and kissing her deeply. His hands stroked her naked back as he pulled her tightly against him. He groaned when their bodies touched; every nerve ending he possessed screamed for satisfaction, possession.

He pushed her over onto her back and cupped her breasts in his hands. Using his thumb to stroke one erect tip, he molded the other in his hand and drew it into his mouth, suckling firmly, using his tongue to excite her. Anna drew a ragged breath and moaned, her hands tangled in his hair as she pulled him closer against her.

Anna's whole body was on fire. His mouth on her breast was driving her insane, his tongue and teeth sending volts of pleasurable sensation deeply into the pit of her belly. She whimpered again and again, her eyes closed, her head thrashing restlessly on the pillow as he continued the sensual assault on her body.

John knew what he was doing to her; he could feel her heated shivers. Her tiny moans of passion were music to his ears. But he wanted more; he wanted her to want him as badly as he wanted her, had been wanting her for far too long. Yet his own hunger threatened to rage out of control. He slid his hand between her legs, covering her completely. Anna stiffened and went still.

He lifted his head from her breast and gazed into her eyes. In the darkened room he couldn't see her face, but suddenly her body relaxed.

Slowly, gently, he began to stroke her, his fingers moving tenderly over the delicate flesh that made her a woman.

Deep ripples of sensation exploded inside her. "That's right, baby," John murmured, his pleasure growing by the second as he felt her reacting to his lovemaking. "It's going to be so good between us, so right. Let it happen," he encouraged as her hips began to move in reaction. "Let it build, let me take you all the way."

Anna couldn't stand it. She'd never felt like this before. From deep inside her, the tension built and built as his hands and fingers excited her beyond belief. She gasped as he leaned over and took her breast between his lips again. He suckled her hard as he slipped a finger inside her, his thumb delicately flicking the swollen bud of female sensation. Anna thought she'd explode. Her hips were moving in wild counterpoint to his rhythmic stroking. Oh, God, she was going out of her mind. She clutched at his shoulders and pressed her mouth against his arm, scoring him lightly with her teeth.

"Come on, baby," he whispered, his own control slipping by the second, "let it go. Give it to me."

Her body was thrashing wildly as the tension spiraled higher and higher, tighter and tighter. Suddenly she cried out as a wave of hot, fierce pleasure hurtled her into space.

Her climax pushed him over the edge. He yanked open the drawer of the bedside table, pulled out a foil packet, lifted his head and tore it open with his teeth. He rolled to one side and a moment later pulled her limp body close against him.

"Oh God," she moaned, "I didn't even touch you."

John chuckled and gently forced her legs apart. "You didn't have to, sweetheart." He eased himself over her and positioned himself between her thighs. Then he gave her a long, hot kiss. "That was just the appetizer," he whispered, raising himself on his arms. "Now we'll get down to the main course."

Anna gasped as he entered her. She wound her arms around his neck as he began kissing her. His body slowly, gently began to move. The embers of passion burst into flame again, and she began thrusting her hips rhythmically as the delicious sensations sent her pulse rate soaring and her heart slamming hard against her rib cage.

John couldn't hold back, his strokes becoming harder, deeper. He jammed his hands beneath her hips and lifted her tightly against him as he felt the delicate convulsions wrack her once again. With a muffled shout of satisfaction and triumph, he let go and gave into the incredible release.

They lay locked together for what seemed a long time. Anna couldn't seem to bring her breathing under control. Lord, this was one for the books.

Holding her against him, he rolled to one side. Lifting his hand, he stroked her tangled hair out of her eyes. "Are you all right?"

"If I was any better, you'd have to peel me off this bed with a spatula," she murmured, snuggling closer and stifling a yawn.

John laughed softly. "Yeah, me too."

Anna wished she could lie in his arms forever. She didn't want to have to open her eyes and face reality, not just yet. What had happened between them was too special, too precious to think about now. She just wanted to feel.

John apparently wanted to talk because he shook her shoulder gently. "Hey, wake up," he ordered. "We've got some serious talking to do here."

"Hmmm . . ." Maybe if she kept her eyes closed, he'd go to sleep.

"Anna," he insisted. "I want to talk to you. This is important. It changes everything."

Her eyes flew open. Changes everything? How? What did that mean?

"Good, I see I've finally got your attention." He grinned at her.

"Are you this chatty with all your women?" she asked waspishly.

"Only the ones I intend to keep," he shot back, reaching over and turning on the beside lamp, "and as there haven't been too many of those, I wouldn't worry about it if I were you. Now, let's get down to the important stuff."

"What important stuff?" She blinked furiously against the bright light.

"You, me, our relationship." John gestured at their entwined bodies.

"Relationship?" Anna stared at him warily.

"Yes, Anna, relationship," he said patiently. "We just made love. In case you didn't notice, it was rather spectacular."

"I noticed."

"Good. Then you'll agree that we've got something going for us. Something more than just landlord and tenant or employee and boss."

She swallowed heavily and nodded. Anna's stomach contracted as she realized just what she'd done. Oh Lord, talk about complications.

"What's wrong, Anna?" he asked quickly as he watched the panic rise in her eyes. "Having second thoughts? It's too late for that."

chapter

seven

"Too late?" Anna queried. "For what?"

"For you to try and weasle out of this," he stated bluntly. "Look, I know you're probably a little shook by how fast things happened between us, but that doesn't matter. Considering how I feel about you, it was bound to happen eventually."

Joy mingled with relief. He wanted her. He had feelings for her. She wasn't just a temporary itch he needed to scratch or an aberrant moment of runaway hormones. But she wasn't quite sure what to say to him. He hadn't said exactly how he felt about her, nor had he told her exactly what he wanted from her.

"Uh, what are you trying to say here?" she finally mumbled.

John put a finger under her chin and lifted her gaze to meet his. "That I want you and I don't mean just for sex." He smiled wryly. "I'd be lying if I said making love to you wasn't important. It is. But I want more than that, Anna. I want a whole relationship. I want to spend time with you, date you, take you places, watch movies. Hell, I'll even help you plant those damned flowers if you want. But I need to know that you're as committed to this relationship as I am."

She stared at him for a few moments, knowing that she was about to agree to something that had the power to change her whole life. Something that had the possibility of bringing her tremendous joy or tremendous heartache. She wished he weren't so blunt. She wished she had time to ease into being with him without the fear in the back of her mind that she might drift back into her old ways and lose herself. But she could tell from the harsh set of his jaw and the determined gleam in his eyes that John wasn't letting her out of this bedroom without an answer. And the truth was, she was in love with him. She had been for a long time now.

"You don't have to worry about how committed I am," she said softly, reaching up to stroke his face. "I want to be with you too."

A week later Anna shouldered the door of the file room open and stepped inside. Dumping an armload of manila files onto the top of a high stool, she sighed and pulled a package of Twinkies out of her skirt pocket.

Life couldn't be better, she thought as she leaned against the open door and opened the wrapping. She and John had been together a whole week now, and already he was such a major part of her life she couldn't imagine existing without him. They ate dinner together almost every evening; either she cooked or he took her out. They had so much in common: they liked the same movies, had the same values, were both basically homebodies and, well— Anna paused and stuffed a bite of cake in her mouth—life just couldn't be better. Naturally, once her classes started, they wouldn't have quite so much time together, but she'd cross that bridge when she came to it.

She heard the outer office door open. She would have called out a hello to Maggie, but her mouth was full. Anna hurriedly tried to swallow her food.

"Hey, Bud, look. There's no one here," a voice said. "I wonder where the princess is. Guess the boss must have given her the day off."

Anna froze at the sarcasm in the man's voice. Embarrassed and a little hurt, she eased behind the closed door. She'd just wait here until they left.

"Knock if off, Len," said another voice, one that Anna recognized. It was one of John's crew chiefs. "Anna's a nice girl."

"I know she's a nice girl. Foxy too," Len replied. "But

you'd think that she was royalty the way John acts around her. He don't even take time to have a beer with the boys now that he's got her livin' with him."

"They're not living together," Bud said. "She's renting his backhouse."

Len snickered. "Yeah, and I bet I can tell you the kind of rent she's payin' too. The flat-on-her-back kind."

From inside the file room, Anna cringed.

"Hey, you'd better watch it," Bud warned. "John'll fire you in a fast minute if he hears you talking about her like that."

"Get real," Len laughed. "It's not like he's in love with her. He's just takin' care of the widow, in every sense of the word if you get my drift."

Anna's hands tightened into fists.

"True or not, he'd have your head if he heard you talkin' about her or any other woman like she was a piece of meat."

"Yeah, he's a gentleman all right." Len laughed again. "Don't look like he's doin' too bad for himself though. She's some looker all right. Smart too. Course I figure it won't last too long. His women never do. Besides, we both know he's only foolin' with her because of what happened to Roger. I mean, I'd feel bad too if I'd just told one of my contractors I couldn't use him anymore and he clutched his heart and keeled over dead."

"Yeah, John took it pretty hard," Bud agreed. "No matter how many times we tried to tell him it wasn't his fault, he still felt bad. And I don't really see why. Roger Trask had been cutting corners and using inferior materials for months before John got tired of warning him and finally fired his butt."

"And now he's really takin' care of the widow." Len snickered again. "Now, that's one responsibility I wouldn't mind havin' myself."

"Come on, let's go," Bud said. "We can't hang around here all day waiting for Maggie to show up. We've got to get out to that Spring Street job."

Anna heard their footsteps leaving the office, but she

stayed where she was behind the door. She was too numb to move.

The moment she'd realized exactly what these men were saying she'd felt nauseated. Could it possibly be true? Then she realized there was no possible about it, it *was* true. John wasn't falling in love with her; he was doing his damned duty. She'd known that Roger had died here, but she hadn't known he'd pegged out right after John had told him he couldn't use his services.

She swallowed the sick bile that rose in her throat. Oh God, she'd made a mess of things. John wanted a relationship all right, she thought savagely, one to ease his conscience.

She slumped against the metal shelves, unmindful of one of the brackets digging into her back. Look what the man had done: he'd given her employment, housing and sex. Everything he thought she'd lost by Roger's death. A hysterical laugh rose in her throat, but she choked it back. She wanted to scream and shout and rage against the man she'd fallen in love with, but she couldn't. He didn't deserve it. The only thing he was guilty of was feeling guilty about her. Feeling pity. Feeling responsible.

And she knew exactly what that felt like. That was how Roger had trapped her.

But she wasn't Roger.

In the wink of an eye, Anna made up her mind.

John hummed tunelessly as he turned into his driveway and frowned as he saw that Anna's old car wasn't parked in its usual spot.

She's probably at the store, he thought, as he climbed out of his car and headed toward her door. They were going to barbecue steaks tonight.

Using his key, he opened her door, stepped inside and stopped dead. John's jaw dropped.

Except for the furniture, the place was empty. Gone were the teapots, the afghan off the back of the couch, the counter appliances and her yarn bag that always, always sat by the side of the wing chair.

Panic flooded him in one fell swoop, and he charged into the bedroom. The closet door was wide open. Empty.

The top of the bureau looked lonely without her hairbrush and curling iron and her perfumes gone too. Then he saw a white envelope with his name on it sitting propped against the mirror.

Stunned and sick with shock, he forced his legs to move. He ripped open the envelope and yanked out her letter.

Dear John:

I'm writing this letter because I don't have the courage to face you in person. I know now that you're involved with me for all the wrong reasons. I'd so hoped that you were falling in love with me the same way I've fallen in love with you, but I realize I've been fooling myself. Please don't worry about me. I've decided to take my Aunt Hilda up on her offer, and I'm going to Alameda to move in with her.

I know you're wondering what's going on here, but the truth is, I finally understand what you're doing, and though I admire you for being so self-sacrificing, I can't let you continue.

You don't love me John and you never will. You're with me for the same reasons I married and stayed with Roger—guilt and pity. And those just aren't good enough reasons to build a future.

When I think back on everything you've done for me, I'm amazed it took overhearing a rather enlightening conversation before I got the point. You got me my first roommate after Roger died, and when that ended, you gave me a job and a place to live. And you did it all because you felt responsible for Roger's death. Believe me, John, you're not in the least responsible. Roger was. Despite his doctor's warnings, he drank like a fish, smoked like a chimney, partied every night till all hours and generally used his heart condition to manipulate others. You had absolutely nothing to do with him dying.

But unfortunately, we're not given the choice of who we love in this life, and because I love you so much, I'm walking away and giving you your freedom.

I will not do to someone else what Roger did to me.

Anna

P.S.
Enclosed is a check for next month's rent in lieu of thirty days' notice.

John read the letter again before crumpling it up in his hand and flinging it onto the floor.

God, when he got his hands on whoever had been shooting their mouth off in his office, he'd strangle him. But angry as he was, worried as he was, he was also higher than a damned kite.

She loved him.

John glanced at his watch, calculated how much of a headstart she had and then raced for the door.

Outside, he glanced at the brand new car he'd hoped to surprise Anna with and grinned. That miserable old heap of hers couldn't possibly beat him to Alameda. He hurried into the house and began yanking off his clothes.

He tossed his shirt onto the floor, picked up his phone and dialed Maggie's number while he went to the bedroom. She picked up on the third ring.

"Maggie, it's me. John." Bending his chin to keep the phone anchored to his ear, he didn't give her a chance to speak. "Pull Anna's employment application and get me the emergency address of that aunt in Alameda." He waited a few moments, then Maggie was back on the line rattling out the address. "Look, I'm taking off for a few days. There's nothing serious pending. Send Hicks out to oversee the Spring Street job. I'll check in sometime tomorrow."

"Where the hell you going?" Maggie demanded. "To Alameda?"

"Yes." He kicked his boots off and hopped on one foot towards his bureau. "And by the way, did you see Anna this afternoon?"

"Of course I saw Anna," Maggie snapped. "You two have a fight or something?"

"Or something," he replied grimly. "Did she leave at her usual time?"

"No, she took off real early," Maggie said slowly, as if she sensed that John was genuinely upset. "She said she wasn't feeling well, so I told her to go home. What's wrong, John? Has something happened to her?"

"Yeah, a bad case of eavesdropping. But don't worry, she'll be fine once I get my hands on her."

chapter

eight

Anna held her breath as her old car turned onto Caroline Street. She eased her foot down on the gas pedal, and the engine flattened but didn't lose power completely. She sighed in relief as she pulled up and parked in front of Aunt Hilda's house.

She'd made it. The minute she got inside, she'd phone a junk yard and have this heap towed off to a land fill. So what if she had to take the bus from now on? That had to be better than what she'd just gone through. Damn. She'd spent the night bawling her eyes out on the Interstate, crawling over the grapevine in the slow lane, with eighteen-wheelers honking at her to get out of the way, and then blown a water hose in Bakersfield. On top of that, she then had to spend half the night drinking lousy coffee in an all-night diner and trying not to cry.

Damn, but she hated being in love. It was the pits, it was lousy, it was the stupidest thing in the universe, and if this was the best that Mother Nature could do to perpetrate the species, it was a pretty poor way to run things. Anna climbed out and slammed the door. She resisted the urge to give her car a good kick . . . With her luck, she'd probably break her toe.

Anna tried to get herself under control. She didn't want her aunt to see her like this. Then she remembered that Hilda was in Mexico. No reason to be strong. She let her shoulders slump dejectedly.

As she stepped onto the porch, she tried to remember just where Hilda kept the spare key.

"Where the hell have you been?" John shouted, stepping out of the shadows.

Anna jumped in surprise and stared at him.

He loomed over her, his hands on his hips and his eyes narrowed. "What's the matter, cat got your tongue? I asked you where the hell you've been." He reached over, grabbed her by the shoulders and shook her gently. "Jesus Christ, woman. I've been half out of my mind with worry. You should have been here hours ago."

Startled by his presence, she blurted out the truth. "My water hose broke. It took a long time to get it fixed and then the car kept losing power and it wouldn't go very fast and truck drivers were screaming at me . . ." Her voice quivered. "Oh, forget it. What are *you* doing here?" She stepped back out of his arms. It was too painful to be close to him, too miserable to know this was probably the last time she'd ever see him. But what the heck was he doing here? "Uh, didn't you get my letter?"

"This one?" He reached into his pocket and pulled out the crumpled letter he'd retrieved from her floor. "What do you think I'm doing here? I came to talk to you. And Anna, I warn you, after a night without sleep and being so damned worried I didn't know whether to call the Coast Guard or the cops, I'm not in a good mood." He waved the letter under her nose. "So you'd better have a damned good reason for writing all this crap."

Anna gasped. "Hey, writing that letter was the most painful thing I've ever done. I'll thank you not to refer to it as crap. I meant every word I said, and if you had any brains at all, you'd thank me for being so self-sacrificing."

"Bull. Look, I've got one question for you, and I want an honest answer." He stepped closer and she stepped back, but he didn't stop until she was backed against the railing. He reached over and flattened his hands against the wood, effectively caging her between the railing and his body. Tilting his head to one side, he gave her a long, level stare. "Did you mean what you said about loving me?"

Anna stared at him. Had she meant it? Of course she

had. Lord, she'd been dreaming about the man for years. Midnight daydreams. Daydreams that had brought her peace and pleasure and joy and which she'd thought, after her grand gesture yesterday, were all that she'd ever have of him. In the miserable hours of last night, it had been the dreams of him that had kept her going. Dreams mingled now with the reality of what he was. John Martell was no longer the phantom lover of her midnight fantasies. He was flesh and blood and heat and passion. He was touch and sound and mind and heart. He was real. He was everything to her, and she loved him more than her next heartbeat.

"Anna, I asked you a question," he prodded. John felt a moment's panic.

"Yes," she finally said, dropping her gaze and studying the tip of her shoe. "I meant it." Anna gathered her courage. No matter how much it hurt, no matter how painful it was, she refused to be with him because he felt responsible for what had happened to Roger. "But how I feel doesn't matter," she continued forcefully, still not looking at him. "Just because I love you doesn't mean we can have a relationship. I know you feel responsible for what happened. I know you've tried to make amends to me because of Roger's death, and I won't let you do it anymore."

"Anna," he ordered softly, "look at me."

She shook her head. She didn't want him to see her tears.

John's patience snapped. He straightened abruptly and yanked her into his arms.

"Hey," she yelped. "What do you think you're doing . . .?"

"I'm holding the woman I love in my arms and trying to talk some sense into her thick head," he snapped. "That's what I'm doing, and you, by God, are going to listen. First of all, I don't feel in the least responsible for Roger's pegging out on my office floor."

"You don't?" She gazed up at him, wide-eyed and apprehensive.

"No. Roger used his heart condition for years to manipulate people. I knew that. I used his drywall company because for a long time he did damned fine work. I only got rid of him when he began cutting corners and using shoddy materials." John gave her a gentle shake. "I felt lousy when he died, but Anna, I've got eyes in my head. Like you said, he smoked, drank, overate and partied himself into an early grave. It didn't have a thing to do with me."

"Then why were you so nice to me?" she asked in confusion. "Why did you suggest I move in with Jodie and then rent me your house and give me a job?"

"Because I was in love with you," he admitted. "I've been in love with you for years."

"For years?" Anna couldn't believe her ears. Not once in all the time she was married to Roger had John ever let on that he cared for her.

"Since the first time I saw you, I think," he explained, then he grinned. "Well, maybe that's not quite true. I was attracted to you right away, but it was only as I got to know you as a person that I really fell for you. But you were married. So I didn't look, flirt or touch. I didn't dare."

"I had no idea . . . ," she murmured.

"Of course not." John shook his head. "I made sure of that."

"But why didn't you say something after Roger died?" she asked. "Why did you wait so long?"

He gave her a mocking smile. "Because I was scared. I wasn't at all like Roger. One part of me was scared that you were only attracted to smooth-talking party boys."

"But I'm not like that at all," she protested.

"Then why the hell did you marry Roger?"

Anna laughed. This was going to be tough to explain. "Try and understand, John. Roger was fun to date, but I knew from the beginning he wasn't the kind of man I wanted to spend my life with. But for some weird reason, he decided he wanted to marry me. When I realized how serious he was getting, I was going to tell him we couldn't see each other anymore. But that night he had one of his attacks and we ended up in the emergency room. Roger was all pasty and white and holding my hand and begging me to marry him. So I said yes. I mean, I couldn't say no—the man was practically on life support!"

"I understand," John sighed. "Roger was a real manipulator."

"True." Anna grinned. "But he was a nice guy. I'll give him that."

"Anna," he began softly.

"Yes?"

"Despite why you and Roger married, there's something I have to know."

"What is it?"

"Are you really over his death? Are you ready to make a commitment to me?" He held his breath.

She gazed up at him and smiled. "Oh yes, John, I'm more than willing to make a commitment to you. Any kind of a commitment you want."

She hadn't finished her sentence when he pulled her close and crushed her against him. Then his mouth was on hers and he was kissing her.

She was gasping for air when they finally broke apart. "There's something I'd better confess," she said when she could catch her breath.

"As long as it's not that you sleep in a sweat suit and woolen socks, go ahead."

"Well, you know how you admitted you've had a thing for me for a long time," she began. She ignored his grin and continued. "Uh, you see, I've had a thing for you for quite some time too. As a matter of fact, I've been having these really great fantasies about you."

"Oh yeah? How long?" His grin widened.

"Three years."

"Aha. So I'm not the only one that's been doing a bit of daydreaming." John laughed and pulled her into his arms. "I'll tell you what," he whispered, "I'll tell you my fantasies if you'll tell me yours."

Anna giggled. "No way."

"Come on, please." He nibbled at her ear, and she shivered. "I bet they were sexy, weren't they?"

"Of course not," she replied and then ruined it by moaning as he used his teeth lightly on the sensitive spot on her neck.

"Liar," he whispered. "But I don't care. Having you in my arms is better than any fantasy I could come up with."

"Oh yes," she murmured. "Reality is much, much better."

His arms tightening around her, he squeezed her gently and then stepped back. Anna's eyes flew open.

"I'm not going to let you distract me with lust," he said pompously. "There's still the little matter of you taking off the way you did and scaring the dickens out of me."

"But I explained why I had to go," she said defensively.

"Yeah, you explained all right. But that's still not the same as talking things out in person." He folded his arms over her chest. "From now on, I want your word of honor that if you've got some flea in your ear, you talk to me. No more little notes left on the dresser. Okay?"

"Okay," she muttered. "And I'm sorry. It was a very childish thing to do."

"Damned right it was childish. And stupid, and I don't ever want you doing something that dumb again."

"You've made your point, John."

"Good. Now," he took a deep breath. "There's something else I have to know."

"What?" She eyed him warily.

"Will you marry me?"

Anna gaped at him. "You want to marry me?"

"That's what people in love usually do," he replied. "You'd better say yes, though. I've already bought you a wedding present," he glanced toward the shiny new red compact parked in front of the house, "and as I've already put five hundred miles on the thing, I don't think they'll take it back."

Anna followed his gaze. "You bought me a car? Oh God, John, you didn't have to do that. I love you. I'd marry you even if we didn't have two cents to rub between us." She rushed into his arms and began showering his face with kisses.

He laughed deeply. "Of course I had to do it. My nervous system isn't up to watching you drive that accident waiting to happen anymore." He held her at arm's length. "I'll make you happy Anna, I swear it. From now on, neither of us will have to love the other in our secret fantasies. From now on, it's for real."

Masquerade

Wendy Haley

chapter

---

one

H e was gorgeous.
      Tall. Lean. Dangerously, broodingly not-quite-
handsome-but-who-cares rugged. The ruggedness was only
enhanced by the soot that streaked his forehead, his green
T-shirt and the knees of his well-worn blue jeans. A working man, she thought. A basic, hands-on kind of guy. And
mad as hell, if that scowl meant anything.

Ellis stared at him, fascinated by the sharp planes of his
face, the flare of his brows and the way the strong August
light cut etched shadows in the hollows beneath his cheekbones. An interesting face. His hair was a rich red-brown
that cast the sun back in ruddy sparks. Her fingers
twitched with the desire to put that face on paper. Too bad
her sketchbook was packed away in her suitcase.

He wasn't looking at her. In fact, the noisy bustle of
New York seemed not to touch him at all; his gaze was
fixed on the cloudless blue sky, his mind apparently fixed
on another scene entirely. She wished he'd look at her.

Her short black hair swung across her cheek as she
shifted her suitcase to her left hand and took a folded slip
of paper out of her pocket. Then she looked up at the address painted on the doorway above the man's head. Yes,
they matched. She tightened her grip on the suitcase handle and walked toward him.

His gaze shifted, focusing on her with an intensity that
made her shiver. His eyes were dark brown, almost black,
and seemed to look straight through to her soul.

"Good morning," she said, a little breathlessly. No,

more than a little. Her hair sifted down over her eyes, and she flicked it away with a toss of her head.

"Hi." His gaze moved downward leisurely, then up again.

She felt the heat of a flush on her cheeks. Good Lord, she was twenty-six years old, much too old to blush just because a man looked at her. But then, no man had ever looked at her quite like *that*. And certainly not when she was travel-worn and tired, her head aching from a long, noisy flight.

"This is Shelton Towers, isn't it?" she asked.

He nodded. She took a step forward, then stopped again when he didn't move out of the doorway. He just stood there looking at her. It was as though he were absorbing her, committing her to memory. Capturing her—every feature, gesture, sight, scent and sound. She felt like a butterfly pinned to a board.

"Coming in?" he asked finally.

She nodded.

"Here, give me your suitcase."

He reached to take it from her, then turned as a man called out from inside the building.

"Ellis, is that you?" a deep, hearty voice boomed.

"Jack?" She peered around the broad-shouldered frame of the man before her to see Jack Giraud, her father's business acquaintance. He looked like what he was: a handsome, wealthy businessman. About ten years younger than Dad, Jack was tanned, fit, distinguished-looking, with those sweeps of silver at his temples. A bit of a shark was Jack, but nice enough to let her use his penthouse for a couple of months while he was in Europe.

Turning his hard blue gaze on the other man, he said, "Take her bag, Langston."

She blushed again, embarrassed by Jack's imperious tone. Langston—Was that his first or last name? she wondered—reached out a long arm and relieved her of her suitcase, then stood aside so she could go in. She smiled at him as she went past, hoping to ease the strained moment, but he just stared at her stonily. The scowl had returned.

She was momentarily distracted by her surroundings. Nice. Understated, but nice. Marble floors the way they made them fifty or sixty years ago, the decor an expensive 1980s version of Art Deco.

"I'll give you a key," Jack said, answering a question she hadn't thought to ask. "Visitors will have to be buzzed in."

"You mean they can't just come up?"

"You're not in Kansas anymore, Dorothy." He put his arm around her shoulders. "How did you manage to get in so early, sweetheart? I wasn't expecting you until late this afternoon."

"The travel agent called to say they had a cancellation on an earlier flight. Since I was all ready to go, I just hopped into the car and rushed to the airport."

"Why didn't you give me a call? I'd have sent the car to pick you up."

"And miss my first ride in a New York taxicab?" she asked, shaking her head. "No way."

Langston moved ahead of them and punched the elevator button. Ellis watched him, noting the stiff, angry set of his shoulders. It was obvious he didn't like Jack, and the feeling went beyond the issue of the suitcase. Strange. Most people liked Jack. Her father used to say that Jack Giraud could charm a snake into buying galoshes.

Suddenly anxious to break the silence, she said, "I had the driver let me off several blocks down. I wanted to feel the city beneath my feet."

"It's just concrete, honey," Jack said.

"Oh, no," she replied. "It lives and breathes. If you try, you can feel its heartbeat."

"That's the sound of the trains." Jack rolled his eyes. "As far as breathing goes . . . If you like smog, this is the right place for you."

She caught Langston looking at her, an unreadable expression in his eyes. "What do you think, Mr. Langston?"

"I was born here," he said. "Smog's in my blood, I guess."

Ellis narrowed her eyes. Was his accent just a bit more pronounced than it had been at first? Then Jack laughed, pulling her attention away.

"Enough!" he said. "I concede the point. Now, Ellis, let's get you settled."

He gave her shoulders a squeeze, and Langston's expression froze into granite immobility. The elevator arrived, its doors sliding open with a swish. Jack escorted Ellis inside. Langston deposited the suitcase at the other man's feet, then turned away.

"Hey," Jack said. "I told you to take care of that."

"My *boss* told me to fix the furnace," Langston said. "Which happens to be scattered in pieces across the basement floor."

Turning on his heel, he strode away. The door began to slide closed again. Ellis watched him through the rapidly narrowing opening, wishing she could see inside that gorgeous head of his.

"Can't get decent service around here," Jack muttered, stabbing at the bank of buttons. The elevator moved upward. "He took over as super last week, and I've had nothing but trouble with him."

"What do you mean, trouble?"

"I asked him to fix a couple of things at my place, and was told I'd be put on 'the list.' And informed that it would take a couple of days to get to me. Harry, the super Langston replaced, was always there the same day."

"There are an awful lot of apartments in this building," she said. "If he's had a lot of calls, maybe that's as soon as he could make it."

Jack pointed to the buttons. Bewildered, she looked along the line of his pointing finger. "I don't . . . Oh," she said. "You're in the penthouse. So, what does that have to do with him?"

"Ellis, Ellis." He smiled. "I don't pay penthouse prices to be put on a list."

Aha! she thought. Evidently Langston didn't intend to

play favorites, and he and Jack had gotten into a battle of wills.

"By the way," Jack said. "I've got a little scheduling problem. I won't be able to leave tonight, as I'd originally planned. But don't worry, I'll be out of your hair first thing in the morning."

"Morning?" she echoed.

"You can have the bedroom, and I'll sleep on the sofa."

"I don't know, Jack. Maybe I should get a hotel room—"

"Look, *I'll* go to a hotel. I promised your father I'd take care of you while I'm here, and dumping you in a hotel room doesn't qualify."

"I hate for you to—"

"Good. Then we're agreed," he said. "I'll take the sofa. Then we'll call your parents and assure them that there's a nice, strong lock on the door."

"I didn't mean to imply . . ." She sighed. "It's just that at home, it would take about an hour for the gossips to get going on something like that."

"Honey, this is New York. We could have a knock-down-drag-out fistfight in the lobby and no one would even notice, let alone gossip about it."

She didn't like it, but there didn't seem to be any graceful way around it. Reluctantly, she nodded.

"Great," he said, grinning the famous white-toothed Giraud smile. "Now for the advantage of my scheduling problem: I get the honor of taking you out to dinner on your first night in New York."

Kyle Langston sat on the basement floor, pieces of the furnace spread out around him. He'd been up all night trying to find what was wrong with the thing. At last, success. If . . . *if* he could get the part he needed, he might just be able to nurse another year out of the thing.

"I don't need this, today of all days," he said to the uncaring metal. "I started out behind, and I'm getting behinder all the time." He glanced up at the narrow window to see that the morning sun was beginning to gild the city. "Besides, there are a lot of things I'd rather be doing on a beautiful summer afternoon."

Like take Ellis on a tour of the city. He could still smell her scent, a flowers-and-musk perfume that reminded him of summer and open fields and carefree laughter. Her hair had glinted blue-black in the sun, and her eyes were the clear, pure green of new leaves. Her face glowed with the sheer joy of being alive.

Something had happened to him as he watched her walk toward him. He'd been changed. Turned inside out by a woman who didn't even know his name. Had someone told him yesterday that it could happen like this, he'd have laughed in their face. Smitten, that was the word. An old-fashioned term for a feeling that was timeless.

Ellis. Ellis what? Who was she, why was she here, and what the hell was she doing with Giraud? She wasn't anything like the series of women who'd been trotting in and out of the penthouse all week. Pretty women, but their eyes had been greedy, their beautifully made-up faces too hard.

Kyle shook his head, remembering Ellis's clear green eyes. There'd been no greed in those eyes, no hardness in the clean lines of her face. Maybe she was Giraud's sister, maybe a cousin or niece. God, he hoped so. It had taken an act of will for him to keep from pulling her away from Giraud.

The phone rang, jarring him back to reality. He wiped grease off his hands as he went to answer it.

"Kyle?" The woman's voice had the whispery quality of someone very old.

"Yes, Mrs. Fischer?"

"I wanted to thank you for fixing my shower yesterday. I'd been trying to get Harry Karlowski up here for almost a year, but he never seemed to have the time."

"No problem. Sorry you had to wait so long. Is there anything else you need fixed?"

"Well, I don't want to be a bother, but the lock on the door hasn't been working properly . . ." Her voice trailed off, as though she didn't quite dare finish.

Very gently, he said, "I'll be up in a few minutes, OK?"

"Thank you."

As he hung up, he reflected on his predecessor's short-comings. Harry hadn't been incompetent, merely lazy. He knew where the biggest tips were likely to come from and scheduled his work accordingly. Mrs. Fischer was frail, gentle, bent from arthritis and on much too fixed an income to be the squeaky wheel that got Harry's oil. It didn't matter that she wasn't physically able to get in and out of a bathtub, or that she'd been taking sponge baths at the kitchen sink for a year.

It wasn't that Kyle begrudged Giraud wanting repairs done quickly. As a tenant, it was his right. But there were other tenants, too, and a lot of them had frankly been neglected. Kyle had inspected every apartment, and assigned repairs according to need. Giraud had gotten testy about it. He'd pointed out that because he rented the penthouse, he was entitled to preferential treatment. Kyle Langston, however, had been brought up to believe that frail old ladies deserved some consideration.

He buckled his tool belt around his waist and headed up the stairs to the lobby. Whistling under his breath, he punched the elevator button. The doors snicked open a moment later, and he found himself face-to-face with Giraud.

"Morning," Kyle said.

Giraud nodded. "Glad I ran into you, Langston. I was just coming down to see you."

Kyle stepped back away from the elevator. Crossing his arms over his chest, he waited for the other man to begin.

"I'm going to be working in London for the next several months," Giraud said. "Leaving this morning, in fact."

"This is the first I heard of it." Something *else* Harry neglected to tell me, Kyle thought. "I suppose you've cleared it with the owners?"

"Yes. I'm paid up through the first of the year. They know that Miss MacKenzie's going to be staying in the penthouse while I'm gone."

"Miss MacKenzie?" Kyle asked, although he knew very

well who Giraud was talking about. Dread settled in the pit of his stomach.

"Ellis," Giraud amended. "You so graciously refused to carry her suitcase upstairs, remember?"

"I remember."

"She's a very special lady, and I want to be sure she's treated properly while I'm gone."

The dread sharpened, and Kyle was surprised to find it had turned into pain. "What's that got to do with me?"

"I saw the way you were looking at her," Giraud said. "Remember one thing, Langston: Ellis comes from a prominent Kansas City family. She's used to nice things and nice people. People," his glance drifted to Kyle's hands, "who don't have grease beneath their fingernails."

Kyle wanted to wipe the smile from the man's face with his fists. Instead, he merely gazed at Giraud with narrowed eyes. "People like you?"

"Of course. I just wanted you to understand the way things were."

"Oh, I understand."

"Good." Giraud took his sunglasses out and slipped them on. "I think it's important for everyone to know where they stand . . . in the scheme of things."

Yeah. The hired hand, the stableboy, the chauffeur . . . and the lady of the manor. Those clear, beautiful eyes, that bubbling joy, that smile, a lie? Disappointment stabbed deep. Kyle turned on his heel and strode away. The traffic noise swelled as Giraud opened the outer door, then faded again.

c h a p t e r

---

t w o

Ellis lay in the center of the bed, listening to the traffic noises outside. She'd heard Jack get up, shower and clank around in the kitchen. He'd left a few minutes ago.

She hadn't slept well. In addition to the fact that Jack had snored loud enough to rattle the door separating them, the black satin sheets had been slick and unwelcoming, and she'd been afraid of slithering right out of the bed. Those would have to go. Today.

Maybe she could get a nice native to tell her where she could get a bargain on percale sheets.

"Oh, brother," she murmured. "What brought that up?"

As if she didn't know. She'd spent half the night thinking about Kyle Langston—she'd wormed his first name out of Jack the night before. In fact, she hadn't paid much attention at all to Jack's charming chatter. He hadn't seemed to notice, fortunately.

She couldn't imagine a woman spending the evening with Kyle Langston and getting away with such absent-mindedness. No, he'd get her total attention, just as he'd give her his. What was the best word to describe him? Intense, that was it. A woman could get caught up in that intensity—caught up, wrapped up and wound tight. It was both frightening and fascinating.

And it was also time to get up and explore the city that was going to be her home. She had to find out how to get to the job she was to start tomorrow; she had to find a grocery store and a dry cleaner, a bakery and a good bookstore. That would be a beginning. Oh, yes, and like any tourist, she wanted to take a carriage ride through Central Park.

Feeling full of adventurous spirit, she threw the covers aside and went out into the other room. Jack had cleaned up after himself, even folded the blanket he'd used. The fragrance of coffee hung in the air.

She turned in a circle to survey the spacious apartment. Jack had expensive taste. Or perhaps his decorator did. Dove-gray carpeting covered the floor, and a pair of burgundy leather sofas flanked the fireplace. The coffee table was a massive piece of marble that must have cost the earth. Lamps, vases, throw pillows and even the paintings were color-coordinated. It all seemed somehow impersonal.

But the far wall was a solid sheet of glass, and beyond it was the soaring skyline of Manhattan.

"And tomorrow, my new job," she said, throwing her arms wide. Carruthers Advertising. She'd come to New York with her degree and her portfolio, and had made the rounds of every ad agency that would see her. No one here cared that Ian MacKenzie was an influential man in Kansas City. No. She'd gotten this job on her own, by the strength of her work. Her parents had been so proud . . .

Something thumped against the front door, startling her. She peered out the peephole, found the entryway empty but for something white on the floor a few feet away. What on earth . . . Oh, right, the newspaper! Jack said he had one delivered every morning.

She went out to get it. The moment she heard the click behind her, she whirled. The door had swung closed.

"Please don't be locked," she muttered.

It was. And here she was, standing in her pajamas. Not one of the nice, plain cotton nightgowns her mother would have bought. Oh, no. Ellis had bought nightwear suitable to an independent New York career girl. And the peach satin-and-lace shortie nightgown with spaghetti straps and matching panties was hardly the thing for calling on one's neighbors. With a sigh, she got in the elevator and punched the button for the floor below.

No one answered at the first two doors she tried. She moved down to the third apartment and tried again.

"Who is it?" a woman called through the door.

"My name is Ellis MacKenzie, from the penthouse upstairs. I locked myself out."

After a moment's silence, the woman said, "I'll call the super for you."

Langston! Ellis thought, panicking. "Could you lend me a robe or something?"

The door didn't open. After a seemingly endless moment, Ellis realized it wasn't going to.

"Stranded," she muttered. "Left adrift to face Kyle Langston in my nighties."

There was nothing to do but go back upstairs and wait. It took Langston probably less than fifteen minutes to come, but it seemed like hours to Ellis. She kept looking around the bare landing, wishing there was a place to hide. Thank God her pajamas were opaque.

As the elevator doors opened, she felt a blush heating her cheeks. Langston stepped out. That dark scowl was in place, and his mouth was set in a grim line. And then he saw her. His eyebrows lifted, and a new kind of intentness came into his eyes. He looked her up and down and back again. Slowly. Leisurely. Thoroughly, as though he were committing her to memory.

Ellis felt naked, stripped bare to her soul. Warmth spread through her, but it wasn't a blush. She was intensely, acutely aware of his nearness, the straight, strong body beneath the T-shirt, the shadow of a day-old beard on his lean jaw, the dark eyes that threatened to swallow her up.

Then she saw his mouth twitch. She took a deep breath. "If you laugh, I'll . . . I'll . . ."

"Have me fired?" His eyes changed. She still felt stripped bare, but now she was sure she'd been found wanting.

Lifting her chin defiantly, she said, "Just open the door, please."

"Yes, ma'am."

He unlocked the door and pushed it open. Standing beside him, Ellis could see what he could see—a straight shot into the bedroom. The black satin sheets seemed appallingly decadent in the morning light. She dared a glance at him, and saw a muscle twitching in his jaw.

"Nice place," he said. "But then you're used to this sort of thing."

"Not satin," she replied without thinking, then blushed.

His eyes narrowed. "Silk, maybe. So, you can upgrade after a while."

Confused, she tried another tack. "Uh, look. Thanks for letting me in. There are a couple of things I wanted—"

"Yeah, I know. The faucet in the bathroom drips, and one of the kitchen cabinets sticks when you open it. Oh, yes, the plate on the bedroom light switch is loose. I'll get to it Friday."

Thoroughly bewildered now, she said, "Okay. But I still want—"

"Look, I've got a lot of work to do. If you find anything else, just leave a list on the table Friday morning. I'll check it out when I come in."

Anger drowned her confusion. "Are you always like this?" she asked, jamming her hands onto her hips.

"Like what?"

"Rude."

His brows went down another notch. "Not what you're used to?"

"As a matter of fact, no. I'm used to gentlemen."

He turned on his heel and walked out. A moment later, he reappeared in the doorway. "By the way," he said, "a lady should know better than to put her hands on her hips while wearing shortie pajamas."

She dropped her hands hastily. Before she had a chance to reply, he turned away again. The door slammed behind him.

"I only wanted to ask you where the nearest department store was," she said to the closed door. "And how much it cost to ride the subway."

It didn't matter, she told herself. She didn't know him,

didn't care to know him, and wasn't *ever* going to know him.

But she felt strangely flat and bereft, and the sunshine didn't seem quite so golden.

Ellis's first week at Carruthers Advertising was a hectic one. With everyone scrambling to meet a deadline, no one had had time to do more than show her the bathroom, coffeepot and the partitioned cubbyhole that was to be her office. As the most junior of junior graphic designers, she'd been loaded with odd jobs, mostly lettering and cleaning up drawings. But she listened and learned, hoping to make herself more useful.

Thursday morning, Ellis was hard at work when an envelope plopped onto the drawing board in front of her. She looked up, registering the secretary who'd shown her around the first day. A plumpish woman with blond hair and faded blue eyes. Ellis searched her mind frantically for the woman's name, and failed.

"Hi," she said. "I'm sorry, I don't remember your name."

"Deirdre." The woman propped her elbows on the top of the partition. "It's been nuts around here. I guess you haven't had time to get to know many of us."

"No one but the other designers."

"And they've only had time to hand you drawings and say, 'Fill in this lettering for me, will ya?' "

Ellis laughed. "That's about it."

"It isn't always like this. Just when we've got a major deadline going." Deirdre pointed to the envelope. "But there's the light at the end of the tunnel. The annual Carruthers costume ball. It's the high point of the year—better then the Christmas party, even."

"It sounds great." Ellis ripped the envelope open and scanned the invitation. "But this is for tomorrow!"

"Sorry. Things have been so crazy around here I just forgot to tell you."

"How am I going to make a costume so soon?"

"You were going to make one?"

"Well, yes. I used to make all my brother's Halloween costumes and the ones for his school plays."

Deirdre yawned, covering her mouth with red-tipped fingers. "Honey, you couldn't wear a homemade costume to this thing, anyway. Half the bigwigs in town are coming, and believe me, those people know how to put on the dog. Try Frame's Costume Shop on Forty-third. He's got a decent selection and prices reasonable enough for us peons. Oh, yeah, get a mask. There'll be a prize for whoever can go the longest without being recognized."

"Frame's," Ellis repeated. "On Forty-third. I'll go right after work."

"And don't forget the mask." With a wave, Deirdre moved on. Ellis sat looking at the invitation for a moment, then sighed and turned back to her drawing board.

After work, she shrugged into her jacket and plunged into the sea of home-bound humanity that filled the sidewalks. One of the first things she'd discovered about New York was that the crowds had a rhythm to them, and that once she matched that rhythm, all she had to do was let herself be carried along. She'd also learned the art of crossing streets: walk out as far as possible without actually getting run down, wait until the traffic pauses, then a quick dart across the street.

Frame's was a tiny shop tucked between a deli and an East Indian clothing store. She peered in the plate-glass window and saw a counter laden with what looked like scarves and belts.

"Looking for something to go trick-or-treating in?" The voice was familiar; the half-mocking tone even more so.

She turned to face Kyle Langston. He wore the omnipresent T-shirt and jeans, but a black cotton long-sleeved shirt gave him an air of dangerousness that was echoed in his eyes. Her pulse kicked into trip-hammer high gear.

"What are you doing here?" she asked, annoyed with herself for having such a reaction to a man who obviously loathed her.

"Just running an errand for someone. Why so surprised?"

"I don't know. I just didn't expect to see you."

"I *do* have a life separate from Shelton Towers."

"I never said you didn't."

She could almost feel the chill in the air between them. Was it because of their antagonism, or was it merely because the sun had sunk below the skyline?

Langston muttered something under his breath, then raked his hand through his hair. "Are you going in?"

"What?" she asked.

"Are you going in?" He pointed to the shop.

"Oh. Yes."

He opened the door. Silently, she went in. Just as silently, he followed her. She looked up at him, startled.

"I'm curious," he said, as though that were an explanation.

"May I help you?" the proprietor asked.

It took an effort of will for Ellis to pull her gaze from Langston and focus on the man behind the counter. He was somewhere in his sixties, small and wiry, his eyes huge and wise-looking beneath thick glasses.

"May I help you?" he asked again.

"I'm looking for a costume," she said.

"What sort of costume?"

"Something unusual."

He snorted. "Look, lady. I'm real low right now. There's a big costume ball at—"

"Carruthers Advertising," she said. "I work there."

"Okay. So you know what a big bash it is. I don't have a lot of choices to offer you this late in the game."

"Come on, help the lady out," Langston said. "She only got in town this week."

Ellis glanced at him, surprised and grateful that he'd speak up for her.

"I didn't say I couldn't do *something* for her," the older man said. "I just said I didn't have much of a selection." He looked her up and down. "You wear what, an eight?"

"Yes."

"I've got Cleopatra."

She shook her head. "There are at least three Cleopatras at every costume party, you know that." .

"So I stock a lot of them."

"And Marie Antoinette," she said.

"You've done this before." He smiled for the first time. "Only thing left is Bo Peep."

"Bo Peep!"

"And I got no sheep."

"Puh-lease."

He spread his hands, his grin widening. "What's it to be, lady? Bo Peep or maybe you can cut two holes in a sheet and go as a ghost?"

She sighed. "Let me see it."

He disappeared into the back room. Langston leaned one elbow on the counter and regarded Ellis with inscrutable dark eyes. She realized she'd never seen him smile.

"A costume ball?" he asked.

"Complete with masks. There's even going to be a prize for whoever can remain unidentified the longest."

"You'll need a wig," he said.

Ellis reached up reflexively to touch her short black hair. "Why?"

"No one would forget that hair," he said.

For a moment she stared at him, astonished by the unexpected compliment. There was no admiration in his expression, however. His gaze remained hooded and impenetrable, and she finally looked away.

"So, you work at Carruthers Advertising," he said. "I've heard of them. Pretty highbrow, aren't they?"

"They're a successful advertising firm, if that's what you're asking." She sounded pompous, even to herself.

The proprietor came back with the costume draped over his arm. With a flourish, he laid it across the counter. The gown itself was powder-blue, with a white insert at the bodice that laced with ribbon. The skirt would come to about mid-calf, Ellis judged, short enough to show the lace-edged pantalets.

"It's very Bo-Peepish," she said. Glancing at Langston, she added, "I'll need a wig."

"Powdered or not?" the proprietor asked.

"Did Bo Peep have powdered hair?"

"You're looking for historical accuracy?"

"Good point," she said. "I've always wondered what it would be like to be a blonde."

"I'll be right back."

Langston held the pantalets up and turned them from side to side. "It's a good thing you decided against the powdered wig, or you would have ended up with Marie Antoinette's hair."

The older man returned, carrying a wig in one hand, a shepherd's crook—or a shepherdess', rather—in the other. "Here," he said, handing the wig to Ellis. "Give it a try. There's a mirror over there by the register."

Ellis tucked her hair beneath the wig and went to inspect herself. Most of the platinum hair was caught up in a coil at the back of the head, with two fat curls to drape over her shoulders à la Scarlett O'Hara. It wasn't bad at all.

"What do you think?" she asked the two men.

"Marvelous," the proprietor said. "You look like another person entirely."

She looked up in surprise as Langston strode across the room toward her. He stopped in front of her, staring down at her for a long, frozen moment. Then he reached out and pulled the wig off. It was a strangely intimate gesture, and she blushed as though he'd removed her blouse.

He brushed a lock of hair back from her forehead. His hand was hot, and so were his eyes. She trembled, taking a deep breath to ease the sudden tightness in her chest.

"I like you better like this," he said.

"You don't like me at all." The words had come unbidden, and she wished she could take them back. Especially since he didn't deny them. Maybe if he had smiled . . .

"Do you want the costume, or don't you?" the proprietor asked.

Again, she had to force herself to look away from Langston. "I want it."

"Okay. And you, young man. Who do you want to be tomorrow?"

"A rich man."

It should have been a joke. But Ellis saw no laughter in Langston's eyes.

"I'm not going," he added.

The older man's face showed his surprise. "No? But I thought—"

"I'm the hired help. Just here to carry the lady's packages back to her penthouse for her."

"It's not my penthouse," she said. "It's—"

"Your *friend's*," he finished for her.

"Right. My *friend's*." Ellis tossed the wig onto the counter and swung around to face him. "What did Jack ever do to you, anyway?"

"Hey, hey!" the older man called. "Time out. What does this look like here, Madison Square Garden? You want to fight, take it outside."

"Sorry," Ellis muttered, taking her wallet out of her purse. "What do I owe you?"

"Do you want to pick it up tomorrow?"

"Well, I'd just as soon take it now," Ellis said. Shooting a glance at Langston, she added, "Seeing that I have the help to carry it home for me."

"I ought to charge you two nights' rental," the proprietor said. "But since you showed proper appreciation for my sheep joke, I'll only charge you for one. It's due back noon Saturday. Say, don't you need a mask?"

She shook her head. "I think I'll make one."

Langston stood silently as she paid, then took the garment bag from the other man and walked toward the door. Ellis grabbed the crook and the wig and hurried after him.

"I can carry it myself," she said, trotting to keep up with his long-legged strides.

"Don't be an idiot," he growled. "It's nearly fourteen blocks."

"I'll take a taxi."

He stopped. "Look. I was out of line in there. I'm sorry."

The apology was unexpected, and took the wind out of her sails. "Apology accepted."

With a sigh, he held out his arm. She tucked her hand into the crook of his elbow, knowing by the storm raging in his eyes that it was a fragile truce. Why should she care? Why should she care if he liked her or loathed her, or why? She hardly knew the man.

But she did care. She did want him to like her. And call it crazy, she wanted him to smile at her, just once.

"Kyle—"

"Let's not talk," he said. "Talking doesn't do well for us."

She nodded, acquiescing. So they walked back to the apartment building in silence. She couldn't keep from watching him out of the corner of her eye. The streetlights cast buttery reflections across the rugged planes of his face and sparked red in his mahogany hair. She didn't understand him. One moment he seemed antagonistic. Then he'd look at her, and it seemed as though his gaze would consume her.

She'd thought herself a reasonably worldly person. But none of the rules about men and women seemed to apply to her strange relationship with Kyle Langston. There didn't seem to be a right thing to say or do, any way to come to terms with him. She felt cast adrift, with no compass and no land in sight.

They parted in the lobby, still in silence. As the elevator bore her upward, Ellis discovered tears on her cheeks.

"I'm just tired," she told herself. "It's been a long, hard week."

At least she hoped that was the reason.

chapter

three

Kyle levered his boots off and let them drop. With a sigh, he leaned back against the headboard of the narrow bed that half filled the tiny basement room that would be his home for the next nine months. A desk occupied the opposite wall, the computer on it casting an angular shadow on the brick.

He propped his head on the pillow and stared at the dark monitor screen, feeling guilty because he should have been working on his dissertation. But his mind kept conjuring Ellis's face for him, superimposing it over what his eyes were seeing. He sighed. This was counterproductive. He'd taken this job because the room and spare time came with it, and because working with his hands gave him peace of mind. It was perfect for him.

He hadn't counted on meeting Ellis. Somehow, she'd taken up residence in his soul, banishing that peace of mind as though he'd never had it at all. She'd also banished the discipline that usually kept him working until long after midnight every night.

She belongs to another man.

It made him crazy, the thought of her loving Giraud. It made him say crazy things, things that could only push her away when he wanted to draw her closer. Even now, he could still smell her perfume. His hands remembered the feel of her silky hair as though she'd been imprinted in his flesh.

"Haunted," he muttered.

Against his wishes, his mind played back the scene in

the costume shop. He shouldn't have gone in, not when the sight of her had made his heart turn over.

He sighed. Bo Peep. She'd fallen into the proprietor's repartee so effortlessly, her eyes sparkling with mischief, her lips curved in a Madonna half-smile. And then she'd put on that damned wig. That had been his undoing. She'd looked remote and cold, the pale hair stealing the warmth from her eyes. He'd taken it off her, reacting with blind, reckless instinct. He shouldn't have. Something had happened when he'd touched her. She felt it, too; the shattered look in her eyes would have made a statue tremble.

She belongs to another man.

Of all the women in the world, why this one? He couldn't begin to give her the things she was used to. The things Jack Giraud could give her.

Kyle closed his eyes, but her face still hung before him. He was working toward a future, but someone like Ellis had it all right now. Money, family with a capital F, a job with a prestigious firm, expensive clothes—upper class all the way.

He'd been burned once by a rich girl. Jacqui. He'd been nineteen, too young to keep from being dazzled by her looks, her clothes and her ennui. She used him to defy Mommy and Daddy, and to make her well-to-do boyfriend jealous. When she'd gotten tired of the game, she went back to the country club and the rich boyfriend. Kyle Langston, caddie, lost his job. It had been a long time ago, but the lesson was still sharp and clear.

How can you judge Ellis by another woman's standards? a treacherous little voice whispered in his mind. When she looks at you, her eyes turn soft and hungry, at least when you don't screw it up by snapping at her.

"She belongs to another man," he said aloud, as though to give the words more substance.

But maybe, the voice replied, he's the wrong man.

"Some women are turned on by the differences," he argued. "Leather as opposed to satin. Cotton as opposed to silk." He drew his breath in harshly as he scrubbed his hand over the sheet beneath him. The memory of the bed in the penthouse, the covers tossed in a wanton sprawl, was visceral in its power to hurt him. "It doesn't last. It's not real. It's only a woman wanting the danger of stepping outside her world."

And some women want the *man*.

"How do I know?"

You don't.

He shook his head. He had to know. His feelings for Jacqui had been puppy love. Eventually, he would have outgrown her. But what he felt for Ellis was real and powerful. The kind that lasted. The kind that hurt. If he let himself go with her, he'd be risking everything.

He had to know. He had to learn Ellis as her friends and family knew her. The real Ellis. And that was something Kyle Langston, building super, couldn't do.

"So, who do you want to be tomorrow?" he muttered.

He sat up suddenly, swinging his legs over the edge of the bed as he reached for the phone.

Ellis rushed home from work Friday evening. Tossing her briefcase on one sofa, her coat and bag on the other, she trotted into the kitchen.

A note hung on the refrigerator door. Kyle's list, with each item checked off. He'd signed the bottom with a bold, illegible scrawl, then added a postscript: "You need a bulb for the center light in the living room."

She made a mental note to pick one up tomorrow. Tonight, however, she was going to have to hurry if she was going to make it to the party on time.

The costume fit well, although the bodice didn't lace up quite as securely as she would have liked. She fitted the wig on, then picked up the crook and stepped back to look at herself in the mirror.

"Baaaaa," she said.

Now for the mask. Retrieving her purse from the living room, she took out the bag of face paint she'd bought on the way home. Bo Peep she might be, but at least she'd have a unique mask.

It took her the better part of an hour to finish. Then she

put her brush down and sat back to look at her image. An intricate design covered the upper part of her face, coiling around her eyes and dipping down upon her cheeks. Her eyebrows had been incorporated into the design, the dark color reflected by tiny slashes of black at her temples and over her cheekbones. She'd used mostly shades of blue and green, with startling accents of yellow that stood out like jewels amid the gentler colors.

She turned one way and then the other, trying to decide if the mask looked more like feathers or a butterfly's wing.

"Doesn't matter," she told her reflection. "I like it. And I'm going to be late if I don't get a move on."

She inspected her costume one last time. On impulse, she went into the bedroom for the pearl bracelet that had been her grandmother's. Its value was mostly sentimental; as family history told it, Grandpa John had hocked his gold pocket watch to buy it as a first anniversary gift for his wife.

She fastened it around her right wrist. "For luck," she murmured.

Tossing her coat around her shoulders, she went downstairs and hailed a taxi. If the driver was startled by her painted face, he didn't show it, just opened the Plexiglas partition so that she could lean her crook over the back of the front seat, then drove away with perfect aplomb. She tipped him well.

It wasn't until she got off the elevator that she got nervous. A muted hum of music and conversation revealed that the party was already under way. Sudden shyness overwhelmed her as she realized she knew virtually no one there.

The elevator doors opened behind her. She made a show of straightening her skirts to let the newcomers pass. Several women moved past her, laughing among themselves. They opened the door and went in, letting a wave of music and loud conversation flow into the landing.

"Hello." The voice was male and low, almost a whisper, and had a hoarse quality to it. A nice voice, nonetheless.

Ellis straightened. "Hello," she replied, coming face-to-face with her companion.

Zorro. Of its own volition, her gaze moved from his wide-brimmed black hat to the sweeping expanse of cape, the belt with its silver medallions and sheathed rapier, the tight black pants and knee-length boots. His mask was larger than it should have been, covering his upper face almost to the thin black mustache that couldn't be real but looked it. Hot Latin eyes stared at her from the eyeholes.

There was something familiar about him, a coiled intentness that was both fascinating and unnerving. Like Langston, she thought, then pushed it aside resolutely. She wasn't going to think about Kyle Langston tonight. She was going to have fun.

"Hi," she said.

"The mask is stunning," he said. "Did you paint it yourself?"

She nodded. "Thanks. I'm—"

"No names, remember?"

"Call me Bo, then."

He smiled, and her pulse rate accelerated. Whoever this Zorro might be, he had a pair of absolutely stunning dimples. A horrified moment later, she realized she'd made that observation out loud.

"Oh," she gasped. "I didn't mean—"

"Obviously," he said, his grin widening. "I'm glad you like them."

There was such teasing laughter in his eyes that she didn't feel like an idiot—quite. "That has to be the single most embarrassing thing I've ever said to a stranger."

"Do you say things like that to people you know?" he asked.

"You're twisting my words."

"Just trying to see if I can make you blush."

"You won't succeed. Red would clash with my paint."

He bowed, sweeping his arm wide in a courtier's gesture. "May I escort you in, Miss Peep?"

"As long as you don't ask—"

"Where are your sheep?"

She sighed. "I knew it. My mother always said you can't trust a man with a skinny mustache."

"Now, *my* mother always told me to look into the eyes. You can trust the eyes, she said."

He was staring at her so intently that she almost asked him what he saw in her eyes. Somehow, she managed not to; that would have been much, much worse than admiring his dimples aloud.

"We should go in," she murmured.

"Yes," he said without moving an inch.

She was stuck, held motionless by that dark, ardent gaze. Her breath caught. Then someone opened the door, and the ensuing blast of sound pulled her out of her reverie.

Silently, he offered his arm. She rested her hand lightly on his sleeve and let him escort her in.

Passing through the door was like leaving reality behind. Carruthers' quiet, businesslike offices had been transformed into a fantasyland. Not by decorations, but by people. Trolls, dragons, fairy princesses. Harlequins, pirates, cavemen, Southern belles, Yankee officers. There were several Marie Antoinettes, and of course, Cleopatras—complete with rubber asps.

Those were the conventional costumes. There were some, however, that had come from less restricted imaginations. *Very* less restricted. Ellis saw a spaceship, a rubber ducky, a Klingon and a bunch of concord grapes. Once, when the crowd around the bar parted briefly, she spotted a large, red lobster deep in conversation with the Tin Man.

"Holy cow," breathed her companion, stepping back to let a vastly oversized Dolly Parton look-alike squeeze by. "I think that was a guy."

"It was," Ellis said.

The dimples came back, and her internal temperature went up accordingly. The music ended, leaving a void that was quickly filled with a muted roar of conversation.

"Would you like some champagne?" Zorro asked.

"I don't drink."

"Neither do I. Ginger ale? Or maybe Perrier with lime?"

She looked up at him, becoming rather lost in those liquid dark eyes. "Ginger ale, thanks."

The crowd thickened as they neared the bar. He took Ellis's hand and tucked it more securely into the crook of his arm. It seemed a casual, almost absentminded gesture, but Ellis felt as though she'd been claimed. A tidal wave of familiarity washed over her, an almost overwhelming sense of déjà vu.

"What do you think that is?" he asked, pointing to a particularly unusual costume.

Ellis turned to look. "A pizza?"

"I don't think so. The edges are too irregular." Then he laughed. "An amoeba!"

"No," she protested. "Who would come as an amoeba?"

"Who would come as a pizza?"

"In this crowd?" She shook her head. "Almost anyone."

"I think . . ." He recoiled as the concord grapes bore down on him in a flurry of purple balloons and Scotch. Pulling Ellis against him, he gently shunted the obviously inebriated partygoer to one side. She got a glimpse of a jowly, purple-painted face as the grapes moved past. Astonishment speared through her.

"I think that was my boss," she said.

"How can you tell?"

"Well, I think the shape of his face . . ." She took a deep breath as the absurdity of it all struck her in a wild rush. Her voice shook as she added, "Although I can't be sure. I . . . I've never seen him in purple before."

He stopped, drew in his breath sharply, then started to laugh. Ellis leaned on his arm as she struggled to keep her mirth from making her eyes overflow. Every time she thought she had herself under control, he got her started again.

"Stop making me laugh," she gasped. "If I cry, I'll ruin my makeup."

"I'll try."

"No," she said as he started toward the bar again. "*He's*

there. If I look at him, I'm going to start laughing again, and I may never be able to stop."

"Come on, let's hide out over there until you get control of yourself."

He led her toward the far end of the room, where it wasn't quite as crowded. They stopped to let a tall señorita pass. Her mantilla and her perfume trailed after her, as well as the glitter of what had to be real diamonds. She turned to look Zorro up and down as she went by. They were a handsome pair, Ellis noted with unwelcome pique. Their costumes couldn't have matched better if they'd picked them out together.

"Friend of yours?" she asked.

He grinned. "No."

"Don't you have friends you're supposed to meet?"

"I might."

But I'd rather be with you. The thought hung between them, as perceptible as though it had been spoken.

"And then again," his dimples deepened, "I might not."

Something stirred the crowd, and a number of people started moving toward the center section of the office. Ellis stood on tiptoes, but she was still too short to see.

"What's going on?" she asked.

A Marie Antoinette, apparently overhearing the question, turned around. "The band is back from their break," she said. "Do I know you?"

"I doubt it," Zorro said.

She shrugged, setting an abundance of décolleté-exposed flesh to quivering. "Can't blame a girl for trying. Some people have fallen for it and told me their names before they thought about what they're doing."

"I'll have to remember that trick," he said.

With a wave of red-tipped fingers, she turned to Ellis. "So, Bo Peep, where are your sheep?"

"I don't know where to find them," Ellis said in a squeaky little-girl voice. She knew this woman; Deirdre was the only person she'd ever met with fingernails that length.

"All right, I give up," Deirdre said good-naturedly.

"Since you're obviously taken, mystery masked man, do you have a friend who might want to dance with a queen?"

"Dance?" he asked.

"Sure. They've cleared out a whole section. You can't expect people to come in gowns and fans and ...," she glanced at his belt, "swords and not let them dance."

"You're right," he said. Turning, he held out his hand to Ellis. "Shall we, Miss Peep?"

She laid her hand in his, shivering a little when she felt how warm his skin was. They reached the dance floor just as the band picked up their instruments. With a shock, Ellis realized that the designers' partitioned offices had been removed to make room for this. Strange, she mused, to think she'd been hard at work here a few hours ago.

The band began playing, a slow, tender love song. Her companion led her onto the dance floor. As he pulled her into his arms, she felt reality slipping away from her. She'd only met this man tonight, but here, held in his arms, their bodies moving in perfect unison, she felt as though she belonged. Again, she felt a powerful surge of déjà vu. Had she known him in another life, perhaps? If there were such a thing, maybe a person kept a memory locked somewhere inside, to be released only in the presence of the one who'd put it there?

"Do I know you?" she asked.

He smiled. "That didn't work before, even with a queen."

"I was hoping to catch you off guard."

"Forewarned is forearmed." His hand spread out over the small of her back. "What are we supposed to do if we identify someone, anyway?"

It took her a moment to turn her mind from the feel of his hand through her gown. "I think there's a list by the door. But to tell you the truth, I only know who the grapes and Queen Marie are, and I'm not about to negotiate that crowd for two names. What about you? Do you recognize anyone?"

"I haven't been trying."

His gaze was warm, attentive, his dark eyes fathomless. Ellis found herself caught up in them again. Against her wishes, heat crept into her cheeks.

"You're blushing," he said.

"And clashing. I must look like a clown with this paint."

"Not at all." His eyes smiled into hers. "You just look like you've been drinking champagne."

"I have to call you something," she said. "What *was* Zorro's first name, anyway?"

"I don't know. Call me John."

"Is that your name?"

"Tonight it is."

She let her breath out in exasperation. "I can't help but think I know you from somewhere—"

"Everyone knows someone named John."

"Stop it," she said. "I'm serious."

"So am I. Besides the fact that you're fishing unmercifully, you're forgetting the spirit of this get-together. Pure fantasy, Miss Peep. Whoever you were today, that person doesn't exist tonight. Tonight, you're a lovely shepherdess who has lost her sheep—"

"No, my mind, if I buy into this."

"But you already have." He raised her hand to his mouth and brushed his lips across her palm, causing a frisson to run up her spine. "Reality doesn't exist. Tomorrow you can be as analytical as you want, but tonight . . . Tonight is mine."

His claim shocked her. Shocked her, and made her heart beat with frantic speed. He leaned close, so close that his breath fanned the hair at her temple. For a moment, she thought he was going to kiss her. Her pulse thundered in her ears, and the room suddenly seemed much too warm.

You don't know him! a tiny, sane voice screamed in her mind.

But something in her *did* know him. Call it heart, mind or soul, some part of her recognized him. She let her eyes drift closed as she felt his breath skim downward over her cheek.

And then a face swam into her mind's eye, an unsmiling face with sharp-angled cheekbones and brows drawn down in a scowl. Kyle Langston. Good Lord, of all the times to think of him!

You don't know him, either.

She drew her breath in with a hiss. The crook slipped out of her suddenly nervous fingers, hitting her partner solidly on his shoulder.

"Sorry," she said.

"Me, too," he murmured, but she didn't think he was talking about the crook.

Then the song ended. Ellis stepped back, shaken by what had happened. For a moment, reality *had* been suspended. She'd let herself be carried away by the sheer power of the moment. It was as though he'd wrapped her in a spell of some kind.

A spell broken by the memory of Kyle Langston's face. Why had he intruded? Why had she *let* him intrude?

"What's the matter?" her companion asked. "You're trembling."

"I . . . I guess I'm just confused," she said.

It was an honest answer, not one she would have liked to make. But she felt stripped bare, exposed to her very soul. A strange notion for a woman wearing a mask.

"I think it's time for that ginger ale," he said.

He took her hand and folded it securely between his arm and his body, a gesture fraught with both tenderness and possession. Achingly familiar, yet if she'd touched this man before, surely she'd know it.

"When's the unveiling?"

"Midnight." She looked up into the half-shadowed eyeholes of his mask. "Then the fantasy ends. I'll know who you are, and you'll know the real me."

"Will I?" he asked.

"What do you mean?"

With a smile, he reached out and ran his fingertip lightly down her cheek. "You can't just whip that mask off, you know."

"If someone guesses my identity beforehand, I won't have to."

"Do you think someone will?" he asked.

"No one knows . . ." She drew her breath in with a hiss. "Trying Deirdre's tactics, are you?"

"All's fair, so they say."

They reached the bar, or rather the end of the line that had formed in front of the bar. The woman just in front of them was dressed as a sunflower, her companion a bumblebee. They glanced over their shoulders at Ellis and Zorro.

"Why didn't you come as a sheep?" the man asked.

"The sheep are lost," Zorro replied. "I, however, know exactly where I'm supposed to be."

"Besides," Ellis said. "If we had, then everyone would have known we're a couple. Couples—"

"Get pegged too easily," the man finished for her. "Tell me about it. We got tapped about a minute and a half after Romeo and Juliet."

They turned around again. Zorro tucked Ellis's hand more securely against his body and smiled down at her. "It's ten o'clock already. Two hours of fantasy to go, Miss Peep."

"Do you think you'll make it without anyone recognizing you?"

"I hope so."

"Why?" Ellis asked. "The prize?"

"Yes." His gaze touched her like a caress, and she knew he wasn't talking about whatever bauble the management planned to give away.

Again, she felt stripped bare despite the mask. Why did a stranger—this stranger, of all the people in the world—have this power over her?

She could leave. Walk out and leave this compelling man behind. It would be the safe thing to do. Maybe, in the real world, she would have. But he was right about one thing: tonight, in this place, reality had been suspended.

No, she couldn't leave. She had to see his face. Tonight, while the magic lasted. And why? She shook her head, exasperated by her own fanciful notion even as she gave in to it. Because tomorrow, if they met, it wouldn't be as Zorro and Bo Peep, who had struck sparks the moment they touched. The fantasy would be lost.

She found that she didn't want to lose this fantasy. It had to end, as dreams always did. But never thrown away.

And then, disturbingly, Kyle Langston's face rose in her mind. Frowning. Disapproving. His eyes seeming to draw her in, consume her. Why, why, why? she railed at herself. He doesn't even like me! Why, with this tall, dashing stranger at her side, did Langston's image keep haunting her?

"Get out of my fantasy, Langston," she muttered under her breath. "You don't belong here."

chapter

four

The ginger ale felt like champagne as it slipped down Ellis's throat. Or maybe it was the man beside her who made her feel so giddy. He watched her as he sipped his drink, and the intimate warmth of his gaze seemed to create a bubble of isolation around them.

"Out there in the hallway ... Why did you stop?" she asked. Why did you pick me?

He smiled. "Instinct. And the pantalets, I think."

"I'm not sure I'm flattered."

"You didn't say it was flattery you wanted," he said. "I'm not very good at it. How about the truth instead?"

She caught her breath. "The truth will do."

"It was your eyes." He reached out and gently brushed his fingertip across her lashes, another of those achingly familiar gestures that made her throat tighten with almost-memory.

"I've never seen eyes that color," he murmured. "The green of new spring leaves, faceted like cracked glass. One glance, and I was hooked. I had to know if they reflected the woman inside."

Ellis nearly sighed when she felt his arm come around her waist. His eyes darkened to obsidian, and molten heat swirled in their depths.

"Do you?" she whispered.

"Hmmm?"

"Do you know the woman behind the eyes?"

He drew her closer, enveloping her in the folds of his cape. The satin lining slipped over her skin, so much like a caress that she shivered.

His eyes reflected his awareness of what she was feeling. "Research takes time."

"How much time? We only have till midnight, you know." Her gaze focused on his mouth. The dimple on the left side was just visible, and she had the strongest urge to . . .

"Hey, Zorro!"

The man's voice jolted Ellis out of her reverie. She saw her companion's gaze shift to a point behind her, saw matching annoyance in his eyes. Swinging around, she faced the direction from which the voice had come.

A cavalier pushed through the crowd toward her, the feather in his hat bobbing frantically. "Hey!" he called again. "Don't run away, you two."

Ellis felt her companion move closer, shoulder to shoulder as though to meet the intrusion with a united front. The cavalier reached them a moment later. Peering from one to the other through the eyeholes of a sequin-studded mask, he said, "Whew! What a crowd. I've been trying to catch up with you since you got off the dance floor."

"It's pretty crowded," Zorro agreed. His hat brim cast a shadow across his face, hiding his eyes. Suddenly he seemed darkly mysterious, more a creature of the night than the green-faced, bloody-fanged vampire passing behind him.

"Hell of a party," the cavalier said. "Biggest collection of movers and shakers I've seen in months."

"Is that what we are?" Zorro asked.

"Yeah. Or believe me, we wouldn't be here."

"What about the Carruthers' employees?" Ellis asked.

The cavalier's feather bobbed. "They're here trying to meet the movers and shakers. What else? Business, sheep lady, up front and personal. New accounts for Carruthers, rich men for the secretaries to meet."

Ellis stared at him, appalled by his cynicism. "You have an interesting perspective on life and your fellow man," she said from between clenched teeth.

"Thanks," the cavalier said. "It helps to have a handle on the world."

"Watch the crook," Zorro said. "It's deadly."

"Yeah, yeah. So Cleopatra said about her snakes." The man snapped his fingers. "I've been watching you, Zorro. Took me a while to figure it out, but I know who you are."

"Oh?"

"You're Colin DeMarco from L and G Electronics."

"I am?"

"Yeah. Don't you remember me?"

"Not in a sequined mask."

"I'm ... Hey, you're not going to catch me so easy." The feather bobbed as he shook his head. "And what about you, Bo Peep? You look awfully familiar."

"Maybe you remember me from nursery school."

He ignored her retort completely. "Come on, give me a clue here. I've been asking people if Colin has a girlfriend—"

"Sorry," she said. "We only met tonight."

He tipped his hat to Zorro. "Congratulations. Well, got to run. See you at the unmasking." He trotted toward the front of the office, presumably to record his victory.

"If that's a 'mover and shaker,' I feel sorry for the future of humankind," Ellis said.

Her companion chuckled. "Fortunately, he's a mover and shaker in a very, very small slice of the real world. He isn't worth the paper he's written on. Forget him; let's talk about something else."

"Okay," Ellis said. "Are you Colin DeMarco?"

He blinked. "That was a hell of a quick feint and thrust for a woman named Peep."

"Are you?"

"No."

"Not tonight?"

"Not ever." He smiled down at her, and it was as if he'd touched her. "You can lower those pretty brows of yours, Miss Peep. I've never even heard of Colin DeMarco. Trust me on this."

Trust, she thought. Now that was an interesting thought. She didn't know his name, didn't know what he looked like. All she had was those dark, dark eyes of his, the eyes that seemed to want so much from her.

She nodded, her head moving almost of its own volition. Trust. Blind faith, more likely. Whichever, she gave it.

"I don't know why," she said aloud. "I don't know you at all."

He took her by the shoulders and turned her to face him. "I'm taking the same chances. You haven't told me anything about yourself. For all I know, you might have a husband, boyfriend, etcetera."

"Of course I don't have . . ." Her voice trailed off as her mind conjured the memory of Kyle Langston again. Now, how could she describe this unwelcome but compelling ghost haunting her subconscious? Definitely etcetera.

But she'd paused too long. Nothing she could say now was going to erase that all-too-obvious moment. Her companion crumpled his cup and tossed it into a nearby wastebasket. When he turned back to her, his eyes held uncharacteristic coldness.

Ellis struggled for words to explain what was happening to her. But how could she explain a non-relationship relationship she didn't understand herself? *I've got this strange, unwilling fascination for my super, who hates my guts but keeps popping up in my mind at inopportune moments?* Now that was bound to go over real well.

Even as those thoughts passed through her mind, the shadow faded from his eyes. "What am I doing?" he said. "I'm trying to bring reality into the fantasy, and it's not even midnight. Forget I asked, Miss Peep, and come dance with me again."

"And when midnight comes?"

"After midnight, all the masks come off."

He held out his arm. Ellis took it, shivering a little as she looked up into the depths of his eyes.

"Do you think it was true?" she asked. "What that man said about the people here?"

"Maybe some of them."

"Did you come here for, as he so subtly put it, 'business, up front and personal'?"

"No." He pulled her onto the dance floor and into his arms. "And I wasn't looking to meet a secretary, either."

"What—"

"You talk too much," he said. "We're wasting time, and ours is precious."

She glanced at the clock. A half hour to go. "Now I know how Cinderella felt."

"Why? Do you think you're going to turn into a pumpkin?" He grinned. "Or maybe a secretary?"

"If I were, would you care?"

"Would you care if I weren't a mover and shaker?"

"How do I know you are?"

"My charm," he said. "And my squeaky-clean fingernails." There was a flicker of something in his eyes that might have been anger. But it came and went so fast that she decided she'd misinterpreted it.

"I think I'm losing the thread of this conversation," she said.

"Then let's just dance." He drew her closer into his warmth, wrapped her up, sent her sliding back into the compelling magic of the fantasy.

And it was magic. Ellis laid her cheek on his shoulder as they danced, letting herself drift on the wings of sensation. She lost her awareness of the other couples around them, heard only a muted blend of music and voices. There was only the man. This man. His arms were strong and gentle as he held her, his breath fanning warm and sweet against her temple. They moved together as though they'd known each other forever. Smoothly, mindlessly, caught up in the fantasy's fragile webbing. She let her eyes drift closed.

It took her a moment to realize that the music had stopped, and took her a moment longer to make herself step back from her partner. She turned to the stage and found the band members gone, the platform occupied by the vast purple shape of the concord grapes. Her boss.

He fiddled with the microphone for a moment, then

said, "Ladies and gentlemen, I fear by this time that you all know who I am—"

"Took us about five minutes to figure it out, Carruthers," a man called. Ellis thought she recognized the cavalier's smug tones. Laughter rippled through the crowd.

"Yeah, yeah," Carruthers said. "Next year I'm coming in a gorilla suit. No one's going to even see my face."

"It's not the face that gave you away," someone called. "It's the belly!"

"Is that you, Tom?" Carruthers cried. "Ladies and gentlemen, I present Tom Benninger. His identity was guessed by six different people."

"Oh, hell," the man said good-naturedly.

"Gather around, everyone," Carruthers called. "I'm going to read the list. If you hear your name and correct costume called, take your mask off. If the guess isn't correct, leave the mask on until I call you up here."

The crowd swirled and eddied, pushing Ellis closer to the stage. Carruthers began calling out names. Groans and catcalls accompanied each unmasking. Soon there were more bare faces than masked, and the air of anticipation rose high.

"The moment of truth," Ellis murmured, glancing around at her companion.

He wasn't there.

Surprise stabbed through her. He'd been there a moment ago; she'd felt his warmth against her back, the swirl of his cape as he shifted position. She stood up on her tiptoes, craning to see over the crowd. He was tall, and that hat ought to have stood out anywhere. But there was no sign of him. Had he gone for something to drink? Had he . . . No. He wouldn't have. Not just now, at the high point of the evening.

But it was her mind that told her all those things. Her heart knew he was gone. Disappeared into the night, like the legend whose costume he wore. And it was her heart that told her he wouldn't be back.

Her breath went out sharply. When she drew it in again, it hurt her chest. The fantasy was over. It had to end, she'd

known that, but she'd expected to learn who the man behind the mask was. She hadn't expected to be left with
nothing.

"So much for luck," she muttered, reaching to touch her
pearl bracelet.

Her fingers met only skin. Frantically, she felt along her
arm, then scanned the floor around her. It could be anywhere; she'd been so wrapped up in the man that she
hadn't paid a bit of attention to anything else.

Tears stung her eyelids, but she managed to keep them
from overflowing. Just. And they weren't for the bracelet;
they were for the end of the lovely dream.

She looked around the room. The masks were gone, but
these were still strangers. And the magic was truly gone;
the costumes no longer seemed quite so clever, the colors
quite so bright. Even Carruthers's purple balloons were beginning to wilt.

"Next is Zorro," he said. "We've got a real mystery
here, two different guesses for one costume: Colin
DeMarco and Mike Figuerera. Come on out, Zorro, and
tell us which you are, or which you aren't." He glanced
around the room. "Anybody see him? No? We'll get on
with it, then. Gotta be here to be in the contest."

Ellis wanted no part of the contest. All her earlier anticipation was gone, having slipped away with the man in the
Zorro costume. Now all she wanted was to go home. She
turned and began threading her way through the crowd.
She almost made it. But then a toga-clad man caught her
by the arm and swung her around.

"Hey, Bo Peep! They're calling your name," he said.
Waving his arm, he shouted. "Over here! She's over here!"

Carruthers peered at her over the intervening crowd.
"Bo Peep? Get your crook up here."

Reluctantly, Ellis began making her way toward the
stage. People turned to look at her as she passed. Her
pulse pounded in her ears, a staccato counterpoint to her
shallow breathing. I shouldn't have come, I shouldn't have
come, played a refrain in her head.

Carruthers gestured impatiently. "Come on, Bo. Up here with me." His balloons quivered.

"Watch out. Don't pop him," someone called.

She stepped up onto the stage. Her boss draped his arm around her shoulders, enveloping her in purple balloons and a haze of Scotch.

"And now for our winner," he said, swinging Ellis around to face the audience.

Somehow she managed to get through the ceremony, stammering her name into the microphone, accepting the prize—an enormous bottle of champagne and an even larger stuffed bear—and making her way off the stage.

Deirdre, thank heaven, came forward to help her. "Are you leaving, Ellis? Here, let me carry some of your boodle."

"Thanks," Ellis said, handing the champagne over. "I don't know what I'm going to do with it. I don't drink."

"Gloat over it for a while, then give it to somebody else for Christmas. That's a great disguise, by the way. I wouldn't have recognized you in a million years."

"I didn't even feel like myself," Ellis said. "Deirdre, I lost a bracelet tonight. It's a double row of pearls with an old-fashioned gold clasp. If you see it, will you save it for me?"

"I'll put the word out. Was it very valuable?"

"Only to me. It belonged to my grandmother."

"Oh, hey. I'm sorry. It'll turn up somewhere, I'm sure."

Ellis juggled the weight of the bear as she pushed the outer door open. Deirdre followed her out. The door closed behind them, cutting off the buzz of conversation inside.

"Did you have a good time?" Deirdre asked.

"I had a great time." Then why did her voice sound so dull?

Deirdre punched the elevator button, then turned to stare at Ellis with too-knowing eyes. "What happened to your friend Zorro?"

"He left." Ellis heard more bitterness in her voice than

she would have believed, and certainly more than she liked.

"I see." Sympathy softened the lines of Deirdre's mouth. "Had a fight, eh?"

"No. Actually, we got along rather well. He just . . . left."

"Men!" Deirdre snorted, tossing her Marie Antoinette curls in a disdainful gesture. "Go figure."

"Yeah," Ellis echoed. "Go figure."

Ellis woke to the sound of someone knocking at her door. With a groan, she rolled over and peered at the clock.

"Nine o'clock," she muttered. "Who's going to visit at nine o'clock on Saturday morning?"

She hadn't slept well. Two men had floated through her dreams, one frowning and harsh, the other clad in a black cape that billowed around him, veiling the night sky.

Fanciful dreams. Frustrating dreams, for they left her more confused than ever. Two men. How had this happened? She'd never been one of those women who could play both sides against the middle. Oh, she'd had her share of dates. But this was more than just dating; Langston and the mystery man had touched something deep and powerful in her, something she wouldn't have imagined in her wildest dreams she could give to more than one man.

The knock came again, more imperatively this time. With a sigh, Ellis flung the covers aside and went to the door. The peephole was just a shade too high for her, making her stand on her toes to see out.

And there, framed in the bull's-eye of the tiny glass, stood Kyle Langston. Her heart skittered into high gear. Jeans, T-shirt, tools hanging in the leather belt around his waist—he was the very image of the man who'd walked through her dreams. The shadow of beard on his chin didn't make him look disreputable; it only accented the angular line of his jaw and made him look even more aggressively masculine.

"Open up," he called. "I know you're there."

"Like you could see me in the peephole," she retorted.

"I've got your light bulb."

"What light bulb?"

"The one for the living room fixture, remember? I left you a note."

She stood for a moment, just looking at him. By rights, she should send him away. Any woman in her right mind would send him away. But when she opened her mouth, what came out was "Give me a minute, will you?"

Racing into the bedroom, she pulled on a pair of jeans and an oversized blouse. A moment in the bathroom got her teeth brushed and her hair combed. All the while, she called herself sixteen kinds of a fool. The man was oblivious to the spot he'd taken in her life and would probably be horrified if he found out.

She opened the door, hoping her face didn't reveal her churning emotions. He stepped inside, his gaze roving from her freshly brushed hair to her bare feet.

"I thought I was supposed to get the bulb myself," she said, striving to retain her composure beneath that intent regard.

"No. Light bulbs are my department."

"At nine o'clock on Saturday morning?"

"Saturday's my busiest day." His gaze moved past her, and she knew he was looking at the stuffed bear that was sitting on the sofa. "Looks like you've got a new roommate."

"I won the contest last night. What do you think of it?"

He walked past her to inspect the bear at close range. "It's big."

"Filled up the whole backseat of the taxi. I had to sit up front with the driver."

His back was to her, so she couldn't tell if he was smiling or not. Chances were that he wasn't; she hadn't been able to get one out of him yet.

So why do you care? she asked herself. But she knew the answer: smile or not, he had intruded in a fantasy that shouldn't have had a place for him, and she wanted to know why.

Frowning, she watched him as he went about his business with the light bulb. She might as well have been a piece of furniture for all the notice he showed her. Finally, she gave up and went into the kitchen to make herself some coffee. The room was small and smoothly functional, from the almond appliances to the matching paint of the cabinets. Ellis preferred her mother's sprawling, lived-in kitchen, where no one minded a bit of flour on the counter as long as bread was baking in the oven. A sudden surge of homesickness tightened her throat.

The thought of homemade bread got her stomach growling; she hadn't eaten since the hot dog she'd snatched on the way home yesterday afternoon. She took bacon and eggs out of the refrigerator.

The sound of hammering drew her into the doorway. Langston was putting up the painting she'd left leaning against the wall. It was the landscape she'd done last summer during a vacation in the Ozarks.

"Hey," she called. "You don't have to do that."

"I don't mind. And with a bare wall right above it, it wasn't hard to figure out where it's supposed to go."

He hung the painting carefully, then stepped back to look at it. "I like this," he said. "It's got a kind of . . . strength. And the way the light hits that old stable, you can almost feel the age of it."

She stared at his back, astonished by his observation. The old stable had captured her with just those qualities. She'd worked very hard to put them on canvas, and it pleased her that he'd seen it. Driven by a sudden, irresistible impulse, she said, "I'm getting ready to put some bacon and eggs on the stove. Would you like some?"

He turned around, his movements betraying his surprise. Well, that makes two of us, she thought.

"Sure," he said. "I'd love some breakfast."

"The coffee will be ready in a minute." She turned back into the kitchen.

A moment later he joined her, and she saw that he'd

taken his tool belt off. He was broad-shouldered and lean, and the sleeves of the T-shirt rode up over the muscles of his upper arms. He smelled of soap and mint and man. She turned away, hiding her sudden nervousness in the familiar actions of turning the bacon as it sizzled in the pan.

"Want me to do the toast?" he asked.

"Sure. The bread's in the refrigerator. Bottom shelf."

He moved around her kitchen with quiet efficiency. It seemed that her skin was somehow attuned to him, tracking him like radar. She didn't have to look to know exactly where he was. Strange.

"How do you like your eggs?" she asked, lifting the last piece of bacon out of the pan.

"Just make whatever you'd planned for yourself."

"Over easy?"

"Sounds great. Where are the utensils?"

"Second drawer on the right." She glanced over her shoulder at him. "Not only do you do toast, but you set tables, too?"

"I'm a handyman, Miss MacKenzie. I'm used to working for my supper."

His expression didn't change, but the atmosphere in the kitchen cooled about twenty degrees. Ellis sighed. Somehow, she always seemed to be a half step off with him. She reached for the eggs and broke four into the pan. A searing gobbet of bacon grease splashed up onto her hand.

"Ouch!" she hissed.

He was beside her in an instant. Pulling her over to the sink, he ran cold water and thrust her hand under it. She gasped. Not from pain, but in reaction to the feel of his arms around her, his lean, whipcord body pressed against hers.

"I'm okay," she said. "Get the eggs!"

But he only left her long enough to turn the burner off and push the pan off the heat. "Let me see that," he said, taking her by the shoulders and spinning her around.

She inspected the red spatter marks of the burn. "It's nothing to worry about. Hardly even hurts anymore."

Gently, so very gently, he lifted her hand. "Yeah, I guess you're right." But he didn't release her; instead, his thumb traced small, intent circles in the center of her palm.

Ellis took a deep breath, then another. He didn't seem to be aware of what he was doing; his gaze was riveted on her eyes. But she was aware. Every inch of her. So this is what it can be like. A shiver ran through her, part dread, part anticipation, part sheer physical reaction. So strong, so powerful . . . so much like what she'd felt last night with another man.

The world seemed to tilt around her, the rules bending, all the things she thought she knew about herself suddenly uncertain. She couldn't feel this way about two men. She couldn't!

"I . . . The eggs are getting cold," she said.

He looked away, releasing her from her frozen moment of revelation. She stepped back, then turned hastily to the stove. The eggs had turned into a rubbery mass. Tossing them into the sink, she started cooking four more.

"Go ahead and sit down," she said without turning. "This is only going to take a minute."

That oversensitive radar of hers seemed to be working overtime; she felt more than heard him walk into the dining area. A moment later, she slid the eggs onto plates and carried them out to the table.

"Thanks," he said. "This looks great."

"You're welcome."

They ate in silence for a moment. Ellis, although she didn't look at him, was overly aware of his gaze on her.

"So, how was the party last night?" he asked.

"Great. I had a great time."

"You don't sound very enthusiastic for a lady who won the prize."

"I lost my grandmother's bracelet there," she said.

"I'm sorry. Was it very valuable?"

"Only to me."

Langston gazed at her for a long, silent moment, then asked, "Did you meet a lot of people?"

"Some." Ellis didn't want to think about the party. She didn't want to think about the man she'd met there. Not now, not with Kyle Langston sitting across the table from her. It was just too confusing. And the more she tried to sort through her feelings, the less sense it all made.

Judging by the look on Langston's face, however, he wasn't ready to change the subject. "I've heard the Carruthers party is *the* place to meet the rich and powerful."

Ellis shrugged again. "I didn't see anyone wearing a sign saying 'Talk to me. I'm rich and powerful.' These are good eggs, aren't they?"

"Is this a hint that you want to change the subject?"

"Yes."

"Okay. Would you like to tell me what's bothering you this morning? You look like you've lost a lot more than your grandmother's bracelet."

"Just a fantasy," she said, pushing her eggs around her plate. "I guess I got a little lonely, and put more stock in it than what it was worth."

"One of the rich and powerful?"

She looked up, surprised by the grimness in his voice. "If I said yes, would it matter?"

"No."

Well, *that* certainly went well, she thought. "So," she said, "what do we talk about now?"

"These are good eggs."

"I already said that."

"So you did." He pushed his chair back, picked up his plate and carried it into the kitchen. "I've got a ton of things to do today. I guess I'd better get going."

She rose to walk him to the door. As she reached for the knob, he turned and looked down at her.

"There's still some paint on your face," he said. "Your mask?"

"I . . . Yes. I must have missed it last night while I . . ."

Her voice trailed off as he cupped her chin in his hand. It wasn't a particularly intimate gesture, or wouldn't have been if someone else had made it. When he touched her, however, it felt as hushed and private as a kiss.

For an instant, she thought his hand trembled. But his face was closed, his expression shuttered, and she was sure she'd been mistaken. He was just rubbing paint off her cheekbone; that was all. The rest was her imagination.

Then she saw his eyes. Dark, molten pools, desire swirling like stars in the sky at night. His hand stilled.

Her gaze focused on his mouth as it drew closer. It was a nice mouth, wide and masculine, without the slightest sign of cynicism. Her eyes drifted closed.

His lips settled on hers, gently, tenderly. She wanted more, more. With a sigh that he caught in his mouth, she twined her arms around his neck and pulled him closer. His fingers speared through her hair to cup the back of her head. She opened her mouth, inviting him in, and he took quick possession. All thought ceased, drowned in a crashing tidal wave of sensation. Ellis sighed again, and this time he echoed her.

With a suddenness that left her gasping, he let her go. She stared at him uncomprehendingly. Then she blushed furiously, aghast at what had happened. Good Lord, she hadn't begun to sort out her confusion about the two men who stirred her so powerfully, and here she'd let him kiss her. She'd let him kiss her like *that*.

"I shouldn't have done that," he said.

"I shouldn't have let you do that."

He took a step backward, his face as hard and unreadable as a statue's. "I'd better get a move on. Don't forget that the costume has to go back by noon today."

Costume! Ellis raised her head with a jerk, caught by a sudden idea. "I won't."

After he was gone, she stood staring at the closed door for a long time. Her father had always taught her to face her problems head-on. And this was certainly a problem.

She had a mystery to solve: why did she have this tremendous attraction to two different men? She wouldn't have peace until she knew the answer.

What she'd do after she had it, well, that was an even bigger mystery.

chapter

five

Kyle sat in the coffee shop across the street from Frame's, wondering what in the hell he'd gotten himself into. Last night had been pure impulse, and all it had done was dig him deeper into the dilemma called Ellis MacKenzie.

Last night there had been times when the world had seemed a million miles away, when there was nothing for him but the music and the feel of Ellis in his arms. For once, there had been no shadows between them, no penthouse apartments and no Jack Giraud.

Last night, Kyle had set out to woo her. And Lord, it had been magic.

Problem was, she didn't know it was Kyle Langston who'd been doing the wooing. She'd probably run like hell if she did.

So tell her the truth.

But pride reared its ugly head. If she was interested in Zorro, it was in the whole fake persona of the man. The "mover and shaker." The acceptable. Not Kyle Langston. Instead of learning more about her, he'd dug himself a hole he'd need a crane to get out of. Hell, after she'd been so taken with his dimples last night, he couldn't even smile when he was with her.

"Want another cup of coffee?" the waitress asked, stopping beside him, coffeepot poised to pour. "Or a sandwich? It's almost noon."

"Just coffee, thanks," he said. "And the check."

The woman fanned herself with the check before laying

it on the table. "Hot, isn't it? And humid. Even the air conditioning can't quite cut this kind of heat."

He nodded absently, his gaze—and his mind—elsewhere. On Ellis MacKenzie, actually. Not for the first time, he asked himself what he was doing. Kyle stirred his coffee fiercely. He ought to have been working on his dissertation. But here he was. And why? Because he'd returned his costume, and upon learning that Ellis hadn't been in yet to return hers, he hadn't been able to leave.

That kiss had been his undoing. That damned, wonderful kiss. It had turned him inside out and upside down, and he wanted nothing more than to do it again. He hadn't meant to. Hadn't meant to go up to the penthouse this morning, either. But last night she'd been so beautiful, her leaf-green eyes frightened and ardent and confused all at once, and she'd felt like a dream in his arms. When they danced, there was no consciousness about it; they had just moved together, so smoothly and perfectly that it had almost felt like making love.

Now *that* was an image to sear a man's soul: Ellis in his arms, skin against skin, her eyes hot with passion. Wanting him. Wanting *him*. Kyle Langston. Not some fantasy man. He shook his head, thinking that things had really gotten bad when he was jealous of himself.

Not himself. It was the mover-and-shaker image Ellis had found so fascinating, the dashing Spanish nobleman with the cape and the sexy mustache. And that drove him nuts. He took a sip of coffee, found it cold and set it aside.

He stiffened as he caught sight of Ellis through a break in the steady stream of people passing in front of him. A glimpse, only; enough to register that she was wearing an oversized blouse the same color as her eyes and a pair of white stretch leggings tight enough to send his pulse soaring into the stratosphere.

He was no green kid. He'd known enough women to realize that no stretch pants, no matter how tight, had the power to make him react like this. No, it was Ellis who made his chest tighten and his palms wet with sweat. She held a line straight to his heart, and every time she tugged on it, he hurt. Just the sight of her made his heart twist with the need to touch her.

Finally, he got a good look at her. She'd broken into a run; her cheeks were flushed with heat, and her hair blew back from her face in dark, shining wings. The costume flapped wildly over her shoulder, the pantalets streaming out behind her like a lace-edged banner. Kyle couldn't help but smile.

Watch it, Langston. Remember the dimples. That smile is a dead giveaway.

Rising, he paid for his coffee, then added the same amount for a tip. He'd worked as a waiter to support his first two years of college, and he had a healthy respect for anyone who could do it for a living.

The thought brought disquietude; had Ellis ever thought beyond penthouses and costume parties? Had she ever looked at a waiter or waitress and seen the person behind the server? And the next, even more disquieting thought: did he want to know if she hadn't?

Yes. Yes, he did. Because he wanted to know if she saw him as Kyle Langston the man. Doctor, lawyer, Indian chief . . . super, he wanted her to care for *him*.

"Well, here goes," he muttered as he headed across the street. "Out of the frying pan and into the fire."

Ellis glanced at her watch as she hurried down Forty-third toward the costume shop. Two minutes to twelve. She was going to make it in time—just.

"Hello!" she panted as she stepped inside.

The proprietor looked up from his ledger. "Ah, Bo Peep. How did your party go?"

"Well, I didn't find my sheep."

"Don't worry, they'll come home—"

"Wagging their tails behind them," she finished. "Do you have any idea how many sheep jokes I had to listen to last night?"

He grinned at her, his glasses winking naughtily in the beam of light from the window. "I heard you won the prize."

"It wasn't hard to stay incognito when hardly anyone knew me to start with," she said. "I felt a little guilty about it."

"What was it this year?"

"A magnum of champagne and a six-foot teddy bear."

"You were lucky," he said. "Last year it was a fifteen-foot pink fuzzy boa constrictor."

Ellis couldn't help but laugh. "Thank goodness for small favors." Her amusement faded. With as much casualness as she could manage, she leaned her elbows on the counter and asked, "Did you happen to rent a Zorro costume to anyone?"

He glanced past her at the front window, then shook his head. Disappointment tightened her throat and put a knot in her chest. It was then that she realized how much she'd been hoping he'd be able to help her.

"You look like you've just lost your best friend," the proprietor said. "What's the matter? Did some handsome Zorro sweep you off your feet?"

"I . . . It's just curiosity. I couldn't guess his identity, and he left before the party was over." A masterful attempt at lying-without-actually-telling-a-lie, she thought.

"You shouldn't be telling fibs," he said, raising his brows. "You're not a very good liar; your face gives you away. And not many people actually blush these days."

With a rueful smile, Ellis put her hands over her hot cheeks. "Didn't you know you're supposed to let people keep their illusions about themselves?"

"Illusions, delusions, whatever." He lifted Bo Peep and went into the back room. When he came out again, he set his elbows on the counter, propped his chin in his hands and regarded her like a wise old gnome. "Personally, I prefer costumes. It's better to wear your illusions than to live them."

"You're a philosopher."

He shrugged. "I just set my sights too high to have illusions. See, years ago, when I was young and foolish, I wanted to be Cary Grant. Every night I slept with my finger in my chin, hoping to make a dimple. When I finally realized it wasn't going to happen, I opened up a costume shop. Now I can help others become Cary Grant."

"Or Zorro?"

"Or Bo Peep."

She understood the wisdom behind what he was saying. But it didn't help her; her problem was too immediate for philosophy. "Are you sure you didn't rent out a Zorro costume?"

The door opened behind her, letting a blast of hot, muggy air and traffic noise into the shop. Ellis glanced over her shoulder, then stiffened when she saw Kyle Langston come in. He still hadn't shaved. With the day-old beard, he looked rugged and dangerous and completely devastating. A rush of adrenaline went through her. And along with it, the thought that there was no one she'd rather see less. Or was it more? The rapidity of her heartbeat could have meant annoyance or sheer joy at seeing him again—or perhaps both.

"What are you doing here?" she demanded.

"I was having a cup of coffee across the street, and happened to see you come in."

"No packages to carry this time," the proprietor said.

"But I've got one to deliver." Reaching into his pocket, Langston pulled out a small ribbon-wrapped package. "This is for you," he said, holding it out to Ellis.

She glanced up at him questioningly, but read nothing in his expression. With a shrug, she untied the ribbon and opened the box. Her pearl bracelet lay inside, nestled in a bed of tissue paper. She nearly laughed in mingled happiness and relief.

"Is that the fugitive bracelet?" Langston asked.

"It is. Where did it come from?"

He shrugged. "I found it on the table in the lobby. Oh,

yes. This was with it." Reaching into his pocket, he pulled out a small envelope.

Ellis opened it. Inside was a note that said, "I found this hooked to the edge of my cape. Last night was pure magic for me. Thank you." And nothing else. No signature, no clue as to Zorro's identity.

She drew in her breath with a hiss of frustration. What was wrong with the man that he couldn't even tell her his name? Was he—Oh, God, horrible thought—was he married?

"What do you think?" Langston asked the proprietor.

"By the frown, I'd say the note didn't tell her what she wanted to know."

"There's the bracelet," Langston pointed out. "She ought to be pleased about that."

"A sentimental bauble," the older man said. "It's a name our pretty lady friend wants."

In other circumstances—in front of an audience that didn't include Kyle Langston, for instance—Ellis might have laughed. As it was, she merely blushed painfully. Slowly, she folded the note and slipped it back into her pocket.

"I'd better be going," she said. "Thanks for all the help, Mr . . . Mr . . ."

"Gabriel."

"Like the angel?"

"I prefer Cary Grant."

Ellis glanced at Kyle, saw that he was watching her and looked away hastily. She felt exposed and too vulnerable beneath that inscrutable dark gaze. "Well, good-bye, and thank you," she said, turning to go.

"I hope you find what you're looking for," Gabriel called.

"I do, too," Ellis murmured under her breath.

For a moment, she thought she'd made her escape. Then she heard the door open behind her.

"Let's take a taxi," Langston said, taking her elbow in a grip she couldn't have broken if she'd tried. "I want to talk to you."

"I can't right now." She felt as brittle as glass, ready to shatter at the first bump.

Ignoring her protest, he hailed a taxi and helped her in. Ellis sighed. It was obvious that arguing with him was going to be useless.

"So," he said as the taxi pulled out into traffic, "tell me about the bracelet."

"The bracelet?"

He crossed his arms over his chest and leaned back against the seat. "Yeah. Who found it?"

"Someone at the party."

"A very cautious answer," he said. "Let me make some deductions here. This 'someone' couldn't be female, because of the blush. And also because of the blush, I'd say this 'someone' had quite an effect on you."

So did you. She remained silent, unwilling to voice that thought aloud.

"So, tell me about him," Langston said.

"I don't know anything about him."

"Come on, Ellis. You must have noticed *something* about the guy; it's not every day you actually get to meet your Prince Charming."

She shook her head. "You're trying to start an argument."

"I'm trying to understand what it is you saw in him."

Those cool, sensible words should have been reassuring. But Ellis saw a light of battle in his eyes that boded ill for the conversation. Annoyance flooded through her, and she lifted her chin defiantly. Who was he to pry into her personal life? He hadn't even asked her for a date! Well, if he wanted information, she'd give it to him. She'd give him more than he'd bargained for.

"All right, I'll tell you," she said, as falsely reasonable as he. "He was nice. Really nice. We hit it off right away. And being with him was oddly familiar, like we'd known each other before."

"That's not reality."

"No, it isn't," she agreed. "But what's wrong with a little fantasy?"

"Fantasy," he said, "is for people in penthouses."

Ellis looked at him with narrowed eyes. "Dreams are for everybody. Can you imagine how terrible life would be if we couldn't step out of the everyday into something completely different, if only for a few hours?"

"You're talking about a different kind of fantasy," he said. "Step out of reality with a book, a movie or a play, yes. Not a man."

"Langston's rules?"

He raked his hand through his hair, and she saw a muscle jump in his jaw. "Was he witty?"

"Very."

"Charming?"

"Yes."

"Rich?"

"I don't know. Probably. He's a prince, remember?"

Moving so swiftly that she gasped in surprise, Langston slid across the seat and took her by the shoulders. "Why did you kiss me this morning?"

"I don't know. It just sort of . . . happened."

"Why?" His voice lashed at her, stung her into answering with reckless truth.

"Because I wanted to!"

"Even though you met this wonderful man last night?"

"Yes."

His fingers tightened. Then they relaxed, spreading out over her shoulders in a possessive gesture. Desire rippled through her in a wild rush, fueled by the hot danger in his eyes. She felt as though she were in the grip of some elemental force, along for the ride whether she wanted to be or not.

"Do you want to kiss me again?"

Her gaze dropped to his mouth. "No." *Yes, she did.*

"Tell the truth, Ellis."

Gazing into his eyes, she had no choice but to obey. "I want you to kiss me," she whispered.

With a sigh that seemed to come from his toes, he claimed her lips. It wasn't a gentle kiss. It held frustration, desire, the need to possess. She trembled, caught up in a whirlwind of his making. Or hers. His mouth moved across hers, opening it. His tongue traced the edges of her teeth, the full, taut line of her lips, then delved deep. Then he retreated far enough to look into her eyes. Their breath intermingled, sweet and achingly intimate.

"Oh, God," she murmured, shaken to her core. "What is this?"

"I wish I knew," he said.

He framed her face with his hands, and his thumb traced the fullness of her bottom lip. Looking into his eyes made her feel as though she'd stepped into a wall of flame. It was dangerous, consuming, utterly compelling. His mouth moved closer. She closed her eyes, giving herself up to him. Wanting. Needing. He had to know how badly she wanted his mouth; the look in his eyes betrayed him. But still he held back, so long that she nearly moaned in frustration.

"Please," she whispered.

"I just want to look at you for a minute," he said, tracing the curve of her cheek with his fingertips. "So soft."

She closed her eyes, winding her hands into his thick, dark hair. "Please."

"God, Ellis!"

His voice was a groan as he came to her again. He fitted his mouth to hers, slowly, leisurely, but with a tightly controlled urgency that made her gasp with reaction. But there was also an abiding tenderness flowing beneath the hot, flaring passion, and it was that tenderness that sent Ellis spinning into a well of sensation.

A sigh escaped her, and she slid her arms around his neck to pull him closer. Every nerve in her body was tuned to him, the musky soap-and-male scent of his skin, the feel of his chest against hers, the rough gentleness of his hands, the taste of him as he explored her mouth. She'd never been kissed like this. It was as though he were demanding everything she had to give, and yet it wasn't a selfish demand, for he was also offering all of himself.

Lost in the sheer wonder of it, she gave what was demanded, took what was offered. He filled her whole world in this moment, sweeping away the feel of the hard plastic seat behind her, drowning the noise of the city in a crashing flood of response. She clung to him, stunned by what was happening to her.

Then he lifted his mouth from hers, leaving her bereft. She stared up at him in bewilderment. Emotion had turned his eyes dark.

"The taxi's stopped," he said.

Ellis glanced out the window and saw the facade of Shelton Towers. Reality again. "Oh." Automatically, she reached for her purse to pay the driver.

Langston's face hardened. "Don't even think about it."

She froze in mid-reach, astonished by the sudden anger in his eyes. He paid the driver, then opened the door and helped her out of the cab.

"Why are you upset?" she asked.

He grasped her by the arm and propelled her toward the entrance. "Why did you assume I'd let you pay?"

"I didn't. Good God, Kyle!" she cried. "It was reflex."

His brows went up. "You pay cab fare for all the men who kiss you?"

"No!" She let her breath out in a hiss of exasperation. "Why are you so upset?"

"I'm not upset."

"Why did you kiss me?" she asked softly.

"Reflex," he said.

"You kiss all the women you ride in taxis with?"

"Only the ones who live in penthouses."

Ellis looked up at him, seeing the lowered brows, the uncompromising line of his jaw. Only an effort of will—and her burgeoning anger—kept her from reaching out to smooth the frown from his face. "Why don't you ever smile?"

"Maybe I don't find reality all that funny."

"Maybe you should."

"I'll give it a try tomorrow. Right now my sense of humor is a little out of whack." He opened the door and urged her inside. "Here you go, Princess."

Ellis blinked in surprise. "You're not . . . coming in?"

"Why do you ask? Do you want another kiss?"

She blushed, and that made her even angrier. "Not from you," she snapped.

"Then maybe you'd rather kiss your fantasy man," he growled.

"Maybe I would." Meeting his hot gaze levelly, she added, "He's much nicer than you."

He grasped her by the shoulders and pulled her close. For a moment, Ellis thought he was going to kiss her again. She ought to protest, pull away, *something*! But she couldn't. She was caught, pinned by his desire and hers. Her pulse pounded in her ears, her breathing accelerated, and a telltale molten river flowed through her core. As annoyed as she was, she wanted that kiss. Ached for it.

All he has to do is touch me, she thought, and I'm lost.

He held her there for a moment, his breath mingling with hers. Ellis licked her suddenly dry lips. His gaze snapped to her mouth, and there was such heat in his eyes that she trembled. Against her will, her eyes started to drift closed.

Then he let her go, so suddenly that she nearly lost her balance.

"Don't you wonder about this?" he asked, his voice harsh and strained. "If you like your fantasy man so much, why are you so damned eager for me to kiss you?"

Ellis couldn't answer, for him or for herself.

Looking truly dangerous now, he strode to the elevator and stabbed the button. "Go on up to your penthouse and your satin sheets, Princess. And watch out for those fantasies; they might not turn out to be all you expect."

He turned on his heel and strode out. A rush of hot air swirled into the lobby, sending a scrap of paper skittering forlornly across the floor. Ellis stood watching it, wondering why she felt as though half her heart had gone out the door with him. She ought to be glad he'd walked out. If she were lucky, he'd never come back.

"You're a fool," she said.

Whether she meant him or herself, she didn't know.

chapter

_____

six

_____

E llis made herself a cup of tea and sat down on the sofa to write a letter to her mother. "Dear Mom," she wrote. "Life in N.Y. is very interesting." And then she went blank.

What was she going to say? That she'd met two men and was afraid she'd fallen for both? Her mother would have a heart attack.

Two men, entwined in her mind and heart. One confused her and infuriated her even as he made her blood sing, and the other . . . She didn't know his name or what he looked like, but he'd made her feel as though she'd known him forever.

With a sigh, she stared out over the city. How could she have gotten herself into this predicament? She was a sensible person, or used to be. But what was "sensible" in the face of such powerful emotions? She felt like a leaf caught up in a tornado, unable to stop, unable even to see where she was going.

Suddenly registering the scratch of pen on paper, she looked down. All her life she'd done this, her hands drawing whether or not her mind consciously directed them. Sometimes, like now, the drawings were devastatingly revealing.

Her gaze riveted to the paper, she laid the pen aside. Kyle Langston seemed to look back at her, his eyes intent, his jaw shadowed with a day's growth of beard. The portrait echoed his brooding good looks, but there was no grimness in the mouth she'd drawn. No, this was the Langston who had kissed her with such shattering tenderness, the Langston who'd taken her emotions and turned them inside out and upside down.

Choose, he seemed to say.

How could she? How could she separate the fantasy from what was real, when she didn't even have a face to put on it?

"Find the face, then," she muttered. "That's what you meant to do before Kyle Langston showed up at the costume shop and turned your brain to mush."

She crumpled the picture and tossed it into the trash can. She managed to get halfway to the kitchen before turning back to retrieve the paper. Cursing herself for ten different kinds of a fool, she smoothed the wrinkles out of it and set it carefully on the coffee table.

She started with the Yellow Pages, intending to call every costume shop in town. After trying three, she gave up. No one was about to give her information about a client.

"Okay, on to plan two," she said, turning to the private listings. As much as she hated to think the obnoxious cavalier might have been right, he'd given her the only lead she had.

"Be there," she muttered under her breath. "Come on, be there."

DeMarco, DeMarco . . . There were lots of DeMarcos. She ran her finger down the list, stopped at Colin. There he was. And he lived right here in Manhattan.

She took a deep breath, then let it out again in a long sigh. This was crazy. Worse than crazy. She couldn't just show up at his home, could she? After all, if he'd wanted to get to know her, he could have brought the bracelet back himself.

"I should let it go," she said. "It was only fantasy."

But it wasn't quite that easy. She couldn't rest until she understood why she'd felt such a powerful attraction to the dark stranger. She had to look into his eyes and see if she felt what she'd felt last night. Most of all, she had to know if the magic still existed, or if it had evaporated like mist in the cold light of day.

As Langston had pointed out in his inimical way, she

had to find out how she could kiss him like that, and yet feel such magic in another man's arms. No, Kyle had made no declarations or promises, and she had no idea what he felt for her. But that wasn't the point; she had to know who *she* wanted.

And she had to choose. For her own sanity and self-respect, she had to settle this issue once and for all.

She went downstairs. Hot, muggy air wrapped around her in a clinging blanket the moment she stepped outside. The sun beat down mercilessly, its heat seemingly trapped and intensified by the towering buildings. The sidewalk was so hot she could feel it through the soles of her shoes.

"Whew! The weatherman wasn't kidding when he said it was going to be brutal," she muttered, abandoning the idea of walking. "Taxi!"

Colin DeMarco lived in an old brownstone in the Village. After paying the driver, Ellis walked up the pair of worn stone steps leading to the tiny entryway. An array of intercoms occupied the wall to her left. What on earth was she going to say to this man? she wondered as she pressed the button labeled "Demarco."

Kyle Langston's face swam into her mind. Intruding, as it had so many times, into the fabric of her fantasy. Why here? Why now, when she was so close to resolving the frustrating mystery?

She thrust the image aside resolutely and pressed the button again. "You've got to be home," she said. "Come on, answer!"

Against her will, the memory of Langston's kiss washed through her. Heat flooded through her in a sweet, hot tide. The sensation was almost unbearably powerful, and for a moment she thought she could feel his mouth on hers, taste his passion and her own.

Was the memory unwelcome? Only in her mind; her flesh retained his touch as though he'd made himself part of her. And it was no fantasy. No, it was real, as real as the beating of her heart.

Something powerful had happened between them without her knowing how or why or when. But it *had* happened. And only a fool would have failed to recognize it for what it was.

Then what am I doing here? she asked herself.

She snatched her finger off the intercom button. But too late; the speaker crackled into life.

"Yes, who is it?"

It took Ellis a moment to get her voice working. "I . . . sorry, I think I've got the wrong place. I was looking for, ah, Kyle Langston."

"Never heard of him."

The speaker lapsed into silence. Ellis stood staring at it for a moment, stunned by the decision she'd just made. With the answer to her mystery almost right under her hand, she'd walked away from it. Impulsively, restlessly, trusting in something she didn't know truly existed. But it felt right.

She turned away. "Okay, Mr. Langston. We've got a lot of talking to do. There's the issue of your, well, as Mom would say, your intentions, and also the obtrusively frequent mention of penthouses. Maybe we'll be able to keep from arguing long enough to figure out what we're going to do with each other."

It wasn't until she was outside that she realized the voice in the speaker had been at least half an octave higher than Zorro's. Whoever Colin DeMarco was, he wasn't the man she'd met last night.

And it didn't matter.

She was going back. Back to Shelton Towers and Kyle. Her pulse raced with anticipation. Now that she'd set the fantasy aside, she was ready to claim the man. Scowls, rough edges, temper and all. She could only hope he wanted her, too. Things had happened so quickly between them . . . But no. She hadn't imagined his tenderness, the way his hands had trembled when he touched her. That was special. Once-in-a-lifetime magic, all the more precious because it was unexpected.

She arrived back at Shelton Towers in mid-afternoon, and the air-conditioned lobby was a welcome haven after the heat outside. As she waited for the elevator, she no-

ticed an elderly woman, her arms laden with a bag of groceries, struggling to open the outer door. Ellis went to
help.

"Thank you," the older woman said, panting with heat
and exertion. "It's terrible outside, just terrible."

"You're right about that." Noticing that the woman's
hands were twisted with arthritis, Ellis said, "Here, let me
carry that for you."

"Oh, I couldn't—"

"I'm going upstairs anyway," Ellis pointed out. "How
much trouble can it be?"

"I'm May Fischer," the old woman said, surrendering
the bag. "And you're a nice girl."

Ellis smiled. "Thanks. I'm Ellis MacKenzie. I just
moved into the penthouse."

To her surprise, Mrs. Fischer blushed. The elevator
doors slid open, and Ellis gestured for the older woman to
precede her inside. Automatically, she reached out to
steady her companion as the elevator began to move upward. The old woman blushed even more deeply.

With Midwestern directness, Ellis asked, "What's the
matter, Mrs. Fischer?"

"I . . . Nothing, nothing. It's none of my business."

"What's none of your business?"

"Ah . . . Well, you're living with Mr. Giraud. I realize
that times have changed—"

Ellis finally caught her breath. *"Living with Mr.
Giraud?"*

"You . . . You're living in the penthouse."

"I'm staying there while he's out of the country," Ellis
said through clenched teeth. "Jack Giraud is a business acquaintance of my father's."

"Oh." Mrs. Fischer's face cleared, and she began to
smile. "I'm afraid we all assumed that you and he were,
well . . . He's had a succession of, er, ladies residing on a,
er, less than permanent basis ever since he's been living
here."

"We're not! I mean, I'm not one of his so-called ladies.
He promised me he'd make it clear to every—" Ellis

broke off as a horrible thought occurred to her. Now she understood Kyle's pointed references to penthouses—and satin sheets. At that moment, she could have cheerfully strangled Jack Giraud.

The lights went out. At the same moment, the elevator stopped, so suddenly that they both staggered. Ellis had to drop the groceries to keep the old woman from falling.

"Oh, no!" Mrs. Fischer wailed. "Not now!"

Ellis slipped her arm around the older woman's shoulders. "So, this is one of the famous New York blackouts," she said with false cheerfulness. "Or are they called brownouts?"

Mrs. Fischer didn't answer. The darkness wrapped around them like velvet. Without the noise of the elevator moving, the only sound was that of their own breathing. Dark and silent, silent and dark. It pressed on Ellis, a heavy weight on her chest. For a moment, she could almost feel the walls of the elevator coming closer and closer . . . With an effort of will, she shook the feeling off. Giving in to an attack of claustrophobia now wasn't going to get them out of there.

"All right, Mrs. Fischer," she said, filling the void with her own voice. "Let's take stock of our situation. I think we had just passed the sixth floor—"

"Seventh."

"Okay. So we're between floors, anyway. From what I've heard, these blackouts can last hours."

"I can't stand this for hours," Mrs. Fischer whispered. "I just can't!"

"Now, don't worry," Ellis said. "You had the foresight to bring a bag of groceries, didn't you? We can have a gourmet feast while we wait to be rescued." Some of the tension went out of the old woman's shoulders, and Ellis gave her a squeeze. "Our best bet of getting out anytime soon is to let people know we're in here."

"There's an emergency phone beneath the panel where the buttons are."

"Okay. Why don't you sit down? I'll be back in a minute."

"I'd rather stay with you." Mrs. Fischer's voice shook just a little. "I don't much care for small spaces."

"All right." Remembering Mrs. Fischer's arthritic hands, Ellis grasped the older woman by the elbow. "Step carefully now; I dropped your groceries all over the floor."

She inched forward, one arm outstretched in front of her, until she encountered a wall. "I wish I hadn't gotten all turned around when we stopped," she said. "I've got no sense of where the doors are."

Blindly, she felt along the paneling. Encountering nothing but smooth wood, she slid a few feet to her left and tried again. Still nothing. It took her four tries to find the panel, then another minute of fumbling before she found the small compartment where the phone was hidden.

"I can't . . . get it open," she gasped, prying at the door with her fingernails.

"Isn't there a handle?"

"Not that I can find. Maybe there's an emergency switch up here somewhere." Reaching up, Ellis pressed every button on the panel. "That's all I can do. Let's sit down and wait."

Ellis eased the old woman to a sitting position, then sat down beside her. Shoulder to shoulder, they faced the darkness together. The air was stiflingly hot. Time seemed to stand still, and Ellis wasn't sure if an hour or a day had passed.

"Are you thirsty?" Mrs. Fischer asked. "There's some apple juice around here somewhere."

"Manna from heaven," Ellis said, setting off on hands and knees to explore the floor of the elevator. "Just stay still so I can find you again."

"Where would I go?"

Ellis smiled. The old woman's voice quivered, but she'd made a joke, and that was a good sign. "I hope you bought some . . ." She broke off suddenly, alerted by a noise overhead. "Hey, did you hear that? Maybe someone's finally looking for us. Help!" she cried, cupping her hands around her mouth. "We're in the elevator! Help!"

"Hang on, I'm coming down!" The man's voice echoed

in the elevator shaft. A familiar voice, one which set Ellis's nerves to singing.

"Kyle," she breathed.

Something thumped down on the roof of the elevator. A moment later, a flashlight beam stabbed down. Ellis covered her eyes hastily as it speared toward her.

"Ellis?"

He swung down into the elevator, landing as lightly as any cat. Ellis sighed as his arms came around her, pulling her close, making her feel safe. It was like coming home. She pressed closer to the hard, lean strength of him, thinking of nothing but how good it felt to be held like this.

"I've been looking for you everywhere," he said, his voice harsh with repressed emotion. He ran his hands over her shoulders and arms and the slim curve of her back, his palms hot even through her shirt. "Are you all right?"

"Fine," Ellis whispered. "Just fine."

He kissed her then, his mouth claiming hers possessively. Ellis forgot everything but the way he felt, the way he tasted.

Mrs. Fischer cleared her throat.

Kyle straightened, then swung the flashlight around. He didn't look in the least embarrassed. "Oh, hi, Mrs. Fischer. I didn't know you were there."

"So I noticed. Help me up, young man."

"This is one heck of a blackout," he said, handing the flashlight to Ellis. "Most of the city is without power, and it's going to be hours before things are up and running again."

Ellis sighed. "It can go back to the Stone Age for all I care, as long as we get out of this elevator."

Then the flashlight beam caught Mrs. Fischer's face, and Ellis was shocked by the pallor of it. She saw Kyle's mouth tighten as he bent to lift the old woman to her feet.

"Okay," he said. "It's a bit of a climb, Mrs. Fischer. I'm going to carry you up."

"Oh, you can't—"

"Why not? You don't weigh as much as my kid sister. Come on, trust me on this."

The old woman sighed. "You're terrible. Are you this persuasive with all the ladies?"

"Only the pretty ones."

He lifted the old woman's hand and kissed it, a courtly gesture that made Ellis's throat tighten. Something about the way he did it was inexpressively familiar . . . With a strangled cry, Ellis dropped the flashlight, plunging the elevator into darkness.

Achingly, tantalizingly familiar, just like the man she'd met last night. Not two men, but one. One!

"Sorry," she muttered, bending to feel along the floor at her feet. Her fingers encountered the smooth cylinder of the handle, and she straightened. "Got it."

The flashlight was undamaged. Her hands shook just a little as she switched it back on, making the beam quiver.

"Is everything okay?" Kyle asked.

"Yes," she said, her voice sounding strangely hollow. "Just fine."

"Okay. Then let's get out of here." He turned back to the old woman. "Do you see that trapdoor, Mrs. Fischer? I'm going up there. When I reach down to you, you grab my hands and hang on. I'll pull you up." With a smile, he reached out and took her hand. "Ready?"

"Ready," she said.

He leapt upward, caught the edges of the opening in his hands, then pulled himself through. It seemed so effortless when he did it, Ellis thought, adding a bit grimly, Zorro himself couldn't have done better.

"Okay, Mrs. Fischer," he called, reaching down through the opening. "Take my hands."

The old woman reached up, but her fingers missed his by several inches. "I can't!"

"Here," Ellis said, "I'll give you a hand."

Going down on her right knee, she offered her left as a step. This time, Mrs. Fischer's hands touched Kyle's. He grasped her by the wrists and lifted her upward slowly. Ellis heaved a sigh of relief when the old woman's legs disappeared through the trapdoor.

Kyle leaned down again. "I'm taking her up," he said.

Ellis nodded; there was an urgency in his voice that echoed her own concern for Mrs. Fischer. "Toss me the flashlight, will you?"

She did, and he disappeared from view. A moment later he reappeared in the opening.

"Are you okay alone for a minute?" he asked.

"Yes. Get going!"

"I'll be back for you." He pulled away again, and Ellis could hear him giving Mrs. Fischer instructions as to what came next. He was calm and reassuring, telling her exactly what to expect. Then the light and sounds retreated, and Ellis knew they were on their way upward.

Alone in the dark elevator, Ellis sat down to think. Kyle had been her fantasy man. Oh, she'd been a fool not to have figured it out earlier! All along, it was he who'd stretched her heart ten different ways, who had intrigued and infuriated her, and who'd touched a level of response she'd never known before.

And why had he played this crazy game with her? Well, she could probably thank Jack Giraud for it. "Whatever the reason, Mr. Langston," she muttered under her breath. "You've got some explaining to do."

Then she smiled, joy coursing through her veins like summer sunlight. The magic was real. She'd doubted it because she didn't understand how it could exist with two different men. But it was real.

Light returned to the square opening in the ceiling, faintly at first, but growing steadily brighter. Soon Kyle dropped down into the elevator. "Hi," he said.

"Hi." Ellis rose to her feet.

She wished he weren't aiming the flashlight on her. She felt stripped bare, her innermost thoughts and feelings exposed to him. But then, she reflected, she'd always felt that way. He reached out, smoothing his thumb along the curve of her lower lip, an inexpressively tender gesture that made her throat tighten with emotion. Truth blossomed in her, bright and warm and solid.

She loved him. Difficult man that he was, she loved him.

"Let's go," he said softly.

Ellis nodded. He leapt for the opening, pulled himself through, then reached down for her. She had to jump to reach his hands. His fingers closed over her wrists.

"Don't worry," he said. "I'm not going to drop you."

"I never thought you would."

He drew her upward steadily. A moment later she found herself on the hard metal roof of the elevator. Cables rose from it into the seemingly endless darkness of the shaft.

Kyle directed the flashlight beam toward a series of metal rungs set into the side of the shaft. Above, the opening to the next floor was a pale rectangle in the darkness of the wall. Ellis swallowed convulsively. Those rungs looked awfully small and far apart, and the opening a long way up.

"Are you all right?" Kyle asked. "I can carry you—"

"No, I'm fine," she lied, moving forward.

"I'll be right behind you. Just take it slow and steady, and remember it's only a fifteen-foot climb."

The rungs felt cool and slick beneath her hands, and she was glad for his comforting presence just below her. She kept her gaze fixed on the light and took the climb one rung at a time. Once, she made the mistake of looking down. Vertigo made the air spin around her, and she clutched the rungs convulsively.

Then Kyle's body came up against hers, enclosing her, making her feel safe. "Come on," he murmured. "Only a few feet to go, Ellis. You're doing great."

She took a deep breath, letting his warmth and comfort seep into her. Then she started climbing again. It seemed like ages before she finally reached the opening, but probably it was only a couple of minutes. Emergency lights bathed the corridor in a welcome glow. She turned as Langston climbed out of the elevator shaft behind her.

"Where's Mrs. Fischer?" she asked.

"This is her floor." With a grunt, he levered the doors closed. "I took her into her apartment so she could lie down. Come on. I want to check on her again."

He took her by the hand and led her down the hallway,

where an open door marked Mrs. Fischer's apartment. Inside, the rooms were crowded with fine old furniture worn to a genteel shabbiness. Mrs. Fischer lay on the sofa, looking small and pale against the cushions.

"You got her?" she asked, rising up on her elbows. "Good. Help me sit up. I feel like my bones have turned to jelly."

Kyle put his arm around her and lifted her upright. "There you go, jelly and all. Are you feeling okay?"

"I'm fine. I don't know whether I'll ever ride in an elevator again, but I'm fine."

"A little adventure never hurt anybody," Kyle said, giving her shoulders a squeeze.

Watching his gentleness, his caring, Ellis felt her throat tighten. It took a truly strong man to be gentle.

The old woman turned to face him. Reaching out, Mrs. Fischer clasped his hand in both of hers. "Thank you, Kyle. I want you to know you'll always be a hero to me."

And to me, Ellis thought.

"I'm just the super," Kyle said, leaning down to kiss the old woman's cheek before getting up. "And I need to check on the rest of the people in the building. Ellis, will you stay with her for a while?"

"Of course." Ellis followed him as he strode to the door.

"I hope you realize what you've got there, young lady," Mrs. Fischer called after them.

Ellis smiled. "I do."

"What's that all about?" Kyle asked.

"Girl talk."

She pulled him to a stop as soon as they were out of Mrs. Fischer's line of sight. Rising up on her tiptoes, she pressed her breasts against his hard chest and kissed first one corner of his mouth, then the other. His hands spread out over her back, pulling her still closer. She let her eyes drift closed as his mouth claimed hers in a kiss that was as raw and hungry as her need for him.

"What was that for?" he asked when the kiss ended.

"What do you think?"

"I don't want to make guesses." His eyes raged with emotion. "I want you to tell me."

"I love you," she said. There. Simply and powerfully, the gift of her heart.

He drew in his breath with a hiss. "Are you willing to give up your dashing fantasy man from last night?

"Yes," she said, gazing up at him through her lashes. But I don't have to, do I? she thought. "Today, I discovered that heroes don't always wear capes."

With a visible effort, he pulled away from her. "Wait for me. If I don't find you here, I'll look for you upstairs." He kissed her again, quick and hard, then turned and headed toward the stairway. Ellis watched him, admiring his cat-smooth movements.

"By the way," she called. "I really like your dimples."

His stride checked briefly, then lengthened again. A moment later he disappeared into the darkness of the stairway.

Ellis smiled.

chapter

_____

seven

_____

Ellis stood in front of the penthouse's big windows, watching night sweep down over the city. The skyline hulked darkly against the violet-stained sky. Even as she watched, lights sprang to life in the darkness like a sudden dusting of jewels. The blackout was over.

"Beautiful," she murmured.

She swung around, registering the sound of a key in the lock. A moment later the door swung open, laying a wedge of light onto the floor. Kyle's lean, broad-shouldered figure cast a dark silhouette in that bright patch.

"Don't turn on the light," she said, moving to sit on the sofa.

"Why not?"

"I like it better this way. There are some candles on the table in front of you. Why don't you light them?"

He closed the door behind him, plunging the room into blackness again. The air was close and hot, but not as much as Ellis's anticipation. A match flared to life in Kyle's hands. As he held it to the candle wick, it cast flickering shadows over his sharply honed face. Ellis drew her breath in sharply. It was all so clear now. How could she have missed the resemblance to her black-garbed companion of last night, even for a moment?

Because she'd let the fantasy blind her to the man. But the magic . . . Ah, that still existed; why else did her heart stutter like this, and her breath ache in her throat?

The man *was* the fantasy, and he was all she wanted.

He lit the last of the three candles she'd set out for him.

Then he glanced down. Ellis smiled at his start of surprise when he noticed the drawing she'd left on the table. After a moment he looked up at her, his eyes black and unfathomable.

"That painting," he pointed to the one he'd admired before. "It's yours, isn't it?"

"Yes."

"You're very talented." He picked up the drawing and studied it. "The mask is a nice touch," he said. "But you forgot to add the mustache."

"Do you know what it was like feeling the way I did about two men?" she asked, unexpected heat tingeing her voice. "I thought I'd gone crazy."

"That makes two of us."

He strode to the bank of windows and stood looking out over the city. Ellis let the silence grow, for it wasn't an uncomfortable one; merely their adjustment to this new reality. She leaned back and watched the play of candlelight upon the walls.

"I went to that party because I thought it was the only way to get to know you. Man to woman, instead of penthouse dweller to building super."

"And I went to Colin DeMarco's house today, looking for the man I met last night."

"What did he say when you charged him with the Zorro offense?"

"I didn't go up."

He swung around to look at her. "What?"

"I didn't go up. I realized that it didn't matter whether I found out who the fantasy man was, because I wanted you. Nothing else."

His breath went out with a hiss. He walked toward her, the crags and valleys of his face stark in the dim light. "The first time we met, I saw you walking down the sidewalk toward me, your face glowing with the sheer joy of being alive, I just . . ." He raked his hands through his hair. "Damn it, Ellis, I've never felt that way before."

"How?" she asked softly.

Reaching down, he drew her to her feet. "I fell in love

with you. At first sight, and it felt like a bomb had gone off in my chest. And then Giraud came downstairs to tell me that you were used to the finer things in life, and that he wanted to be sure you weren't the sort to be bothered with a guy with grease under his fingernails—"

Ellis put her hand over his mouth. "Tell me again."

"What?"

"That you love me."

He slipped his arm around her waist and pulled her close. His other hand stroked her hair away from her cheek, another of those incredibly intimate gestures that so revealed his feelings. "I love you," he murmured, his breath hot and sweet upon her lips.

"And I love you," she whispered, gazing at the hard mouth so near hers. "Even if you think I'm a snob."

He drew back to stare at her. "What?"

"You think I'm a snob. All your comments about penthouses and satin sheets—"

"Pure jealousy. Until Mrs. Fischer read me the riot act, I thought you and Giraud were lovers."

"—and let's not forget the stuff about grease under the fingernails and not a few mentions of princesses—"

"So I was wrong. You're not a snob. And you're not Jack Giraud's latest squeeze."

"No. And yes, my father is rich. He's influential, and he has quite a few business interests. His favorite, however, is the free clinic he began fifteen years ago and supports almost single-handedly. You see, he grew up poor and hard, and he's never forgotten his roots."

"I'm beginning to see," Kyle murmured.

"My father is the last man in the world to look down on another person for what he does or how much money he makes. He judges a person for what's in here, and here." Ellis tapped her heart, then her head. "And so do I."

Kyle opened his mouth to say something, but Ellis put her finger across his lips to stop him.

"Let me finish," she whispered. "You're not wrong in thinking that I do care about the finer things in life. But tell me—what is finer than love?"

"Nothing," he said. "Nothing at all."

She closed her eyes, wanting him to kiss her, then opened them again when he chuckled.

"Greedy, aren't you?" he asked.

"About some things."

"I've got something to tell you first." Taking her by the chin, he tilted her face up. "I'm not quite what you think I am, either." He smiled. "Don't look so alarmed. I just wanted to confess that I'm not exactly a super—or won't be once I finish my dissertation."

"Doctor of what?"

"Psychology. I want to counsel troubled teens."

Ellis took a deep breath. "Any other deep, dark secrets you'd like to confess before we get on with it?"

"Get on with what?"

"The kissing."

"No," he said, framing her face in his hands. "No more secrets. For the rest of our lives."

"What are you saying?" Ellis gasped.

"I want to marry you," he said. "Why are you so surprised? When lightning strikes, it strikes fast."

"Not lightning," she murmured. "Magic."

"Besides, I have a bet going with Mr. Gabriel. He bet five bucks that you'd turn me down."

"What?"

Before Ellis could muster her outrage, Kyle pulled her up onto her tiptoes, molding her body to his lean, hard frame. His eyes were tender and passionate and roguish all at once. Ellis felt herself softening, heat pooling in the center of her body. Then he smiled, and she knew she was lost. Those dimples . . .

"I love you," he said. "How about it, Ellis?"

She wound her arms around his neck, spearing her fingers into his thick hair. "I've always believed in magic."

He claimed her lips with a kiss that was staggering in its intensity. With it, he gave her all of himself, heart, mind and soul, and demanded the same in return.

Ellis gave it, knowing it was forever.

Behind Closed Doors

Catherine Palmer

chapter

one

"Whatever Wyatt Noble wants, he gets." The manager of the Hartley Rio Grande Hotel dropped a thick file folder on Sarah Ellsworth's desk.

"Is that hotel policy," she asked, "or simple fact?"

James Baca smiled. "Both. Headquarters in Dallas added a note to Noble's dossier before they sent it to us. When he's traveling—which is most of the time—Wyatt Noble stays in Hartley Hotels exclusively. Plus, he has instructed the seven newspapers he owns to conduct their professional development meetings at establishments within the Hartley chain. That includes seminars, conferences, and social gatherings."

"The works." Sarah tapped the edge of the dossier on her desk to even the pages. "I get the picture."

"We're to treat Wyatt Noble with utmost cordiality while he's here in El Paso. No requests denied. No expense spared."

"I assume he'll be staying in the Presidential Suite."

"For two weeks." James Baca ran a fingertip across Sarah's gleaming desk. "He purchased the *Tribune* about a month ago, and he's planning to look in on his newest investment."

As executive assistant in charge of rooms, Sarah kept a schedule of hotel events, blocks of rooms reserved, and notable guests arriving. She mentally reviewed the list of conferences that would take place at the hotel in the coming months. "Wyatt Noble's visit coincides with the annual convention of the Texas Press Federation."

"He's president of the organization."

She checked her leather-bound schedule book. "The Press Federation has reserved fifty-eight units that weekend. I'll make sure everything runs smoothly."

"I have no doubt about that."

"Any special word on Wyatt himself?"

"Most of it's in the dossier. He's a bachelor. A loner. He's made some bold business moves as owner and publisher of Noble Newspapers. Buys failing papers and turns them around. Always sells for a profit. He's made a mint to add to the gold mine he inherited from his oilman father. Wyatt Noble could throw his weight around, but I doubt you'll hear much out of him. He's considered a lone wolf. Just keep up your usual standards."

Sarah stood as her supervisor left the office. "You can count on me."

Beige—in carpets, curtains, and upholstery—imbued the two-thousand-square-foot Presidential Suite with an aura of understated elegance. As Sarah walked through the rooms the following afternoon, she checked off each item on the list she had compiled from Wyatt Noble's dossier. His file had given her an intriguing picture of a man who had been born with a silver spoon and had made the most of his advantages. A graduate of the University of Texas at Austin, he had earned an MBA. Though he could have moved into an executive position with his father's oil company, Wyatt Noble had charted his own course in a specialized field—newspapers. At thirty-eight, he had solidified his position as a force among United States media goliaths.

As Sarah inspected the master bedroom—fresh sheets, fifteen cedar hangers, silk laundry bags, shoeshine kit, a basket of fresh fruit—she tried to picture the man who would live in this suite for the coming two weeks. Personally responsible for guests who stayed in the executive rooms, she always found herself speculating about these people who were from a world so different from hers.

Wyatt Noble's dossier had painted the typical picture

of a wealthy, educated, respectable man. Sarah formed a mental image of William Randolph Hearst—or rather Orson Welles in the role of Citizen Kane. She envisioned Wyatt Noble as rotund, impeccably dressed in dark suits and narrow ties, slightly balding, chomping a fat cigar.

Was there a "Rosebud" in Wyatt Noble's past? Probably not. Sarah chuckled as she looked over the bathroom. The mirror was spotless. The end of the toilet paper had been folded into a neat V. The gold fixtures gleamed. The basket of men's toiletries she had ordered specially prepared by the hotel gift shop sat at the end of a vast marble counter.

Maybe there was no long-lost child's sled to haunt Wyatt Noble, but he did convey an air of mystery. Why had such an eligible man never married? Why had he chosen newspapers over the oil business? Why did he own no real estate—other than the large ranch near Waco that he had inherited from his father? The list of items at the end of his dossier suggested possibly the most curious, most compelling aspect of the man.

Executive guests often requested a selection of personal preferences which the hotel supplied. Usually these included expensive wine, caviar, champagne, dozens of roses, chocolates, and the like. A few times Sarah had spent hours driving her little Chevy all over El Paso trying to fill an extraordinary order for such items as a special brand of oysters, or a large dog kennel and basket. Once she had been obliged to replace the shantung silk bedroom curtains with black velvet. On another occasion, she'd hand-picked from a bowl every licorice-flavored jelly bean, for a musician who had a superstitious aversion to them.

Wyatt Noble had made the expected request for daily copies of the *Wall Street Journal, USA Today*, and the *New York Times*. Of course, a newspaper publisher would keep tabs on his competition. But the rest of the dossier list didn't fit with Sarah's image of him as an early twentieth-century press lord.

As she inspected the suite's kitchenette, she noted the

case of Seven Rivers brand chile salsa Wyatt Noble had asked for. The hottest strength. Bags of blue-corn tortilla chips were stacked in the cupboard over the sink. Bottles of Pop's root beer chilled in the refrigerator. On the white counter sat a canister of loose Earl Grey tea.

What kind of man ate fiery salsa, drank root beer, and sipped English tea? Sarah shook her head as she left the kitchenette. On the long dining table at which hotel guests often hosted private dinner parties, she had placed a bundle of fresh wildflowers. As she studied them, Sarah wondered what it was in Wyatt Noble's file that had compelled her to pick the flowers from her own garden and bring them to the hotel. Was it his down-home love of salsa and corn chips? Or the image of a solitary man drinking hot tea alone in this vast suite? Or the extra-large white towels he had requested—the sort a person could snuggle up in after a hot shower when there were no warm arms to do the job?

Whatever it was, Sarah hoped the flowers wouldn't wilt before Wyatt Noble checked into the hotel at six that evening, after his flight from Albuquerque. As she gathered the slender stems and began to arrange them in a cut-crystal vase, she wondered whether he would even notice the extra care she had taken to make his stay at the Hartley satisfactory. To the chips, salsa, and tea, she had added southwestern snacks such as piñon nuts and frijole dip. The refrigerator now contained not only the root beer, but also a jar of jalapeño jelly and a bag of flour tortillas.

Sarah knew she was not nearly as educated as Wyatt Noble, nor had she been born to the privileges of wealth and society that opened doors for the kinds of people who stayed in her suites. But she knew how to make those people contented guests.

From the day she had graduated from high school she had worked for the Hartley Rio Grande Hotel. She had spent fifteen years climbing the ladder—from maid, to housekeeping supervisor, and finally to the management position she had coveted. Now she attended evening classes in business administration at the University of Texas at El Paso. Her ultimate dream? To head the personnel department at a hotel within the Hartley chain.

Sarah knew she could do it. As executive assistant in charge of rooms, she had learned to be a good motivator and an excellent manager. She was careful, thorough, never impulsive. She supervised more employees than any other upper-level administrator in the hotel. So if her instincts told her that Wyatt Noble would like wildflowers, she mused as she selected a bluebonnet, he would have them every day.

She was sliding the bluebonnet blossom down among a spray of baby's breath when the door to the suite swung open. Sarah glanced up, surprised at the intrusion. A man strode in—no luggage, no attaché case, not even a key.

"I'm sorry, sir," she began, "but this is Wyatt Noble's suite—"

"Good. I'm Wyatt Noble."

She should have known. Orson Welles, William Randolph Hearst, and Citizen Kane evaporated. Wyatt Noble wore the larger-than-life air of all-fired, flat-out, down-home Texas. This was no pudgy, dark-suited businessman. In everything from his black Stetson to his cowboy boots, his presence said independent, self-made, indestructible.

A black leather coat covered shoulders twice as wide as his silver-buckled waist. His white button-down shirt was tucked into knife-creased Wrangler jeans. A medallion of turquoise and sand-cast silver fastened a braided leather bolo tie with long silver tips.

Eyes the color of faded indigo assessed Sarah, took in her tailored plum-colored suit, the dossier and notebook in her hand, her hair, mouth, and eyes. His gaze lingered on her face.

"I beg your pardon, Mr. Noble," she said when she found her voice. "I understood you'd be arriving after six. I was . . . I was inspecting your suite."

His eyes dropped to the vase she had been arranging. "Wildflowers."

"I thought . . . I . . ." She wished she had ordered the usual tea roses and lilies. The wildflowers seemed too personal, as though she'd given him a part of herself. "I . . . we . . . the hotel likes to provide fresh flowers for our executive guests."

"Where did you buy them?" He was walking toward her. He took off his Stetson and pushed his fingers through hair as black as a Texas night.

She wanted to lie, tell him she'd ordered them from a local florist. But she'd never covered the truth. "I picked them in my garden. I bought some wildflower seeds this summer, and I seem to have grown a meadow. More than I know what to do with."

"So you brought them to the hotel." He placed one hand on the table and leaned toward the vase, but his eyes never left her face. "I like that. I like . . . wild-flowers."

She kept expecting him to lower his head and sniff the bouquet. He was so close, hovering over it. Instead he stared at her, that indigo gaze moving from her mouth to her eyes and back to her mouth again. Her linen blazer felt hot, stifling, even though she had preset the suite's temperature at a comfortable sixty-eight. The file folder went damp beneath her palm. Usually adroit in awkward situations, she couldn't think of a thing to say.

"Your house must be interesting." He was coming around the table toward her. He still hadn't smelled the flowers. "I can't imagine a house with a meadow of its own."

"A small meadow," she corrected, mashing the tip of her thumb on the end of her pen.

"A small house? You live alone, then." It wasn't a question.

"I have a dog." She wouldn't back away from him. Men like Wyatt Noble stayed in the hotel's suites all the time—men with blue eyes and blue jeans. She could handle this. "I trust your stay at the Hartley Rio Grande will be satisfactory, Mr. Noble. As executive assistant in charge of rooms, I've seen to it that everything on your dossier—"

"And your name?"

"Sarah. Ms. Ellsworth," she amended. "My office is to the left of the registration desk in the lobby. If you require anything from housekeeping—new towels, laundry service—just give me a call. Extension 217. We certainly want to make your time at the Hartley Rio Grande as pleasant as possible."

Her words sounded hollow and artificial. He had pulled the bluebonnet from the center of the arrangement and twirled it between his thumb and forefinger. She couldn't help but notice his hands, strong and tanned. Not the pasty white, softly immaculate fingers of most executives.

"Bluebonnets." He lifted his eyes. "These used to grow everywhere at home. They'd lie across a field like a blanket. Jacob's horses would dip their noses down into the blue as if it were a mountain lake."

"Jacob?"

"Jacob Noble. The man who . . . my father. He had a lot of horses. Arabians."

"Did you ride?" A momentary panic shot through Sarah the instant the question was out. She wasn't supposed to become personal with guests. She'd helped write the hotel policy that stipulated employee decorum. Stay distant. Polite but detached.

"Not at first. Scared to death of them." He grinned, a slow smile that tilted one corner of his mouth. "But I learned. Jacob got me out there and taught me how to ride. From the time I was thirteen on, hardly a day went by that I wasn't on a horse. You ride?"

She knew she should give a quick, monosyllabic answer. Yet somehow it felt natural and easy to talk with him. She shook her head. "I wouldn't know the first thing about mounting a horse. I was brought up in the city. East El Paso. Ysleta." She wondered if the name meant anything to him. Did it tell him that her family had been of the working class, that she'd grown up in a tension-filled environment, that things hadn't come as easily for her as they had for him?

His blue eyes were far away. "I lived in the city for a while, too. Tough."

She wanted to laugh. What did Wyatt Noble know about a tough life? Did he understand what it was like to watch your father work in a factory that offered no way up, no way out? To never have the chance to ride horses, or study at a university, or lie in a field of bluebonnets? But there was something in his stance, something in the way he looked at her—seeing inside and through and beyond her—that froze her derision and made her wonder if he really did know.

"Here, Sarah," he said, slipping the bluebonnet stem into her lapel. The warm pressure of his fingers went straight through to her skin. "Thank you for the wildflowers."

"You're welcome." She curled her knuckles around the sharp edge of his dossier. "Hartley Hotels is proud to be of service to Noble Newspapers, and we're particularly pleased to be hosting the Texas Newspaper Fed—"

"Did you know your eyes are the exact color of rainwater? An oak rain barrel used to sit beside our cabin in the mountains. I'd hitch myself up and look over the edge—scared to death I'd fall in but too fascinated to pull back. I'd gaze down into the rainwater. I could see things . . . the blue-brown reflection of the sky, the dark brown bottom of the barrel . . . I could see myself in the depths. All those layers. Your eyes—"

"Luggage!" she exclaimed as the bellman towed a rolling cart through the open door of the suite. Whirling away from Wyatt Noble, she grabbed the back of a chair for support. She could hardly breathe. The more he'd talked about her rainwater eyes, the more she had thought she was going to drown in his . . . those blue, stormy, hungry, consuming eyes.

But luggage wasn't something to exult about. "Now that your bags have arrived, you can settle into your suite," she amended. "I'm sure you must want to rest after your flight."

"I'm not tired." A hundred messages hid behind his words.

She tried to form her lips into a smile. "Again, we do welcome you here at the Hartley, Mr. Noble. I trust you'll have a pleasant stay."

She hurried across the room, hoping her knees would hold up. The bellman stared at her, and she was sure her cheeks must be flame red. Behind her, she heard Wyatt Noble call out.

"Thank you. Good-bye . . . Sarah."

She had let down her mask. That was the problem. Sarah stacked and restacked the pile of brochures on her desk. In fifteen years of working at the Hartley, she had re-made herself, yet with one look into the blue eyes of Wyatt Noble, she had cast away that facade and thrown her world out of kilter.

To her employees, Sarah was not a woman who had barely graduated from high school before going to work full-time. She wasn't someone who had worked long, hard hours to help her family pay the medical bills from her father's illness. She wasn't a person who lived with memories of meager meals, hand-me-down dresses, shoes that pinched. To her labor force, Sarah was simply Ms. Ellsworth. Boss.

Oh, they were aware she had worked her way up. They understood—because she had chosen to tell them—that she knew their daily routine inside out. She had chapped her hands scouring the same toilets and bathtubs they now cleaned. She could fold and tuck sheets into hospital corners with the best of them. She knew how to remove hard-water spots from a shower, how to vacuum a carpet and leave it without footprints, how to sift an ashtray next to an elevator and imprint the hotel's famous H insignia in the white sand. But that was all they knew of Ms. Ellsworth.

She had crafted her mask, and she kept it always in

place. She performed her duties to perfection. Most significantly, she never did anything on the spur of the moment. She was thoughtful, careful, deliberate. Never hasty. Never careless.

So why, she asked herself as she adjusted the corners of the stack of brochures, had she blithely pulled off her mask and cast it aside in the presence of Wyatt Noble? Sinking into her chair, she stared at his dossier. A newspaper mogul she'd never met in her life knew more about her than did her employer of fifteen years. This blue-eyed stranger knew she lived alone, had a dog, had grown up in the city, hadn't ever ridden a horse, and grew wildflowers. Personal things.

Sarah drew the bluebonnet from her lapel and touched the silky foliage. Rainwater eyes, he had said. He could see layers of things in them, see the sky, see himself. The way he had looked at her . . . never taking his gaze away . . . as if he were trying to memorize her mouth . . . She had felt the touch of his hand through her linen blazer and her blouse. Even now, the pressure remained, warm and strangely electric.

She wanted to see him again. She wanted to find out if the same thing could happen twice—this odd, dizzying, whirling sense. He had felt it, too. She knew he had. Men didn't just start babbling about a stranger's eyes. She could picture him now, up in his suite. Dipping a fingertip in that red hot salsa and putting it to his tongue. Running a shower. Peeling off that leather coat. Gazing at the wildflowers and thinking of her.

Stop! Sarah slapped her palms down on her desk and rose to her feet in the same motion. This whole thing was ridiculous. Wyatt Noble was a complete stranger. He was a world apart educationally, financially, socially. She'd never been a romantic dreamer. Life was too hard. Too real. A woman who had goals to attain didn't roam around with her head in the clouds. She didn't waste time in fantasy. She certainly didn't believe in love at first sight. Utter nonsense.

Sarah grabbed her schedule book. It was time to update

her lists. Time to check in on the new housekeeper she'd hired for the twelfth floor. Time to reorder toilet paper, cleanser, soap. Time to phone the linen supply company. Time to get back to reality, and time to forget about a man with black hair, a compelling touch, and eyes of faded indigo.

chapter

t w o

Sarah waited until she was sure Wyatt Noble had gone to the *El Paso Tribune*'s offices the following morning. As the employee elevator whisked her up eighteen floors, she studied her checklist for the executive suites. A descending line of neat X's told her everything was in order. On a rolling metal cart, she had placed every item she would need to restock the rooms.

The owner of a Mexican shoe factory and his wife occupied the west wing. They wanted current magazines and fresh flowers supplied to their suite every day. On the lower shelf of the cart, Sarah had stacked the latest issues of *U.S. News and World Report*, *Time*, *Ladies Home Journal*, *Redbook*, and *Victoria*. A bouquet of pink roses stood in an enameled vase beside the periodicals.

A soap opera actor, in town for a grocer's convention, had taken a suite in the east wing. He wanted his bar restocked daily, red satin sheets on his bed, and cartons of mail—scripts, publicity materials, fan letters—taken up to his room for his perusal. On Sarah's cart, bottles of beer and wine clinked between a swath of folded crimson satin and a canvas mail pouch.

A singer who had enjoyed moderate success on the pop charts was staying in the north wing during her appearance in a musical at the civic center. She had kept the hotel laundry busy with scads of sequinned, lace, and feathered evening gowns. She insisted that her suite smell like vanilla and that a bubble bath be waiting for her after every performance. A potpourri pot, a bottle of liquid scent, and a crystal jar of bath beads nestled in one corner of the cart.

Then there was the south wing. Sarah lifted the bunch of wildflowers she had picked in her garden that morning and recounted the jars of salsa, bags of blue corn chips, and extra-large white towels.

His eyes were the exact color of the bluebonnets.

No. Sarah clenched her jaw as the elevator doors slid open, and she wheeled her cart into the hall. *Don't think about him. Don't remember the scent of his leather coat. Don't recall the way his hand raked through his hair. Don't imagine his slow grin or hear his deep Southern voice.*

As if the very thought of Wyatt Noble could pursue her, Sarah barreled the cart down the hall, past the heavy wooden double doors to his suite, and into the north wing. For a good hour, she tended to the other executive rooms, inspecting the previous housekeeper's work and adding the hotel's special touches herself. Finally, when she was convinced the entire eighteenth floor was empty, she wheeled her cart into the south wing.

Her knock sounded hollow on his door. *His* door? Hundreds of guests had stayed in the Presidential Suite, and suddenly this was *his* door? Sarah grinned ruefully and knocked again. When she heard no response, she inserted her master key and opened the door an inch.

"Housekeeping," she called loudly. The word literally echoed around the cavernous suite, bouncing off the high ceiling and bare beige walls. "Housekeeping."

With a quick breath of relief, Sarah pushed the door wide and rolled her cart into the suite. An empty suite meant peace, quiet, and efficiency. It meant she could soon get back to all the other items on her daily schedule. It meant she wouldn't have to think about Wyatt Noble. She bent to pick up the wildflowers . . . and he walked out of the bathroom. Bare-chested, jeans-clad, his face half hidden by white shaving cream, he held a dripping razor.

"Mr. Noble." Sarah's fingers tightened on the bundle of flowers. "Please excuse me. I knocked and called—"

"Good morning, Sarah." He rubbed his hand over his

damp chest. Dark curls, springy and masculine, outlined the sculpted muscle. "You brought more wildflowers."

"If I'd known you were here—"

"I was shaving." He shrugged, and his grin beneath the mask of white foam nearly melted Sarah's knees. "Can't hear much in that bathroom with the water running."

"No, I'm sure that's true. Again, please excuse my intrusion. I'll come back in an hour."

"That's okay. Go ahead with whatever you wanted to do. Don't pay any attention to me."

As if that were possible, Sarah thought, trying to keep her eyes blank and her face expressionless. The man was a veritable Apollo, standing there half-naked in those skintight jeans. His wet hair was the color of ink, and his eyes held the heat of a blue flame.

She cleared her throat. "Actually hotel policy stipulates—"

"What's your position with the Hartley anyway?"

"Executive assistant in charge of rooms." The long title sounded tangled and awkward as she tried to speak like a professional. "Housekeeping."

"You do good work."

"Thank you. We certainly try to ensure that our guests are comfortable."

"I'm comfortable." He leaned one shoulder against the bathroom door frame. "You comfortable, Sarah?"

"Well, of course—"

"The suit looks a little stiff. I like the color. Green. It does nice things to your eyes. But I'd ditch the jacket if I were you. You look a little flushed. Hot."

"I'm not hot."

"Maybe it's your hair."

"What's wrong with my hair?" Off balance again, she lifted a hand to the hair that she kept blunt-cut at her shoulders and brushed to a silky chocolate shine.

"It doesn't go with the suit. Too soft. Very feminine and loose. You ever wear T-shirts?"

"When I'm gardening, or walking."

"You walk?"

"Three miles a day. There's a track at the high school near my house."

"Take your dog?"

"On a leash."

"Too bad. Don't you wonder how he'd feel to be set free sometime? Just take off flat-out after a jackrabbit or a prairie dog? Ears flying, tongue hanging out. I used to have a dog—"

"What kind?"

"Mutt. He'd go with me when I rode. There'd be the three of us, the horse, Chaucer, and me."

"Chaucer? You named your dog Chaucer?"

"I figured he'd seen some things in his time. Roamed around a little. He was a rascal, too. You know, Geoffrey Chaucer was a real character himself. Ever read *The Canterbury Tales*? 'The Miller's Tale'—now there's a story that wouldn't make it into most libraries today if anyone bothered to read it. Ever read 'The Miller's Tale'?"

Sarah shook her head. Of course she hadn't read Chaucer. Oh, maybe something in high school, but it hadn't penetrated. Not deep enough that she would name a dog after him. She was miles apart from Wyatt Noble. Maybe she had fallen into conversation easily—too easily—with him again, but it was clear their common ground had an abrupt limit.

"I'm sorry, but I do need to get back to work, Mr. Noble," she said, turning the cart to face the door. "I'll return in an hour."

"I could use some of those towels." He came toward her. She inadvertently glanced at his chest, damp and glistening with water droplets. "If you don't mind."

"I brought them for you. For your suite." She handed him a stack of thick towels, but when she pulled her eyes up to his, she still felt uncomfortable.

"Might as well stay and finish what you came for, Sarah. I'll be in there shaving. Won't bother you a bit."

"Well . . ."

"Okay." He flipped a towel over one shoulder and turned to the bathroom. As the door shut, she was left with a vision of his back, an expanse of smooth, hard flesh ridged with bone and muscle that tapered into a fine pair of masculine buttocks.

"Oh, Lord." Sarah whispered the words that were a prayer for strength, control, distance. This couldn't be happening. She was thirty-three, for heaven's sake, far past the giddy teenage stage when boys were all that mattered. She was even beyond that serious marriage-driven age, that time when the longing for a husband, children, abiding love, and commitment were a palpable force. Her drive to succeed in a world that threw obstacles in her way at every turn had seen her past all those phases. She had turned her thoughts away from men, from sensuality, from the need for family, and had settled into being a single woman. Content. Assertive. Successful.

Now she was staring at some stranger's buttocks! She was literally shaking as she wheeled her cart across the room. Wyatt Noble. What was it about him that had done this to her? She threw open the refrigerator door and counted the jars of salsa. He'd opened one and eaten part of it. Now she was thinking about his mouth! The taste of fire on his tongue. Good heavens.

Sarah set a new jar of salsa beside the first. He'd tasted the jalapeño jelly, eaten a couple of the tortillas. They were the extras she'd put in. Had he noticed? Rolling her eyes at her own wayward thoughts, she checked his cupboards, counting the bags of blue corn chips. He'd drunk a couple of root beers, and she replaced the empty bottles with full ones to chill.

Taking out her checklist, she scanned the kitchen to make sure her employees had left it clean. The only thing out of place was a note lying beside the sink. Sarah turned to go. Policy forbade reading guests' messages or in any other way prying into their personal lives.

As she wheeled the cart past the sink, her eye fell on the first word. "Sarah." Printed in a bold, black hand, in block letters, it clearly said her name. Should she read it? Was she the only Sarah in his life? She leaned closer.

"Sarah, thanks for the extras in the kitchen. You know how to make a man happy. W."

Grabbing her cart, Sarah propelled it out into the living room. She didn't know how to make a man happy! Didn't know the first thing about it. Wyatt was wrong. She'd dated a few men, and every relationship had ended badly. She seemed to attract men who wanted to control and mold her, men who wanted her to be someone she wasn't. She put up with it for a while, then when things got too intense, she ended the relationship with a swift coup de grace.

As she set the stack of crisp newspapers on the low coffee table in the sitting area, Sarah heard the bathroom water cut off. Okay, he might come back out into the suite, but she could handle this. He was an attractive man. Acknowledged. He was kind. Anyone who would think to write a note to the hotel housekeeping service must be considerate. Or at least a good motivator. He was easy to talk to. But so was her dog.

She checked off the items on her living room list. It had been vacuumed, dusted, polished. The curtains had been pulled back to let in the morning light. Everything was in order. Except for the old gray sweater draped over a chair. Sarah touched it. Hand-knit. Well worn.

As she headed for the dining area, Sarah passed one of the leather couches. She glanced down at the book lying on a mahogany side table. *Business as Usual.* Of course, Wyatt Noble would read some nonfiction thing that showed no imagination. An empty mug that smelled of black tea and bergamot oil sat beside it. Beneath the first book lay another, its paperback cover peeking out beneath the hardcover. Sarah glanced up, made sure that Wyatt was nowhere in sight, and slid the business tome to one side.

A Western novel in shades of brown, yellow, and gray was spread open flat on the table. A gunslinger, legs in a wide stance and six-shooter aimed straight ahead, stared out beneath his battered brown Stetson. Behind him, a black stallion reared and pawed the air with its hooves.

A Western. Now, that was refreshing. A man who read fiction had an extra spark. He wasn't all careers, goals, money. He pictured a world where good guys fought bad guys, where a man could win a woman with his bravery rather than his bank account. And that teacup. The scent was definitely Earl Grey. Sarah formed a picture of Wyatt Noble—old gray sweater, cup of steaming tea, nose buried in a good category Western. Warm . . . considerate . . . thoughtful . . . gentle . . .

"You read?"

Sarah's head shot up. "Oh!" She shoved the business book so hard it shot off the table and landed between her feet. Hot as a Texas summer, she grabbed the book and slammed it down on the Western. "Yes, I read. Novels. Romance, mystery, fantasy."

"Fantasy." He was standing by the couch, hands slid casually into his pockets. An easy grin softened his features. "I've been doing some fantasizing myself."

Sarah ran her fingers down the length of her hair. "I'm sure you have a strong ability to picture the trends your business will take, Mr. Wyatt. Well, if you'll excuse me, I'll replace the old flowers, check your bedroom, and be out of your way."

"You're not in my way. I told you that. In fact, I was hoping you'd drop by this morning."

"Checking on the suites is my job, Mr. Noble."

"Name's Wyatt. You can call me that, if you would." He followed her to the dining area. "I was afraid I might miss you, so I left a note."

"Yes."

"Did you see it?"

"Yes." Here she was, admitting she'd read a personal message, caught red-handed studying his personal reading matter, talking with him so easily that he wanted her to call him by his first name—breaking every rule in the policy manual she herself had written!

"I stay in hotels a lot," he was saying. "You're the only

one who's been sensitive to what I might enjoy. A personal touch. That's rare."

"I've been at this for fifteen years."

"You started in hotel management right out of college? You're not that old."

She glanced up. He had rested one hand on the back of a chair. He looked wonderful—a soft denim shirt buttoned to the throat, a pair of jeans, a brown leather belt, brown boots, a black wool blazer—and it was time to put back the distance between them.

"I didn't go to college, Mr. Noble."

"Wyatt."

She pulled the wilted wildflowers from their vase. "I worked my way into this position."

"On-the-job training. Some of my finest employees have that background." His blue eyes were as depthless as a lake. "I admire spunk. The independent spirit. The person who fights the odds, takes a chance at a dream, and wins. I'd call you a winner, Sarah."

"I would, too." She set the bundle of fresh flowers in the vase and then met his eyes. "And I won't let anything jeopardize my dream."

"What's your dream?"

He was following her into the bedroom! Sarah swallowed. "What's yours?"

He gave a low laugh. "I'm thirty-eight, and I've already got it. You know that old saying, 'A man's reach should exceed his grasp, or what's a heaven for'? Who wrote that?"

"I wouldn't know."

"Browning, I think. Anyway, I reached, I grasped—"

"And you captured your dream. Now nothing's left."

He sank down into a wing chair and stared at her. She stared back. For that single instant, the room took on a music of its own, the throbbing, pulsing drumbeat of her heart. She tried to swallow, but her throat felt like a dry towel. He was sitting there, strong, powerful, wealthy, larger than life. And she had found the single chink in his armor.

"I'm looking," he said slowly. "Looking for something to put meaning, fire, back in the old dream."

"You haven't failed at anything else. You'll find it."

"I'm beginning to think so." He stood, pushing up from the armchair like a self-propelled rocket. "Sarah, I've been wanting to ask you—"

"I'm sorry, Wyatt," she cut him off. "Mr. Noble."

"Wyatt."

"Anyway, I really have a thousand things to do today. Your bedroom is in order, and the kitchen is restocked." She rounded the cart and headed out the door. He was right behind her. "Your newspapers are on the coffee table. Here are the rest of your towels."

She swung around, arms outstretched, and shoved the towels right into his stomach. With a grin, he took them. "Thanks."

"Is there anything else I can do for you? Anything you need?"

"Anything you could do for me? Well . . ."

"All right, then." Flushed with heat, she pushed the cart into the hall. "The Hartley wishes you a pleasant day."

"Bye, Sarah." His voice tapered off as she hurried toward the elevator. "I'll look forward to seeing you again."

Sarah went through her day reciting a hymn of denial. She didn't feel anything for Wyatt Noble when he looked into her eyes. He hadn't meant anything personal in those comments about her hair, about the fantasies he'd been having. He hadn't left that note for any reason other than the hope of continued good service. He didn't mean what he'd said about hoping to see her in his suite that morning, about looking forward to seeing her again later. Not in any significant way.

She certainly felt nothing for him—other than a simple male–female attraction. Plenty of men were as genial to her as Wyatt Noble. She had read innuendo into everything. She exaggerated the significance of his behavior and words. The feelings that careened around inside her were simply a result of working too hard, going for too long without a vacation, laboring under too much stress from her evening college courses. Something! Anything!

Okay, okay. Maybe there was such a thing as love at first sight, and maybe it had happened to her. Maybe she was falling in love with him. Maybe she did cherish his old gray sweater and his worn leather boots. Maybe she had always wanted a man who read novels and drank tea and cared about her dreams. Maybe she'd longed for a man who could make her heart stop at the sound of his voice, whose smile set a fire in her breast. And maybe Wyatt Noble was a man just like that.

But maybe he wasn't.

Whatever was going on, she had to stop it. As she sat at her desk a few minutes before the end of her workday, Sarah counted the number of uncharacteristic things she had done. She'd snapped at one of her new employees, who had inadvertently watered the silk trees in the atrium. She had stammered through a phone conversation with the linen supply company because she was thinking about Wyatt Noble's bare chest. Worst, she had forgotten a meeting with James Baca, and the hotel's general manager had come searching for her, only to find her sitting on a window ledge and staring blankly down at traffic twelve floors below.

The fact was, she decided as she gathered up her briefcase and purse, she had let her imagination run away with her. Even if Wyatt Noble had some attraction for her, which he didn't, she wasn't the type for a brief two-week fling. Not with any man, and especially not with a hotel guest.

If she ever did let someone into her life, she would want commitment and permanence. She would want a long relationship, months of dating, a slow-paced engagement, a carefully thought-out future. Wyatt stood for everything but stability. He was a footloose bachelor with no permanent home and a lifestyle she could never relate to.

No, she decided as she shrugged into her jacket, Wyatt Noble was impossible. She would forget him.

She reached for the doorknob, and her door swung open.

"Hey, Sarah," he said, sweeping his Stetson from his head and engaging her with a lopsided grin, "know of any place around here where a man can get a good home-cooked dinner?"

chapter

three

"Denny's," Sarah said, wishing she'd put on lipstick. Wyatt was staring at her mouth. "Country Kitchen. Western Sizzler."

"I was thinking Mexican." He stood in the doorway, his big shoulders blocking her path. "Enchiladas. All those tortillas and the salsa in the fridge. You make me hungry, Sarah."

She blinked and twisted her purse strap. She was definitely reading into everything the man said. "There are several Mexican food places within walking distance of the hotel. Or you could put in a call for room service. I'm sure the hotel chef would create something special for you. The Hartley's food service has won numerous awards, and our chef—"

"Can you cook?"

"Of course, but—"

"Would you mind giving me some culinary advice before you head home? I've got a hankering for enchiladas the way Dorothy used to make them."

"Dorothy?"

"My mother. I bought some cheese, canned hot sauce, and corn tortillas at a little place downtown. I figured I could put together something to bake in the oven in my suite."

"I'm really not all that good with Mexican food." The thought of being alone with Wyatt under other than professional circumstances sent a knot of trepidation and excitement into Sarah's stomach. "The hotel chef would be more than happy to advise you."

"If you'd drop by on your way out," he said, as if he hadn't even heard her, "just to make sure I'm on track, I'll do the cooking myself."

"I have to make a final check around the lobby area—"

"Fine! I'll see you upstairs in a few minutes, then." He gave her a jaunty thumbs-up and vanished.

Sarah leaned back against the wall and groaned. She was going up to his suite. To cook enchiladas with him. This was not good.

"Sarah?" James Baca stuck his head through the door. "You still here? I noticed your office was open."

She practically jumped to attention. "I was just leaving. Heading out to give the lobby a last look."

"Is everything all right, Sarah? You're a little flushed."

"Everything's fine. Everything's in order."

"I saw Wyatt Noble in here a moment ago. Is he satisfied with our service? Any trouble there?"

"Oh, no. He's very pleased."

"Let's keep it that way."

"Whatever Wyatt Noble wants, he gets."

James smiled. "I can always count on you, Sarah. How's school these days? Class tonight?"

"Not tonight." *Thank goodness,* she realized, *since she was going to spend the evening making enchiladas.* "My classes are great. Straight A's."

"I've been looking over my employee schedule. You're due for a salary review, Sarah. I'll be keeping my eye on you, and we'll talk in a couple of weeks. How does that sound?"

"Wonderful, Mr. Baca. Thank you."

"See you tomorrow, then."

He exited, and she hurried out behind him. As she locked her office, Sarah pictured a pay raise—money well earned, and essential to her progress in school. Would she still be eligible for a pay hike if she were caught fraternizing with a guest? Would she be eligible if she refused to fraternize and the esteemed guest caused a big stink about it?

As she scanned the lobby and then entered the open elevator, Sarah made up her mind. This was a business call. She was simply meeting a patron's request. Simply making sure that nothing Wyatt Noble desired was denied.

Heavens, that didn't bode well. A row of blinking white lights marked the elevator's progress as it skimmed up eighteen floors. What if Wyatt desired things she wasn't prepared to give? What did she really know about the man anyway? What kind of person was he at heart? He certainly knew how to get his way, how to win at all cost. What if he wasn't as noble as his last name suggested?

Uncertainty curling through her stomach, Sarah knocked on his door. A moment later it swung open, and all her fears evaporated. Wyatt stood there, black hair tousled, a splash of red chili sauce down the front of his shirt, and the smell of burning tortillas wafting from the kitchen.

"Problems," he said, grabbing her arm and propelling her across the open floor. "Big problems."

"Your oil's too hot." She slid the sizzling pan off the burner.

He jerked a white towel from a hook and draped it on the counter. She set the pan on the towel to cool, then took stock of the situation. "If you fry your tortillas too hot and too long, they'll turn stiff and brittle. You can use them as chips to dip in your salsa." She slipped out of her jacket and rolled up her sleeves. "But if you want to make enchiladas, cook the tortillas only for a couple of seconds. They'll be tender, soft, pliant."

"I like the sound of that."

She caught the look in his blue eyes. Picking up a pair of tongs, she turned back to the stove. "Here, watch this."

He leaned over her shoulder as she demonstrated, placing the pan back on the burner, dipping the tortillas back and forth in the hot oil, and then laying them gently in the baking dish. She could feel him close behind her, his chest brushing her back, his breath warming her hair.

"Make a layer of tortillas," she said, "then cover it with enchilada sauce."

"Cheese next?"

They reached for the bowl of grated cheese at the same

time, and their fingers touched. A jolt of electric energy shot through Sarah's hand. She jerked back. "Go ahead," she said. "You put it on. Be generous."

She watched his long, tanned fingers lift a handful of cheese and scatter it across the red sauce. "Onions?" she asked.

"Not tonight."

She shut her eyes as his hand slipped around the curve of her shoulder. "Why don't you put on another layer of tortillas?" His mouth hovered just behind her ear. "I'll watch you."

She worked at his dinner and tried not to notice the way his fingers molded her satiny blouse, heated through the fabric, set her skin on fire. His thumb lay along the sensitive curve of her spine in a warm, firm pressure. She layered the tortillas, then ladled the hot sauce. He leaned against her, so close she could feel the hard outline of his thigh, as he reached for the cheese. His hand scattered grated fragments across the thick red liquid.

"I'll put this in the oven." She slid out from between him and the counter, balancing the heavy dish. As she walked across the kitchenette, she heard him open the refrigerator door.

"I bought some margarita mix. Made us a couple of glasses." He handed her a tall lime-colored drink rimmed in salt. "Thanks for helping me out with the dinner. I'm a whiz at scrambled eggs, but this was uncharted territory."

She took a sip. Half the glass and her world would be swirling. "Well, now that things are under control—"

"Would you join me, Sarah? I'd like your company at my table."

"That's very kind."

"I'm not saying it to be kind. I'd like you to stay for dinner. I enjoy talking with you. You're interesting. Intelligent. Beautiful."

"Mr. Noble, please."

"Call me Wyatt, Sarah. I'm no stranger."

"I met you twenty-four hours ago. You're a guest at the hotel where I work."

"And you enjoy spending time with me, getting to know me the way I like getting to know you. We have something in common."

"Hardly."

"You sense it, too, but you won't let yourself be with me long enough to find out. You're just as curious as I am about why it happens."

"Why what happens?"

"Why when we look at each other things start to get tangled. Why when I touched your shoulder a few minutes ago, you trembled."

"I didn't."

"You did. You're wondering about me—where I come from, what makes me tick. Just like I'm wondering about you. You want to know why we belong together."

She caught her breath. "We do not. We come from completely different worlds. We're light years apart."

"You're wrong, Sarah. There's something between us, and you know it."

"No." She set her drink on the counter and grabbed her jacket. "I don't do this kind of thing."

"What kind of thing?"

He was following her across the room toward the door. *Fall in love,* she wanted to say. *Give myself to a man who can't give anything back.* "Flings," she said, turning on him. "Affairs. One-night stands."

"I don't do that kind of thing either."

"Good. Then, you'll understand why I'm leaving now."

Before he could respond, she slung her purse over one shoulder and hurried down the hall, leaving him to eat his enchiladas alone.

Sarah spent a restless evening. Final exams were less than a month away, and she tried to study. She had papers to write, statistics to compile. Laundry had piled up, so she set the washer running. She swept, mopped, dusted. She ate a bologna sandwich that tasted like cardboard.

Her dog sensed her unsettled spirit and begged for a walk. While leading Reba around the block, she realized she had named her own dog for a poet of sorts. A musician. A country troubadour. And her dog, like Wyatt's, was a mutt.

Coincidence. Maybe she and Wyatt did have a few things in common. Daily, mundane sort of things. Not the major, life-shaping events that made a person into who she was. Maybe they both did feel something when they looked at each other, when they touched. What was so shattering about that? Maybe she had secretly fallen in love with him. A mild crush at age thirty-three. These things happened. He would leave in two weeks, and she'd get over it.

She slept badly, and dreams invaded—her recurring vacuum cleaner nightmare. She was vacuuming the crowded lobby at the Hartley, and all of a sudden she realized she was stark naked. She ran for cover, and the vacuum's cord popped out of the wall socket. It slung around like a lariat. Knocked over lamps and brushed pictures off the wall. Snagged Mr. Baca around the neck. Then the vacuum started sucking things up. Tablecloths. Curtain hems. Bedskirts. Bigger things—couches, her Chevy, the silk trees in the Hartley lobby, her house, Reba.

Reba! Sarah sat up in a sweat and lugged herself out of bed. This had to stop. If she was having her vacuum cleaner nightmare, things were really out of control. She was vulnerable. Wyatt Noble had clearly found the chink in her armor, too, a chink she hadn't even known was there.

She dressed for the day, pulling her hair into a tight bun at the back of her head. Her stiffest suit was a dark pin-striped gabardine with a tight straight skirt and a jacket that looked as if it had once belonged to a gangster. She wore it with black stockings and a pair of spiky heels. A slash of dark red lipstick, and she felt tough again, invincible.

As she drove to work, she recited a litany of affirmations—a jumble of scripture verses she'd learned in Sunday School. "Wait for the Lord; be strong and let your heart take courage," she mouthed as her little Chevy chugged through the heavy morning traffic. "And He has said to me, 'My grace is sufficient for you, for power is perfected in weakness' . . . for when I am weak, then I am strong. . . . Finally, be strong in the Lord, and in the strength of His might."

By the time she pulled into her parking space at the hotel, she felt peace descend like a soft, warm cape around her shoulders. This thing with Wyatt was not so big, not so catastrophic that she couldn't handle it. It was a slight bump in the path of her life. With divine strength and her own good sense, she could drive right over it and continue on her way.

Sure enough, things went better from the moment Sarah walked into her office. She gathered her checklists and had a short meeting with her senior staff. She called in her supply orders without a fumble. She loaded her cart for the executive suites and rode the elevator to the eighteenth floor with nary a tremble.

When she knocked on Wyatt's door and got no answer, she poked her head in. "Housekeeping," she shouted at the top of her lungs. He had gone for the day. She rolled her cart across the carpet, placed new towels in his bathroom, added fresh bars of specialty soap to his basket, and set his stack of newspapers on the coffee table.

Okay, maybe she did pause for a moment to sniff the cologne bottle on the bathroom sink. And maybe she hugged his damp towels as she carried them back to her cart. She did study the portrait of the elderly couple on his bedside table and read the inscription, "To Wyatt with our love, Jacob and Dorothy."

She was wondering why a son would call his parents by their first names when she walked to the dining room table to replace the wildflowers. Then she saw the note. "Sarah," in bold, black ink.

Her heart began to do a two-step. She picked up the folded paper and opened it. "Sarah, please meet me here at the suite at noon. Wyatt."

She slid the note into her pocket. This was all right. He might want to order some extra newspapers in the morning. Maybe he needed some laundry specially cleaned. Or maybe he wanted to talk about last night, to apologize for his lack of discretion.

Her cart almost empty, Sarah wheeled it into the kitchenette. She restocked his root beer and piñon nuts. Then she lifted the foil on the pan of enchiladas. One small corner had been cut out. It looked so cold, forlorn. A pang twisted her heart as she imagined Wyatt seated at that long table all alone, eating that square of enchiladas and drinking his root beer.

Well, anyway.

She rolled her cart out of the suite and down the hall to the elevator. She had other things to think about.

Noon rolled around faster than it should have. Sarah knocked on the door of the south suite, then crossed her arms like a barrier over her chest.

"Hey, Sarah." He opened the door, a soft smile lighting his features. "How're things going today?"

"Very well, thank you. I trust everything is in order here in your rooms?"

He motioned her to one of the long couches. She brushed past, ignoring the mingled scents of his cologne and his leather coat. As she seated herself, she realized he was still standing. He looked dominating, powerful in his black coat and boots. Feeling the urge to pop back up and meet him eye to eye, she instead stared at his long legs as he strode back and forth.

"Things are fine here," he said. "The enchiladas were great, by the way. Just how I like them."

"Is there something you need for the suite? Do you have a special request?"

He stopped pacing, and his smile went lopsided. "You might say that. I wanted to talk to you for a minute."

"If it's about last night—"

"No, it's about tonight. Sarah, I'd like you to accompany me to the banquet and dance for the El Paso Arts Patrons Society this evening. In fact, while I'm in the city,

I'd like to take you to all the evening events on my schedule. I have something nearly every night—galas, gallery openings, cocktail parties, you know that kind of thing. The more I thought about it last night, the more I realized I'd like to spend that time with you. I enjoy being with you, and I think you're very attractive."

Sarah shut her mouth and swallowed. She unknotted her fingers from the sofa upholstery. Like champagne bubbles, her desire to see more of Wyatt frothed up inside her. Long, slow hours they would spend together. She could revel in the sound of his voice instead of trying to dredge it up in the middle of the night. She could fairly wallow in the scent of his skin, drown in the blue sea of his eyes. Those brief snatches of conversation she'd been clinging to could stretch on and on. She could explore him, find out who he really was, discover what it was that drew her with such fervor.

He could have picked up the phone and called anyone. In two seconds flat, Wyatt Noble could have a date for his upcoming events. But he wanted her.

She cleared her throat, searched for words. And all the reasons she should turn him down flooded in. All her college classes met at night. This evening her statistics professor planned to prepare his students for a test the following session. A long term paper and two presentations were due in the next two weeks. Not to mention finals at the end of the month.

What came first in her life? Heady romance? Secret love? Or the reality of her need for an education, her ambition to better herself, her determination to succeed in a world that predicted failure.

"I'm sorry," she said, standing. "Thank you very much for your kind invitation, but the general manager of the hotel has made it clear that his employees are not to fraternize with guests. He wouldn't approve of my attending the banquet or any of the other events with you. It wouldn't be professional."

"There's no problem." He gave an easy shrug. "My corporation does a lot of business with the Hartley hotel chain. A hell of a lot."

She stared at him. Was that a veiled threat? Was he actually implying that he would take his business elsewhere if she didn't go out with him? Mr. Baca would be very unhappy if that happened. Noble Newspapers was a solid, reliable, and productive account. She'd probably lose her job.

A chill crept through Sarah. Wyatt was forcing her hand. He knew he could get whatever he wanted by throwing his money and power around. She had to work hard for everything she earned, but he could manipulate and bend people to his will with the sheer weight of his influence. Maybe she had been attracted to the man, but she resented the idea that she had to stop her world because his was more important.

"Well," she said, tight-lipped. "Since you put it that way, I accept."

"Great. I'll pick you up in the limo at seven. What's your address?"

"I'll meet you here at the hotel." He wasn't going to find her house, that was for sure. She walked to the front door on pencil-stiff legs.

"See you this evening, Sarah," he said. "In the lobby by the piano. I'm looking forward to it."

She wasn't. She walked away without a backward glance.

Sarah spent the afternoon—when she should have been working—in an attempt to cover her bases. She caught James Baca on his way to a meeting and quickly explained the situation.

"Wyatt Noble wants to date you?" he asked, blunt as ever.

"In a manner of speaking. It's more like accompanying him to the events on his social calendar."

"Sounds like dating to me."

"Well, I certainly haven't encouraged his behavior, sir.

Not in any way. I'm perfectly aware such action is against hotel policy. Besides, with my evening classes, I really don't have the time to go anywhere with the man."

"I understand your problem, Sarah, and I trust that you wouldn't violate our standards. But since Mr. Noble seems to have his mind made up about this, let's not rock the boat. We'll bend our rules a little. Noble Newspapers is a valuable client. We don't want to lose them."

"Yes, sir. I see."

He gave her a weak grin and went into his meeting.

Her resentment only grew as Sarah called her professors and detailed her predicament. Because of her exemplary grades, they told her, they would agree to work around each conflicting date that arose. She would, however, still be responsible for the same material as all the other students in the class.

Of course, yes, of course. At home, she rifled through her wardrobe. Her closet was hung with a small selection of business suits she had chosen with great care, one by one, over the years. Each was tasteful, timeless, expensive. Each had required her careful budgeting of a salary that was more appropriate for khaki skirts and sweaters. She had worn her suits in all seasons, accessorizing with light cowl-neck sweaters in winter and cool blouses in summer. Three pairs of faded jeans lay in her chest of drawers along with T-shirts bearing logos from the walk races she'd participated in.

That was it. There were no cocktail dresses, ball gowns, froths of swishy silk. How did Wyatt have the nerve to expect her to fit in with all those society types at his events? It galled her to think of having to climb into a limousine and spend hours at some dinner, when she didn't belong. She wasn't part of that world. She wouldn't have a clue what to say. She would be completely out of place—and it would show.

Annoyed, she jerked her best black suit out of the closet and tossed it on the bed. With the shimmery turquoise blouse she had bought for an employee Christmas party—

and worn five years straight—she decided the outfit might pass. She pinned a rhinestone brooch her mother had given her to one lapel, fastened a pair of small silver earrings on her ears, and stepped back into her spiky pumps. It was going to be a long night.

chapter

four

Stetson in hand, Wyatt rose from his seat the moment Sarah entered the lobby. At the nearby piano, a man in a tuxedo played a waltz that echoed the musical cascade of water running over stones in the atrium's fountain. Wyatt took a step forward, then stopped, his blue gaze locked on her face.

Her chilly reserve trembled slightly as she absorbed the full impact of the man awaiting her. He stood tall, tanned, and massive-shouldered in his Western-cut charcoal suit, white shirt, and black boots. A gleaming silver bolo tie embedded with a chunk of green turquoise dominated an image that said money, power, rawhide toughness, and a steel will.

"Hey, Sarah." The gentle, welcoming timbre of Wyatt's deep voice belied everything in his body language. "I'm glad you came."

What choice did I have? she wanted to ask. But he took her hand in both of his and drew her toward him.

"You look beautiful tonight." He was smiling down at her, his eyes dark navy. "You just knocked me flat when you walked in. I never met a woman who could do what you do for a black suit."

"I'm glad you like it," she said, her back stiff. "You're going to be seeing a lot of this outfit in the next two weeks."

His smile faded. "I didn't think about . . . I hope I haven't made things hard on you, Sarah."

"I've worked through it." She couldn't make herself let him off the hook. She gave him the hint of a smile, but she knew stubbornness was written all over her face. Wyatt was probably accustomed to people kowtowing to him left and right. Though Sarah always had respected authority, she knew she couldn't sit still and be walked on—not by anyone. Her independent and self-assured spirit had been the downfall of every relationship she'd ever had with a man. And it would probably put a quick end to Wyatt's fascination with her.

"I've learned to be resourceful and adapt to difficult situations," she said. "It's my job."

"I figured you could handle a curveball," he shot back. "Otherwise I wouldn't have asked you out."

"I take it you throw a lot of curves."

"Curves are my specialty." He gave an appreciative glance at the full rise of her breasts beneath her turquoise sheath. Then he lifted his eyes to her face, and he gave a quick wink. "May I escort you to the limousine, Miss Ellsworth?"

Cheeks uncharacteristically flushed, Sarah took his extended elbow. She slid her fingers around the warm, hard muscle beneath his jacket as he led her down the marble steps and out onto the sidewalk.

For the first time in fifteen years of working there, Sarah understood how it might feel to be one of the wealthy guests who patronized the Hartley Rio Grande Hotel. The doorman gave her a polite bow. The driver of the sleek silver limousine held open a leather-padded door. People on the sidewalk stopped and stared. Children pointed.

Sarah ducked her head and entered the dimly lit interior of the luxury sedan. Two long leather seats faced each other with an expanse of blue-gray carpet between. A small teak bar held chilled champagne, long-stemmed glasses, white napkins. The seats were low, and Sarah had no option but to stretch her legs across the floor. Wyatt slid in next to her, too close, and put his arm on the back of the seat behind her shoulders.

"Champagne?" he asked, reaching around her and confining her within the bulk of his body.

She shook her head. "No, thanks."

"Not even root beer?" He pulled open the door of the tiny refrigerator and held up a bottle of Pop's. In a moment, the two champagne glasses were filled with foamy caramel soda. He handed one to her and lightly clinked it with his. "Here's to the future," he said. "Here's to us."

He heart hammering against her rib cage, she took a sip. The liquid burned as it slid down her dry throat.

When she lifted her head, he placed a finger on the corner of her mouth and ran it across the thin line of foam on her upper lip. Then he licked the tip of his finger. "Delicious," he whispered.

"You're outrageous, you know that?" she returned.

When he chuckled, she let out a shaky breath and averted her eyes to the window. He was doing it again—pulling her out of her detachment. If she tasted good, he smelled like heaven itself. As he settled next to her for the short ride, she drifted in the male scent of his clean skin. There was something about the cut of his suitcoat, about the shaven angle of his jaw, about the curl of black hair that fell over his forehead, that sparked a white-hot flame inside her. Did he know what the sight of him, what the sound of his voice, did to the pit of her stomach? Did he have any idea of the turmoil he had unleashed? Did he know that from the moment he had walked into that suite and placed a bluebonnet blossom in her lapel she had been lost to him?

Lost in a man. Every iota of feminine assertiveness rejected the concept. Yet in the limo, leaning against Wyatt as the driver maneuvered the streets of El Paso, Sarah realized that losing one thing might mean finding something else.

Wyatt Noble, like no man she had ever met, had stirred to life a hidden urge inside her heart. Though she had known him only a short time, he had touched her. He had unlocked her womanly need for closeness with a man, for fellowship, connection . . . passion.

His large frame lounged across the limousine seat as he talked about his father's ranch, regaling Sarah with stories of how he had learned to ride a horse. The streetlights caught his eyes and his smile. When he laughed, the sound tumbled down into her heart. His big hand stroked her shoulder, and she began to relax.

"You could learn to ride," he said as the limo slid up in front of the El Paso Convention and Performing Arts Center on the Plaza near the Rio Grande. "I'd teach you."

She glanced at him in surprise. "The only place I know of with horses is Sunland Park Racetrack. I don't think I'm quite up to quarter horse racing."

He laughed. "I'm talking about my ranch. Near Waco."

The door swung open, and he exited to the sidewalk without further explanation. Sarah scooted unglamorously across the leather seat. Wyatt had toasted their future. Now he was talking about teaching her to ride horses on his ranch. What was going on here?

"There's the mayor," he said, taking her arm. He settled his Stetson on his brow and adjusted the brim. "I reckon he'll be after me for a contribution tonight. Never fails."

As they climbed the steps, the mayor spotted them. Sarah swallowed at the knot in her throat.

"Howdy, Mayor." Wyatt greeted the man. They shook hands. "City's looking good tonight."

"Thank you, Wyatt. Glad to know we've got a fine new owner for the *Tribune*. Noble Newspapers has always supported my party's causes."

"We support whatever's worthy, Mr. Mayor." He turned to Sarah. "I'd like you to meet Sarah Ellsworth. She's a native El Pasoan."

"Miss Ellsworth." The mayor took her hand and nearly squeezed her fingers off. "So pleased to know you. You're a very lucky young woman. You've snagged yourself a fine man here."

"I'm the one who did the snagging," Wyatt countered. "I'm the lucky one tonight."

The mayor laughed. "Of course! Certainly! And Miss Ellsworth, your father is . . .?"

"Mike Ellsworth. El Paso Natural Gas." *You never met*

him, Sarah added mentally. *And he never contributed a dime to your worthy causes except by paying his taxes.*

The mayor tapped his forehead for a moment. Then he clicked his fingers. "Michael Ellsworth, yes indeed!"

"Sarah's with Hartley Hotels." Wyatt's arm around her shoulders tightened. His blue eyes lingered on her face. "That's where we met."

"Wonderful! Superb! A fine establishment. Wyatt, while you're here for the convention, I trust you'll take a good look at your investment in El Paso. We're certainly a progressive city. I intend to see that our economy grows and thrives, and I'm sure you'll want to support that."

"Strong businesses make good advertisers. You know I like to see business booming. Especially my own."

The mayor laughed as Wyatt started into the Arts Center's foyer. "You're my kind of man, Wyatt. With my re-election campaign gearing up, I hope you'll keep me in mind."

"I expect my reporters will cover all the candidates so well that no one in El Paso will forget any of you." Wyatt gave the mayor a smile that reflected none of the warmth Sarah felt when he looked at her. "Give the *Tribune* a call when we can be of service."

"Thank you, Wyatt. Thank you very much."

"Conflict of interest," he said under his breath. "As if the owner of a newspaper would give money to a political campaign."

Without breaking stride, Wyatt steered Sarah into the Rudy Montoya Room, where a throng of people mingled, chatted, and sipped drinks. The Arts Patrons Society was not a large organization, but clearly these were El Paso's elite. In a breathtaking whirl, Wyatt introduced Sarah to various members of the city council, the CEOs of most of the major industries in El Paso, the president of the university, the owner of Sunland Park Racetrack, the commander at Fort Bliss, and enough doctors and lawyers to fill out the gathering. Wyatt knew many of them by name. And they knew him.

Sarah smiled until she thought her mouth would crack.

Her black suit was completely out of place, of course. The women in the room displayed a rainbow of chiffon cocktail dresses that shimmered and swished as they sashayed from group to group. Many of the men, like Wyatt, wore clothing that reflected their Texas heritage—boots, Stetsons, even the occasional pair of jeans. The Levi Strauss Company was, after all, the fifth largest employer in El Paso. But even casual style came across as haute couture.

The banquet dinner was served at a collection of long tables. White cloths had been set with fine china. Candlelight reflected the weighty diamonds sprinkled on fingers, necks, and ears. Soft violin music set an artsy, romantic mood, and the meal emerged from the kitchens—course after course of steaming delicacies on silver trays.

"What are you thinking about?" Wyatt whispered during the lengthy speech that involved the introduction of various noted artists and performers in El Paso. He took her hand beneath the table and wove their fingers together. "Sarah?"

She shrugged. Honesty at all cost. "Actually, I was wondering what kind of cleaner they use to get these floors so shiny. Before that, I was calculating how much it cost to feed all these people tonight."

He chuckled, seemingly unfazed by her mundane, practical thoughts. "A pretty penny, I reckon. I feel like a stuffed turkey myself."

"You're no turkey, Wyatt. I, on the other hand, could best be described as a flounder."

"Sarah, you've charmed the socks off these folks. If anyone's floundering, it's me." He leaned against her ear. "I've been sitting here all night trying to figure out how to break through to you. You're holding back."

"Of course I am," she returned. "What do you expect?"

"Everything."

She glanced at him, expecting to find a teasing sparkle in his eyes, a flirtatious wink. His blue eyes fixed her with a look that was depthless.

So close she could feel his breath, his mouth breathed the next words. "Will you dance with me, Sarah?"

Before she realized the society president's speech had ended, Wyatt had lifted her against him and moved her out onto the dance floor. They floated amid the sway of silk dresses, lost in each other's eyes. Sarah knew something was happening to her . . . something foreign and frightening, yet so exhilarating she could barely breathe.

Her senses took on a life of their own—a mixed, mingled, crazy jumble of impulses. The scent of Wyatt's skin seemed to take on color, a warm gray-blue that set her heart hammering. The spark in his eyes glimmered to the music in the room, a melody that offered the promise of a golden tomorrow. When he spoke against her ear, she heard no words, but the sound of his voice went down her spine like a cascade of warm syrup.

At some point in the mindless blur of passing hours, she fled to the bathroom, only to find herself leaning against the cool marble wall as she panted for breath. *What was happening?* she repeated to herself. Her comfortable world of memos and checklists, toilet-paper orders and mop handles had evaporated in the heat of Wyatt Noble's touch.

She took off her jacket and mopped her neck with a cool, moist towel. This had to stop, or she would do something she might regret. She already regretted everything about the man who was waiting for her outside. And she wanted him. More than anything she'd ever wanted in her life.

Holding her jacket like a shield in her arm, she returned to the hallway. "Wyatt, I'd better go home now," she said. "I have a busy day tomorrow."

He ran one finger up the side of her damp neck. "Sure, Sarah." But he made no move to leave. "I hope you had a good time with me tonight. I enjoyed your company."

"It was very nice."

His grin tilted up at one corner. "When you said that, you looked like you just ate a raw persimmon."

"I'm not much good with people like your friends in there." She looked over his shoulder at the swirling ballroom. "I don't really relate."

"Relating's not the name of the game. And it *is* a game.

It's called mingling, networking, doing business. Once you know the rules, it's no big deal. You say howdy and put on a smile. You make professional connections. You eat some good food. But you never get down to what really counts."

She studied his face. "And what really counts for you, Wyatt?"

He threw back his head and looked at the ceiling. "Ah, Miss Ellsworth always gets right to the point, doesn't she?" He faced her again. "What really counts used to be that scene in there. Making connections. Making bucks. Proving I could build something out of nothing. Then a few years ago, my father died. I put his business in order. Sold off part of his estate. Set Dorothy up so she wouldn't have to concern herself over the details. After things had settled down, I stopped and took a good look at things. I held in my hands everything Jacob had worked his whole life to earn. A pile of papers, bank accounts, numbers. But he was gone. Flat gone."

Sarah bit her lower lip at the pain written in his eyes. She understood something of his loss. Her father's illness had taken a deep toll on her own family.

"It was Dorothy who set me straight," Wyatt continued. "She caught me one day, drunk as a skunk. I was down in the basement sprawled across the floor with Jacob's awards and trophies scattered around everywhere. I'd been going through boxes of the damn things, trying to pack up after the funeral. I'd been drinking for days. A certified binge. I didn't want to think what I'd been thinking. Couldn't let myself feel what I was feeling. That afternoon in the basement, Dorothy flopped down beside me . . ."

He stopped talking and smiled. "You'll have to meet Dorothy. You two would get along great. Anyhow, she told me to wise up. Jacob might have put a lot of stock in his millionaire status, she said, but he'd learned that there was more to life than oil wells and deals. Jacob had taken his love away from those material things and had put it where it counted. On his faith in God. On Dorothy. And on me."

"Well, you're his son."

Wyatt gave a mirthless laugh. "Yeah. Anyway, I thought

Dorothy was full of it. Nothing was more important to me than my corporation. Noble Newspapers was all I'd ever wanted. It was my total dream. A few years went by before I began to figure out what my mother had been talking about that day in the basement. I quit drinking. Switched to root beer. Joined a church. Started going back to the ranch to visit Dorothy more than once a year. And began looking around for something else."

"Something that really counts."

"Someone." He put his hand on her bare shoulder. "I'll take you back to the hotel now, Sarah."

Driving home through a midnight mist that had rolled in off the river, Sarah replayed the evening with Wyatt. Weird, very weird. She had started out mad as heck about his overbearing attitude, his disregard for her personal life, his ability to use his money and power to mold the world to his own desires. She'd ended it wanting to spend the rest of her life with the man!

In between there had been the otherworldliness of the Arts Patrons gathering. Those glittering people. A dinner that could have fed Somalia for a year. A dance in which smells had sound, sight had a scent, her senses had gone into overdrive. And then that conversation with Wyatt in the hall outside the women's rest room.

What was going on? She had acknowledged a secret infatuation with him. After all, he was incredibly handsome, kind, gentle, intelligent, courteous. What more could a sane woman want?

But he was toasting their future. He was inviting her to his ranch to teach her to ride his horses. He wanted her to meet his *mother*, for heaven's sake!

And he hadn't even kissed her.

Sarah stayed up most of the night studying for the statistics test she was to take the following morning at seven. Her professor had agreed to open his office early so he could monitor the exam. Bleary-eyed, she drove to UTEP and fought her way through the endless problems on the exam.

Later, as she inched through traffic on her way to the hotel, a deep purple anger bubbled up inside her. Anger at herself. *This* was her reality. Not last night. She lived in El Paso, Texas, not on some horse ranch in Waco. She headed Housekeeping at the Hartley, and she had worked damned hard for that position. Every cent she made went into house payments, food, business suits, and her college education.

Was she going to blow all that for a dream man with a lazy smile and sexy blue eyes? A man who offered nothing? Who promised nothing? A man who would take his root beer and his Stetson and ride right out of her life in a matter of days?

Feeling like her reserve was on empty, Sarah dragged into her office and dropped her attaché case on her desk. This had gone far enough. If she had bombed that stats test, she would never forgive herself. Never forgive Wyatt Noble. She didn't have time to prance around at society balls.

She picked up her phone receiver and punched the buttons to Wyatt's room. Nothing. When she didn't want him, there he was. When she needed to talk to him, he was nowhere to be found. She flipped through the phone book until she found the number for the *El Paso Tribune*.

"Who may I connect you with?" the woman on the other end asked.

"Wyatt Noble, please. Tell him Sarah Ellsworth is on the line."

"One moment."

Sarah listened to an orchestra playing "Love is Blue" for a moment. The receptionist came on again. "I'm sorry, Ms. Ellsworth. Mr. Noble won't be in today."

"He won't? Well, where in the heck is he?"

"I beg your pardon?"

"Um. I'm with his hotel. Do you know how I could reach him?"

"Oh, his hotel. Mr. Noble is spending the day with Ms.

Mercer, the publisher of the *Tribune*. I believe she's taking him on a tour of the city, and they'll be having lunch together at the Tigua Indian Reservation. If you'd like to leave a message, I'll try to reach him for you."

Sarah pictured Eleanor Mercer. Twice divorced. Harvard grad. Tall, buxom, gorgeous. Her picture was often in the society section of her own newspaper.

"No, that's all right, thank you," Sarah said. "I'll speak with Mr. Noble when he returns for the evening."

She hung up and flipped open her case. As she stared down at the pile of papers—study notes, memos, checklists—Wyatt's words filtered back to her. *I held in my hands everything Jacob had worked his whole life to earn. A pile of papers, bank accounts, numbers. But he was gone. Flat gone.*

Was this all she was living for—this bag full of checklists? This position at a hotel populated by nameless unknowns? She had no more relationship connections in her life than Wyatt had. Not unless she counted a dog and a family she ate dinner with once a month or less.

"Sarah, we've got trouble on eight." James Baca stuck his head through the doorway. "Ashtray spilled over on a guest's tapestry luggage. Sand, ashes, cigarette butts everywhere. I've got the guest; you get the ashtray and the luggage."

"Yes, sir." Sarah jumped to attention.

It was the vacuuming nightmare come to life.

J ust before quitting time, Sarah plodded back into her
office. Her lack of sleep was taking its toll, and she still
had the entire evening to look forward to. Or dread, as the
case might be.

Wyatt hadn't returned to the hotel all day. Just as well.
Sarah knew she was too mixed up to talk rationally with
him.

She would lock her office and dress in the black suit she
had brought from home. If she ordered a tray of tea and
scones from room service, she could eat in silence and try
to collect herself before heading off to the latest event on
Wyatt's dance card. This one involved the opening of a
new oil-painting exhibit at the El Paso Museum of Art,
followed by a semiprivate dinner with the president of the
Chamber of Commerce.

Sarah sank into her chair and bent to work her feet out
of her high heels. Not that she didn't like art, she thought
with a weary sigh. In fact, she had excelled in her high
school art classes, and she would have taken a second major in fine arts at UTEP if she'd thought it could benefit
her career. Instead she was minoring in finance.

Sacrifice had been the name of her game. Not mingling,
networking, good-ol'-boying with big shots. Not dabbling
in artistic realms. Her focus had required trade-offs, giving
up pleasure for reality. She didn't mind. It was all going to
be worth it when she took her place as personnel manager
at the Hartley.

Sarah wiggled her bare toes. Another night with Wyatt
Noble. How could she keep distant? How could she pre-

vent that whirlwind of emotion that threw everything, including her entire life's priority system, into chaos?

"Hey, Sarah."

At his voice, she lifted her head. "Wyatt? I thought the exhibit opening wasn't until ..."

Oh, the man was a killer, all blue eyes, denim, and leather. She involuntarily rose from her chair as he came across the room, his smile warming and comforting the troubled edges of her heart. *This* was why she couldn't stay detached.

"You look like you've had a long day, Sarah," he said, taking her hands between his. He propped one hip on the corner of her desk. "Can I buy you a drink? Root beer?"

She couldn't help but laugh. "I'm fine. Really. It was just this stats exam this morning, and then ashes on a suitcase this afternoon ... I have a dream, see ... sort of a nightmare actually ..."

His hands slipped up her arms. "Tell me about your dream, Sarah."

"Oh, it's nothing."

"Sure it is. If something's bothering you, I want to know about it. I've been thinking about you all day. I feel like I might have ruffled your feathers without meaning to. I'm not used to ... well, considering other folks' feelings much. Usually I just set a goal and slug my way through any obstacles until I get it."

"And I'm your goal?" she asked. "I mean, I'm flattered that you've been thinking about me today instead of about ... other people ... other things. But at the same time, I resent the idea that I'm some kind of impersonal objective."

"Whew, Sarah. You always get right to the point this way?" He gazed at the floor and shook his head. Then he laughed. "Yeah, I guess you do. That's what I like about you. That's why I'll have to admit that you are my goal. Sorry if that sounds a little mercenary, but that's how it is. I want you."

She swallowed. "For what?"

"Everything." He shrugged. "And I suspect you're

enough like me that you don't take kindly to someone messing up your plans. Throwing you off-kilter. So, here's what I've done."

Uh-oh. She didn't like the sound of this.

"I've assigned you the use of a limo and driver. I realize you have a car, but all these extra evening gigs might put a strain on you time-wise. A limo can get you where you need to go, and you won't have to think about a thing."

"Well, thank you. But I—"

"I've added your name as my guest at the country club. Swim, use the sauna, the running track. Whatever. Unwind. It'll do you good." He stood and jammed his hands in the front pockets of his jeans. "And I set up an account for you at Papillón. Mercer told me it was *the* place to shop."

"Papillón . . ."

"Look, I love that black suit. Don't get me wrong, Sarah. Whatever you choose to wear is fine with me. You look gorgeous right now with your shoes off and . . ." He took a deep breath. "I'm not used to this kind of thing. It's been a long time since I tried to make anyone but myself happy."

"Wyatt—"

"I'm not buying you off, okay? If you don't want to spend my money at that boutique, that's dandy. But if you're in a bind because I asked you to go to all these functions, just . . . Hell. I'm botching this."

A smile tickled her mouth. He looked like a discouraged little boy trying to win a sweetheart with a mud pie. "I'm not offended that you set up an account for me," she said. "Of course, Papillón . . ."

"Is there someplace you'd rather—"

"No! Heavens. Papillón is fine. In fact, I'll drive over there right now. Or maybe I'll take a limo. Good grief."

They stared at each other.

"I just want you to be happy, Sarah," he said. "I want you to feel comfortable . . . with me."

"I do." Her shoulders lifted in a sigh. "That's the strange part about it. I do."

"Good. So, go shopping. Buy whatever you want." He gave her his jaunty thumbs-up. "*Carpe diem*, you know."

"No, I don't know." She shook her head. "And that's why I shouldn't feel comfortable with you, Wyatt. We're from different worlds. You're educated. I'm still struggling—"

"I don't give a flip about how much school you've had. We're coming at life from the same angle. We can talk. We understand each other." He walked to the door. "*Carpe diem*: seize the day. Life's too short to fool around, Sarah. See something you want? Go after it."

As he left her office, Sarah felt the echo of his words. *You are my goal. Sorry if that sounds a little mercenary, but that's how it is. I want you.*

Dressed in a scintillating blue cocktail gown that skimmed her ankles and shimmered with sequins at her breast, Sarah wandered through the El Paso Museum of Art. Wyatt couldn't keep his eyes off her. So much for the geometric iron sculpture in the lobby. So much for the rows of abstract paintings staring down at them from the gallery's walls. So much for the genteel crowd of art patrons, several of whom had been at the banquet the evening before.

"Now, there's quite a canvas," Sarah commented as they strolled down the wing.

Wyatt tore his gaze away from her face for a second, glanced at the painting, and gave the picture a gruff *hmpf*. "Eyes on the same side of his face. Very Picasso."

This time, Sarah did know the reference. "I like Picasso. His paintings give life a different angle. A fresh perspective."

"Isn't it a flounder that has both eyes on one side of its face? That would tend to give you a different angle on things."

She chuckled. "Maybe you could use a new perspective, Wyatt."

"I like things just the way I'm seeing them right now."

He shot her a sly grin. "So, you want this painting, Sarah? I'll buy it for you. Hang it in your living room."

He dug into his jeans for his wallet.

"No!" She grabbed his hand. "Don't do that, Wyatt. Sheesh, you scared me half to death. I don't want the painting. Really, it's too . . . big."

"It's ugly," he whispered. "Damned ugly. I wouldn't even hang it in my barn. Scare the milk cows dry. Come on, let's step out into the fresh air."

Taking her hand, he led her through the crowd and out a side door. Evening had lit the sky with a soft pink hue that frosted the tops of buildings and reflected in a thousand windows. They strolled down the street, studying shop windows, absorbing the calm that was slowly seeping through the vast city.

"Never thought I'd like El Paso," Wyatt commented as they wandered hand in hand past a bakery. "Too brown."

"Brown?"

"The city is brown. The Franklin Mountains are brown, barren, rocky. The buildings are brown, shades of tan and beige. The river's brown. Even the sky. It's brown."

"Not every day. Most of the time it's a brilliant blue like—" She caught her breath. He stopped and turned to her. "Like your eyes."

"Sarah . . ." His hands found her shoulders, her neck. He drew her against the length of his body. "Sarah, I—"

"Wyatt . . ." She shivered as his hand slipped up into her hair, his fingers sliding apart to cup the back of her head. She touched the front of his coat with her fingertips.

He tilted her head up, forcing her eyes to meet his. His free hand found her back, her waist, the smooth curve below it. He pulled her closer, settling her against him. "That's better," he murmured.

"Always taking what you want . . ."

"You want it, too."

Her eyelids drifted shut as his mouth brushed across hers, his lips warm, firm. At the contact, she felt a tremor run through him, and he caught her more tightly, molding his mouth to hers.

The intimacy of the kiss took her by surprise, threw her off guard. She clutched his lapel as his lips parted, slanted, sought her with a ravenous hunger. He deepened the kiss, and she couldn't help responding, meeting him with the pent-up need that had driven them together like comets on a converging course.

He broke apart, breathing hard. She could feel his heart thundering against her open palm.

"Sarah?" he questioned. When she couldn't answer, he pulled her hard against him a second time. He cupped her head, thumbs under her jaw, as he explored the tender, sensitive secrets of her kiss.

She slid her hands beneath his jacket, around the solid bulk of his chest, to his back. His muscles beneath her fingers were hot, bunched, jolted with electric tension. She kneaded them in rhythm with the dance of their kiss, a sensual, melting waltz.

When his lips moved away from her mouth, he nuzzled her cheek, her ear. His breath sent shivers coursing down her spine and tipping the crests of her breasts. His hands stroked her bare shoulders, and she couldn't suppress the image of his fingertips caressing the silky skin beneath her dress.

"Yes, I do," she whispered. "I want it, too." She slid closer, aware of her urgent need for the pressure of his body against hers. Her thigh touched his, and she heard him groan her name, a muffled sound that came from somewhere deep inside him.

"*¿Rosas?*" The husky little voice was so close that Sarah stiffened in surprise. "*¿Señor? Rosas para la señorita.*"

Wyatt drew back and peered down at the thin arm thrusting upward, and the determined fist clutching a clump of long-stemmed red roses. A little boy, brown eyes luminous and black hair shiny in the lamplight stood just beneath his bouquet.

"*Rosas para la señorita,*" the child repeated. "*Para tu amor.*"

"*Amor*, is it?" Wyatt gave Sarah an assessing frown, as though he could read the answer in her eyes.

She inadvertently looked away, unwilling to let him see the unspoken truth. Before she would let him know how deeply she had fallen for him, she wanted more from the man than a single kiss—earth-spinning though it had been.

Wyatt rumpled the child's hair. "*¿Quanto vale sus rosas, niño?*"

"*Un dólar para una rosa.*"

"Hard-driving businessman," Wyatt confided to Sarah. "He wants a buck a shot." Taking the bundle of roses, Wyatt held them up in the streetlight, as though carefully examining them for flaws. He made as if to choose one. Then he rejected it and started to select another. Finally he pulled out his wallet, peeled off a large bill and slapped it in the boy's open hand.

"*Todas las rosas, hombre.*" Wyatt laid the roses in Sarah's arms. "*Para mi amor.*"

The boy's face broke into a disbelieving grin. "*¡Gracias! ¡Gracias, señor!*"

As the child took off down the street, Wyatt turned back to Sarah. "Now, where were we?"

"On our way to dinner with the president of the Chamber of Commerce, I think," she said softly.

"I don't think so." He caught her against him, crushing the roses, and kissed her again.

She could hardly believe that the overpowering flood of desire rampaging through her was happening a second time. Sliding her fingers through Wyatt's hair, she abandoned the bouquet that was wedged firmly between them, and drifted into his drugging kiss.

Lost, she swirled through the blue lights, aware only of the scent of his leather coat, the spicy-clean fragrance of his shaven jaw, the drugging perfume of pressed roses. His warm hands seemed addicted to the bare flesh of her back above her bodice, alternately massaging and then feather-stroking the sensitive skin.

He turned her into the darkness of an overhanging shop entrance, and leaned her against the glass window. His body felt hard, demanding, yet she knew he was holding back with a barely leashed restraint.

"Sarah," he said when they broke apart, both struggling for air. "Sarah, I won't ask more than you're willing to give, but I swear—"

"No." She shook her head, fighting to keep her values above her desires. "Wyatt, I won't . . . I can't . . ."

He laid a finger on her lips. "At least we know what it'll be like when we do." Taking the crushed roses from between them, he slipped his arm around her shoulder and led her out onto the sidewalk again. "Let's go to dinner."

They ate at Pancho Villa's, a dimly lit, fine-cuisine restaurant named for the infamous Mexican raider who had often been an unwelcome visitor in El Paso. Sarah tried her best to concentrate on the round of introductions as she met the intimate group of dinner guests that evening. She was seated by a youngish red-haired woman bent on engaging her in conversation.

"I haven't seen you at our Junior League meetings, Sarah," Joscelyn Peacock confided over the soup course. "Aren't you a member?"

Beneath the tablecloth, Wyatt wove his fingers through Sarah's.

"No, I'm not," she returned. "I work, and there really isn't time for much else in my life."

"Oh, you *work* at the Hartley! Silly me. Somehow I had the idea that your family . . ."

"No. My father's with the gas company."

"That explains my confusion. I bet you haven't lived here long enough to join all our organizations, sororities, and clubs." She waved a long-nailed hand over her soup. "As an executive, your dad must have moved you around a lot. You've probably lived everywhere. Lucky you. I grew up in li'l ol' El Paso. My family owns The Haberdashery. You know, the men's clothing chain?"

"Yes." Of course Sarah knew. Her marketing class at UTEP had focused on El Paso's most successful enterprises, and the finance class she was taking at the moment involved a detailed examination of area businesses. The Haberdashery was always listed as one of the highest moneymakers in the national retail garment industry.

"Anyway," Joscelyn said with a sigh, "we were stuck here all my life. Trade with Mexico and all that. And I just *had* to go and marry Bill Peacock, didn't I? Oh, well."

Sarah took a sip of soup. She couldn't imagine a woman like Joscelyn regretting having married the CEO of El Paso's most successful plastics company. "According to my study of local finance," she said, "the plastics industry here has grown more than nine hundred percent since 1982. There are approximately forty plastics processors that employ more than two thousand people in the area. That's really something to be proud of."

Joscelyn stared at her. "Well, sure."

"I mean, more than six hundred injection molding presses producing more than a hundred million plastic products a year? It's almost mind-boggling. Your husband manages the company that showed the greatest growth for a three-year period."

Joscelyn looked across the table at Bill Peacock, as if seeing her husband for the first time. "Anyway," she mumbled.

"I realize plastics are controversial these days," Sarah continued, aware that Wyatt and several others had turned to listen to her. "Yet we can't function without them in our society. I'm sure people have no idea how vital plastics are. If the general population were better informed through the television and print media, we might see a strong increase in plastics recycling, as well as greater support for local industry."

"Are you suggesting an advertising campaign of some sort, Miss Ellsworth?" Bill Peacock asked from across the table.

"It could only help. According to my research, you have the funds. The time is certainly right. People are becoming more and more aware of plastics, but usually in a negative light. The disposable diaper issue is critical right now. You need to illustrate the value—the absolute *necessity*—of your product not only in daily life, but in health care and other vital areas."

"Excuse my frankness, Miss Ellsworth, but by any chance are you with Dunwitty?"

She glanced at Wyatt and couldn't help but laugh. "Robert Dunwitty Advertising? No. I'm just interested in seeing El Paso grow."

"Do you have a background in business promotion that would enable you to work on an ad campaign of some sort?"

"My focus is personnel."

"*There*, Bill," Joscelyn put in. "She's a people person, just like me. So stop trying to coerce her into talking about business, business, business. I swear, the man has a one-track mind. Now, Sarah, why haven't I seen you at the country club?"

"We just joined," Wyatt stated before Sarah could open her mouth. "At first I didn't see much point. But now that I'm thinking about relocating here in El Paso—"

"You are?" Sarah interrupted.

"Uh-oh, is this something you two need to talk over in private?" Joscelyn teased. She dug her elbow into Sarah's side.

"I've never invested in housing," Wyatt continued to the whole group. "My mother lives on the family ranch near Waco. I've got a vacation cabin in the mountains of southern New Mexico."

"Ruidoso?" Joscelyn queried.

"Great place. But I'm considering a more permanent residence or two. How's the housing market in El Paso?"

The conversation quickly broke apart again, into a discussion of various neighborhoods, builders, legalities, and financial details. Sarah focused on her soup. Wyatt was thinking of buying a house in El Paso? *I'm thinking about relocating here.* What could that mean? He had been hinting broadly of more than a passing interest in her—but they'd known each other less than a week.

She was imagining things. That had to be the explanation. A man like Wyatt Noble was as concrete, down-to-earth, and responsible as she was. He never rushed into things. He couldn't be anything but shrewd and prudent to have become as successful as he was. Certainly a woman he had kissed only twice in his life wouldn't cause him to have a sudden radical personality change and become impulsive, wild, careless.

Sarah studied Wyatt during the main course. He had engaged Bill Peacock across the table in a discussion of the current state of journalism. They moved from that subject to business, comparing investment potential, the stock market, the economy. On any other night, Sarah knew she would have jumped feet-first into the conversation. There was nothing she liked better than the intricacies of the business world. Tonight had shown her she could hold her own with a man like Bill Peacock, who was undoubtedly much better educated than she.

But what about Wyatt? Could he really be serious about a woman with a head for high finance—rather than one whose main interest was joining country clubs and sororities? Sarah had a suspicion that Wyatt was most attracted to the kind of woman Bill Peacock had married.

In fact, Joscelyn's qualities were just the attributes Wyatt had most encouraged in Sarah. If Wyatt were the settling-down kind—which he wasn't—he would want someone beautiful and reasonably intelligent. She would be someone who could grace his arm at social functions, who could "knock the socks off" his associates, and who would enjoy the luxuries of a limousine, a country club membership, and a charge account at Papillón.

He wouldn't want a woman whose goal in life was to manage personnel at a hotel in downtown El Paso. A woman in the middle of a college career. A woman who intended to obtain a master's degree before she was through. A woman who liked her little house and her long-haired mutt, and who didn't give a rip for high society, fancy cars, and silk cocktail gowns. He wouldn't want Sarah.

"I'll look for you at our next Garden Guild meeting, Sarah," Joscelyn Peacock said as they rose from dinner.

"We gather in a different member's home each month. It's wonderful! You get to see the latest in interior design and enjoy a lovely catered brunch. There's the flower thing, of course, but don't worry about that. We all have gardeners."

"Of course," Sarah said, imagining society matrons gathered in her tiny one-bedroom house with its tag-sale furniture.

"Sarah has her own meadow," Wyatt boasted to Joscelyn as he walked Sarah to the door. "Native wildflowers. You wouldn't believe the bluebonnets she grows."

"A meadow?" Joscelyn regarded Sarah as though she were from another planet. "Well, my goodness."

"You ought to schedule her to give a program at one of your meetings. Shake things up a little bit, wouldn't it?"

Joscelyn laughed uncertainly. "A meadow . . . like with weeds?"

"Some of the most beautiful wildflowers are actually considered weeds," Sarah said. "The morning glory, for example, is termed a primary noxious weed. Farmers despise them. But in a suburban lot, they can be pretty spectacular."

"Morning glories." Joscelyn was still pondering that one as Wyatt and Sarah left Pancho Villa's and climbed into their limo.

"You got awfully quiet in there," Wyatt remarked as the limousine eased through the lamplit streets. "Something bothering you?"

Sarah studied the blue-lighted outline of his face. His expression showed serious concern, and her efforts to distance herself once again began to waver. He had nestled her against him, and the warmth of his body beneath his leather coat had a soothing effect on her jangled nerves.

"You took me by surprise," she said. "I didn't know you were looking into buying a house here."

"Is that a problem?"

"Not for me."

"You sure about that?"

"Of course. You can do whatever you want, obviously. It doesn't affect me one way or another. I just thought El Paso was a little 'brown' for your taste."

He grinned. "You might say I've seen the light on that issue."

"Why El Paso?" she demanded, turning suddenly to face him. "Why here?"

"Right to the point, Miss Ellsworth? As always. No wonder Bill Peacock was so impressed. If you'd agree to it, he'd hire you to run an ad campaign for him."

"You're off the subject, Mr. Noble."

"Okay. Why El Paso?" He tapped his fingers on his thigh. "Nice city. I own a newspaper here, by the way."

"I'm aware of that."

"Kind of makes a man think about sticking around to keep an eye on things, you know?"

"You own six other newspapers. You don't have homes in those cities."

"Well, El Paso. Let's see ... strong economy. Pleasant folks. Good restaurants. Fine hotels." He looked at her. "And you."

She let out a shaky breath. "That's what I want to talk about."

"I figured."

"Look, Wyatt, I agreed to go with you on these social engagements only because ... well ..."

"Why did you agree to that, Sarah?"

Because I fell in love with you the minute I saw you. Sarah leaned her head back on the seat and shut her eyes. "Because you asked me. Because Noble Newspapers is too valuable a client for Hartley Hotels to lose. Because I was told not to rock the boat, to do whatever you asked. Anything to keep you happy."

Wyatt stiffened. "Who the hell told you that?"

"My general manager. But it hardly matters. Wyatt, you made it clear to me you could pull your account with us if I wasn't cooperative. You hold a lot of sway with the Hartley. I couldn't upset that relationship by turning you down."

"Bull." He set his jaw and glared at the Stetson on his knee for a full minute.

Sarah felt her insides turn to jelly. So the real Wyatt was emerging, the angry, stubborn, driving force who had built an empire at any cost. Now the truth about him would come out.

"I would never, *never* use my power or my money," he said, punching out every word with his index finger, "to make you do anything. Got that?"

She nodded. His eyes were a glittering blue, his words tight. The limo swung into the hotel drive.

"I asked you to spend time with me this week because of *you*," he continued. "*You and me.* Is that clear?"

"Yes." She felt like a wayward subordinate at a board meeting.

"Now, you'd better make up your mind whether you

came along because some damned GM told you to, or because of me. You and me."

He stuffed his Stetson on his head as the limo door swung open. Before she could give him an answer, his big shoulders were disappearing into the night. Sarah unknotted her fingers and followed him.

For a moment, they stood on the sidewalk staring at each other. The limousine pulled away; the doorman gave up holding the door open and went back inside the hotel.

Sarah shivered. "Well," she said, thinking about garden guilds, sororities, her college degree—all the reasons it wouldn't work.

"Well?" he demanded.

She let out her breath. "Oh, Wyatt . . . it's you. You and me." Then before he could say anything, she turned and ran all the way down to the parking garage.

At home later that night, Sarah debated allowing herself to sleep in the following morning. It would be Sunday, but she was too tired to go to church, she reasoned. All week she'd slept poorly, staying up late with Wyatt Noble and then lying awake for hours afterward. Now she had a stack of homework to complete, bags under her eyes, and a stomach that rolled like a tilt-a-whirl.

But the next morning, Sarah's resolution to sleep a few extra hours was shattered by the shrill chirp of her bedside phone. Swimming out of the depths of her dream, she fought with the cord.

"It's the vacuum cleaner cord," she finally mumbled into the receiver. "It's all tangled. My hands are tied, see. I'm gonna fall . . ."

"What?"

At the sound of Wyatt's deep voice, Sarah's eyelids shot open and adrenaline surged through her veins. "What?" she said back. "What what?"

"Sarah, is that you? Did I wake you up?"

She grabbed her alarm clock. "Eight-thirty! Do you realize what time it is?"

"You just told me. Sarah, you're usually at work by this time of morning. Sorry, I didn't expect . . ."

"No, it's okay. Did you want something from me?"

"I could think of one good answer to that question." He fell silent a moment. "Anyhow, the reason I called was to ask you to recommend a church I could go to this morning."

Sarah rubbed her eyes. "Take your pick. Yellow pages are full of them."

"Where will you be?"

So that was it. She had weakened last night, and now he was homing in. But what did he really want from her? She still wasn't sure. The image of the runaway vacuum flitted through her mind.

"I had planned to sleep in," she said.

"You're awake now."

"No kidding. So, is church on your agenda or something?" she said, suddenly irritated. "Am I obliged to go with you, like it's part of the week's itinerary?"

He was silent for a moment. "You always this grouchy in the morning, Sarah?"

"I'm not grouchy. I'm just . . . confused." She sighed. "Okay, I guess I'll go to church after all."

"Great. I'll pick you up. What time?"

He was so persistent. Sarah fingered the quilt her mother had made. For some reason, she still didn't want Wyatt to see her home. This was her last private domain. He'd invaded every other carefully guarded space in her life. On the other hand, the Hartley was far out of the way from her church. Giving in, she told him to pick her up at nine-fifteen, and gave him her address.

After a quick shower, Sarah slipped into one of her few dresses, a simple springtime cotton shift with tiny flowers sprinkled on a white background. She was brushing her hair when the doorbell rang.

"Hey, Sarah." Wyatt was all smiles as she pulled open the door. "Wow, you're beautiful. Gorgeous."

"Thanks." Somehow when he said it, she felt it.

She stepped out onto the sunlit walk and spotted the

uniformed chauffeur, and the long silver sedan parked in front of her house. *Oh no, not the limo.* Sure enough, three of her neighbors had emerged onto their porches. Old Mrs. Hernandez across the street was peeking through her curtains. But Sarah's discomfort softened when Wyatt slipped his hand around hers and gave her a gentle kiss on the cheek.

"I'll rent a car for next Sunday," he said, walking her to the limo.

"Next Sunday you'll be winding up the Texas News Federation conference."

"The Sunday after that, then."

"You'll be gone, Wyatt." She looked into his blue eyes, even though she knew he might read the pain in hers. Every moment she spent with this man was going to make his leaving that much harder. Not only did he stir her womanly desires, but he had become so much more to her than just a handsome man. As he held open the limousine door, she climbed into the familiar interior.

Church only confirmed Sarah's unhappiness about his imminent disappearance from her life. Wyatt slipped easily into the comfortable, open atmosphere of her adult Sunday School class. He revealed a strong knowledge of Biblical scripture, and he didn't hesitate to enter the lively discussion around the table. After the lesson, he snagged a donut and cup of orange juice from the refreshment table, and joined the department's teacher and several of the other men in an evaluation of the Diablos, El Paso's minor league baseball team.

"Great guy," the leader whispered to Sarah as they headed upstairs for the church service. He winked. "Keep him."

When they had settled into their cushioned pew, Wyatt again took Sarah's hand. They shared a hymnbook, their voices joining in the songs of praise. Writing on the back of the bulletin, Wyatt took notes on the pastor's sermon. He occasionally elbowed Sarah about some point he considered of interest, then indicated his note on the subject so she could read what he had written.

Sarah, on the other hand, was having a terrible time concentrating. For one thing, Wyatt smelled like heaven itself. Every time he leaned against her to whisper in her ear, she had to catch her breath. His skin was so smooth, his jaw so clean, it was all she could do to keep from kissing him right there in church. His black hair gleamed, and it set up a contrast that made his eyes look like bright sapphires. When he smiled or spoke, she found her attention wandering away from what he was saying and settling on his lips. Just the thought of sliding into his arms and feeling his mouth meld with hers sent an uncomfortable warmth through her.

This was not the kind of thing to be dreaming about in church, and when the pastor invited people forward at the end of the sermon, Sarah considered walking the aisle to confess her wayward thoughts. Not that her minister would have condemned her, of course. Though he spoke strongly against sin, he gave equal time to love—of all kinds. In fact, more than once the minister had preached about the importance of finding the right kind of person to share life with. Wyatt Noble more than fit the bill.

Sarah wandered out of the church in a kind of daze. Being at Wyatt's side felt so normal it was positively eerie. He greeted the minister, congratulated a choir member, and rumpled a child's hair on the way to the limousine. Everyone stared, of course, as Sarah climbed in with Wyatt, but she realized that even this was beginning to feel right and comfortable.

"Lunch?" he asked as they sped down the suburban streets.

She shook her head. "I need to study, Wyatt. I have an accounting test tomorrow."

"I'll help you study. You show me the material, and I'll ask you questions."

"Don't you have something better—"

"*No.* I don't have anything better to do than spend time with you, Sarah. We don't have very many days left."

"Which is exactly why you shouldn't come to my house." She ran her finger down the gold-edged pages of her Bible. "I'm feeling uncomfortable about this whole thing."

"You're feeling *comfortable*, Sarah. As comfortable with me as I feel with you. Let me spend the afternoon with you."

Of course he was right. She had just admitted to herself how at ease she felt with him. What she didn't feel at ease with was his leaving. If he pushed for more time with her, she didn't trust herself to keep her distance. And what she gave him of her heart, she knew she would lose in the end.

"Wyatt—" she began.

"Sarah, please." He took both her hands in his. "Something's happening here. Something I've never felt. Look, I'm thirty-eight years old. I thought I'd been through everything. Done everything. But this . . . this between you and me . . . this is something new. Don't nip it in the bud just because you're afraid."

"I don't want . . . I don't want to be hurt, Wyatt." She shut her eyes and let out a breath. *There*, she had said it, letting him know how much she cared and how deeply she would feel his loss.

"Important things cost," he whispered. "You have to take the risk if you want the prize. The higher the stakes, the greater the reward."

"And the greater the pain of failure."

"You're not a woman to run from pain, Sarah. You've got more strength than anyone I know. Come on. Take a chance."

As the limousine pulled up alongside the curb in front of her little house, Sarah relented. "Okay, you can help me study. Send the limo back to the hotel. But I want you to understand that if things start bothering me, I'm driving you home."

"Home?" He followed her out into the noon sunshine and stepped into her wildflower meadow. "I think I'm home right now."

Sarah fixed a quick taco salad for lunch. They ate in her dining room, an intimate nook decorated with striped mauve wallpaper, a floral border, a round oak table, and softly padded chairs. After they cleared away the lunch, Wyatt insisted on washing the dishes while Sarah gathered her textbooks.

The living room had once been a formal parlor, and Sarah had furnished it bit by bit—plump sofa and chairs she had reupholstered herself in cabbage-rose chintz, a low pine coffee table, a beaded vintage lamp, and walls painted a pale, pale pink.

"This is you, Sarah," Wyatt said as he settled on the floor across the coffee table from her. "Soft, feminine. You wear those suits every day, but your womanliness shows through. Here in your house, there's no hiding."

She opened her accounting notebook. "There's some hiding."

"Tell me your secrets." He covered her hand with his and forced her to meet his gaze.

"Didn't your parents teach you the old rules? If you tell, it's not a secret anymore." She shoved the open text in front of him and pointed to the review pages. "Here. Start testing."

He gave her a long look, then dipped into the study. Sarah was surprised at how successful their united venture was. Wyatt had taken accounting courses, but he enjoyed the review, and he was able to help Sarah when she got stuck on a problem. She popped a bowl of popcorn, and as the afternoon waned, they slogged through the unit until she was certain she knew everything.

"When's the test?" Wyatt asked sleepily. He had stretched out on the floor, his head on a sofa cushion. The accounting text was propped on his stomach.

"The class is taking it tomorrow night, but my prof is giving it to me early. I'll meet him at seven in the morning."

Wyatt eyed her. "I really put you out, didn't I? You've missed a slew of classes. You've been making up your work on the side. I bet you haven't been getting any sleep—and I woke you up this morning."

She had stretched out perpendicular to him, their heads

meeting at a right angle. "It hasn't been so bad," she said. She rolled onto her stomach. "I'm keeping up. And I really have enjoyed the evenings out."

"In spite of Joscelyn Peacock?"

"I meet Joscelyn Peacocks every week in my business."

"Why didn't you tell her what you do at the Hartley? You evaded the subject with Bill, too."

Sarah shrugged. "I told you I like to have my own secrets. It's easier that way. I don't fit in with Joscelyn and her group, Wyatt. I'm a working woman, not a socialite. Besides, I'm not nearly as educated as the people you associate with."

"You may not have a string of degrees behind your name yet, but you're every bit as intelligent as anyone in that room last night. More than most. You blended. You're no different from Bill Peacock or Joscelyn or me."

"Oh, come on." Sarah rested her chin on her folded knuckles. "I'm the daughter of a gas-meter reader and a housewife. I have two brothers and a sister, none of whom made it past high school. I had barely graduated myself before starting my job as a housekeeper at the Hartley. I cleaned ashtrays in the halls. I scrubbed toilets. I dug hair out of shower drains."

"Bleaggh." Wyatt made a face that sent Sarah into giggles.

"See?" she went on when she had composed herself. "My whole frame of reference is different from yours. Your father is Jacob Noble. Noble Oil. You grew up riding Arabians. You had the finest education money could buy."

"I was born in Galveston, Texas, and I had no father," Wyatt countered, his voice almost a whisper. He lowered his eyes, and the fun left his face. "There's no record of the man who gave me life. I was taken from my mother when I was two years old. The police found me alone in an empty house. I had been there almost a week with nothing to eat and only water from a leaky faucet to drink. My diaper hadn't been changed all that time. I was dehydrated, anemic, bruised, and malnourished."

Sarah swallowed. The man lying beside her on the floor

was no longer the brash lone wolf of the newspaper empire. His blue eyes reflected the hurt of his past. "Social services placed me in a foster home," he continued. "I lived there almost a year. The social worker didn't want me growing too attached to those folks, so they transferred me to another foster home. I was moved from family to family, house to house, city to city, school to school, until I was thirteen."

"Thirteen!"

"I've seen it all." He shook his head. "You want to talk secrets? There are things I've been through I don't even remember. Stuffed them away and they're not coming out. Ever. Oh, social services sent me to counselors. To help me cope, they said. I learned all the jargon after a while. It got to be kind of a joke. I could analyze the counselors as fast as they could do me."

"Wyatt . . ."

He was looking at her again, searching her face. "Does this make you want to stay away from me, Sarah?"

"No," she whispered. "Of course it doesn't."

He took her face in his hands and gently rubbed her cheeks. "And it doesn't matter to me where you come from either."

"So Jacob Noble adopted you when you were thirteen?" she asked.

"It was easy street from then on. I'm lucky enough to have been given a strong dose of intelligence, so I never had trouble with school. Loved reading. English. Debate. Math. Chess team. I took accelerated classes in every subject."

"Why did you choose newspapers over the oil business?"

"It interested me more, and I guess I have a flair for it. Jacob never pushed me in any direction. He and Dorothy were the most important factors in my life, Sarah. They gave me everything they had. More than money. A strong marriage to model. A spiritual life to hold up as an example. A work ethic to follow. Love and acceptance. Oh, they gave me love in great barrels full. I'm blessed, Sarah, and I know it. I don't take anything—or anyone—for granted."

His eyes told her that she, too, had become precious. As his lips met hers, she finally pushed away the last barrier holding them apart. Wrapping her arms around his neck, she eased against him. His kiss deepened, and she met the sweet, sensual caresses with equal fervor.

"Sarah . . . Sarah," he murmured in her ear. His hands covered her back, molding over her shoulders, trailing down her spine. His fingers worked into her hair as her lips taunted him with swift, urgent kisses.

"Wyatt, I've been so scared," she whispered. "I've felt so out of control."

He touched her lips with his fingertip. "My strong, beautiful Sarah. Don't be afraid."

She clutched his back as his hand slid around her waist and up, slowly up. His breath came deep and ragged. His mouth searched hers. He eased his palm over the rise of her breast, topped the crest, cupped the heavy swell. She felt a melting heat as his body moved against hers with a hard, demanding pressure.

"Wyatt." His fingers teased her, tightening her nipple into a firm, swollen bud. Dismay swept down into the pit of her stomach. She could so easily lose her way in the flame of his passion.

"I won't take advantage," he assured her, though his words were hot on her neck, and his urgency pressed the tender flesh between her thighs. "But, Sarah . . . I have to touch you. I've been in hell."

"You don't know how it's been for me. I can't sleep. I can't eat. Ohh, yes . . ." He opened the buttons on her shift, and his warm hand found its way inside. As he cupped her breast, their mouths came together again, hungry, aching with pent-up desire.

His fingers stroked around and around the globe of pale flesh until they found the sensitive center of her desire. Then he brushed his palm over her taut nipple, back and forth, until she felt her hips began to sway against his thigh. She slipped her hands around his neck and worked them into his coarse black hair. He toyed with her, rolling her budded nipple between his fingers, stimulating every nerve to its tightest point.

When she was sure she was lost to him, he spread her bodice and found her other breast. As he gazed down at her in the soft lamplight, she gloried in the proud thrust of her own womanliness. He had brought her to this, and she felt tremendous power even in her weakness.

As his head bent toward her breasts, she kneaded the muscles of his back. His mouth found her nipples . . . wetted, lapped, savored them. Damp with need for him, she couldn't think how she could possibly keep the slender thread of control she still clutched.

"Wyatt," she ground out.

For a moment he couldn't respond. His body pushed hard against hers, and she could clearly feel his own need. His mouth moved over her breasts, his breath heated, his hands cupping and releasing her. Finally, when she began to tremble with need for release, he pulled away.

"Sarah," he groaned. "Sarah, I've never lost control this way. I want you so bad I can taste it."

He rolled onto his haunches, cocked his knees, and hung his head as he fought for air. She struggled up and buttoned her shift down the front. Her breasts were barely contained, her swollen nipples jutting through the thin fabric.

"I'll drive you back to the hotel." Weak-kneed, she grabbed her purse and somehow made it to the front door.

As she stepped outside into the cool night air, he caught her from behind. "Sarah," he said. "This is it."

Blind with elation, fear, uncertainty, sensual ardor, she hurried to the car. *This is it.* This is what? The beginning? The fulfillment of a secret dream? Or a brief interlude before the end?

For the next three evenings, Wyatt and Sarah spent no time alone together. Wyatt was completely up front with Sarah about his feelings. He wanted her. He wanted her too much.

As deeply as she desired him, Sarah fully agreed. They had to keep a rein on things. She understood that with this distancing, Wyatt was telling her he couldn't get too involved before he had to leave. She knew this wasn't only to protect him. It was intended to spare her the distress of their separation ... although she could have told him it was already too late.

Monday night they attended a dinner of local apparel industry leaders. Chief executive officers for Tony Lama, Levi Strauss, Farah, and several other successful garment makers wanted to meet the new owner of the *Tribune*. The newspaper was an influential element in their marketing strategy. Sarah enjoyed conversing with Joscelyn Peacock's father, a genial man with none of his daughter's flightiness.

Tuesday evening Wyatt and Sarah dined with leaders in the medical manufacturing field. Sarah was introduced to the CEOs of Johnson & Johnson, Baxter Healthcare, Becton Dickinson, and Davol. Other executives represented the sterilization companies of Isomedix, Griffith Micro Science, and Dynatech Scientific Laboratories.

Wednesday evening the dinner hour was reserved for defense contractors. El Paso's proximity to test ranges had brought manufacturers, world-class technicians, and engineers to the area. Trying to decode the military lingo,

Sarah had a headache by the time dessert was served. The pain grew worse when Wyatt asked her later if she would accompany him on a house-hunting venture the following afternoon.

Though Sarah had always been blunt, she couldn't make herself confront Wyatt with her questions. Why was he looking for a house in El Paso? How did he feel about *her*? What were his plans for the future? Did she fit into them? Maybe she didn't want to hear his answers.

They spent Thursday afternoon riding around with a real estate agent and traipsing through one vast executive home after another. They explored houses on the east slopes of the Franklin Mountains, the side of the city that boasted Fort Bliss, the largest air defense center in the United States. Then they drove across to the west side of the mountain range, where suburbs stretched for miles and a mall had recently been built.

"So which house did you like best?" Wyatt asked that evening in Sarah's office. She was clearing her desk before checking out for the day.

"Which one did *you* like?" she returned as she slid two files into her attaché case. "It's your taste that matters, not mine."

He was sitting on the corner of her desk, idly sorting her pens. "I asked you first."

"Frankly, I thought most of them seemed a little cold."

"Couldn't you warm them up so they'd feel the way your house does?"

"You might if you hung some wallpaper and bought a few rose-printed chintz pillows for your couches."

"What about that place in the valley, down by the river? The one with the horses? Did you like that?"

Sarah reflected on the large old home with its arched porticoes and clay tile floor. Though it was the least expensive, it had been her favorite. The agent, she presumed, had shown it as the poor example by which to judge all the following fine homes.

"I liked that house, Wyatt," she said, trying to block the

sadness from her voice. "I'm sure you'd be happy staying there when you were in El Paso for a visit."

"Sarah, listen." Wyatt stood and took her shoulders. He looked away for a moment, unable to speak. Then his blue eyes searched her face, and he pulled her into his arms.

His kiss was deep, penetrating, possessive, and Sarah responded to the core of her soul. With the agony of losing this man slicing into her like a knife, she wrapped her arms around his chest and sank against the full length of his body. He wove his fingers through her hair, stroking and squeezing it. His lips grazed her cheek, tormented her ear. Breathing hard, he kneaded his hands down her back.

"Wyatt," she murmured, her reserve shattered by his touch. She explored his chest, memorizing the solid muscle with her palms. As his hand covered her breast, she shuddered with the burst of flame that skittered across her skin and then seared the core of her stomach. Sorrow and passion mingled, each making the other seem all the more intense, and she fought the sudden blur of tears.

Wyatt burst out of the kiss, tearing his lips from hers and physically setting her away from him. "Listen, Sarah," he said, struggling for breath, "the Press Federation people are coming in tonight. I have meetings all day tomorrow—"

"And all day Saturday," she whispered. "Yes, I know."

"But there's the banquet Saturday night. You'll be with me for that, won't you?"

"Wyatt, I—"

"Sarah, please." He shoved his hands into his jeans' pockets. Ill at ease, he searched for words. "I want . . . I want you to meet my associates in the business. Publishers and managing editors from all over Texas will be here. In the ballroom next door, the local Concert Guild is holding its annual fund-raising ball. We can slip over there after the federation's awards presentation. We'll dance, Sarah. Just the two of us."

She swallowed at the dry lump in her throat. Their last night together. Wouldn't it be simpler to end it now? To get the pain over with, and not add another memory to have to erase?

"Oh, Wyatt, I don't—"

"Sarah, I'm asking you. Please."

"Okay, okay." She felt the tears begin to swim. Her voice sounded wavery. "But would you mind leaving me alone right now, Wyatt? I have some things to do here before I can leave."

"Sure." He went to the door. "Saturday night, then."

She nodded calmly, but as he closed the door, she crumpled onto her desk and gave in to the pain.

"I don't think we should skip out of here," Sarah whispered Saturday night as Wyatt edged her toward the door of the Coronado Room at the Hartley Hotel. "The emcee announced a hospitality room on the seventh floor, and I'm sure everyone will be expecting you. The *Trib* just won all those awards—"

"Let's go dancing, Sarah," Wyatt breathed in her ear. "My arms have been empty for two nights."

Trepidation creeping into her stomach, Sarah gave in to his request and accompanied him down the hall to the De Soto Ballroom. She had spent the last two days trying to convince herself that people didn't fall in love this deeply in such a short time. She had told herself that though Wyatt seemed to match her in intelligence, interests, spirituality, even background to some degree, they had little of real significance in common.

But when he led her onto the dance floor and took her in his arms, every reasonable doubt vanished. The band played a familiar Texas waltz, and Wyatt drew Sarah close against his chest as he moved her to the rhythm. Again, it seemed to Sarah that they blended perfectly, their feet stepping out the one-two-three so easily that they didn't have to think. Others in the room danced apart, but Wyatt held Sarah so close she could feel the brush of his jacket against her cheek and smell the scent of cologne on his skin.

"I've missed you," he said against her ear. "Couldn't wait for this moment."

She shut her eyes, so afraid the tears would start up again. Years ago she had put her emotions on a back shelf, but in the last three days she had cried buckets. His fingers felt strong woven through hers, and she was sure his hand on her back could hold her up through anything. When the band segued into a two-step, he kept her close. In some ways, this dance was even more sensual. Sarah could feel his thighs brushing against hers, her breasts tipping his chest.

"You've meant so much to me, Sarah," he whispered. "Everything about you . . ."

But all she could hear was the finality in his words. This was the closing speech of a kind man. Someone who wouldn't hurt her for the world. Yet it *was* the end.

"When I arrived in El Paso, I thought it was going to be another one of those dull, mindless visits." His mouth formed the words, and Sarah followed the movement of his lips in sad fascination. "And then I met you. I never expected anything like this. You took me off guard."

She tried to smile as his blue eyes captured hers. "I've got to admit you've been something of a surprise, too."

"Yeah." He stopped dancing and held her close. "Oh, Sarah—"

"So what's next on your agenda?" she cut in, with a forced brightness in her voice. "You've been talking about your mother. Will you go to Waco next?"

He let out his breath and started dancing again. "Houston. I'm looking into purchasing a small paper there. I'll be a week or so going over details."

She fought the lump forming in her throat. "Staying at the Hartley, I hope?"

"It won't be the same . . ." The music slowed, and Wyatt held her away from him. "I'll get you a drink, and we'll go out on the balcony."

"You know, I really ought to be heading home." She looked out over the crowd to keep him from seeing the tears in her eyes. From a distance Joscelyn Peacock spotted her and waved. *Oh, no.* She started in Sarah's direction, bringing a group of friends with her.

"I've had a long week," Sarah said quickly, "and I'm so tired I could—"

"I want to talk to you, Sarah. Stay until I've had my say. Will you give me that?"

She clenched her jaw and nodded. Of course, she'd give him his moment, his own swift and gentle coup de grace. "Sure," she managed.

He tipped her chin and brushed his lips across hers. "Back in a minute."

She watched bleakly as he walked away toward the open bar.

Joscelyn Peacock descended. "Sarah, I'm so glad you and Wyatt dropped in on the Concert Guild ball." Silver sequins shimmered with each breath. "Ladies, I want you all to meet Miss Sarah Ellsworth. She's Wyatt Noble's . . .?"

"Friend," Sarah finished.

Joscelyn gave a breathy laugh. "It looked like more than that, Sarah, the way Wyatt was holding you tonight." When Sarah didn't respond, she pressed on. "Anyway, I wanted you to meet some of my dearest friends. This is Madeline James, Frances Foley, Dianne Steele, Erma Meyer, and Angela Bartlett. We're in everything together."

Dianne Steele wore a gentle, welcoming light in her soft brown eyes as she shook Sarah's hand. "Are you interested in joining a service sorority, Sarah? We have several active organizations here in El Paso."

"She *works,*" Joscelyn commented, one eyebrow raised.

"Oh, really?" Madeline James asked, with feigned interest. "How interesting. Where?"

"Right here at the Hartley," Joscelyn said.

At this news, the women glanced at one another. Dianne smiled. "You work at the Hartley? Are you the manager?"

Sarah saw Wyatt over Dianne's shoulder. He was headed toward her, a drink in each hand. She looked at the circle of women. "James Baca is the manager of the hotel," she informed them. "I'm the head of Housekeeping."

"Housekeeping . . ." Madeline's mouth parted.

"Then you're nothing but a *maid*!" Joscelyn exclaimed. "Why on earth would a man like Wyatt Noble be seeing someone he has nothing at all in common with?"

An icy river slid down Sarah's spine. "It's not what you do that counts, Joscelyn," she retorted. "It's who you are. Excuse me."

She knew Wyatt had seen her face, the stricken look she couldn't hide. Turning, she left the women behind as she headed for the door. She might have denied Joscelyn's words, but they held a ring of truth that had haunted Sarah ever since she met Wyatt. The taunt seemed to seal the distance that could never be bridged.

"Sarah!" His voice stopped her. She turned, determined to accept gracefully this ending to their brief time together. "Wyatt, I—"

"I love you, Sarah," he whispered, and he pulled her into his arms and kissed her fully, deeply, possessively.

With stunned looks on their faces, Joscelyn and the other women parted as Wyatt led Sarah out onto a balcony. He shut the long French doors behind them, then took Sarah's hands and kissed them.

"Wyatt," she tried again. Her tears refused to hide. She sniffled, and he gathered her close, kissing her damp cheeks, her eyelids, her mouth.

"I love you, Sarah," he repeated. "I don't care what other people say or think. Never have. Don't you know that by now?"

She sucked in a shuddering breath. "I don't usually . . . cry . . ."

He grinned. "Might as well shed a few tears when the man who loves you asks you to marry him."

"Marry you . . ."

"You're the best thing that ever happened in my life, Sarah. If you'll have me, I want to make you my wife."

His blue eyes were soft, loving through the blur of her tears. "I love you, Wyatt. I love you so much." She sniffed again. "Yes, I'll marry you."

"The sooner the better." He settled her against his chest,

and she could feel the heavy throb of his heart. "Our marriage, our bond of love, will stand through eternity, Sarah. That's my vow to you."

She shut her eyes, and as his hands slipped into her hair, she seemed to see a meadow dancing with golden butterflies . . . wildflowers sunning their faces against the blue sky . . . and a thousand bluebonnets nodding in the breeze.

#1 National Bestselling Author

SUZANNE FORSTER

SHAMELESS

"A stylist who translates sexual tension into sizzle and burn."–*Los Angeles Daily News*

Jessie Flood is a woman used to scandal. She shocked the town of Half Moon Bay, California, when she implicated her childhood friend, Luc Warnecke, in her stepfather's murder. Then, Jessie gave birth to an illegitimate child and married Luc's multimillionaire father. Now newly widowed, she's the head of the Warnecke media empire. But there's one person from her former life from whom she cannot escape–Luc, the man Jessie nearly destroyed. Even as they face each other as dire enemies, they cannot deny the powerful hunger that drove them together.

___ *0-425-14095-4/$4.99*